anthology

Indignor House

Fall 2024

anthology

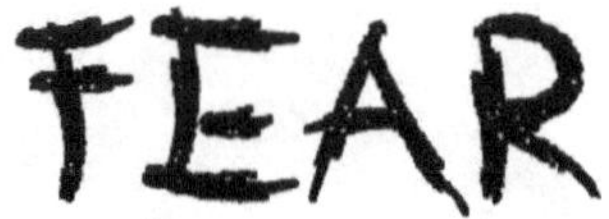

© Copyright 2024
First Edition

ISBN 978-1-953278-54-8 Hard Back
ISBN 978-1-953278-55-5 Soft Back
ISBN 978-1-953278-56-2 E-Book

Published by

INDIGNOR HOUSE

Chesapeake, VA 23322
www.indignorhouse.com

Cover Design: Indignor House

"Monsters are real, and ghosts are real too. They live inside us, and sometimes, they win."

Stephen King

Contents

Contents - Continued

Contents - Continued

An Introduction

We write to share stories and to give warnings. Through the simple act of placing words to a sheet of paper, wisdom is sometimes shared. Therefore, what inspires us? A dream? A thought? A fear?

What do most of us fear? Harm? Okay, then which type of harm, emotional or physical?

Fear, the easiest of human manipulators. If you can make others afraid of death, you can easily control them. Create the concept of a plague, or war, or aliens, and boom, the world is yours to control. Blast the news with these concepts, make your people fear the future, and they'll demand to remain in the past.

How to rule the world in three easy steps. Let me help you.

1 – <u>Make people afraid</u> – again fear is our friend. Use the media, written or verbal, doesn't matter how, just do it.

2 – <u>Create an illusion</u> – make your people look over there when you do something over here. They'll never know.

3 – <u>Give small gifts</u> – when you give, they stop trying to make, when they stop trying, they rely on you to survive.

Once you have their fear, attention, and gratitude in your hands, you can conquer the world. Next step? Hire people to keep your three steps moving. Then, people will demand to lay their spoils at your feet. In fact, they will wash your feet for you.

I remember graduating from high school and afraid of college. Although I graduated from high school with honors, I honestly did not believe I was smart enough to continue my education. Therefore, I enrolled in a junior college. When they handed me my degree, I was afraid to enroll in a four-year university. But I did, and eventually they too, handed me a degree. Again, I was afraid to continue. Eventually, the university handed me another degree. Now, four degrees later, I still feel dumb at times – afraid to continue, but also afraid to stop.

What did the college environment teach me? It taught me to question everything. People will talk and talk, they will raise their voices if they believe no one is listening. They will eventually scream out their demands. They will order you to believe everything they say. Why? Because the one who can scream the loudest knows the most? Nope, just reply with, "Why?"

Through these pages, we will examine many types of fears. Fear is not just an unknown monster lurking behind a door. Then again, a lot of things can be lurking behind a door. And sometimes, we honestly do not want what lurks behind a door. Remember the game show that asked which door you wanted? My answer would have been, "None!" I'm no dummy.

Therefore, when you open the internet or newspaper or news channel, instead of believing everything you read or hear, ask *Why?*

I would bet that the author of those reports would have no answer. Life is nothing more than an illusion, a simple trick of the shadows or hand.

AN INTRODUCTION

Enjoy your fears as you flip through these pages and determine which of our stories you can relate to.

Lynn Yvonne Moon
Indignor House
Chief Executive Officer

The Dream

Lynn Yvonne Moon

I hear everything they are saying, but I can't understand a word. Are they speaking English? Yes … yes they are, but … at the same time, the language is different … almost foreign. The muffled sounds are echoing, the pain … the sound hurts my ears … but the voices are crystal clear. It must be the level of the noise that's causing the confusion … blurry vision, nothing … I can see nothing. Vagueness … haze everywhere or … no wait, the room is exactly as it's supposed to be … but where am I?

I can hardly sense my hand against my face. Am I dreaming? Yes, that must be it. I am having a dream. What's the last thing I remember? Think … think! Oh yes, making love by the fire. But when did I go to bed? I can't remember. Maybe I was carried to my room. No, I wouldn't have slept through that, I'm too light of a sleeper.

"Objection!"

A deep voice echoes through my ears. My stomach tightens as a peaceful calm surrounds me, and I fall into a twilight sleep.

"Order! I demand order. Attorneys approach the bench … now!" It's a woman's voice, but I don't recognize it. Whose voice is it? It sounds familiar, perhaps the television, did someone leave it on all night?

What's wrong with me? My head, my god how my head hurts. There's a brightness around me, it must be morning. Did I oversleep again? I really must get moving. My god my head hurts.

"Your Honor, please!" a voice yells. "We all know how long this will take if we cannot get through at least one question without this constant interruption."

I glance at my hands. They are shaking. I'm not in my bed, I'm not in my house. But where am I? Looking around, I realize it's not the television that's making the noise that hurts my ears. The sound is coming from all around – front, back, and sides. The tips of my fingers tingle. I rub them together, trying desperately to stop the strange crawling sensation that's running up and down my arms. I reach out for my warm blankets to pull them close. I want to feel safe and secure. But my blankets are not anywhere near. I have to be sleeping, I just have to be.

The room spins and a gnawing sensation nags from deep within. Floating and twirling, my mind runs wildly. I feel confused and sick. This has to be a dream, nothing else can explanation these weird sensations. I reach out again for my covers but feel something hard instead of soft.

The dresser? Am I touching my dresser? What's my dresser doing way over here?

The more I grope at my surroundings, the more I realize I'm not in bed. Chaos – confusion is terrorizing me – sickening me. I can't think clearly. My hands reach to scratch my head, but instead, I press them tightly against my eyes, trying to stop the wild spinning.

The noise – muffled words – shuffling shoes – *stop – please stop!* I'm sitting in a chair. *Get a hold of yourself.* Hard wooden arms rigidly hug me. *But I don't own any chairs with hard wooden arms. I'm in a chair, a real hard chair.*

Fear rises from deep within my soul, spreading violently throughout my veins, attacking the farthest and deepest points of my sanity.

"Your Honor, that wasn't a question," a voice pleads. "It's clear that he's leading the witness. I object."

I take a deep breath and let it out slowly. Blinking several times, my eyes focus, somewhat. I skim the room for something familiar … anything familiar, but I freeze.

I do not know where I am or why. It's impossible to comprehend anything. I've never seen this room before. This is definitely the first time I've been in this place. But how can that possibly be? No … something's not right, something's all wrong.

A table, a wooden table is before me. It's definitely not my kitchen table. Next to me is a man wearing a dark suit with a red tie. He's verbally arguing with the man standing in the middle of … of the …

"Courtroom!" I scream.

The voices around me rise to the level of utter chaos before the judge slams her hammer against her desk. "Order! Order in my court. Bailiff!"

"She spoke!" A reporter shrieks from behind me.

The man sitting next to me grabs my arm. "My god …" he whispers, "… can you hear me?"

"What's going on … where am I?" I ask. "Who are you? What is this place?"

I jerk my arm away and scoot back. With my sudden reaction, the Bailiff rushes to my side. My fear is growing faster than my mind can comprehend.

"What's happening?" I scream.

"My god!" the stranger next to me repeats.

"Order … I demand *order* in my court!" the judge yells as the other voices continue to grow louder and louder.

The people behind me are moving about and talking out of sync. The confusion and disorder is growing more uncontrollable. The judge continues to yell but no one is paying her any attention.

For the woman who has been silent for the last several months is suddenly speaking. The crazy, evil, and comatose woman who slashed her children into tiny unrecognizable pieces while they slept and who stabbed her husband over a hundred times is suddenly awake and speaking.

I grab my ears and scream. I scream for my husband to help me. "John! John, where are you?"

Asphodel Road

Jon Pierre Carter

I felt someone watching as I drove down Asphodel Road. No one was with me and not a soul on the road. But I couldn't shake the feeling of prying eyes. My headlights pierced the dark, revealing a scarred road with veined cracks that resembled an alligator handbag, with blood smeared along the sides in a blotchy abstraction. I assumed the gleaming, crimson pools were from a recent roadkill and nothing more. Memorials made from makeshift crosses lined the grassy shoulders like a well-groomed cemetery, making me think twice about speeding along this narrow and winding road.

I hit the brakes as a coyote darted into my headlights, its skin pinkish grey with patches of dull fur. The creature must be suffering from a disease, perhaps mange or rabies. Its limbs stiffened, forcing it to hobble in a pathetic wobble. It vanished into a cluster of contorted trees.

An eerie feeling hit as I set the car back in motion. It felt like someone or something had just invaded my soul. A parasite, picking apart my innermost thoughts, awakening parts of my past best left forgotten. It felt as if my clothes had been torn away, leaving me naked for the world to see.

A woman stood on the side of the road under a flickering streetlamp. Her dark hair draped solemnly over her shoulders. She waved a hand. A default suspicion compelled me to speed past without a second thought, but regret set in. She could be a stranded motorist in distress. Despite my reservations, I wanted to help. As if an unseen force held me captive, I pulled over and waited. I peered through the rearview mirror as she hurried to my car.

Her knee-high boots emitted the sound of galloping clicks with each hurried step. She opened the passenger door and her wide eyes stared at me. She climbed inside, kicking at the crumpled cheeseburger wrappers and crushed coffee cups that littered the floor.

"Apologies for the mess. Been on the road for a while. The name's Carl."

"Sarah … and let's be clear about some things. I won't do quickies or a half-and-half or any weird stuff. I just needed a ride."

"That's … that's not why I picked you up. I just want to help."

She studied me with clear, blue eyes as pristine as the backdrop of a winter's sea. My sister had those same eyes. The girl appeared to be in her mid-twenties. A gaunt face with sunken cheeks and peppered skin that aged her prematurely. She retained a natural beauty – a hooked nose, high cheek bones, and black hair that gleamed with a brilliant sheen of a vinyl record. The door closed, casting her into the shadows.

Sarah stared out the passenger window. "I'm sorry. Men don't usually give me a ride unless they want something. My car stalled around here somewhere. I got lost taking a shortcut through the forest. My flashlight died." She held up a small, green cylinder. "Been on foot for … don't know how long. I'm exhausted."

"Where do you need to go?"

"Anywhere but here."

"You and me both," I whispered. "Feels like someone's been watching me."

"The locals say this road is haunted, yah know. Nothing good ever happens out here. Even the animals act funny. Motorists sometimes disappear. People been murdered too. See all those crosses? Those aren't just accident victims. This road attracts the worst, like a magnet or something."

"Ghost stories. Every small town has 'em. The name of this road … Asphodel Road … reminds me of the Greek underworld."

"Underworld?"

"Asphodel Meadows … where the soul dwells in limbo … according to the ancient Greeks anyway."

She laughed. "Mr. Smarty Pants?"

"If what you say is true," I replied, "should I be worried … about you? Are you one of those sinister characters that prowls the night?"

"I could ask the same about you." She smiled.

She had me there. If Asphodel Road attracted brute forces, I was certainly a prime candidate for the road's hellish embrace, synching in with the other malcontents traversing these grounds at ungodly hours.

An icy silence followed. Frank Sinatra played from the speakers, interrupting my strained pause. His velvety tenor somewhat soothed my nerves. I hummed.

Sarah snickered and shook her head.

"Not a Sinatra fan?" I asked.

"A bit old fashioned, don't you think? How old are you?"

"Thirty-two. But I consider myself an old soul. Sinatra's my hero. Good-looking, charismatic, dashing, and bold. Contrast him to me … no contest there."

"Ayn Rand said that a man who doesn't value himself cannot value others. You're not the only one who reads."

I laughed. "No offense, but I'd never peg you as an Ayn Rand fan."

"I used to read a lot … business and self-help mostly. I love inspirational quotes from successful people. Too bad none of it stuck, considering how much I screwed up *my* life."

"Then, we have something in common." I sighed.

"I had my dreams mapped out. Break into modeling, start my own agency, and be the talk of *tinsel* town. But life got in the way, yah know. So … what's your story? You don't seem like most guys I meet. You go to college or something?"

I took college classes while serving a five-year prison sentence for grand larceny, but I refused to disclose that little detail. "A few courses, but I read a lot in my spare time. Wanted to be an English professor, but like you, fate refused to shine favor on me."

I contemplated my life trajectory. My fate was anyone's guess. I'd been driving for days. To be honest, I wasn't sure why I took this route. I had to get out of town after I – after the *incident*. What made me turn on Asphodel Road was anyone's guess.

"You have family nearby?" I asked. "Anyone that can help?"

"I have a brother but haven't talked to him in years."

"Why haven't you talked to him?" A biting silence filled the car. I wanted to snatch my question back from the ether, but it was already out there, traversing the turbulent waters and breaching an unspoken barrier. "I have a little sister," I said. "Her name's Emily. She followed me around like a puppy when we were kids. We never had the happiest of childhoods, so I was her protector. When I turned seventeen, I ran away from home. Lived on the streets for a while. Did what I had to do to survive. Haven't seen her since."

"How long has it been since you've seen her?"

"At least fifteen years. She was ten the last time I saw her. I traveled outta state. She's probably forgotten all about me."

"You should have stayed in contact with her," Sarah stated.

I sighed. "You're probably right."

"Why did you abandon her?"

The question cut deep. "The abuse became too much for me, so I left. I wanted to take Emily with me, but … I was just a kid."

"Sounds like you were only thinking of yourself."

"You don't mince words, do you."

She didn't answer. Her condemnation had surprised me. Perhaps my story reminded her of unsettled memories. I wanted to know more about her, but it felt as if I would be committing a capital offense. Not to mention that the eerie feeling of being watched had suddenly returned.

I was driving down the same stretch of road for a while now. It felt as if I was driving in an endless loop, never reaching the end and only to start back at the beginning. I glanced out my side window and it seemed as if the same trees enshrouded in the night were passing by again.

I jolted as something scratched deeply into the side of my neck; a wild animal digging its curved nails into my skin. The tires squealed as I slammed on the brakes.

Sarah glared at me. "What's wrong?"

I stepped outside and yanked open the back door. Nothing! Sarah jumped out and rushed to my side.

"What happened?" she asked.

"Something scratched me." I rubbed my neck, checking for blood. "You didn't see anything?"

Sarah shook her head.

I held out a clean hand and shrugged.

"I told you, this road is haunted," she said.

"Don't start that again."

A howling echoed from somewhere behind the trees. The all-too-familiar scream of a coyote. When one grew up in the backwoods, one knew the howl, high-pitched akin to a woman's plea for help. But the nocturnal calling suddenly morphed into a cackling; a human laughter swirling within the chorus of yowls. Goosebumps ran up my back. Something was near, and it was staring at me.

Everything about this area looked completely distorted. The leafless trees resembled bony talons. The air carried a sweet but pungent aroma of death – a slight hint of sulfur. A rotting carcass must be close. The soft wind whistled, playing tricks on my mind as if warning of impending danger.

The fluorescent glow of my headlights filled the road. A pair of reflective golden eyes glared back. At first, I dismissed them as the eyeshine of a possum or coyote, but the eyes were not at ground level. The orbs reached as high as a man who would stand over seven feet. It must be a small animal perched on a branch. The thing's unblinking eyes remained fixed, waiting for me to make a move.

Sarah's drawn expression hit, and my protective instincts kicked in. I pulled her in close. We crawled into the car and locked the doors. I flashed a mini light on the creature, unable to make out the form. The glaring gold eyes simply vanished before reappearing after I moved the light away.

"It's an evil spirit." Sarah grabbed my hand. "But you have power over it. Stand your ground and tell it to go away."

The cackles, growls, and howls grew louder. The phantom eyes inched closer. The trees rustled, and a thunderous stomp boomed, rocking the car.

I sped down the road, continuously looking into the rearview mirror. I needed to know if that *thing* was following. Nothing. My speech sounded hoarse and shaky. "What was that *thing* back there?"

"You shouldn't have panicked. Your fear gives it power. You shouldn't be afraid. A living person has control over the dead. They can only harm you if you let them. It was FDR who said that the only thing we have to fear is fear itself. Don't let the fear consume you, Carl."

"There has to be a rational explanation," I said. "Just an animal of some kind. My eyes must have missed it."

"There's no point in running. It'll only follow us wherever we go. Confront it and banish it."

"If what you say is true, then why haven't you banished it?"

"I never said it was going to be easy."

I slammed on the brakes. "I don't know what you're getting at, but I want no part of this."

Sarah averted her gaze and paused. Perhaps searching for the proper words? "About your sister. If you had another chance to help her, if she was in trouble, would you?"

"What does she have to do —"

"Just answer the question." Her brow hardened and her words became quick and sharp.

"Of course, I would."

Sarah's eyes looked deeply into mine. "I need to show you something." She placed my hand on her icy chest.

A vibration ran up my arm and down my back. My eyelids felt suddenly heavy and burned with fatigue. A white flash filled my view.

I stood silent in the living room of my childhood. My little sister, Emily, was playing with her teddy bear. Her plump face brimmed with exuberance. Her hair shown like the sun's rays. A bucktooth smile that could brighten anyone's day lit her cheeks.

My father stepped boldly into the room. He grabbed her arm and slapped her across the face. The same fiery beard covered his lower jaw and that stubborn pot belly still spilled over his belt. He manhandled her with arms as thick as tree stumps, hands as meaty as a bear's paw.

I felt the shackled hopelessness that always anchored me to her frail body, the torrent of abuse subduing her sunny aura, darkening her soul. Each night she prayed, prayed for my return. But I never did. The abuse only grew worse as she entered her teenage years. Pa would come to her room each night.

Don't show me this!

He would cover her mouth and enjoy his forbidden desires.

I froze, feeling the agonizing betrayal. *He couldn't sink any lower.*

I now stood in the backyard of our single-story house. The yard was spacious encircled by a grand forest. It was a humid, summer night, with fireworks crackling in the distance, the sky filled with sparkling lights. Pa sat drunk in the middle of the yard, watching.

Emily stepped outside, holding Dad's hunting rifle. Pa never saw it coming. The gunshot blended with the pops and crackles of the night as the back of Pa's head blew open. His body slumped to the ground, the beer foaming near his hand. Emily stood over the twitching corpse and stared. I should have felt something over my father's untimely fate, but I felt nothing.

As Emily disappeared into the house, a thin black mist swirled. The cloudy blockade locked onto my muscles, clenching and pulling. A dark intelligence seeped through my pores, reading my emotions with empathic precision – a blend of hate and resentment, harmonizing into a vengeful maelstrom that polluted the air with a sulfuric tinge. A blinding light and another force warped me back onto the street. I stared at the headlights reflecting against the road.

Glimpses of Emily's life flashed like a sliding projector's screen. She had sold herself to make ends meet, pawning ill-gotten loot with a gang of strung-out transients – all the while embarking down the primrose path of opioid bliss. As the years melted into the universe, an unforgiving street life consumed Emily's youth, her blonde hair coated in a matte-black finish that matched her now darkened features. With skin dulled to a pale grey, the moisture had deprived and shriveled her like a prune; cheeks receding from a plump rosiness to a hollowed tautness that shaped her mouth into a fish-lip pucker. The Emily of yesteryear no longer existed, and in her place rested a despondent woman with empty eyes. A fate dipped into an outlaw lifestyle only to reforge into a familiar face – Sarah?

The memories hit and my heart sank at the sight of her ungodly fate. An irate client strangling her in a dingy motel room. He appeared to be a family man; middle-aged with a hefty physique and sporting a balding dome. He was the type one would greet at a bank or a park.

"No!"

I reached out to stop him, but my hands fell through the man's neck. Nothing was solid. It was simply a vision from Emily's past reduced to a simple thought. Emily lay motionless on the bed, her eyes and mouth closed, a calm serenity across her face. She had finally found the peace that she never knew in life.

The man dug her grave in the woods with a rusty shovel, the area lit only by a lantern.

I shouted obscenities, trying to grab him as he erased my precious sister from existence with fresh dirt and dead leaves. He walked gently on the forest's curvy path, using the lantern as a guide. I followed. His Chevy truck was parked on the side of the road. I watched as he drove away. Only a reflective road sign glared – Asphodel Road.

Emily had mentioned that this road attracted the worst type of people. Men such as the one that murdered my sister and who eluded accountability. I could only hope that karma doled out proper justice to her killer.

Sarah nodded.

I turned away and stared at the road. "Emily? Is it you? Did that man really kill you? Is Asphodel Road your grave?"

From the corner of my eyes, I saw her nod.

My tears escaped, and I lowered my head. "I'm sorry I wasn't there. Why didn't you tell me when I picked you up?"

"You'd never believe me. Besides, I was still angry. I called you here because I need your help. You must free my soul from this place. I'm confined here for eternity, where Pa torments me because I murdered him. Only you have the power to stop this because you have the breath of life. For over five years, I've walked this road and I don't understand the dark force that lives here. But I've seen how the living can conquer the dead."

I took a moment. "You said this road attracts evil men. I don't think you lured me here … I think the road did." I choked on my words, struggling to utter my confession. "I'm on the run because I killed a man. I gambled to pay off my debts. I did a B&E for quick cash. The homeowner surprised me from the hall. We struggled and I shot him. He was just an old man. I regret it every day."

Sarah sighed. "That's terrible. I'm not going to judge. You saw my past. I need you to be strong for us both. Be the brother I need you to be. Pa is inside you now. I can feel him."

I thought about his penetrating eyes. I blinked several times as the image of my father suddenly appeared behind Emily. He was surrounded by that same baleful mist from our backyard. His eyes were black as obsidian, foam dripped from peeled lips, a row of fangs protruded from his smile. Emily squirmed as he grabbed her from behind, burying his canine teeth into her throat. Her face twisted and she screamed. I reached for her but a white light blinded me.

I was back in the car again. I jumped out and shouted. "Emily!"
No reply.

My legs shook, my adrenaline surged manifesting inside my shaking fits. I cried out her name into the wind. The night choked back a blackness that should have left me helpless if it were not for my high beams. I was now standing on a different plane of existence, a world farthest from the sun with its merciless freeze and never-ending silence.

A woman's voice sailed through the air, high-pitched and piercing from the shadows. Emily cried out from a distant dreamland. A familiar essence that lingered, a hostility as thick as stale perfume, reminding me of Pa's head in our yard and the back of his head gone.

Acidic disdain hovered in the air like an electric current, the pinch of sulfur stinging my nose, frothing like cream. Pa's unearthly seed had germinated into something I couldn't understand, but it made me shudder. My father, an otherworldly spirit confined to this hellish road chasing Emily, playing an endless game of cat-and-mouse.

Emily needed me to confront this darkened force, but my cowardice prevailed. I hurried to my car, locking the doors. I took a deep breath, ignoring my pounding heart. Staying on Asphodel Road, I drove until a large sign blocked my path.

Dead End

Behind the sign was nothing more than a barrier of brush and endless trees. I grabbed my mini flashlight and the beretta. The glowing gold eyes stared at me.

Fear swelled in my gut. I wondered if my father's primal spirit dwelled within those glaring eyes. My words quivered. "Dad, is that you?"

I shined a light on those wicked eyes that inched ever closer. Emily cried out from somewhere in the darkness.

"What would Frank Sinatra do?" I asked.

I stepped closer to the glowing eyes until his sloshy footsteps echoed and the monster took form. Bright pink flesh contrasted eerily against the dark night, a bipedal beast with the head of a long-snouted coyote, red foam dripping from its mouth, jagged long teeth, eyes beady as black marbles. The body decaying, fur just barely clinging to the bone. One side of its ribcage exposed, the arms scrawny. I thought about my father's fate, his corpse at the mercy of these famished animals.

But here stood my dad. The true manifestation of his vile essence – disease-ridden like a rabid coyote, decayed as a rotting carcass. This road must have given him a physical form, and the form he chose was the most horrid imaginable. His spirit must have absorbed Mother Nature's unflinching cruelty – the ferocity of the predator and the dark clouds lurking over all woodland creatures. Instead of recognizing the unbridled beauty, he chose to harness the dark side. The forest of Asphodel Road was the perfect breeding ground to feed his spirit, nurturing his perverted thoughts, allowing his rotting soul to fester, providing a form befitting his foul deeds. My dad was no longer a malicious human. He was now something feral and inhuman.

But within that animalistic scourge rested the heart of a bereaved man who never healed from his wife's death. He was abandoned by his only son and murdered by his only daughter. What little humanity he held in life he had discarded in death, adopting a mantle so horrifying it petrified me into a fear-induced paralysis. All communication between my mind and body severed like the purgatorial phase between sleep and consciousness. I heard Emily's disembodied voice, urging me to move.

I broke from my stupor and fired shots into the creature's chest, ignoring my ringing ears. The creature stumbled when the bullets hit, black fluid dripped from the wounds. Judging by his decrepit exterior, he had no beating heart, no blood flowing in his veins. Nothing but tattered flesh and bags of bones with diseased blood, black as death itself.

The creature moaned a low-pitched giggle, reminding me of a laughing hyena. The body jerked uncontrollably, the head jittering. The walking corpse barreled my way like an oncoming train. I fired more shots. The demon attacked, digging it claws deeply into my abdomen. Pain exploded and I collapsed, losing my gun and flashlight. The animal locked its jaws on my arm with the strength of a crocodile. The acidic saliva ate at my flesh. I kicked and finally the creature released me.

My sister's advice about the living having power over the dead echoed through my dimming brain. She was powerless over this monster because she had no life force. But my breath was more potent than any weapon I could hold. My use of the gun stemmed from a place of fear, not out of bravery. I pressed through the pain and spoke from the heart

"I'm standing my ground, Dad! I'm establishing boundaries. You no longer have power over my life."

The creature paused and Pa's face materialized. His eyes now glared at me. He stepped back, a flicker of emotion revealed – fear. I pushed through the pain, struggling for a breath, relying on sheer adrenaline.

"I'm no longer running. I banish you to the outer darkness. You'll no longer torture me or Emily. God, free us from this demon's torment, free us from our father. Bestow mercy on us. Please forgive us for our crimes. Forgive *me* for the man I killed."

Like a recoiled snake, the monster aimed for the trees, emitting a dull growl. The creature's skin peeled like a molting snake's until nothing remained but a skeletal form. The animal collapsed and slowly dissolved from existence, leaving only a pair of gleaming eyes that eased into the shadows. When the eyes finally vanished, a light lit the world. But the physical pain was too much for me to ignore. I heaved and breathed in deeply.

Emily's cheeks were flushed, but her eyes held a renewal with a glossy vigor.

My mission was complete. "I'm here for you, Emily."

Her words sounded thick with emotion. "Thank you, brother."

A dull ache pulsed through my body. I wasn't going to make it.

Dead End

I thought about Sunday school and our fire-and-brimstone teacher who talked about the wages of sin and how it related to death. I paid for my sins but hopefully achieved something greater — a redemption perhaps.

I had read the Quran when serving time. It said that God *or Allah* used hellfire to cleanse criminals and sinners in the afterlife. That some people did good deeds on Earth and didn't need hell, but others needed the flames to purify their souls. The punishment ended eventually and that was when the sinner would be reborn. That was the *God* I wanted to believe in.

"I want you to live," Emily whispered.

I faded in and out, hearing her prayers. But I couldn't make out the words.

I now stood on Asphodel Road next to Emily, staring at my lifeless body. My eyes closed, looking peaceful. I had somehow adopted a new body. An essence now solidified that hovered between two planes.

When Emily smiled and we embraced, my soul relaxed and a diamond-shaped light formed. I should have been afraid, but the aura's warmth drew me in like a moth to a flame.

Emily looked at it. "I've never seen this until now. What do you think?"

I squeezed her hand, just as I did when she was small. "I don't know what to think, but let's find out together."

24

Lynn's Thoughts …

As I read through the lines, I could actually visualize myself inside a car, at night, and alone. But what the author never said was where the driver had come from or why. Leaving that little detail out helped to create the scene that soon haunted me.

Was it the drive itself that took our character into the next realm of existence or was it the evil monster, his father? Was Carl already dead before he even started down that road? Did the road ever exist in the first place?

Bringing in the Greek philosophy on the underworld allowed the reader to take a glimpse of where the story was taking us. The author then flips by contrasting this theory with Ayn Rand and her thoughts on *Objectivism.* Clever, indeed. Rand was an advocate of reason and somewhat rejected faith. A dualism that could make one contemplate – *at what point does death override life?* The Greeks believed in an afterlife where the soul was judged at the time of death. Rand believed that if man was to survive life, that man would need to live by *his* reason and not just by *his* faith. But who's reason and who's faith? Man's or God's?

Our author brings to light in this short piece how the soul can and will separate from the body. Therefore, I've often wondered if our judgment equated to our guilt through our physical existence and not the spiritual. Or in other words, the guilt of what we did or did not do while alive. If Earth was created for us to learn and grow, then once our life ended, how would we eventually judge ourselves?

The father in this story, was he sorry for what he did to his children, or was his pain too great? What was he actually guilty of doing or not doing? Was he guilty for being a bad parent, or was he guilty of not accepting his fate – that of losing his wife?

Many unanswered questions in this piece. Many thoughts to contemplate.

26

ATA NOR

Michael A. Wexler

The blackness of the forest stretched out forever unbounded.

The warm and humid air caused my skin to glisten and my hair to hang in my eyes. The twigs beneath my leather boots were too damp to crack. I gripped my sword and moved through a dark, unwelcoming world – a silent carpet of spongy earth and soggy mold.

Soon enough, I would find light in the fiery pit of the great beast ATA NOR.

The path was rough through the dense brush and cramped with trees. My nervous ears listened for padded footfalls that threatened each step in this realm devoid of life. Nothing dared to live within the domain of ATA NOR. I knew that, yet I chilled to the illusions taking root in my imagination.

I often fretted over fanciful evils that did not exist.

This will not do.

I halted, squaring my shoulders and tilting my head, as a forced growl sent my overwrought fears scattering across my subconscious.

Were there not enough to challenge my courage in the nearness of Ata Nor? Did I need to burden my task with ghosts and phantoms?

Calmed, I took up the trail.

My thoughts wandered. I reflected on my long fighting days and the vast regions and wild kingdoms I had traveled. The wars I had fought and triumphed in – Ljfar to the west and Griev to the east. I had battled the wild, unnamed barbarians of the frozen north and the dark-skinned horseman of the arid southern deserts. Always had I entered the lists with courage and determination. Except for here inside the hot, lonely jungles leading to Ata Nor. For the first time, I felt fear. I advanced upon the undefeated emissary of death and I had faltered.

I thank the Gods there is none to see.

Again, I shook myself.

"I must advance. I held the trust of my village and honor demands I go forward!"

Faint at first and then growing ever stronger, a noxious puff of poisonous vapors touched my senses – spewed from the bottomless pit of my faceless demon. There was nothing supernatural or imaginary in that rush of heat, stinging my flesh and burning my eyes. Even at a distance, I felt a presence of evil, a taste of death. I paused, listening. Did Ata Nor cry out, egging me on? Was the wind kicking up, or did I feel the foul breath of the undying beast blowing a warning?

"Turn back or die!" a voice screeched.

The ancient ones of my tribe had warned of the wailing spirits of lost souls who had fallen into the pit, devoured by the endless bloodlust of the final conqueror, ATA NOR. I steeled my soul and pressed on.

I reached a dense and twisting part of the forest. The gases that rose from the pit of ATA NOR descended thick and choking, a heavy canopy of blackened treetops blocking an escape. I forced my lips to clamp against the acrid fumes, yet they seeped within me like hungry serpents sent to strangle and kill.

Following the curve of the forest, I bent low against the billowing smoke limiting my vision. It took me unaware when the unholy vanguard of ATA NOR emerged from the dark billows – naked sirens calling, coaxing, beckoning me forward – their voices a low, throaty hum.

I counted five. Slender, lithe goddesses clad in silken sheaths, their ivory limbs waving me on, long blonde hair waving in a thick and suffocating wind. I stepped closer, watching their opal eyes that seemed to smile. I stopped, fighting the draw. As swift and inviting those eyes had become, a rippling sea of fiery globes burst forth, filling my path.

My nerves strained, my muscles flexed. Hesitation shed, I sent my great sword slicing into the ethereal images. Unaffected laughter echoed as they were not real. My sword arced and the creatures vanished, a puff blown to hell.

Again, the low growl of an angry beast escaped my parched throat. The crisis had passed. My blood ran hot again. I had allowed myself a second stumble into the trap of my imagination. Was it my mind failing or my strength fading? Or was it the fabled torture of ATA NOR that the old men of my village had foretold? An agony of fear that the beast inflicted upon his intended victims.

"Hear me, ATA NOR!" I yelled. "I do not intend to be a victim! I am a man amongst children who does not shrink from fairy tales and childish make believe. I fear neither the dark nor the unknown and stand tall, braced for combat, equal to the trial ahead."

Of all the young men in my village, it was I that the elders had chosen to end the reign of ATA NOR – chosen because I alone dared to go.

I remembered old Basamet sitting with me the hour before my departure. How many years had Basamet been the tribal elder? It seemed he was gray and withered since I was pink and suckling at my mother's breast. But his eyes, his eyes never lost the glow of youth. Now, invested with the wisdom of age, his eyes sparkled, so much so that the whiteness of his beard looked almost absurd, as if it should be as black and youthful as those dark eyes.

"You go upon the noblest of missions," said he.

"Is that but another word for dangerous?" said I.

There came a sudden darkening to Basamet's countenance. The sparkle transformed into a cold light that did not attempt to hide the truth.

"I have sat as we sit many times in my long lifetime," he said in slow, measured words. "In each instance, having this last talk with the chosen warrior. Each meeting proved a prelude to death, a horrid death for which I have no description. The men, to the last, were both brave and confident they should succeed where the others failed. Is it not the same with you?"

"Could it be another way? If the wolf feared its prey, it would die of starvation."

"You have the power of youth," said he, "as did those before you. Choosing you came easy, for you have oft demonstrated your skill upon the hunt or the contests of war defending the holy ways. But this, this journey to the pit of ATA NOR –"

"It is different?"

Basamet nodded. "Triumph now, and become the greatest warrior to stride the Earth. Fail —"

"Fail and I am but one in a line of boastful pretenders."

"Fail and you are dead, and within a few full moons, forgotten because your name, the mere speaking of it, is a reminder of the profane power of ATA NOR."

I smiled at Basamet and replied, "I shall return in triumph! With ATA NOR defeated and our people free of his bloodlust. All this I shall accomplish, ancient one."

"If you live."

"I shall live."

I went forward with a sharpened sword and ready dagger, leading a celebratory procession to the edge of our black and dismal forest. Watching as the cheering crowd withdrew, quiet and quick, shrinking from my view, their terror of these woods and what lurked within written large upon their faces.

War-weary faces.

A war not of man against man, but man against the supernatural, the faceless demon ATA NOR.

I had set forth upon my quest in a strident mood — my confidence bolstered by my youthful vigor and the pride of an unbeaten warrior. A poise sobered by the bleak reality of the lonesome woods, the heavy boughs hanging close, the looping vines requiring constant avoidance, the rich stink of the still unseen pit of the beast.

But no forest runs forever, no more so than any single journey. The faint glow accompanying the pit's vaporous mist was just visible in the dark, and with it, the full measure of my youthful bluster returned.

ATA NOR drew close, and I welcomed him.

A welcoming rush transformed into a pressing concern for what had begun as a gentle mist and flowing smooth, now swooped and swirled as flying wraiths blowing hot across my brow. The tenacious fog thickened. I wiped at my sweat and shivered at the clinging dampness. I dried my hands against the bole of the nearest tree lest my sword should slip in a moment of crisis.

The trees thinned. The beginnings of a glade, an open space of fifty yards at the edge of which sat a yawning pit of shimmering flame. I had found it, the burning home of ATA NOR.

The legends are true, for I confess to my doubts.

As Basamet had lamented in the memory of an aging man, no human foot ever known to come this far and return. No eye of man ever seen the great beast and lived to recall his face or describe his voice. Even the oldest of the village men could not prepare me for what I might meet. The villagers only knew that, in the depth of the darkest night or by the light of the brightest sun, ATA NOR would come, invisible and irresistible, to carry away another victim. His voracious appetite for human flesh was never satisfied. He would steal a life, leaving behind a bereaved and shattered community. ATA NOR picked no favorites. Man, woman, and child all succumbed, young, old, hero, and coward.

Humanity is full of each.

Yet it seemed there were never enough souls to satiate the hunger of this greatest of devils. ATA NOR would come, silent and soundless, and someone would die. Their deaths were as inevitable as the grief that followed.

The sight of the great flaming hole flooded me with an unfamiliar hesitancy. I had battled the beasts of the fields and the men of the mountains and valleys. None had taken the better of me. Never had I hesitated. My victories had created a fearsome warrior, the best of the best – the one selected to vanquish ATA NOR.

Yet I wavered. Was this fear? I felt different, a difference expressed in a more cautious, more calculating approach to an unknown enemy.

Yes, that is it.

Caution – not fear, as the village elders had warned. I was advancing against Satan himself.

I raised my sword high. "My faith lies in my blade!"

I stepped without the benefit of the moon or stars, the light of that gaping pit as my guide. Shoulder's squared, I advanced. My feet seemed possessed of their own intent.

I smiled.

Though my soul perceived an evil presence, I sensed no unholy demon, no supernatural being. I crept forward to the very edge of the abyss, leaning forward as far as the inferno permitted, fighting the searing heat, looking, searching. I saw nothing but the fanning flames falling away.

"ATA NOR!" I cried. "Come forward, face me, and we shall learn if good or evil, courage or fear is the greater power. Of which shall carry the day."

A few loose boulders lay to hand. I hefted one and heaved it into the pit. It disappeared in a hissing noise, not unlike an angry serpent. I waited. ATA NOR did not respond. I wondered if he had vacated his ghastly hole and was now abroad in the village seeking fresh prey.

The truth did not matter. I would wait for ATA NOR until the first rays of dawn dictated that the night should end, after which I would return to my hut and tell my tale. I would delight the women and children and bask before the warriors. Then sleep, venturing out upon the morrow and every morrow after, until ATA NOR was dead – or was I?

Surrendering to the intense heat, I backed away from the pit's edge, the foggy mist enveloping me again. I cursed and sought to cool myself by reentering the forest, a small, uncluttered plot. But the mist pursued. It came at me with a heavy cloud now laden with bits of ash impossible to escape lest I retreat from the woods, and this I could not do. I vowed against it and stood firm.

"I should conserve my strength," I mused, for without cause I felt weary.

An unwelcome stab hit my ribs causing my thoughts to harken to a recent battle with the valley tribe. The dozen men I had killed and the balance sent fleeing in terror at my ferocity and the ferocity of my tribe. With a low snarl, I sat cross-legged upon the forest floor, my great curved sword resting upon my knees – the sudden slack in my vitality a puzzlement.

I touched my right side, where a random sword had penetrated my guard. A deep wound, but one expected such injuries in battle. It was no worse than a dozen such injuries sustained in past skirmishes, a wound to endure in silence.

I grew sleepy. I growled.

A long overdue breeze blew, freeing the smoke and stench. It was pleasant and pleased me with its caress. It carried strange new scents upon its breath. Flowers laden with memories of forgotten places, worlds of my youth and conquests.

A sense of unreality swept upon me, a sudden realization that I had seen so much in my young life, known so many faces and souls, and yet, I was alone. I was always alone. What kind of life had that loneliness wrought?

Is there love?

I had known the company of women far and wide but never love. Never one beauty above another. Was there hate? I had warred often and killed many men. Did I hate them? Did I know a single soul long enough or well enough even to care that they had died?

No.

I slew from duty, not hate, and with the blind anger of others forced upon me. It was them, the war bringers, I should despise. For never did they fight but sent the young and ignorant to their deaths while they grew fat and old and rich.

I saw figures upon the breeze, men running, swords swinging, racing along a line of destiny that ran back to my earliest days. It was as if a door had opened upon my entire existence, and through it poured every life I had encountered and affected.

Across that door hung a filmy curtain against which the wind blew to the effect of a gutted candle. I heard a murmur of voices that sought to counsel and console me.

Console me of what?

I did not create the wars. I but fought them – the honorable calling of those sworn to duty.

"Duty or slavery?" a voice asked.

The sound broke the vale of sleep that had stolen over me. With a start, I awoke. My head filled with that questioning voice. With an effort, I surged to my feet to cast aside my sordid dream, and then I saw it, no, not it, I saw *her.*

An involuntary gasp escaped. Who would not start? The swirling mist had congealed into a solid form in the center of the small space I had picked to rest. Though more haze than stone, it shimmered and shone. A human figure, a woman, beautiful beyond conception, inching toward me, reaching out.

This vision, this naked, vaporous entity, for it could not be real, stretched out her arms to wrap around me, to draw me in close. I saw hard nails of great length, stained blood red and tipped with fire.

Impossible.

The same for her eyes. They lit and sparked, flushing her cheeks, highlighting a curved mouth with lips burned crimson and tinted orange, blue, and black.

I would not countenance this illusion. I proclaimed it a trick of ATA NOR, casting a hypnotic spell to disarm an opponent and render them vulnerable. No, I would not have it. My sword flew, cutting through the steaming mirage. The air moved, and the flames rippled and danced, but the illusion remained.

A tinkling of laughter joined the crackling blaze that expanded and contracted and again moved to engulf me. And I knew.

She was ATA NOR!

"You will not possess me, ATA NOR!" I cried, standing tall and refusing to retreat. "Show yourself in your true form. My sword awaits. It can kill as swift and sure as any conjure you throw against me."

The odd fiery figure ceased dancing. The flames dimmed and cooled. With it came a lighting of the darkness. Even the well of fire from which ATA NOR had emerged looked cold.

Could it be that it iced?

I stood awed, peering into the incalculable depth of mist and light around me.

From the very heart of the specter, there came a voice. "There is nothing to fear. There is nothing to fight. It is your time, noble warrior." The beautiful woman had returned, smiling.

My sword struck out, guided by instinct, carving through the renewed form that was not a mist but solid flesh, bone, blood, and muscle. My cut rose up and veered sideways through a white, enticing neck that sparkled with pearled dew. And when that mighty blade again found air, the naked figure of ᴀᴛᴀ ɴᴏʀ stood as before – no blood, no injury, no change.

"There is no need to strike," sang the phantom. "Embrace me, warrior. Is that not the journey's end you seek? Come, fear not. Your struggles end here. Nestle against my breast, and all shall be as ordained."

"I ordain who and what shall be my struggles. I embrace the victory of today and the challenge of tomorrow. And this victory shall be the death of you, ᴀᴛᴀ ɴᴏʀ."

For a reply, the vision laughed and flowed as if cast upon a vast wind. She engulfed me, and though I pushed hard against her, I could not move. My chest burned, my limbs trembled. I lost my sword. The lethargy I had grappled with in the forest returned – twice fold.

ᴀᴛᴀ ɴᴏʀ softened and became lithe and supple. Loveliness beyond description. I lost all fear and felt an overwhelming desire to surrender. I gazed up. The first faint rays of the sun smiled down upon us. Clouds moved apart, and a piece of heaven opened.

My eyes watered with the first dew of the day.

The beckoning morning called to me as nothing had called to me before. In the arms of ᴀᴛᴀ ɴᴏʀ, I began to rise. The tiredness fled. The pains of my wounds earned over a lifetime of attack and defense evaporated. A great peace came upon me, contentment I had never known before.

As we rose, I gazed down and into the shadowed forest. I saw not an empty woods but an open plain sunbathed and littered with the remains of a great battle that had not been there moments ago. And – there was the flaming pit of ᴀᴛᴀ ɴᴏʀ, which I now perceived as filled with flailing corpses.

"You look upon both sides of death, warrior."

A vague remembrance crowded my mind. I understood the flash of crashing bodies, banging swords, flying knives, and grunting men, and there was nothing to fear from Ata Nor. The beast of the pit would not rise for me. I should never see nor know his distorted visage, his clutching hands.

I flew with an angel.

Indeed, my struggles had come to an end. A far greater power than man's ego had judged me and made a decision.

I felt a final, everlasting pity for the doomed souls that had caused the great battle from which I now lifted. I experienced a wrenching sadness that the people of my lifetime did not know nor appreciate the beauty and tenderness that could be theirs if they could find the wisdom to live in peace. The warmongers, the greedy and the self- serving, they, not I, would know Ata Nor.

Here, the great flaming pit of hell awaited the likes of Basamet.

I allowed myself to fall limp and nestle upon my angel's breast. I felt her heart beating loud and strong even as my heart slowed, faded, and came to an end.

Lynn's thoughts …

An interesting twist about life and death. I was expecting a dragon or monster at the end of the path for this nameless character. Instead, I meet his conscience and doubt over his life of being a warrior. If I stand back and contemplate about the battles fought throughout time, how many of those who ordered those battles were actually part of those battles? It is quite simple to send another to do your bidding, but it is quite different to do it yourself.

I am not sure, but could Aᴛᴀ Nᴏʀ represent man's cowardness as he battles for power and control?

Our main character is wandering through a dense forest afraid of the evil he must fight. In the end, we perplex that perhaps the old man, Basamet, was actually that evil force. Afterall, he was old and had lived through many battles before. Which I can only concluded that he must have sent others to do his dirty work – to fight his wars.

Therefore, was there ever an actual pit of fire that let to hell or was the actual battle, the fighting and deaths, the imaginary pit?

Michael Wexler added a little flavor of the old style of speaking in his dialogue in order to set the stage and date of his story. But then I ask, do not battles still exist in our world today? And within those battles, how many rulers are at the front fighting?

What would have happened during WWII if no one came to the party? What if everyone just stepped back and dropped their weapons? What would the rulers have done? There would have been no one to kill the ones protesting. Unless the rulers picked up the weapon themselves. And how often does a ruler actually step forward to murder another? Are they not the ones ordering others to kill?

Interesting concept, Michael. Now let's ask, what about the fate of these warriors? Will they be judged harshly for killing, or will they be rewarded for following orders?

The Black-Eyed Kids

Nicole Duffeck

"We're lost," Nicole stated. She was tired from riding in the car for the past twenty hours. Not feeling angry or annoyed, it was just a passionless statement.

"Think you might be right," Nathan replied.

They were attending a conference in Atlanta and had decided to carpool rather than fly. Neither were keen on falling twenty-thousand feet in a sardine can. But at this point, Nicole would have gladly taken her chances, because she would already be in bed after nursing a few Mint Juleps.

"It would be wonderful if we could find a gas station or someplace to ask for directions," Nicole said.

"There must be a town nearby. We're still on the highway … I think."

"Have you seen any road signs?"

"No, nothing."

"No place in America is this uninhabited." Nicole was trying to muster a little sense of optimism.

Nathan grinned.

At least, Nicole thought it was a grin. But it was hard to tell in the dim light of the dashboard. It could have been a grimace or a scowl. She turned on the radio and was met with a blast of static. "Whoa, how deaf are you?"

"It was a good song, and you were in the store … needed something to entertain me." Nathan frowned, raising a 'brow. "Not sure you're gonna find anything this far out."

Nicole admitted defeat and turned it off. There were only two stations, albeit fuzzy – a fire and brimstone preacher or country music. Both made her cringe.

"We must be in banjo county," Nathan stated.

"Probably best to not pull over if you see shirtless men in overalls."

"Why? You afraid Bubba will whisk you off your feet to his pig farm?"

Nicole swatted his arm. "Keep driving, Regis. I'd like to find the hotel before the conference is over."

"Holy heck," he said. "I think we're in luck. I see lights."

"You sure it's not Jed and Bubba shining for deer?"

"Positive. I see a gas station."

"Ah, finally. Neon salvation."

"Hopefully, they're open," Nathan replied.

The tires bumped into the gravel, and the car jostled through the ruts and potholes. The building was open.

"There's a higher power after all," Nathan said.

The dashboard clock showed just after three in the morning, so unless the place was open at an ungodly hour, it was a 24-hour establishment.

"Want to come in?" Nicole asked.

Her nerves felt on end, something about the place gave her the creeps. It could have been she was lost and nine hundred miles from home, or it could have been the rundown gas station with the antiquated pumps, or it could have been something else. But it was intangible, something that permeated the environment, the soil, and the groundwater.

"No, let me keep some semblance of dignity and pretend we're not together."

"Ouch! You mean you're embarrassed to be seen with me?"

"No, would rather not be the lost guy from the north. It's okay for women to ask for directions but not so much for men."

"Be back in a minute," she said through the open window.

The air was still and humid but far from quiet due to the constant buzz and hum from cicadas, crickets, and mosquitos all accompanied by the deep bass of toads.

She hurried across the parking lot. Nearly tripping over the cracked curb, she sighed. She pushed the door open, and a bell chimed. Behind the counter a young woman looked incredibly bored. Nicole stepped up to the counter and the woman glanced up from her magazine.

"Help, yah?" Her accent was thick and almost sounded fake as if mimicking the Beverly Hillbillies.

"Yes, I need directions. Going to Atlanta and got a bit turned around."

"Happens all the time." The young woman pulled out a map from the carousel behind her. "A dollar-four for the map, directions are free." The woman shrugged.

Nicole handed her two singles.

The woman shamelessly pocketed the bills. "Thanks for the tip." She unfolded the map and pointed. "You're here. You need to follow this road another twenty miles. It'll connect to the highway. Take a left and you'll get to Atlanta."

"Appreciate it." Nicole smiled.

"Mmmm, one last bit of advice, and this is for free. Don't sit in the parking too long."

"Why not?" Nicole frowned.

"Just not the safest place." The woman replied, flipping her magazine back open.

Nicole hurried out the door, the bell chiming. The gravel crunched as she ran. "Hey … I think we should get outta here." She raised the window.

"Why? What happened?" Nathan's eyes narrowed.

"Nothing happened, just that the clerk said it's not safe."

"If I see headlights, we'll take off." Nathan studied the map. "Where did you say we were again?"

Nicole pointed. "We need to …"

Tap – tap – tap.

Inside the darkness and just past the edge of the halo from the yellow lights stood two children. The girl looked to be about thirteen. The boy about eight.

"Holy Christ," Nathan stated, lowering the window. "You nearly gave us a heart attack. What are you doing out here?"

"Please let us in," the boy said, his voice sounding robotic, eyes lowered. "We're lost and need a ride home."

Nicole froze. She couldn't move.

"How did you get out here?" Nathan asked.

Nicole's tongue felt stuck to the roof of her mouth. She tried to speak but couldn't.

"Please let us in," the boy said. "We're lost and need to get home."

Nicole's arms itched, her heart pounded, she wanted to run, to escape, but could not move.

"Nicole …"

Their clothes. They both appeared to have walked off a stage of a Victorian set. The boy was wearing faded, brown knickers, a long-sleeved white shirt, and a tattered cap that looked older than him. The girl wore a yellow-gray frock that was patterned in delicate flowers that fell to just above her ankles. No logical explanation for why these two were dressed the way they were.

"Where are you coming from?" Nicole asked not understanding why she even asked.

"Please let us in," the boy said, looking up.

The boy's eyes were devoid of expression and color. They were pitch black, all black, no white.

Nicole screamed "Nate! Drive! Get outta here!"

Nathan sped out of the parking lot, fishtailing onto the road.

Tears ran down Nicole's face.

Nathan's jaw looked clinched, his knuckles white. He must have seen it too.

"What was wrong with them?" Nicole asked.

Nathan remained quiet.

"Nate?"

"No idea. Vampires maybe or changelings? No clue."

"Did you feel something?" Nicole asked.

"What do you mean?"

"Were you afraid?"

"When I saw that kid's eyes, yes."

"The clerk at the station said to not stay in the parking lot. Said it wasn't safe. I wonder if that's what she meant."

"I really have no desire to turn around and ask."

"If you said you were going to, I'd get outta the car and walk the rest of the way to Atlanta."

They drove in silence. Nicole barely aware of where they were. Nathan focused on the road, occasionally, he would glance in the rearview mirror.

"We turn here," Nicole said.

Nathan jumped. "What was the name of that town?"

"I don't know. The clerk just pointed to a spot on the map and I didn't see any name. Why?"

"I want to avoid it on the way home."

"I'm not sure if I want to know what those kids were. They felt evil." Nicole said.

It was just before dawn when they pulled into the hotel. After entering their room, Nicole fell on the bed. "Next time, we fly," she stated.

"I'd still take my chances with the Children of the Corn." He winked.

Nicole giggled. "More like Children of the Cotton. We're in the south, yah know."

Tap – tap – tap.

Nicole froze.

Nathan peered through the peephole. "There's nothing here." He pulled the door open. "Nothing."

Nicole sagged with relief. She couldn't understand why she believed the kids would have followed them to the hotel. Then again, they weren't natural and therefore didn't have to operate by natural law.

Nicole looked up and down the hallway. It was silent except for a faint murmuring. She couldn't make out the words, just a low voice or voices. The hair on her arms stood but she chided herself. This was a hotel and there were TV's and people moving around.

"Want some breakfast?" Nathan asked.

"No thanks. I'm too tired and keyed up to think about food."

"Suit yourself. I'm going to the continental breakfast. See what they have to offer. Probably stale donuts and those tiny boxes of cereal."

"Very tempting, enjoy." Nicole settled on the bed.

Nathan said his goodbyes and left, gently closing the door.

The elevator with freshly cleaned glass gave him a moment of pause. He studied his reflection, making a mental note to start visiting the gym more often. He pushed the button and waited.

A movement from behind caught his attention. Not wanting to be rude, he ignored it. Continuing to study his reflection, he paused. He wasn't alone. The children from the nameless town stared at him with their vacant eyes.

"Can we come in please?" the boy asked. "We're lost and need to go home."

48

THE BLACK-EYED KIDS

Lynn's thoughts …

Oh, the black eyes of the children. Wherever that town is, we will definitely pass on by. The author brings the chill of the unknown, of what may or may not be dangerous. From inside a car or room, we sometimes feel safe. But what lurks just beyond – that is another question.

The black-eyed children started showing up in the 1980's, originally in Texas and inside the vast wilderness, and some of those roads do seem to ride into the sunset with nothing around.

But a fable is just a fable, a story told to frighten those sitting around the campfire. Then again, are black-eyed children just a story?

Many will categorize these children next to Bigfoot or the abominable snowman. Where others will claim they do exist. Theory has it that once you invite them in, your life is over. The children will approach and knock on a door or window. They are always asking for help. They claim to be hungry or lost. It was once written that a woman who had a kind heart and never said a word ended up with them on her backseat.

According to legend, if we are indeed *taken* once we invite them in, how was she able to claim they ended up on her backseat? Just saying.

Our author uses the dark road and eerie gas station as the backdrop. No blood, no one died, and no one was kidnapped. But the story still gave us a moment to pause and reflect.

How safe are we on a deserted road? How safe are we at night or alone? Perhaps this is a good reason to always keep our windows up or down if one is in a house.

Good read.

50

Bloody Mary

Marcus Hysmith

Saturday night they had a sleepover – Janey, Kim, and Sarah, seventh graders and best friends. They were at Janey's house. Her dad had rented a stack of VHS horror movies. It was 1988. Hellraiser – Janey's third time seeing it but the other two hadn't. She insisted it was her favorite movie of all time.

Janey loved being scared. The electric shock from the unexpected and dangerous seemed to fuel her. Nothing was dangerous in watching a horror movie – any more than when her father snuck up and said, *boo* – but the emotions were riveting, arbitrary as it may have been. It momentarily pulled one out of everyday life – just for a second – long enough to elevate a heartbeat with an immediate giggle.

Such fun.

Dad moved the color television from the kitchen to her bedroom. With popcorn and ice cream by their sides, they had planned on staying up all night.

Janey farted.

They giggled until it became no laughing matter. They ran into the dark hall to escape the fumes, whispering to not wake her parents.

"Damn, Janey," Kim whispered loudly.

"Oopsy. Must have been the fart fairy. Stinkerbell!"

The girls groaned.

"Open the window," Sarah stated.

Janey pulled her shirt over her nose, braving her way back into the room. Her eyes watered. She pulled on the blinds, revealing the pitch-black yard. She opened the window, fanning with a pillow. "All clear!"

"You're an idiot," Kim replied.

"I know." Janey laughed. "I'm okay with that."

They hit rewind on Hellraiser, retaking their positions on the floor.

"I saw Kevin crunching on you," Sarah said to Janey.

"No way?" Janey replied, seeming to be excited.

"Big way. At lunch yesterday. He stared at you with his mouth open like he'd just seen a ghost." Sarah nodded.

"Barf." Kim pretended to throw up. "That's not a good kind of staring."

"No, it was," Sarah replied. "But I know he likes you."

"I was wearing my blue dress," Janey said.

"Dork. Boys don't care about that," Kim replied. "I don't think they even notice what we're wearing."

"Like he'd seen a ghost?" Janey said. "Like, he was scared?"

"More like in shock. Like *hubba hubba* staring." Sarah laughed.

"You're shitting me," Janey replied.

"I wouldn't shit you, you're my favorite turd," Sarah said.

"Why won't he talk to me?" Janey asked.

"Because boys are loco and afraid of girls," Kim replied.

Janey giggled. "What do they have to be scared of?"

"Don't know, but you're getting married." Sarah hugged herself.

"Ew," Janey and Kim moaned.

"There's no denying it, you're in love," Sarah stated.

Sarah and Kim tickled Janey, forcing her to escape. "Stop it. I have to go to the bathroom." She left, giggling.

"Have you heard of the game *Bloody Mary*?" Janey asked.

The girls shook their heads.

"You say it three times in front of a mirror in the dark, then Mary, the Queen of England, appears." Janey nodded.

"Mary Queen of Scotts?" Kim asked.

"No, the other one. I think Henry the VIII's daughter." Janey smiled.

"You've done it before?" Kim asked.

"Nope." Janey shook her head. "Takes three to make it work."

"Screw it, let's try," Sarah said, standing.

"Okay," Janey replied, "but we have to whisper 'cuz … my parents."

They stepped into the bathroom and closed the door. Janey turned off the lights. The only light seeped in from under the door. They could barely see themselves in the mirror.

Janey pushed the two aside, placing herself in the middle. "We have to hold hands." They took each other's hands. "Now, we stare into the mirror and focus on our foreheads. Don't look away!"

They did as she said.

"Here we go. All together …"

They spoke at the same time. "Bloody Mary … Bloody Mary … Bloody Mary."

They stared at their foreheads, but nothing happened.

"I don't see anything," Kim said.

"Keep staring," Janey ordered. "Don't break your concentration. Sometimes you have to do it a few times."

"Bloody Mary … Bloody Mary … Bloody Mary."

They paused between each incantation. They felt a heavy silence as they stood on the edge of the abyss. After a couple of times, Janey's heart pattered.

Mary Tudor's face materialized in the mirror. Faint at first, clearing with each second. The girls tightened their grips, holding their breaths. Mary's face split and blood splattered against the mirror. The lady's screams echoed through the small room.

The girls wailed like Banshees, darting to the safety of Janey's bedroom.

Dad stomped down the hall. He flung open the door and stared at them. "What the hell are you doing?"

Janey pointed at the bathroom, her hand shaking. "M-M-Mary!"

"Janey?"

Janey shook her head. Tears ran down her cheeks.

He looked in the bathroom, flipping on the light. "Really, nothing's here?"

The girls shook their heads.

"Bed! That's enough for one night."

"Daddy," Janey pleaded, "we saw *Bloody Mary* in the mirror!"

He sighed. "No, Janey. That's your imagination. If you stare at something long enough your mind plays tricks. Now, bed!"

"No way, Daddy," Janey cried. "It happened."

"Seriously, Mr. Hutchins," Kim stated, "we all saw her."

"We can't hallucinate the same thing," Sarah said.

"Girls!" he stated. "There's no such thing as ghosts. Watching those horror movies was probably a bad idea. Now sleep!" Shaking his head, he gently closed the door.

Windsor Castle - 1555

Mary Tudor, Queen of England and daughter of Henry the VIII, sat screaming in front of her mirror. Her voice echoed from the stone halls, making its way under the door to the ears of the guards. They ran inside only to find her cowering in a corner.

"M'lady?" the guard asked. "What is it?"

"Little girls!" she whispered.

The guards looked at each other and shrugged. The room was empty except for Mary Tudor.

"Fetch Madame Clarencieux," the guard ordered.

The man left. Susan Clarencieux used to be Mary's lady-in-waiting. But was now the Mistress of the Robes. She was Mary's best friend.

Susan rushed in and knelt next to Mary.

"Little girls!" Mary whispered. "Little girls!"

"What's happened, M'lady?" Susan asked. "What little girls?"

"Little girls," Mary repeated.

"Where are these little girls?" Susan asked.

Mary pointed at her mirror.

A table, holding a small mirror, stood against a wall. It was pointless to look behind it. She did look under it, however, and around the bed. "I don't see any little girls."

"In the mirror! They were in the mirror!"

Susan looked in the mirror but saw only her reflection. "Were they ghosts?"

"Yes! Ghosts!"

"They're gone now. Ghosts can't hurt you, M'lady. They are only apparitions."

Mary nodded but frowned. "I must confess. Fetch Lord Gardiner."

"Very well," Susan replied. "But you don't blame yourself for seeing ghosts."

Mary sighed. "Fetch him at once!"

Lord Gardiner was wearing his sacraments, carrying his Bible. "What is it, M'lady? What is troubling you?"

"I saw the ghosts of three little girls wearing odd clothing. In that mirror. They were saying *Bloody Mary* over and over again. When I screamed, they disappeared."

"You've seen ghosts," Lord Gardiner replied. "Not uncommon in this castle."

"But their clothes."

"No matter. Never hurts to confess, but I don't believe you brought it on yourself."

Two days later …

Mary combed her tangled hair, while looking in the mirror. She shuddered as she combed – not sure if what happened two days ago actually happened or if she had imagined it. She was either haunted by ghosts or cursed with madness.

She closed her eyes, took a deep breath, then opened them –

Three little girls stared back, screaming, "Bloody Mary … Bloody Mary … Bloody Mary!"

Mary screamed. The little girls screamed.

The guard entered only to find Mary cowering in the corner.

"Little girls!" she whispered and pointed.

The other guard was already fetching Madam Clarencieux.

"M'lady," Susan asked, "did you see the ghosts again?"

"They were different girls this time. But girls wearing odd clothing."

Susan helped her to her feet. "They are only ghosts. They can't hurt you."

"Please … send for Lord Gardiner."

"M'lady –"

"Send for him!" she screamed.

Lord Gardiner stood quietly and listened.

"These aren't ghosts!" Mary stated. "They don't look anything like someone who had died here." She stopped pacing and glared at the man. "They are a message! A warning! We must no longer tolerate Protestantism. I wish for those who hold influence over non-Catholics to be put to death at once."

"This won't be popular amongst the people, M'lady."

"Damned being popular. God is telling me what I should do. And … I shall do it!"

"M'lady," he nodded.

Three days later …

Mary, confident that the trouble was abated, spread balm over her skin to lighten it. She hadn't been sleeping much lately with all the executions and unrest.

"Bloody Mary! Bloody Mary! Bloody Mary!" Three little girls stood wide-eyed staring at her.

Mary couldn't move. She threw the mirror and it shattered. The guards entered and the scene repeated itself.

"We must set an example," Mary stated. "Round up as many known Protestants as possible and burn them at the stake!" She raised her arm in the air. "Make sure Thomas Cranmer watches it all. He must know what trouble he has brought to his queen."

Thomas Cranmer was the Archbishop of Canterbury and considered the leading opponent of the Papacy in all of England.

"M'lady," Lord Gardiner nodded.

Mary glared at her guard. "Every mirror … break every mirror!"

Perplexed but dutiful, the guard never thought to question her order. He had the mirrors in the castle removed and broken.

The lords and ladies had no idea what was happening. Rumors spread that Mary had seen a ghost who called her *Bloody Mary*. The name, unfortunately, stuck. Everyone called her *Bloody Mary* behind her back. They assumed she had gone mad.

Four days later …

Mary ate alone in the small room next to the kitchen. She had prayed before tasting the mutton. Glancing into the silver tray, she froze.

"Bloody Mary! Bloody Mary! Bloody Mary!" Three little girls stared at her, chanting.

Mary threw the tray at the wall. She ran from the castle, ripping at her greying hair.

The kitchen staff stared out the window and shrugged. Mary Tudor, Queen of England and daughter of Henry the VIII, had definitely gone mad.

BLOODY MARY

Lynn's thoughts …

I remember my school days, but I do not remember learning about Mary Tudor in such a manner. Perhaps insanity does run in the Tudor family?

The short story follows three little girls having a typical sleepover. I doubt if any young girl never tried to summon Bloody Mary at least once. Never worked for me. But I guess it worked for someone at some time. Back to the story. The little ones, playing in the bathroom, summons the evil queen. But according to Marcus, it was prior to Mary's murderous rampage.

The time theory paradox! Or, that aged ol' question, what came first, the chicken or the egg. If these little girls had never tried to summon Bloody Mary, then Mary would not have gone mad and murdered her citizens. But if she had not gone mad and murdered her citizens, then she would not have been given the name, Bloody Mary. So which came first?

The idea of having something to allow us to peek into the past would indeed be a marvelous experience. But I would bet anyone that people of the past were not that different from the people of today. The only difference you ask? Technology!

The root of all evil. The more we advance, the more insane we become. And the more insane, the more advanced, and the more advanced, the more evil, and so on, and so on, and so on. I'm dizzy now.

Honestly, what difference does it make whether we lived in 2024 or 1024 – Mary reigned from 1553 until 1558, by the way. People's fears and anxieties are what seem to destroy them while destroying others. I would argue that fear is fear whether you were born today or a million years ago. The only difference is how we turn on the lights.

Brightmore

Onyx Rebel

The phone pinged.

I paused as I reached for a crystal that had caught my eye. A message about an opening for a Certified Nurses Assistant (CNA). The job market was scarce these days, no luck in finding other work. Being a CNA was the only thing that paid my bills. Although I loved helping others, working as a CNA was physically taxing. Why, just the other day, I rolled a woman on her side who was at least three times my size. My back hurt for the rest of the night, and to top it off, the pay wasn't great. The assignment was at a new facility.

```
Brightmore - third shift - 10 p.m. to 6 a.m.
```

The only good thing about working for a staffing company was that I could make my own schedule. Accepting the position, I finished shopping for the crystal. I owned many different ones, but something was urging me to pick up the black tourmaline. My ring broke a few months ago. Unfortunately, this shop didn't have a ring, but I selected the smooth black tourmaline, adding to it a piece of labradorite. It was pretty. Usually, I carried a protection pouch when working at a nursing home. But I had to be careful. You see, I was an empath and not the best at blocking out others' emotions – not yet.

I parked in the lot at exactly 10 p.m. I had tried to arrive earlier but overslept. A big dinner of a cheesesteak and fries made me sleepy. Thankfully, my snacks and sandwich were already packed. Unfortunately, my protection bag was left at home. It charged by the sunlight and was still on the windowsill. As I stepped out of my car, someone was heading to theirs. Entering the front door, a chill ran up my back. Most facilities were cold, but this place was different. It was freezing.

"Welcome to Brightmore!" the receptionist stated. "I'm glad you're able to help. The name's Katie. We're always a little short staffed for this shift. It's not a difficult one. Most of our residents will be asleep. You have rooms 300 through 315 … 310 and 313 will need to be checked every few hours 'cuz they're bedridden. Look in on the others as you see fit."

"Thank you, I'm glad I can help. Why are you always short staffed on this watch?"

"Oh … you know … some people just have an over-active imagination." She looked away as she clicked something on her computer.

"Over-active?"

"Yeah, a few have said weird things happen at night. They get freaked 'cuz people have died here. In fact, a woman died just last week and now no one wants to work this shift." She laughed, nervously.

"Understand. Death is a part of life. I accept that. I won't run and will let you know if I have any trouble." My hand rubbed against my chest where my protection bag should have been.

The third floor was quiet. Like most nursing homes, the place had an old, decorative carpet and cream walls. Random paintings and worn chairs lined the halls. A faint hint of pee seeped through the air. The difference between private and government nursing homes? Public ones had bare floors and a stronger stench of urine. On the bright side, the residents usually had the supplies they needed. Private facilities, on the other hand, tried to resemble a home with carpets. And one could enjoy the aroma of a fresh-scented, lavender cleaning solution.

The common room was on my right. Another CNA was sitting there, looking bored. After introducing herself, she left to check on her residents. I found the hall that led to my rooms. It was to the left of the elevators. Her hall was to the right.

I started by peeking into my rooms. The first two residents were sleeping quietly. When I walked into room 303, an instant chill hit. Somehow, this room seemed darker than the others.

The bed was near the far wall with a dresser next to the closet door. No one was in the bed. A rocking chair by the one window was dimly lit from the outside light. A woman with long white hair and staring at her lap was rocking, but only slightly. Her hair covered her face.

"Ma'am?" I asked. "Are you okay? Would you like to rest in your bed? Be more comfortable."

No response.

I reached out and brushed my fingers across her hand. She lifted her head and grabbed my arm. I froze. Her eyes were pure white, no pupils. I pulled away, but she held tight.

"Let me go, please!" I begged. "We need to keep our hands to ourselves."

She remained quiet.

The coldness of her touch seemed to be growing. I was focused on prying her hand away when she grabbed me with her other one.

I yelped.

"Your life is bright and warm," she whispered. "It calls to me."

What the fuck! I yanked myself free, feeling a slight sting from her nails that were long and thick. *Great, infection.* "Ma'am, are you okay? You cannot grab me like that." I rubbed my arm.

She remained quiet.

Shaking my head, I left her alone to rock. "That was weird."

It was freezing in her room but warm in the hallway. Giving myself a mental reminder to check the temperature in her room later, I peek in on the other residents.

Room 313 was bedridden and needed to be changed.

"She wants your warmth!" the woman whispered. "She wants your warmth!"

I shrugged off the woman's words and checked on my last few residents. Entering the common area, I spotted a fish tank.

The fish were lively and of different colors. I could never tell saltwater from fresh, but an angel fish seemed happy. Watching the critter zoom from vine to vine, it took me a second to notice the eerie reflection.

The strange, old lady from room 303 was now standing behind me. I turned and stared. My hands shook. But no one was there. I glanced around believing she was hiding. But no one. Brushing it off as my nerves, I decided I needed to eat.

It was only midnight. Wanting to keep busy, I read until it was time to check on my residents again. The other CNA was on the couch. She looked tired.

"How's your night been?" I asked.

"Not bad. Just taking a break. And … you?"

"Okay, one of my residents got a little handsy … but nothing crazy."

"With *that* hall? No one likes … ever since … oh shit." She pulled out her phone. "It's my kid. Gotta go." Her worried voice echoed through the hall.

I headed to room 313. Entering, it felt like someone was watching me. But the woman looked as if she was asleep. Adjusting her blankets, I paused.

"She wants your warmth!" the woman whispered, her eyes closed. "She wants your warmth!"

I turned to leave but the woman grabbed my arm.

"She wants your warmth, don't let her take it!"

"It'll be okay," I whispered. "She can't take my warmth."

"Say a prayer," the woman said.

I left her to sleep. As I passed room 303, the same chill as before made me shiver. I paused and the squeaking chair echoed into the hall. Wanting to check her room temperature, I entered. No thermostat on the wall.

"What the fuck, why's it so cold in here?" I rubbed my arms. On the door were scratch marks. My fingers reached out but stopped. A cold breath was now hitting my neck. I turned, but the woman was still in the rocking chair.

Sighing deeply, I turned to leave. Taking a step, a strong grip held tight. The woman was now behind me. Her head tilted and mouth opened. Those same white eyes stared at me. I pulled on the door and darted into the hall. Glancing back, I sighed again. She was in the chair by the window, rocking. I closed the door.

It was almost six in the morning, and I slowly made sure my nightly duties were done. I headed to the nurse's station to give the next CNA my report. The receptionist asked how my night went.

"Everything was fine, but Ms. Ray in room 303 was freaking me out."

"Room what?" she asked.

"303," I repeated. "Ms. Ray … small woman with long, white hair? Guess she's blind 'cuz her eyes look odd. She sits in that rocking chair all night."

Nervously, she laughed. "That room is vacant. Did the other CNA's put you up to this? Ms. Ray died last week. She wasn't blind, but she was a little odd. Always complained that someone was trying to take her warmth like they did to her mother."

I stared at her. "Well, someone was in *that* room."

"Who told you about her?"

"No one. I saw her … I just … I have a headache." I handed her my report and walked out as another CNA walked in.

I sat in my car and breathed deeply. Feeling confused, I was not sure what was going on. I knew I had seen someone. Was she just in my head?

Gospel music playing through my speakers on my way home somewhat calmed me. The first thing I wanted was to sage myself and hold my bag. A squeaking sound, just like that of the old rocking chair echoed through my ears. The figure of an old woman sitting by the window grabbed my attention. She was staring at her lap.

"I'm so cold," she whispered. "I just need to be warm."

A stinging on my wrist made me look. A red mark where Ms. Ray had grabbed me earlier now appeared. My protection pouch was still on the windowsill. I reached for it, feeling a cold hand on my arm.

I started and grabbed the pouch, both landing hard on the floor. Gasping, I stood. My heart raced as I clutched my sage.

Never again would I walk out of my house without my protection bag. The fear of that old woman's spirit remained heavy on my mind.

I also knew I'd never go back to Brightmore ever again.

Lynn's thoughts …

Ah, the old woman in the rocking chair story. Why is it that everyone is so afraid of old ladies? Do they remind us of an old witch? Why are we not afraid of old men?

The concept of someone in a room that we tend who was never there to begin with is a haunting idea. Being as forceful as I am, I probably would have gone back to that room immediately to validate everything. Then again, perhaps I would have lost my warmth.

The concept of death and spirit tends to engulf the concept of fear. Perhaps it's the notion of growing old? I will admit that as the years pass, I do often wish I could turn back time, but would I honestly want to live it all over again? Maybe we should embrace death and not fear it.

Our character held a warm and loving attitude toward the aging in her care. I am sure being a CNA is difficult work and hard on the back, but when does tending to another differentiate from caring for ourselves? Could our author be alluding to how death can become a comfort, a warmth, that we all eventually seek?

Humans struggle through life. We work, we live, and we die. Some earlier than others, but eventually, we all will be standing at death's door. The question is, how will we address our end? Do we address it as a fear, as isolation in a chair by a window? Or do we embrace it as when crossing a finishing line?

The concept I found in this story blends life and death, mixing it with a little faith. Was there a woman in 303, seeking warmth? Or was it our character's imagination running wild? Maybe we all need a protection bag, but I do not believe that bag will ever carry anything that will protect us when our time is up.

68

BuckEye

Roger Guffey

The birth of Jeremiah Walker, my grandfather, was an auspicious event. From the moment he was born, floating precariously between womb and world, he was still enrobed in his intact amniotic sac. Such en caul births are extremely rare, and according to folklore, these children are gift wrapped presents from *God* who endowed them with preternatural traits. They are believed to be prophets, particularly receptive to the voice of *God*.

Jeremiah was a precocious child who walked at eleven months and spoke coherently at fifteen. He was reading at two, a skill augmented by listening to fairytales and scriptures recited from the bible by his parents. They believed his gifts would best be served if he walked a spiritual path that was in harmony with the omniscience – the deity who spoke to him in his dreams and prayers. By the time he was twenty-one, he was an ordained minister. He could have had a lucrative career in the ministry had he so desired, but he felt it blasphemous to take money for spreading the word of *God.* Instead, he felt compelled to strengthen his connection to Provision by sharing his vocation as a carpenter in emulation of Jesus himself.

When World War II erupted, my grandfather enlisted as a chaplain who would comfort those fighting the Nazis who wanted to rid the world of the Jews. After Germany surrendered, he volunteered to serve in the Pacific Theatre. Truman's decision to use nuclear weapons, although bringing a speedy end to the war, horrified him. He returned home a changed man who redoubled his efforts to expand his ministry. He married my grandmother, Alice Turner, who blessed him with two daughters and a son. The son would eventually become my father. The returning troops started families that needed houses and carpenters to build those houses. My grandfather started a construction company where my father eventually learned the trade. After graduating from college, my dad expanded the family business and Grandpa devoted more time to his ministry.

After the war, Grandpa began an unusual ritual that frustrated his family and friends. His actions were loaded with secrecy. Every August sixth, he made a solitary pilgrimage to a safety deposit box. When my father turned twenty-one, Grandpa invited him to accompany him to the bank, an outing that lasted until Grandpa died.

Dad did not pursue the ministry, preferring to put his eggs in the basket of secular capitalism, although he did attend church, tithed offerings, and performed incidental repairs. When I was born, my mother named me Jeremiah Walker the Third and educated me in the faith that had served our family well.

When I stayed with my grandparents, Grandpa passed along our family history and the lore of our generations. As the years rolled by and Grandpa cut back on his preachings, the charlatans on television who claimed to cure people of illnesses infuriated him. Especially, when they claimed *God* talked to them. I asked my grandfather why it bothered him so much.

His eyes flashed an anger I couldn't understand. "Because," he said, "they're using *God's* name in vain for profit and fame. These false prophets are constantly begging for money even though they already have mansions, jets, and yachts. Jesus never asked for money and never charged fees for his miracles. You'll never hear me making those wild claims, because *God* does not work that way. Isaiah warned us 'For my thoughts are not your thoughts, neither are your ways my ways, declares the *Lord*. For as the heavens are higher than the Earth, so are my ways higher than your ways and my thoughts than your thoughts.'"

I looked at him, wondering. "But Grandpa, everyone says *God* speaks to you."

He smiled. "I believe *God* speaks to us all, but he speaks in the same still voice he used when he spoke to Elijah. I'm not a snake-oil salesman trying to profit from our conversations. But sometimes *God* tells me to do or say things to advise others. At times, he tells me to keep my own counsel and not reveal what he tells me. "

That explanation satisfied my curiosity until I was about sixteen. Like most teenagers, I doubted the teachings of Christianity. When I confided my feelings, he would simply smile and speak in his same gentle voice.

"All people have doubts at some time," he would say. "The weakest faith is that which is never tested. When I was in the army and saw all the suffering and destruction, I wondered why *God* allowed such horrors to happen. The worst was in Japan after they dropped the atomic bombs … unfathomable deaths and sufferings. The heat burnt shadows of people onto their walls. Those shadows are still there. Hundreds of thousands of souls just evaporated. And survivors …" – he shook his head – "… dying horrible deaths from radiation poisoning. Even today, babies are born with birth defects and people die of cancer. Count yourself blessed that you never experienced any of that."

My mind whirled, trying to envision what he was telling me.

Grandpa took a deep breath. "The military tells us that those atomic bombs probably saved a million troops from dying in traditional warfare. That is hard to wrap my mind around ... sacrificing a hundred thousand to save a million?"

"Did you ever ask *God* why he allowed that to happen?"

"Of course, but that was when I realized I was asking the wrong question."

"What should we be asking?"

"We should be asking, why did *mankind* allow that to happen?"

I nodded. "That is a good question."

He paused as his eyes glanced over his wire-rimmed glasses. "Sometimes when I'm meditating, I wonder if *God* or Satan ever got tired of people blaming them for the things we could have prevented. We do have free will."

"Have you ever heard *God* speak to you so clearly that you had no doubt it was his voice?"

"Yes, but most people struggle to distinguish their will from *God's* will. More often than not, we humans insist on doing our will and then claim it was *God's*. We're really good at deluding ourselves, but when that happens, it never ends well."

"Then I have to ask, did *God* ever tell *you* a secret you cannot share?"

"Yes." He glanced out the window and the conversation was over.

Throughout the years, I developed an obsession to find out what my grandfather's secret was. I tried to wheedle little details of his epiphany until I finally summoned the courage to ask.

"Grandfather, does your secret have anything to do with your safety deposit box?"

He laughed. "Maybe yes, maybe no. All things come to he who waits. You'll know the truth when you turn twenty-one."

Grandpa eventually grew old and broke his hip a few months before I turned twenty. A few weeks later, he died of pneumonia, and whatever his secret was, he took it to his grave. I couldn't sleep because the puzzle gnawed at me. Eventually, I sought counseling, which did little to assuage my angst.

The solution arrived on my twenty-first birthday. After celebrating with family and friends, Dad tapped me on my shoulder and smiled. "Grab your jacket."

We drove to the bank in silence. The manager retrieved the key, and the dual locks turned, opening the box. Dad motioned for the man to leave. Satisfied we were alone, he lifted the lid and pulled out a small, black box. He flipped it open and held out a buckeye.

"Now that you're of age, I can tell you my father's secret."

My heart pounded and my eyes widened.

"When he returned home from his tour in Japan, your Grandpa took a walk to enjoy the beautiful autumn colors. He paused to rest under a buckeye tree, and a buckeye hit him on the head. He picked it up and heard the voice of *God*.

"As long as you keep this buckeye in your family, the world will be spared from a thermonuclear war that could destroy mankind. You cannot reveal the details of this covenant. When a child turns twenty-one, only then do you pass on this wisdom."

I snickered. "Come on, you don't believe any of this, do you?"

My father returned the buckeye to the black box. "This buckeye is now eighty years old and shows no signs of aging. It's as pristine today as when Grandpa placed it here. I once asked a professor about how long buckeyes last. He said that eventually, the nut would dry and the shell would deteriorate. Here we are eighty years later and no thermonuclear war."

I laughed again.

"But here's the catch. You cannot tell anyone about this or remove it from the bank. It's a secret only *God* and my dad shared. The fate of the world depends on *you* keeping the secret."

I stared at my father, trying to comprehend. "Are you listening to yourself? You're an intelligent and successful businessman. A pillar of the community and a deacon in the church. What's next? Ouija boards and tarot cards?"

"All of my life, my father believed he heard the voice of *God*. He never deviated from his story and I never had reason to challenge him. But I'll tell yah what …" – he handed me the little box – "… if you're so sure your Grandpa was just pulling our legs, here's the buckeye and the box. Throw it away, if you dare …"

Damn it. I was afraid he was going to say that.

BUCKEYE

Lynn's thoughts …

Fear comes in all kinds of shapes and forms. Can we hold the future of mankind inside a little, black box? Not sure.

The buckeye tree is the official state tree of Ohio and earned the name because the nut resembles the eye of a deer. It is watching you. Carrying a buckeye around inside your pocket is supposed to bring good luck. They are poisonous and we cannot eat them. But a squirrel can.

Odd how the world is sometimes. Supposedly, God created the world on one of his better days. Wait, was there a day before the world existed? Interesting question.

Edgar Cayce said that God created the world as a training ground for our souls. Definitely, feels like one at times, and sometimes it feels that I'm barely passing. If one accepts the existence of a soul outside of our flesh and bones, then what would there be for us to do? I'm sure souls do not have a day job. Then again, who else would clean the streets of heaven?

Our author creates an interesting dilemma. The future of whether or not a bomb is or is not dropped rests exclusively on whether a buckeye nut remains inside a little box. That is what the words say. But in reality, if we dig deeper, we could claim that this story is about faith. If we believe and live a righteous life, then we continue on after death or so the good book claims. If we do not believe in the word of God, then our existence ends. If the nut is our faith, do we keep the nut in the box or do we throw it away?

In other words, do we challenge fate? If there is a God, and we throw away our nut, then we supposedly will die forever. If we keep the nut in the box, then we live forever. And that ultimate secret – does even God exist?

Hmmm … I think I'll keep my nut for now. How about you? Do you keep the box?

Child of the Night

Kyle Connor

They wouldn't listen. Desperate words clawed from my chaffed throat, but my pleas fell on deaf ears. I kept screaming. Why were they ignoring me? I begged them to stop. To explain why they were doing this. Undeterred, they forced me deeper into the darkness.

I thrashed, frantically, but their grips only tightened as they pressed on. Nearly twice my size, they scarcely notice me struggling. They had not yet seized my hands. Maybe it wasn't too late or at least to knock some sense into them. Nothing made sense.

I slapped and yanked, but they held firm.

What do I do?

Four hands pushed me to the cold, solid floor.

This isn't real.

An ephemeral moonbeam reflected the metallic bars that now encage me.

This isn't real.

The heavy door creaked shut.

This isn't real.

My denial quieted, stripped from reality as a terminal echo reverberated through the basement – the harsh click of the lock.

They stepped back, traversing through the solitary ray now permeating the aged window.

I glimpsed at their faces. My whimpering broke the silence. "Why are you doing this?"

"For your own good," the man said.

The voice was so familiar; but I couldn't place it.

This isn't real. "Mom?"

"I know it's scary, baby," my mother replied, "but this is to protect you."

"You call this protection!?" I kicked the bars, but the cell proved unyielding.

"No need to get all worked up," my father said. "This'll be a lot easier if you just relax."

They were crazy! My parents were actually crazy people. *I've got to get outta here.* If only they could see me, see what they were doing to me, then maybe they'd snap out of it. "Dad! Can you turn the lights on? The dark's scaring me."

"The sky should clear any minute now. Light will be shining your way soon. Hang in there."

Do all crazies act this casual? "Mom, what're you doing?"

"Setting up the camera, baby."

"Camera? Why do you need a camera?" This was bad. This was getting *real* bad.

"It'll be easier for you to understand. You'll see in the morning."

Oh god. I didn't want to ask. *I've got to get outta here. Think!* "My throat hurts. Can I have some water?"

"Sorry kiddo, no bathroom breaks," my father said. "Best not to fill up your bladder."

Oh god. I'm going to be sick. Wait, that's it! If I'm sick, they'll have to let me out. My fingers stiffened as I shoved them down the back of my throat. Retching, I knelt over.

My father laughed. "Kudos for trying, but you won't be playing hooky tonight."

Damn. What the hell is happening to them?

Just a few minutes ago, Mom was cleaning up after dinner, and Dad was watching the game. Everything seemed so normal.

So normal.

A loud beeping shook me back to reality.

"Alright," she said. "It's recording."

"Why are you doing this!"

"Baby, we told you. I wish you would listen," she replied.

"I'm listening, Mom!"

"Now that you're thirteen, you'll go through some … *changes.*

Changes … what is she talking about?

"Since tonight's your first, we're …"

Oh fuck. That was not what I wanted to hear. This was some *sex* shit. I just knew it. I didn't want to know it, but I knew it. I can't do this.

"… growing hair over your …"

They're losing it. I'm losing it. Keep it together.

"… around the same time each month …"

Don't listen. This isn't happening. Have to …

"… you'll grow …"

Breathing too fast …what're they …

"… rt craving …"

I can't …

"… ll mo …"

What's 'at? Somethin' movin? In here? Not sure … wait … yes … yes. There it is again. Something's shaking. It's me. I'm shaking!

My eyes adjusted, and the iron bars creaked as my crooked and hairy fingers grabbed hold. The exposed studs lining the basement – *I can see them through the walls?* Scarcely illuminated by the dim moonlight, yes, but perceptible. *How can I see through the walls?* My parents, I could see them too. *Is that them?*

The light was playing tricks, now.

Yeah, that's them.

Their voices, but it didn't sound like they were talking, no they were —

Chanting?

Couldn't tell. Whatever sickness had overtaken their sanity, I had caught it. My fear suddenly vanished, replaced by a suspicious promise. A promise of — strength. It whispered to me, assuring that with the power came a surrender. It tempted me with the offer of a new life, a new purpose.

Is this my madness?

My parents' shadows shook me from a deeper introspection. With a queer look written all over their faces, something between pride or joy or euphoria, they were just too excited about my change.

Change?

They were singing now. But another voice bellowed. A voice I never heard before. But it was *so* familiar. The voice didn't sing, it beckoned.

The clouds parted, and the basement of my indoctrination appeared. Yet my gaze remained fixed to the sky, oblivious to the twisting and pulsating of my muscles.

The moon! The enchanting full moon.

I welcomed it from deep inside. The light penetrated my soul, merging with a dormant force — an inner force. An unrealized depth of my fusion erupted — mounting, surging, awakening.

Basking in the glow, I released. I felt alive. The skin from my former self now gone, casting away all confusion. The night's call was clear, beautiful, strong.

Tonight, I shall respond!

With a pride that out-shown my parents' pride, I joined their harmonious song. A nocturnal serenade to our family pack now becoming one symphony, one long *howl* at the moon.

81

82

Lynn's thoughts …

I always loved a great vampire story – oh wait, this is about a werewolf family. It is fascinating how a vampire's considered sexy and alluring, but a werewolf is what – just a dog? Why couldn't we have a series on werewolves?

Although a simple story about a young girl coming of age as a werewolf, could we also not compare this story to parents dealing with the everchanging emotions of a young teen? In many ways, I say that there is no difference.

I raised four children. Each one I wanted to lock inside a cage at one time or another. If we think deeply about it, didn't our teens change with the full moon? Didn't they grow fangs, long hair, and run wildly through the dark, devouring life? Didn't they change? Then eventually, they would settle down and return home, tired and exhausted, after having consumed only God knows what.

The author honestly captured a family protecting their child coming of age. So very relevant in today's society. Our young are easily swayed by many external forces – school, work, friends, commercials, social media – that at times parents simply do not know what to do or where to turn.

It would be so much easier if babies simply came with an instruction book. Our new widescreen television came with an instruction book. My cell phone came with an instruction book. Therefore, why don't children arrive with one?

Perhaps a thought for a future short story?

84

Choices

Nicholas A. Tseffos

His watch beeped.

Neil Casperson hit the snooze, staring at the whiteboard and drawing a line through two of the twenty items on his priority list. He had rearranged the tasks and renumbered them, looking for ways to optimize his research. He scratched his salt-and-pepper beard, realizing he'd missed a variable in his experiment. His thoughts percolated to the *what-ifs*.

He erased half the board.

Beep –Beep – Beep.

He swiped his watch again with a straight finger.

Five droopy-eyed lab assistants stood at the whiteboard, holding steaming cups of coffee in one hand and a donut or laptop in the other.

A car horn blared, and Neil glanced out the window. "Shit, I'm late."

He circled three items on the whiteboard, tapping the marker over each. "Stay focused here … here … and here. I won't be gone long … hopefully no more than an hour. If you need anything, don't be afraid to call my cell."

The phone vibrated inside his pocket, but he ignored it. It was important to not miss any last-minute changes to his instructions.

"I know we haven't slept much in the last couple of days," he stated. "If you need to grab a quick nap, use my office couch." He set the marker in the tray. "Any questions?"

A woman with her blonde hair pulled back in a ponytail glanced at the door. "Neil, your wife's here."

Vicky stood holding Olivia, their one-year-old with pigtails that stuck straight out. They wore matching floral sundresses and white sandals. Vicky held a look that Neil had seen a lot lately.

Neil shook his head. "I have to go. Keep me posted."

The windows in the minivan were already down. Neil sat in the driver's side as Vicky buckled her seat belt. Olivia sucked her thumb. He started the car, staring straight ahead, mentally going over the list on the whiteboard. He wondered how long it would take his team to recalibrate the experiment and gather the data he needed.

Vicky sighed. "Why didn't you answer your phone?"

I don't need this right now.

"I said I'd pick you up at nine. Why weren't you ready?"

Neil shook his head. "I found something. Something I missed last time. This could be a big deal –"

"Your son's a big deal," she stated. "He's expecting you to be there. It's the last game of the season, and I'm done making excuses about why you can't be there. Your family has to come first sometimes."

Neil concentrated on the road. "I think we're on the verge of a breakthrough."

"That's the same thing you've said for the last six months … and nothing has changed."

He slapped an open hand against the steering wheel. "Why the hell do you think I work so hard?"

"Keep your voice down and don't swear in front of Olivia." She shook a finger at him. "I'm tired of you hiding behind that line of …" – she made rabbit ears with her fingers – "… providing for your family." We need more than a paycheck. These kids deserve more … I deserve more."

Neil pursed his lips. His face reddened. "Like I don't know that? Come on, Vicky, you're overreacting."

"Then prove it. Stop acting like nothing matters except for your work and your reputation as the Wiz-Kid of MIT."

Neil clenched his jaw.

Neil lowered his daughter into a backpack, hoisting her on his shoulders. He buckled and cinched the straps as her legs kicked like a cowgirl wanting her horse to gallop. She giggled, tugging on her father's ear.

"Olivia, honey, please." Vicky gathered a blanket, water bottle, and sunscreen stick from the back of her minivan. She pushed the button, and the door closed. "Be gentle."

Neil grabbed Olivia's feet. The backpack pulled tight against his shoulders, and he assumed she had just arched her back. He yawned, trying to rid his mind of the argument with Vicky.

Olivia tangled her fingers in his curly hair and yanked.

A group of dads had gathered on the far side of the chain-link fence separating the fields from the parking lot. They'd be discussing the opposing team and the starting lineups. He dreaded the small talk and the testosterone-filled rants that were waiting for him.

Work crept back into his mind. Neil never wanted to be that boss that came in late and left early. The unrelenting manager who never paid his employees a compliment and took credit for their work. A guy who forgot about his subordinate's birthday or didn't listen when they had an idea or an opinion. Yet today and at a critical point in their experiment, he abandoned them. Without success, he'd have to shutter the lab and let everyone go. Then he'd be looking for a new job.

He followed Vicky to the field. As a soccer ball rolled into the street, Neil raced for it. A car screeched just avoiding the ball. Vicky waited as the thing angled her way. With her hands full, she kicked it to the young girl waiting for it.

Neil took several items from his wife's hand. "I'm sorry. I was out of line in the car."

"You're tired and stressed. Can we just try and enjoy Jack's game? Then you can head back to the lab."

The argument in the car haunted him. Her tone implied he didn't care about his family. Did Vicky actually believe he was one of those guys who only cared about bragging rights? A guy who believed whoever died with the most toys won?

They headed for the soccer fields swarming with ten-year-olds wearing shorts, shin pads, and colorful jerseys. Neil raised his hand to shade his eyes. His son, Jack, was wearing white at the far left pitch.

Jack flashed him a toothy grin, giving a windmill wave.

Neil waved back. He lifted his chin to feel the sun on his face. Maybe Vicky was right. This was what he needed.

The team warmed up, and Neil paced the sideline with Olivia on his back. He encouraged Jack to kick through the ball. The phone rang in his pocket.

Maybe they had a breakthrough.

"Really?" Vicky stood beside him and scowled. "I thought we talked about this."

Neil wiped his mouth, hoping his decision to not answer wouldn't slow down his lab's progress. He hit the silence button and slid the phone into his pocket.

The white team's goalie, a kid a head taller than the other players, practiced kicking balls out of the net.

Jack stooped to pick up an errant ball.

The goalie struck a line drive.

Neil watched as the ball slammed into his son's head. Jack crumpled.

Neil sprinted onto the field. Olivia bounced, squealing as if on a ride in an amusement park. He held her legs as he shouldered through the boys. He expected Jack to have the wind knocked out of him or a lump on his head that required ice. Blood poured from Jack's nose; his face swollen and his body twitching. He made a raspy, gurgling sound.

Neil's breath quickened. He knelt. His panicked brain couldn't recall the EMT training he had received in the military.

Jack stopped twitching. His body stilled.

Neil reached for his son. "Jack?"

Olivia's weight shifted. Her hands yanked his hair, forcing him off balance. With one hand on the ground, he snapped open the waist buckle with a loud click and rolled his shoulders to release the straps, placing Olivia and the backpack on the ground.

Another soccer mom knelt, lowering her ear over Jack's mouth. She rested two fingers on his wrist. Placing her hand behind Jack's head, she extended his neck up. "We need to get him to a hospital."

How soon can an ambulance get here? Maybe I should drive him myself? Faster that way.

He laid his hand on Jack's chest and felt a slight movement. The boys huddled with their parents. A few were crying, others stood silently.

"Vicky? Vicky, where are you?" Neil needed her support to get through whatever would come next.

Vicky stood behind him, flanked by two other mothers. Tears ran down Vicky's cheeks, her expression showed the same terror he'd seen when her father had a heart attack.

Their eyes met, and he pointed at Olivia, still in the self-standing backpack.

Vicky swiped at her cheeks, lifting Olivia.

Neil leaned closer to Jack.

A coach spoke sharply on his phone, "We need an ambulance at West High School. Field number two."

Neil couldn't remember if his son's blood type was O or A. He wanted to cradle him in his arms.

Jack moaned.

Neil held his cold hand. A chill ran through him, imagining his son in pain. "Hang on, Jackie. The ambulance'll be here soon."

Jack's eyes fluttered as he gasped for breath. He turned his head, revealing the outline of a jagged bone on the side of his face that had broken through the skin.

"Jack … Jack." The woman cradled his neck. "Don't move. I've got yah." She whispered to Neil, "It's a good sign that he woke up."

Neil shook his head. *Why don't I know how to help my son the way this stranger is?* "I … I don't know how to thank you."

"I'm an ER nurse. This is what I do."

How lucky was he that a nurse was at the game? Neil took a stuttered breath. Vicky's face was white. She was gripping Olivia against her chest, rocking her back and forth.

"He's going to be fine," Neil said, trying to convince his wife and himself. With a PhD in physics and biology, he knew the complications could be endless, and the long-term outlooks were too many to calculate.

Sirens and flashing lights. A police car was stopped in the street.

One minute, I'm waving at my son, and the next, we're on our way to the hospital.

The crowd parted. Two EMTs stepped through, carrying large square boxes and backpacks, setting them down next to Neil.

Hurry up!

"Hey, Mike," the woman holding Jack's head said.

"Laurie …" The EMT gave her a slight smile. "What have we here?"

"Stable. Breathing on his own," Laurie stated the words calmly as if addressing an old friend. "Lost consciousness. Possible facial fracture and concussion."

Oh my god, is this really happening?

Neil stood, his nerves feeling off. He wrapped an arm around his wife as the EMTs lifted Jack onto the gurney.

The sun felt warm, yet he shivered. Adults patted him on the back and spoke words of encouragement that made no sense. He couldn't focus on anything except the surreal scene playing out in front of him.

Vicky wiped her eyes. "I'll ride with him." She jumped into the vehicle. "Take Olivia and meet us at the hospital."

His son never wanted to play soccer. The speech Neil had given about team sports and the bond it developed seemed silly now. Jack's first game he sat on the field and picked dandelions. Neil told his son about the winning goal he'd scored at the championship game in college. He had bribed Jack with ice cream after each practice.

This is all my fault.

Neil bear-hugged Olivia as he sprinted to the minivan. His arms burned from holding his growing daughter. His run slowed to a fast walk.

He strapped Olivia in her car seat.

God, let him be okay.

He started the car.

Olivia cried.

Neil turned a corner, keeping an eye on the ambulance.

Olivia screamed louder.

"Honey, listen to Daddy." He glanced in the rearview mirror.

Olivia thrashed her legs, her hands yanking at the shoulder straps.

"Everything's gonna be all right. I'll get you a treat when we get to the hospital."

Ignoring the tow-away sign, he parked. The EMTs raced the gurney carrying Jack into the hospital. Vicky walked alongside, holding Jack's hand. With Olivia's arms wrapped around his neck, Neil ran through the double doors.

A nurse placed a hand on his chest. "Are you the father?"

"Yes, where is he?"

She pointed.

He entered the small room, still wrestling with Olivia.

Bright lights flooded his senses. Confusion scrambled his thoughts. A nurse blocked his view of his son. Errant lines continuously drew across the monitors mounted on the wall. LED lights blinked yellow and blue. The sound of bongs and beeps filled the spaces. Red gauze spotted the gray tile floor.

Neil stepped closer.

Vicky held Jack's hand. His white shirt was now streaked red.

A nurse adjusted an oxygen mask over the swollen face. An ER doctor checked his vitals.

Jack thrashed side to side. His voice sounded garbled. "It wurts, moo. It weally wurts."

"I know, honey. But you can't touch your face." Vicky glanced at the doctor. "Can't you give him something for the pain?"

"Not with a head injury. We have to wait until the specialist can evaluate him."

Neil took another step. His son's cries felt like acid running through his veins. "How long will that take?"

"The doctor's in surgery and will be down shortly. We're lucky he's in the hospital today."

Olivia pushed off Neil's chest. He set her down, and his hand grabbed Jack's foot. Minutes ticked as they waited for the surgeon. If this were *his* lab, he'd rearrange tasks, reassign his staff, and change priorities to get his son to the top of the list. But it wasn't his lab, and he wasn't in control. He lowered his head and waited.

A man wearing a white lab coat and black scrubs entered. He had a shaved head, dark beard, and the body of a marathon runner. He placed his hand on Jack's arm. "Calm down, son. Let me take a look."

Jack was breathing hard.

Neil let go of Jack's foot and fisted his hands, trying to stay calm.

"My name's Matt." He pulled a penlight from his pocket, flashing it across Jack's eyes. "Follow the light ... good. What's your name, son?"

Jack looked like he was trying to form the words. His lips moved slightly. Tears ran down the side of his cheeks. "Yack."

Neil fought the urge to not cry.

"Stay strong, Jackie," Vicky whispered. "Mommy and Daddy are here."

Olivia was playing with the bloody gauze.

I can't do anything right.

First, he bribed his son to play soccer, and now his daughter could catch a bacterial infection. What would the doctor and nurses think of him allowing his child to play on the dirty, emergency room floor? He picked her up.

"Jack, you're going to be fine." The doctor rested his hand on the boy's shoulder. "I need you to stay calm while I talk to your parents. Can you do that for me?"

Jack's eyes darted from Vicky to Neil.

"I'll stay with you, honey," his mother said. "Dad can talk to the doctor."

Neil trudged into the hall, wishing Vicky was holding his hand. They never made decisions about their children alone. Olivia began a swimming motion to escape her father. He held her across his chest with her arms and legs dangling. He knew the doctor was trying to console Jack and never tell a child the truth. Neil's feet felt like cement blocks as they strolled to the reception area.

The doctor opened a small consultation room and motioned for Neil to sit.

Neil glanced around to ensure the floor was safe for Olivia. She bopped around the room on stiff legs, falling, catching herself with hands on the floor, before rolling to a sitting position. She'd fling her hands in a *ta-da* motion.

The doctor smiled. "I need an MRI to confirm my diagnosis, but I think his nose and jaw are broken. Standard procedure is we plate the bone to stabilize the area."

During stressful times, Neil tried to keep his emotions out of his decision. He tried to do the same with the doctor and shifted his thinking from a father to a scientist. He focused on the technical details of biology, bone, cartilage, and how white blood cells healed the body. The surgery made perfect sense.

"I'm worried about a brain bleed. I've called in a neuro-consult. Once we have the MRI, I'll brief you before the surgery.

I'm sending him to radiology, and I'll have my assistant book an OR."

Neil slumped, feeling light-headed. All his life, he relied on the principles of physics and the building blocks of biology to interpret the world. He was never at a loss for questions to drive a hypothesis or to find solutions. With a simple kick of a ball, everything had changed. His ability to interpret the surgeon's statement seemed foreign as if he had just arrived on an alien planet where nothing he had learned applied.

"Whatever we find, Mr. Casperson, you should know that the first week after surgery will be the roughest. We'll do everything possible to keep Jack comfortable."

"Um … ah … will he make a full recovery? Any restrictions?"

"Let's see what the MRI shows before I answer that question." The surgeon stood. "As soon as I can, I'll give him something for pain."

How am I going to tell Vicky about Jack?

He followed the doctor, realizing he had forgotten Olivia. She sat on the floor, sucking her thumb.

What's wrong with me?

He pulled her fingers from her mouth and headed to the bathroom.

I hope she doesn't get sick from the bloody gauze.

Neil stood at the bathroom door as two nurses rushed Jack's bed to an elevator. An ER doctor pressed on Jack's chest, pumping up and down. Jack's body rocked with each thrust.

Neil charged at the gurney.

Vicky's eyes were swollen. She stood behind the doctor with her arms crossed. "He just blacked out. They have to ease the pressure in his head."

A brain hemorrhage.

The worst-case scenario. Neil reached to touch his son, but the gurney sped past. He and Vicky followed only to be stopped by a nurse.

"No children allowed on the surgical floor," the nurse said. "The front desk can direct you to the waiting room down the hall."

"I love you, Jack," Neil said.

The doctor pumped on Jack's chest.

Neil's stomach tightened. He needed to throw up.

Neil checked his watch, questioning whether his son was still in surgery. Vicky was curled up on the sofa. Her hand covered her eyes as if the lights tortured her. What would he do if the doctor told him that Jack wouldn't recover? What would it be like to go home without his child? How would Vicky react when her world fell apart?

Olivia sat on the floor playing with a package of saltines the nurse had given her. She squeezed the plastic and smashed the crackers into bits, sucking on an open end. The crumbs spilled on the floor.

Neil's phone vibrated again in his pocket. He looked at the caller ID. It was his assistant. He hit the silence button, and instantly, a text arrived.

```
We overcame the software issues and
have proven our cellular aging
hypothesis. Where are you? We are
about to break out the champagne. We
don't want to celebrate without you.
```

Neil stared at the screen. In the past, a scientific breakthrough would cause him to phone the dean, write a paper, and submit it to a science journal, and of course, plan a party for his employees. He ran a hand over his head, returning his phone to his pocket.

A moment that would have had him dreaming about a Nobel prize had instead reminded him about missing Jack's parent-teacher conference, or the speaking engagement at Harvard when he told Vicky on Jack's second birthday, 'He won't even know if I'm there or not.'

How could I be so insensitive?

He hugged Olivia. Did his career matter? The long hours. His drive to exceed expectations and not let his team down. The fame he garnered as being one of the rising stars in the technology world. None of those *things* could save his son.

A woman wearing a blue cap and mask approached.

His heart raced, anticipating the news.

"I'm Jack's neurosurgeon."

Vicky crossed her arms.

"The cranial pressure has been relieved, and his heart's back in normal rhythm. Dr. Swanson will proceed with the facial reconstruction. It'll be a couple more hours."

Neil studied the small woman. "He's going to be all right?"

A slight smile drew on her face. "Yes, Mr. Casperson, we have accomplished what we wanted from a neurological perspective. He's in Dr. Swanson's good hands."

He clasped his hands over his mouth. "No long-term issues?"

"As far as we know, he should be fine. Both physically and cognitively."

Neil closed his eyes, praying the next surgery would have the same outcome.

Jack showed up in the ICU a few hours after surgery.

"Everything went as planned," Dr. Swanson said. "He'll be transferred to the children's ward within the hour. Kids are resilient. I expect Jack to remain with us for about a week."

Neil opened his mouth to thank the doctor but couldn't find the words. Instead, he shook his hand.

Vicky gave Dr. Swanson a two-arm hug.

"If you need anything, have the nurse page me." Dr. Swanson nodded.

Vicky glanced at Olivia who was playing on the floor, squishing saltine crumbles into her hair.

"It's my turn. I'll stay with him," Neil said. "Take Olivia home." He hugged his wife. He kissed her neck. "I'll call when he gets to his room."

Neil paced in front of the nurse's station. His head ached from lack of sleep, but he wanted to be there for Jack, assuming his son would be scared and confused. Without Olivia or Vicky, he felt like a child lost at the mall looking for help.

He pulled out his phone and typed the dean a message.

```
I'm taking leave and will fill out
the paperwork later. Not sure how
long I'll be out. Please respect my
time, and no calls or texts. I'll be
in touch over the next few days.
```

Neil promised to stay with Jack until he could return to school. With the experiment a success, he had directed his assistants to take over. She could talk to the dean, write the research paper, and throw a party for the lab. But all of that could wait until tomorrow.

The aroma of coffee filled the air. A full pot was sitting on a warmer beside the ice and vending machines. He grabbed a large cup, dropping in two ice cubes, and filling the rest with coffee. He downed the cooled liquid, feeling a surge of energy. Two nurses wheeled Jack into his room. His face was bandaged like a mummy with eye slits.

"Mr. Casperson," the nurse said, "would you like me to bring in another bed? You're welcome to stay the night with your son."

"Thank you," Neil replied. "I don't want to leave him again."

Lynn's thoughts …

All parents are supposed to go first. The thought of losing a child is probably one of the worst fears the world could hand us. And – when our children are hurt, we tend to blame ourselves.

As Neil struggled with his little girl, I kept wondering if she was the next to be injured. He sat her down at the soccer field, by the emergency room gurney, in the consulting room, and she played with crackers in a wrapper. Her nine lives were just about up.

Thank goodness, she survived the ordeal.

Sometimes, we do not know what we have until it is gone. An age-old statement, but quite truthful. Life is short but our goals are also short. However, which comes first? Which takes precedence? Balancing life with family can be a difficult decision. We never know where our life path will lead. And Nicholas, our author, does a great job of explaining it. Neil wants his experiment to be successful, a breakthrough, perhaps a cure for cancer. But at was price does Neil have to pay for this success?

Learning how to balance our goals with our time for family may be difficult unless we set boundaries. Neil finally learns the lesson of balancing when he accepts the hospital bed. Sleeping next to his child is something every parent does. But for Neil, that first night will be quite an experience.

Fear is not always a monster lurking inside a closet. Fear can also stem from our faults, whether on purpose or by accident. Then again, are goals considered a fault or a responsibility? And when does working hard cross over that invisible line? That is a question everyone must face at some point in their lives.

102

The Coffin Club

P. K. Granger

That's odd. A voice message for Uncle Otsey?

People sometimes adopted the respectful approach, which left them cloaked in uncertainty, and Uncle Otesy was always alone. Thus, no one ever left messages.

I slid down the hill on a seldom-used footpath, bypassing the tourist-clogged sidewalks of New Alesund's harbor. Morning drizzle and low-hanging branches nibbled at my thoughts. A tingling sensation gripped my chest as a wayward blackberry vine coiled around my arm. I moaned, but for only a moment as the aroma of commercial fishing and the distant barks of sea lions eased my tension. Straightening my collar, I slowed my pace. The path now wound through various anchors, nets, and traps – stuff commercial fishermen once used but were now worn beyond repair.

A loose pile of weathered gray rope propped open the rear storeroom-turned studio of Salty Blue's Marine Supply. Classic Elvis music flew by as I stepped closer, vibrating past and over the long-abandoned pier. Rumors persisted that the Coffin Club, a handful of hobbyists building their own, had won the keys in a poker game. But in truth, it was Salty's curiosity that drove the deal and which now piled their inventory high on the back shelves.

I rapped on the aluminum door. "Uncle Otsey said to stop by?"

Cade and Sally, tenured members, were wiping stain over Frank's new casket. The myrtle wood glistened in the morning sun, and the room, filled with do-it-yourself coffin kits, hobby tools, and old furniture still looked empty.

"Morning, Tye." Cade wiped his fingers with a rag. "You remind me of the faded pumpkins the grandkids scattered across my yard."

I chuckled. "Wednesday and a week already. What's up?"

Cade continued to wipe his hands in a precise and deliberate manner. Coffee and the vibe of unwelcome news swirled between the stench of stain and the vibrations of Elvis. Sally sat on a bench with a manual in her hand, frowning.

"We weren't sure you'd get the message." His gaze remained fixed on the floor. "What with his medicines and …"

Sally laughed. "We hoped you would."

Cade always listened to the local gossip, which nudged the uncertainty of Otsey into varying levels of disapproval and fear.

I glanced around. "My Uncle's treatment's complex. He feels good. No delusions."

Uncle Otsey definitely considered his smokes as recreational. The edibles and prescriptions were therapeutic. My schedule brought me through town a handful of days each month. I coped with my uncle most of the times. But it was at night when I would toss and turn.

Cade cleared his throat. "Frank relapsed."

Despite the energy and spryness of the club members most had health concerns.

"We finished his casket, but here's the problem. We can't find his bracing packet." Cade shook his head. "The past six weeks, Frank's been confused."

The four kits I delivered in August sat on metal rims of sawhorses – braces glued tight.

Sally's graying 'brows arched into her hairline as she jumped up from the bench. "They're doing that expensive gene treatment … up at the nursing home. Still fighting death. But others died when …"

Cade's grip tightened on the rag. "Can you give me a bracing from your truck? We'll pay."

I rubbed the back of my neck before tugging my shirt collar back into place. The delivery truck held preordered complete kits. No extra parts. Already my boss tracked my work, making cuts here or there. He always picked at the little stuff. With no way to guarantee that replacement brackets would arrive before the designated owners needed them, red flags ripped through me. I glanced at my boots and sighed at the wet leaves sticking between the laces.

"Cade, uh, I've got no pay grade … not for shorting others." My eyes drifted to the coffee pot and the berry muffins. "Call my boss … you're a repeat customer and hold more influence than me."

Elvis now sounded louder than ever.

Cade frowned.

My face felt burnt. "I'm here until the weekend." I scribbled my number on the bulletin board. "Just call."

Sally pulled Cade aside. "One more thing –"

"Sally! I told you not to bring this …" Cade pulled his arm from her grip.

"I'm right." Sally's eyes narrowed.

Cade walked back to Frank's coffin.

She frowned, holding the gaze. "People are being murdered!" She stated.

"What?" I asked.

She threw her fist in the air. "The workers at the nursing home ignore us, act like we're half-senile retirees with a coffin fetish."

I smiled a half grin.

"But you …" – she pointed – "… a handsome man. If you sit with 'em, they'll talk all night."

"I have a girlfriend," I replied.

"Oh, no romance." She stuffed a couple of twenties in my jacket. "Eat pizza with the night shift. Reassure 'em Frank's friends appreciate their care." She leaned closer. "But find out what they know."

I shook my head. "I do deliveries, not detective work."

The music stopped, leaving the room stuck in a silent haze.

The arches over Sally's eyes flattened. "Selling yourself short? You Barcets solve puzzles. Otsey did that in the military, yah know."

Otsey had never talked about his army days. His past was not a part of my vocabulary. "Then ask Otsey for help," I stated, pulling out the bills.

Cade motioned me to the coffee and muffins. "Better if we collaborate with just you."

Sally spread a faded green ledger across the table. "I tracked the deaths from Astoria to Reedsport. Goes back for a year. At the funerals –"

"You attended the funerals?" My mouth felt dry.

Sally jabbed her finger against the paper. "The recent ones, best information comes at the wakes." She pointed at a few names. "These people died before their time."

I glanced at the ledger and skimmed across the names, dates, times, and locations. The last column described diagnosis and prognosis. Four of the names lived in the area. Fluorescent pink highlighted eight names of those who had died in the past seven months.

"Show it to the police," I stated.

"Tried." Sally patted my hand. "Besides, we have a sheriff." She shrugged. "Profiled us as death-conspiracy nuts."

"Labels hurt?" I glanced at Cade, who was studying the stain.

Sally shook her head. "In my nightmares, Frank's a dead duck lying on a hospital bed."

I rubbed the side of my face. A while back, the club gave me a beater Chevy pick-up to drive around town. A coffin delivery truck with the side panels plastered with *Final Journey – custom coffins, urns, and kits –* invoked wisecracks, stares, and pranks. More than once, I had to fight off the vandals. I leaned over Sally's notes and sighed. "They all died between midnight and four in the morning," I whispered. "Can you find someone to sit with Frank at night?"

She nodded. "Sure."

"We'll need harder evidence," I said, pausing at the door.

Sally's face lit. Her hands clasped under her chin.

Cade frowned. "Sometimes, a long shot works."

Pumpkins lined the entry of the one-room annex that was attached to the fire station that also served as the local sheriff's office. An officer's feet rested on the chipped Formica desktop. While leaning back in a swivel chair and thumbing through his phone, he nodded at a clipboard. I jotted down my contact information and reason for the visit. Officer Reynaldo set his phone on the desk. With the mention of the coffin club, his feet thudded across the hard vinyl floor.

"Those death watchers?" His skepticism was written all over his face.

I leaned on the counter. "More of a social, crafty group."

"Oh?" He shuddered. "I was in one of their houses once … my wife's cousin. Coffin laid in the den." His body rocked. "Filled with board games; Monopoly … Life. It was used like a footlocker. Boards and pieces painted inside the lid with family photos." The officer's hair stood in spikes. "Like they were in the middle of a game."

I grinned and shrugged. "Yeah. Their coffins remind them to live. You know, treasure each day?" *Hmm. Better not mention Cade and Sally's names.* "They try to make things better for whenever the inevitable comes. In their unique way, the idea of their friend dying scares 'em."

He glared out the window, his attitude somewhat floating across the parking lot. "The sheriff checked with the other departments along the coast. No investigations of similar cases. The nursing home claims the timing when people pass is unpredictable."

The tension in my neck softened. I took a long, slow breath. "Could you help the club?" My phone vibrated, but I focused on the officer.

"It's hard. We all try. The 'cap, he told us to patrol past the care center. Me? I'm thinking of a needle. An oddity noticed during the day … no way. Nights, maybe." He peered over his glasses. "Midnight to five, we make emergency-only calls. No haystack patrolling." His shoulders sagged. "Not in the budget."

Walking back to my truck, I checked the messages. Cade's terse, subdued voice indicated that the replacement brace would arrive in about a month.

Otsey's wood-framed house rested alongside a stream that flowed to the Pacific. A tiny tsunami could definitely obliterate it. I stuffed my hands in my pockets and walked along the bank, ignoring the faint mist.

Mercury mirrors shattered the shoreline. Seagulls yakked above the roar of the breakage. To the south, I spotted a pile of driftwood. My uncle seemed to be moving logs. Two years of building driftwood sculptures had made him strong.

"Did you pick up the plastic?" he asked by way of a greeting. His eyes twinkled. He was standing beside four upright logs, each with an end buried in the sand.

"No litter."

A hazy trail of smoke followed Otsey as he moved to the stack of driftwood. His to-do list seldom included standing still while talking. "'Least you're trained." The wind caught his empty clam bucket, banging it against a log. "What'd your Type-A coffin lovers want?"

"Your medicine freaks 'em out. Should you smoke out here?"

His hand rolled a joint as he balanced a log across two others, pretending not to hear me. Otsey never argued. I sat on the sand, summarizing the day.

My uncle frowned. "Up there?" He waved a seven-foot stick to the south and at the town's nursing home where the roof peeked just above the tree-lined ridge.

"Yeah?"

My uncle stood silently. His eyes seemed to glaze over as he stared at the roofline; obviously, brooding thoughts unrelated to his driftwood. I gave him time and space to exist at his own pace.

"Sometimes, I work farther south. More tourists there. They always stop and talk." The lines on his face grew faint. "Clear view of the old folks. It overlooks the beach. A night aide props open the emergency door and strolls out every hour to meditate for the length of a cigarette. There's a sliver of light around the door. A couple of times …" – he scratched behind his ear – "… the light escaping around the door grows larger." After pulling an unidentifiable, edible concoction from his pack, he shoved it in his mouth. "She's deep in the trance out at the back edge … when the ninja creeps inside."

"Ninja?" *Jeez.*

"Quick, dark." He nodded, picking up another stick. "I assumed a pill-fleecer?"

My hands gripped my knees. "Are you sure?"

"Not my business." He searched his pockets. "A bit too subtle for revenge." He shrugged. "Love makes no sense either. Maybe means nothing." He took measured deep breaths, obviously fighting past memories. "I work on the darker nights when they can't see me."

"Say what?" I frowned.

"Not what, boy, when. Full moons bring out the crazies. Might wreck my sculpture."

The next storm would return the structure to driftwood – a version of natural ebb and flow. "Uncle Otsey, what month was it?"

"Hmm … sleeping on the sand?" His eyes lit. "August. The night Brother Bob dropped by with the black cod." Otsey dug in his pocket again. "Smoke?"

I shook my head. Thinking of the pink highlighter on the list, August twelfth shined out.

"You staying awhile?"

"Yeah." The driftwood shifted into a sculpture as somber as the Pacific water. "Power motivation makes little sense. Are these killings for mercy or money?"

Otsey paused, wiping his finger across his lips. "Drugs … probably for comfort."

I pulled on my gloves and zipped up my jacket. "Thanks. Is your trellis an entry from the sea?"

Otsey withdrew to an impervious place next to the logs, sand, and water.

The Net-A-Whale Tavern featured a midweek deal – beer, fish, and chips. Tonight, every table was full. Conversation fought for airspace with the flatscreen televisions. Sagging strands of bare vintage bulbs hinted at lighting. Paper witches and ghosts hung between the faint shadows bouncing against the walls. The place reminded me of a mixture of sea air and stale fries.

I ignored the sticky sounds from my boots as I aimed for the far side of the bar. Four regulars with the best view of ESPN were debating the probable winners of the upcoming football game. Erica, the bartender, nodded. Descended from Norwegian fishers, her source for cheap, but fresh fish, kept her in business. She slid a beer my way.

I picked a place to rest. The wiry guy across the bar and next to the only other empty barstool twirled his whiskey glass. A constant motion with an attitude. The local foursome finished their predictions, and the wiry guy motioned for a refill.

He leaned a little closer to me. "Are those undertakers friends of yours?"

People recognize me? Other patrons glanced in my direction. I smiled since everyone here seemed to know everyone else. "Not sure. I do know where the back doors of the funeral homes are."

"Hell of a job." The man laughed.

"Sally came in an hour ago," Erica stated. "She's asking people to sit with Frank at night. Says you're finding out what's going on up there."

I grabbed the counter to keep from falling over, while my mind blanked at a response.

The man slapped his hand on the counter, sending an awkward moment into the air. "He won't live long … up in that care center!" He wiped his chin. "They ever try to send me there, I'm stepping into the Pacific!"

"It's that bad?" I sipped on my beer, fighting the urge for a refill.

He frowned. "I heard the rumors about the deaths." He waved his empty glass in the air. Other glasses rapped against the wooden tables. The wiry guy glared at me before returning to his whiskey, holding the place's attention. "Heard of anyone sneaking out there in the early morning hours?"

I fingered the bills in my pocket.

A jersey-clad husker frowned. "Place smells of rotten."

The man across the bar laughed. "Nope. Our sidewalks roll up early these days." He signaled for his tab. The conversations, along with clanks of silverware, refilled the room.

I pull a couple twenties from my pocket. "Erica, two pizzas to go. One veggie. One pepperoni."

I strolled through the mist to Otsey's place, past assorted lights and abandoned jack-o'-lanterns, shaking off the tightness growing on my back. My uncle's house loomed in the darkness, a closet rectangle. The quarter moon, low on the horizon, suggested the way to the beach. Otsey sat on a log under his sculpture with a blanket around his shoulders. His face glistened from the sea's mist. His clam bucket seemed empty.

"Here," I said, offering him a couple slices of vegetarian pizza. I tightened the collar around my neck.

He eyed the darkness of the coastline. His cheeks grew pale and caved inward as if aging at that particular moment. "The ocean's loud," he said.

It sounded the same as always to me. "Frank's getting weaker." I sat beside him.

"He's never around anyway." He finished the first slice. "Learn anything? Whisper, I've got a headache."

"Two people in their seventies died sooner than anticipated. An oncologist talked to the head nurse. Specialists never show up at nursing homes. State inspectors arrive unannounced. Means a family member probably complained about the care. Normally, they'd find pages of deficiencies, but this place came out squeaky clean." I paused. "No ninjas spotted."

"That's the point of sneaking around … ninjas." He grinned and wiped his mouth with the back of his hand. "A skilled bunch of spooks." Otsey's eyes gleamed despite the low light. "What's your plan?"

I stared at the black ocean. "Looked for witnesses. Tried social media."

"Computers …" Otsey slapped his hands against his legs. "I'm about action." He lowered his voice. "How does one fight a ninja?"

I now stared out at the midnight ocean. "You feeling okay?"

He pulled an edible from his backpack. "Tye, one thing. Bang … no hesitation. That's problem-solving." He winked. "Works on ninjas too."

It was late and Otsey was talking in riddles while ignoring my questions. He often read me better than I liked. "I'm giving the club a bracing kit."

"Let's go tonight. No witnesses."

I laughed and nudged the sand with the toe of my boot. "What about you?"

"Oh, no need to worry about me. I'll explain to the jury that my medicine robs me of recollection."

Despite Otsey stopping to tie his shoe and study the harbor's lights, we reached Salty Blue's in under an hour. He was stuck on a monologue. His tension seemed to electrify the air. It was now darker than an evening blackout and more quiet than a moth. Not even a sea lion barked.

Whatever possessed me to bring him along?

Salty Blue's rear yard popped into brightness as the motion sensor lit. I was blinded for a few seconds as Otsey disappeared between the dense piles of maritime relics. The key was hidden behind a rusted anchor alongside the storeroom door. I placed the bracing unit inside.

I bent down to the anchor returning the key as something hard slammed against my back. My head hit the jagged metal edge and I sighed. "Otsey! It's me!"

A knife blade flashed. I clutched a wrist and pushed. As I kicked at the guy, the knife hovered just inches above my heart. A hand squeezed on my neck. I twisted and shoved, banging the man's wrist against the edge of the anchor. I'm choking out jagged breaths. At last, my kicks hit. His kneecap snapped. The dude fell, screaming, holding onto his now ailing leg.

Otsey stepped out from the shadows, carrying a rope and the knife. His complexion a buttered mellow. "Recognize 'im?" he asked.

"In the bar … tonight … whiskey-sipper." My voice creaked. I fingered my neck.

Otsey laughed. "Tye, you fight good. Now, I'm taking over." He yanked the guy's head back, placing the edge of his knife near his bulging eyes. "Watched you following us, ninja-man." Otsey's voice pitched. "Most fun I've had since they discharged me. Why'd you kill those people?"

"Can't say."

Otsey laughed again. "They all claim that … at first." He dragged the blade closer to the guy's ear. "But never in the end." He switched to a guttural growl. "Four minutes of intact body parts remaining."

A thin line of blood ran under the edge of the knife.

I touch Otsey's arm.

He winked. "Go home, son. I want to enjoy this one alone." Otsey grinned. "Let's call you, Bait." My uncle's hysterical laugh had returned.

Bait searched the area, before closing his eyes. "I called the cops," he said. "Thought you were stealing."

Otsey slammed the butt into the side of the guy's head. Blood oozed in his hair. "Bait, speak no lies … not tonight." Otsey dug his fingers into the guy's neck.

"I'll call the police," I stated.

"No," Otsey yelled. "Cops stick to the rules."

Bait couldn't see Otsey's cheek where a slight dimple had appeared. It was Otsey's poker bluff. He lashed Bait to the crab cage. "Decide your destiny." My uncle tugged the struggling mess to the neglected fishing pier. "Three body-intact minutes left."

I tugged on my side of the cage. Bait jerked from inside, but the ropes held tight. The rotting pier creaked as we stepped on it. Bait's eyes bulged. He sputtered incomprehensible words. The sea lions barked, shattering the night. The circular cage swung close to the water's edge.

Otsey radiated craziness, leaning over Bait. "Around here, the sea lions and crabs feed on scraps from the packing plants. Trained scavengers. Down on the bottom, your body'll disappear. Your choice, Bait. Speak or sink."

The pier swayed with our weight.

Bait struggled.

"I'm the same no matter," Otsey stated. "Post-traumatic stress gets me another peaceful involuntary commitment." My uncle grinned, his voice carried a boisterous joyful tone. "Your choice. Silence means to sink."

"They sent me a padded, red envelope," Bait yelled. "Used a bicycle courier."

"And?" Otsey asked.

"It had a name, location, syringe … and cash." Bait's stutter sounded raspy. "The person was dying anyway. I just inject into the IV." His face quieted as his eyes closed. "That's all. They sleep … forever."

Otsey held out the knife. He stared at the pitch-black water of the bay and shook his head.

"Who hired you?" I asked.

Bait's face brightened. "I'll give you a grand from the next case. Spend it any way you like."

"No deal." I shoved Bait and the cage closer to the edge.

Bait's head now hung only inches above the water. "All the money then, ten grand?"

"Who hired you?" I asked again.

"Don't know," Bait yelled. "No names given except for the targets!"

Sounds believable.

Otsey stepped on the cage, stabilizing it on the pier, but leaving Bait hanging over the dark water.

Time for the police. As I reached for my phone, the rotted pier emitted a screech, shifting with the water. I grabbed Otsey's shoulder to avoid him toppling off the edge. The wooden planks halted Bait's slide.

Bait's eyes bulged. "Pull me back!"

I leaned over the man. "You don't confess, and we explain we found you feeling remorse, slicing your wrists. Understand?"

"Is everyone in your family crazy?" he asked.

My uncle held up the knife.

"Okay." Bait gasped but his eyes lit.

What's he thinking? My heart pounded. The sea lions sounded closer. My body shook. "There's gotta be more. You wanted leverage? Someone sent you a red envelope and you just followed what it said?"

Otsey lifted his foot. The cage and the man splashed into pitch-black water. The color drained from Bait's face as my uncle jerked on the rope. The man's face balanced just above the waterline.

"Someone who looked like me … the envelope for two of the runs …" – seawater slapped against Bait's face – "… I followed him, a man in a charcoal suit … Coastal Budget Insurance." His words spewed making little sense, blurring together.

"Yeah," I said. "And?"

"Pull me back!"

Otsey and I dragged the cage onto the pier.

Bait coughed and spit. "I needed proof of the hush money. The guy is the finance officer. Took his family on vacation to Hawaii. I searched his house. Found papers taped on the backside of a desk drawer. Memos from his boss and an audit of the company." Bait stopped talking.

"That's a long stretch," I stated. "All this during one burglary?"

"Not a heist. Had lots of time with no alarms. You tell the cops, and I'll say you're lying."

"Don't threaten me," I stated. "You're the one in the cage. What'd you find?"

"The memo said he'd be fired if the company paid claims due to his contracting mistakes." Bait shrugged despite the rope. "He wanted to keep his job. Hired me instead. There's a list of names and claims to be paid. I recognized the ones with check marks."

"All this because the company's stuck paying claims until the contracts expire?" I asked.

"Death's cheaper." Bait's eyes are half closed now. "Audit showed the guy modified the coverages after the lawyers wrote it. Screwed it up."

Anger and exhaustion racked through my body. "You make any copies?"

Bait nodded.

As flashing red and blue lights crossed the bay bridge, I yanked Bait from the pier. Otsey flipped the empty cage and rope into the water.

Otsey walked the footpath toward home.

I followed.

When we reached the top of the hill, he paused. The aroma of mint had replaced the salty sea breeze as he sucked on a candy, an oblique mask etched across his face. Deep in thought and worn by the night, we stood unable or unwilling to move. The eastern lights, outlining the coastal mountain range, echoed in the distance. Sea lions slipped into the water, and a pair of fishing boats eased away from the dock.

Otsey pulled his jacket tighter around his neck, cramming an edible into his mouth. He was quiet, his thoughts somewhere else. We both felt numb. As the silver gleams tinted the seawater pink with the sunrise, the Coffin Club's obligation to support, to make things better, consumed my thoughts.

"That's what you did?" I asked. "In the Army?"

Otsey winced. "Variations of … tonight you stopped dreadful things from happening. Focus on that, not me."

"We did it, not me." Thoughts of the price my uncle had paid, still paid, kept me watching the glimmering water as it retook the broken trails of boats and sea lions.

"You should go," he stated. "Not sure how I might feel."

Otsey wanted me safe. "Okay … I'll get my truck. The mist should stop soon. I'll drive by. If the clam bucket sits on your porch, I'll stop. We'll dig for dinner. If not, I'll keep going."

Otsey nodded. "No promises." His eyes looked moist.

"We're good." I walked silently beside my uncle. "As long as you stop signaling that fake poker bluff … I need to win on my own at times."

Faint dimples crossed Otsey's cheeks. "With luck, tomorrow, I'll build a driftwood sculpture."

Lynn's thoughts …

Do we ever know the true history of our relatives? With so many years between an uncle and nephew, how much of that life was lived as a secret? In our story, a nephew learned of people dying unexpectedly in an old folk's home. Wanting to dig a little deeper, excuse the pun, he asked for help from an aging uncle. Little to be known from our main character, his uncle was somewhat of an expert in pulling information from an unwilling participant. A trait he had learned while serving our country. A talent unknown to the nephew.

The fear of death is real to many. But when death arrives before our time, that fear becomes more of a fact. It's interesting how so many of the young actually believe it's okay to allow our elders to die. But then, when those young become old, their ideals and conclusions on death somewhat change.

Cloaked in uncertainty is what our author called it. I would argue that our children honestly do not understand life or how to deal with it, and that is where the uncertainty comes from. Instead, the young boast about their unrealistic achievements, which are important to them, but in reality, lack validity when compared to actual life.

The fear in this story does not pertain directly to death but alludes to the unknown. A simple fact of not knowing who our relatives were prior to us entering this world. History can be changed if those in charge should decide to change it. For the young may never know what had come before. Not if it is erased. If rumors exist along with photos, who knows?

I believe that is how monsters are born and survive; through the words and photos of the past. Uncle's passion for his smokes and edibles probably stems from hiding from those monsters that lurk in the shadows. I believe those monsters are sometimes called regret.

the CURIOUS case of JOSEPH NESSEN

Georgie Svrcek

From the desk files of the late Dr. E. G. Sterling

Capgras Syndrome is a psychiatric disorder characterized by the belief that a loved one – be it a parent, child, friend, or spouse – has been replaced by an impostor. It often happens with schizophrenia but could appear in others with neurodegenerative disorders such as dementia or traumatic brain injuries. The condition was rare with little understanding and research. I, myself, only encountered one patient throughout my psychiatric career who came close to fitting the diagnosis.

I was called to the university hospital one night to perform a psych evaluation on a patient – Joseph Nessen.

Joseph was recuperating from surgery after an automobile accident. Though there was no evidence of trauma other than a concussion, he began exhibiting unusual psychological symptoms, namely, he was insisting that the woman whom he had awoken to each morning was no longer his *real* wife.

I entered Joseph's room and he was alone. His left arm was in a sling and his leg wrapped in thick, white gauze.

"She stepped out of the room," he stated before I had the chance to introduce myself. "You know ... to give us time to talk."

I sat on the chair next to his bed.

"I'm not crazy," he stated.

"I don't like that word, crazy," I replied.

Joseph rolled his eyes.

"I'm Dr. Sterling. Tell me about what you're feeling. That way I can grasp the sense of what's happening."

"I can't describe it. It's a gut feeling." He shifted his position and winced as he lifted his leg. "There's something different about her. Something's off. I don't know why or how, but that's not my wife. That's not Ingrid. It's somebody else."

"Is there anything in particular that makes her different?"

He remained silent for a moment. His gaze aimed at the end of the bed. "Ingrid has a birthmark just above her right collarbone. I've seen it many times. But with that lady, it's just ... not there. She looks like her, but she's not her." He used his free hand to fidget with his gown.

"The mind can play incredible tricks on a person. Especially given that you were badly injured in the crash. Your brain may be convinced she always had a mark when in fact she never had one."

He glared at me; his eyes shining with tears. "You don't get it. I knew you wouldn't."

"I understand this can be scary and confusing, but I'm here to help. You're not the first who's had this happen."

He fixed his gaze back on the end of the bed. "Get out, please."

"Joseph ..."

"I said, get out!" A single tear rolled down his cheek.

I sighed, pulling a business card from my pocket. "I'm here if you ever want to discuss this with someone. No judgment, just a space to work through your feelings and maybe find some answers." I set the card on the small end table.

I wrote a prescription for a mild antipsychotic, though I wouldn't have been surprised if he turned it down. I left the hospital, almost certain I'd never hear from the man again. Therefore, it was to my surprise that I received a call a week later. He explained that the feelings hadn't left and that he needed someone to talk to. He said he wasn't looking for me to fix the problem, but to just listen and understand. I agreed to the terms.

He arrived with a light blue cast and crutches. He sat on the leather couch across from my desk, instantly launching into a detailed explanation of what was going on. What it felt like to wake up next to a stranger that appeared so familiar. The unease he felt as they wheeled him out of the hospital.

Given his insistence during our first meeting, I was surprised he had returned home, but he assured me he had no other choice. The woman was adamant that she *was* his wife. It seemed to him like the only thing he could do was play along. Now, he was at home with her, and it was all too clear that she was, in fact, an impostor. He described in detail the way she used to smile – a little higher on the left and showing off her gums – and that the other woman's smile was more even and smaller.

"It's unsettling, almost eerie, to see her smile like that."

When I stated that injuries could affect our memory or perception, he shut me down, insisting he no longer felt the effects of the concussion. Therefore, his intuition was real. I thought better of pressing the issue.

By the time he returned for another session, I had decided to adjust my approach. It was obvious I would be unsuccessful in reversing his delusion. Therefore, I might have more success in helping him cope with the discomfort than actually addressing the cause.

"She folds the laundry differently now."

I attempted to shift the topic to how he might go about living with this new person. He was resistant, arguing that my job was not to fix him but to just listen. I explained I had no interest in denying his experience and only wanted to help him find a sustainable way to exist in this new reality. He seemed a little taken aback by that statement.

"I just want to be with *my* wife," he said.

"I know, and you can be. Just a different version of her."

"But I want the real Ingrid. I want things to be like they were before." His voice wavered as he spoke.

"Let's take one step at a time." I couldn't say that he left my office buoyed by our conversation or more distressed than when he arrived. The longer our sessions continued, the more entrenched his beliefs became, despite my best efforts. Each week, he brought new evidence of his not-wife's facade. He explained how his *real* wife had an affinity for animals. She could approach any creature on the street and it would immediately accept her affection. On a recent walk with this new one, a cat hissed and ran away.

I tried to brush it off, explaining that every cat isn't friendly, but he silenced me, declaring he knew what he saw. The next week, he explained that his *real* wife was never good at singing – it was a bit of a joke between them. Yet he overheard this new one singing while making dinner one night. Her voice nothing like the way it was before. This new woman was clearer and more melodic.

I noticed a change in his behavior by our fifth session. He silently entered my office, only nodding in response to my greeting. I asked how he was feeling, but he didn't say a word. I waited and after a while, he spoke.

"I think she hates me."

"What makes you say that?" I asked.

"I'm doing everything I can," he said, looking at the wall. "I'm doing my best to live with her and take things for what they are but it's hard. She's losing patience." He took a sharp inhale. "She's upset I won't be with her, that I won't touch her. That I'm still ... *thinking* like this."

"Did she say what she wanted from you?"

"She snapped at me last night," he replied. "Said I just needed to get over myself and accept that she was really my wife or I was going to end up alone. Said she'd leave me."

I started to reply but he cut me off.

"Ingrid would never have talked to me that way."

"Perhaps you could consider this woman's feelings. She clearly cares for you, and it must be hard to hear you don't feel the same toward her."

He shifted his gaze and glared at me. "You think this is hard for her? I'm the one who lost my wife and is being forced to live with a faulty copy, and you want me to care about her feelings?"

"It might help if you approach this relationship with an open understanding. Things might feel less foreign if you treat her like she's just another person."

"But she's not just another person." His voice grew louder. "She has all these things about her that make her look like Ingrid, but there's enough inconsistencies that I know they're *not* the same. She's too close to be just anyone, and she's too different to be her. I don't know if I can keep living with someone like that."

"We can work on bridging the gap between the two. We can get you to the point where she feels like your wife again. You just have to think about her as –"

"I don't want to *think* about *that* woman! I want *my* wife back!" He grabbed his crutches and stormed out of the room.

I sat silently for a moment, unsure of what to do. I wasn't even sure he would show up again, but sure enough, the following week he arrived for his appointment. He had started to change. He was losing sleep. His appearance seemed haggard as dark circles grew under his eyes. When he spoke, the words were more erratic and disoriented.

He talked about the missing birthmark on her neck and how he scoured through their pictures to find proof that it was once there. He explained how he observed her behavior throughout the day and marked the times when he noticed something different, something sinister, that proved she was being deceptive. As the weeks progressed, he talked about the research he was collecting on doppelgangers and lookalikes and the fascinating things he was discovering – of twins who swapped back and forth, of a teacher who was seen in two places at the same time, of people who saw their spouses in one room only for them to enter the house from somewhere else. I did my best to redirect his thoughts, to offer logical explanations, but my efforts felt pointless. I was less of an outlet for his emotions and more of a faceless sounding board.

He grew utterly obsessed with uncovering the truth about this other woman, and with that obsession, he was becoming more paranoid and delusional. The more stories he read, the more conspiracies his mind created.

First, his *new* wife was an identical woman who had kidnapped the real Ingrid out of jealousy. Next, she was not a person at all but a humanoid robot created as an experiment to mimic human conduct. Finally, she was a clone, genetically engineered to spy on him and collect his personal information and secrets.

I watched with each passing visit him becoming convinced that this new woman, this not-wife person, was there to kill him. I should have acted. I should have placed him on a mandatory psych hold or insisted that he be medicated. For the life of me, I cannot explain why I didn't. Perhaps, I naively hoped I would say something during one of our sessions that would work, and he'd return more lucid and under control.

Since he arrived each week on time, a part of me must have believed I was making a difference. How foolish I was. I should have done something. I finally offered my home number and encouraged him to call if he needed to talk, which led me to the culmination of our time together.

It was early morning, almost three, and a few days after our last appointment. The piercing sound of the phone jerked me awake. I answered, and without hearing a voice, I knew it was Joseph.

"I know it's not her, Dr. Sterling," he whispered, his voice low and shaky. "I know that's not *my* Ingrid. I'm done pretending."

I shot out of bed, gathering my things. "Joseph, I need you to think about what you're saying."

"I don't need to think about it anymore. I refuse to let that *thing* pretend to be *my* wife." He growled.

I darted into my office, rummaging through the filing cabinet for his folder. "Can we just talk about this for a moment? Can you walk me through what you're feeling?"

He laughed.

I pulled his file from the stack, retrieving the intake form.

"You already know what I'm feeling. It's all I've been talking about for weeks. I'm done talking. I'm done sitting on a couch and explaining how I feel. I'm tired of you telling me to have pity on her. She's figuring it all out. How to eliminate me. I'm done being afraid. I've had enough, and I'm finally going to do something about it."

I was out the door.

"Do you hear that, bitch?" he yelled. "I said I'm going to do something about it!"

"Joseph!" I stated as I climbed into the driver's seat.

The call ended.

I took off, dialing 911. Luckily, he lived nearby and I was familiar with the neighborhood. Within minutes, I had arrived. There was only one car in the driveway, and the lights were off in the house. I might have believed that I was at the wrong place had it not been for the blood-curdling scream. I sprinted up the walkway and pounded on the front door.

"Joseph!"

I tried the handle and it was unlocked. As I stepped into the dimly lit living room, my eyes fell upon a body – half in and half out of the bathroom. The head was split and she was bleeding on the hardwood floor. Blood was splattered along the walls. I stepped closer and that was when I noticed Joseph. He was standing silently, holding a knife in one hand and a picture frame in the other, leaning on a crutch. He dropped the knife and it clattered across the floor.

I did my best not to jump.

"It wasn't her," he whispered. "It was never going to be my Ingrid."

"I'm sorry, Joseph," I replied.

"I did the right thing," he said.

The sound of sirens grew louder as red and blue flashes streamed through the open door.

I stood quietly as two officers pinned Joseph's arms behind his back. Just like the knife, the picture frame fell and bounced across the floor.

"It wasn't her!" he yelled. "She was going to kill me! I did what I had to do!"

I stepped closer to the body as his screams softened. I had never met Ingrid in person. But she seemed like a lovely lady only with blood pooling around her head. Without thinking, I picked up the frame and studied the photo of Joseph and Ingrid from years past. The two were at the beach. Joseph sported dark sunglasses and Ingrid was wearing a floppy sunhat. Her thin bathing suit straps revealed her chest, including her collarbone, above which rested, just as Joseph had described, a small brown dot. I glanced down at the woman on the floor, and my mind froze.

The collarbone of this body was smooth and pristine; illuminated by the faint, ghostly glow of the outside lights and devoid of any marks.

GEORGIE SVRCEK

Lynn's thoughts …

Devoid of any marks, *hmmm.*

To not be believed or to be believed – how *do* we perceive the world in which we live? The ability to perceive is nothing more than our awareness of the objects that surround us, or conditions, or forces, all experienced through sensations. It is just our capacity to understand.

To that point, who has the right to interpret our perceptions? After all, how we relate to our world is actually controlled from inside our minds. Who has the right to warp or attempt to warp what is or is not inside our minds?

I had to look up *Capgras Syndrome.* It's an interesting condition. Jean Marie Joseph Capgras explained his study on the syndrome in his paper, *The Illusion of Doubles.*

Oooh, a doppelganger – the evil twin. The one who does the nasty deeds and blames the innocent one. Supposedly and under the multi-verse theory, we exist inside various realities at the same time. But if those realities should collide, a doppelganger will appear.

Sometimes I wonder if half of our world leaders are now their evil twins. It would explain a lot. Although, how much reality could really be included in that theory, probably none.

The fear of confusion within our thoughts would indeed bring terror to anyone. After all, it's all we have in this world – our perceptions. To experience the horrors of illusions simply enter a house of mirrors. We will see ourselves extending into the forever ether. We actually experience our multi-verse traveling into the future and past at the same time. A concept that is somewhat difficult to grasp.

Then again, what is reality? Is it what we see when our eyes are open, or is it what we perceive when our eyes are closed?

134

Dead Rat

Linda Balboni

I woke feeling good, watching Good Morning America while sipping coffee. This day felt just like any other day until around noon. With Christmas only a week away, I had planned to paint my nails a crimson red. But a sharp pain just under my ribs that spread to my stomach hit.

Perhaps my scrambled eggs and toast were not agreeing with me or perhaps it was gas pains.

I always had a strong stomach, could eat anything spicy with no issues. My thoughts, however, were soon replaced with more pain. I rested on the couch hoping that would help. I tried walking it off, icing the area, a heating pad, but no relief. It was time to visit the emergency room. The monster raking havoc inside would not stop.

I collected my pocketbook and phone, and headed for my car, clutching my stomach.

"Are you okay?" my husband asked. "What's going on?" He ushered me to his truck.

Tears rolled down my cheeks.

"Should I call an ambulance?" he asked.

"No," I replied. "Just drive me to the hospital!"

Every bump was excruciating. The pain grew to where I could hardly breathe.

As my husband checked me in, I made my way to the ladies' room, becoming close friends with the toilet. My mind reeled as I tried to make sense of this throbbing pain. For six hours, I sat in an uncomfortable chair in a crowded waiting room, feeling as if I had just stepped into hell.

Finally, I was in a room. My blood was drawn by a rude phlebotomist, who was obviously having a bad day. An EKG was next. The nurse who performed the test left me exposed until I pulled the johnnie back to cover my breasts. She practically yanked me from the gurney when the test was complete.

If looks could kill, I would be dead about now. No compassion. A full moon hung in the black sky, and I kept thinking that this must be Hades.

"I want to go home," I stated, aiming for the exit.

My reluctant husband followed.

A rainstorm hit the day before and with no power, our basement had flooded with six inches of water. I inched my way into a pitch-black house, holding my stomach.

I didn't have the energy to change my clothes but tried desperately to become comfortable. I stayed on that couch that night. Tuesday morning, I felt worse and prayed I would make it through the day. The phone rang. It was the incompetent hospital.

The nurse insisted I should return because my white cells were very high and other tests were abnormal. I was very weak and could hardly move. On Wednesday, when I made my way to the bathroom, I was horrified to see that my urine was a tea color.

I was terrified there was something seriously wrong. To make things even worse, our water was cold. I washed with the limited resources I had. With no appetite, I made my way back to the couch.

I waited as long as I could, but I had to return. We did, however, switch hospitals. The one closest to our home was not listed in my insurance's network, and I was worried about coverage. After the horrible treatment the other day, it didn't seem to matter anymore.

We entered and my pain was relentless. My son was there with a worried grin. He gave me a hug. Trying to hold back the tears, I followed the nurse to a room. I kept thinking of how fortunate I had been throughout my life, no serious health conditions for over sixty years. My mind raced as I thought the worst. My pancreas, my intestine?

"Hi, I'm Steve and I'll be your nurse!" A nice young man with a caring and compassionate attitude greeted me.

My daughter and son-in-law soon arrived and remained by my side. They took turns holding my hand, assuring that I was safe. After several tests, it was determined I had a serious infection.

"You have a very angry gallbladder," a doctor stated.

To say I was shocked was an understatement. The doctor advised that surgery was imminent and wanted to schedule it for tomorrow.

"But I must make Christmas cookies!" I said.

The doctor smiled. "I think the cookies can wait another day or so."

When my family left for the night, I was reduced to a young, frightened girl, feeling alone inside a scary world. I watched a little TV. My brain reeled, trying to remain calm. Visiting the bathroom with my new friends – a pole and bags of fluid to combat the infection – was quite the challenge. Keeping everything in place while maneuvering back and forth soon became a tad bit easier, but was becoming more and more annoying.

After a sleepless night, Krista, a sweet nurse, entered. She carried a tray with a shot for who knows what. Laurie, my day nurse, soon entered like a warm breeze, wearing a large smile. Her headband was adorned with sparkles.

"You're surgery is scheduled for eleven."

I quietly accepted what was about to happen. I was wheeled to pre-op and the kind-hearted staff greeted me. I could not hide my fear as tears wet my eyes. A nurse held my hand, telling me – just like Bob Marley has sung – 'Every little thing's gonna be alright!'

Her words comforted me as the mask was placed over my face. Then lights out. I woke in the recovery room, feeling numb but pain-free. I was thankful I had made it through the operation. A strange memory from the twilight was of SpongeBob SquarePants smiling at me.

Why? Did I see yellow in my dreams?

The surgeon had said everything went well. My gallbladder was quite infected and to the point of gangrene. He had referred to it as a *dead rat.* I had heard this statement as they wheeled me out of surgery. The thought made me pause, knowing how serious my condition had been. I was wheeled upstairs to my room and was soon enjoying a warm blanket.

Laurie, the day nurse, entered to welcome me back. She took my vitals. The medical staff was kind, but there was something very special about Laurie. I nick-named her, Laurie Sparkles.

I was soon released and returned home. I didn't want to take the pain medication. But the pain was unbearable.

The phone rang and I answered.

"How was your night, did you sleep?" Laurie Sparkles asked.

I explain the deep pain.

"This is no time to be a hero. Take the medication every four hours."

I tried the medication, but the pain persisted.

The surgeon ordered an endoscopy to make sure there were no additional stones lodged in my track. Unfortunately, there wasn't a specialist who could run the test where the surgery was performed. I had to accept my fate. I would be returning to the first hospital where they treated me so poorly.

Once secured in the ambulance, I stared out the window feeling every jolt as the rain pelted the windows. The attendant asked how I was doing. She shared her experience of having her gallbladder removed. We compared notes and before I knew it, I was entering the other hospital. I was alone again, except for a man in the next bed. He looked disheveled and was moaning in pain. My heart ran cold even though my maternal side wanted to comfort him. My thoughts turned to apprehension as once again I would be under anesthesia and worried about what could happen, and how things could go wrong.

How could I ever leave my beautiful son, daughter, and my husband? The love I held was immeasurable and precious. A week ago, I was living life with no thoughts of hospitals, pain, or surgery. I reflected on how instantly everything could change with the trajectory of one's life.

"It's time to go!" a friendly voice said.

My eyes welled with tears as I held down my panic. In the operating room, a rather serious anesthesiologist gave me a quick synopsis of what was about to happen, not caring that my face was bathed in tears. As the mask rested on my face, another dark thought hit, but I was out.

It seemed like only seconds before I woke in recovery. Everything had gone well. I felt an overwhelming sense of relief.

My deepest worries were replaced with gratitude as I looked forward to seeing my family. They transported me back to the second hospital with my waiting Laurie Sparkles. The ambulance ride was rocky but I didn't care. I was relieved that this procedure would be it for my unexpected ordeal, and I could return home. The thought of being in the hospital on Christmas brought stark sadness. I held everything within my power to heal. Once in my room, I marveled at the flower arrangements my son's friends had delivered. The fragrance was refreshing. I found no words to express how touched I was. A fresh start, new beginnings, and a time to revel in the enormous delight that life brought.

My thoughts turned from dread to positive. The first time in days that I hadn't felt hopeless. Laurie Sparkles entered, greeting me with a huge smile. She was positive about the results of my endoscopy and before long a surgeon's assistant entered. I was now free of additional stones.

I had slept well that night, hoping to return home the next day – just before Christmas.

Laurie Sparkles checked my vitals and was glad to see that everything seemed normal. We had a nice conversation and I told her how much I appreciated her kindness. And that her name, Laurie, made me smile. It was my beautiful sister's name. My Laurie had passed five years earlier and I felt an odd spiritual connection to this woman.

"What was her middle name?" Laurie Sparkles asked.

"Ann."

She grabbed my hand, tears in her eyes. "That's my middle name! Did she die from cancer?"

I nodded.

We both cried, knowing in our hearts that my sister's spirit, my Irish Twin, had come through Laurie Sparkles to make sure I would be okay. Such an angelic feeling that no mere words could explain how we shared a belief that this was beyond explanation. Something divine.

My lunch arrived, and I ate what I could. Laurie Sparkles wished me a Merry Christmas just before she headed home. My daughter had arrived to pick me up, and I held my discharge papers close to my chest with excitement.

I sat on my couch, remembering how the pain had felt. My husband helped me wrap a few presents. I was just elated about spending Christmas with my family.

I was still weak from the surgery, but my joy replaced my struggles as my children arrived to celebrate. My family prepared the dinner, and we enjoyed Eggplant Parmesan, pasta, salad, garlic bread, and delicious Ricotta Surprise pie.

It was one of the most treasured Christmases I'd ever remember. Such generosity and love, much more than I could have expected. Christmas was always a special family holiday for us, but I was especially thankful for my fast recovery. I was truly blessed by a light brighter than the North Star.

DEAD RAT

Oh, the fear of our bodies giving out. It's a little interesting that I had my gallbladder removed years ago. I kept telling my doctor about a pain in my right side, but he didn't believe me. It took six months of complaining before he would order a test. The next day, I was scheduled for surgery. The surgeon told me later that I was just in time. My gallbladder was about to rupture.

What is it with the medical profession these days? They seem to be rolling downhill. Could it be from the insurance industry not wanting to pay for procedures? If that is the case, then why are we paying our monthly premiums?

Linda does a great job of demonstrating how hard we try to stay away from hospitals. I could never explain how horribly I was treated in several hospitals throughout my life. And I am sure, many of our readers have had the same experiences.

Pain and not knowing is a deep-rooted fear. A fear that in many ways mimics that monster that hides in the dark. Linda compares her fear to that of a dead rat. Something she heard while waking from surgery. When something inside of us is dying, in many ways it is similar to a dead rat.

Family is crucial when we are ill. Although, we can experience a little jealousy as they stroll through the room healthy and with energy. The relief we feel as we heal can definitely be described along the lines of spirituality.

Our author brings spirituality into her story through the introduction of the deceased sister, matching her soul to the sparkling nurse's. Those friendly nurses do add a touch of the divine to our hospital visits. Especially, since we feel so helpless. There is no way we could fix ourselves. We therefore rely heavily on the medical profession. Too bad not all of our medical staff are as wonderful as Laurie Sparkle.

144

Dem Bones

Michael G. Whitfield

The elbow is connected to the humerus until it's not. The humerus being the bone from shoulder to elbow, followed by the ulna – considered the forearm, extending to the wrist. Proper to say the *elbow* is a joint. Ligaments connect bone, muscle, and tissue.

'Dem' bones' is God's logic having designed the human body. Required knowledge under normal circumstances in a basic anatomy class. Ghoulish to speak of in polite conversations. None of it matters in ripping a body apart. Grisly, dismembering me and mine, the hands of a group of incompetent undertakers.

Can't tell you where 'I' is, actually. Should say, wherever I am, there are no days, no nights. Dark all the time, pitch black. As for bones, got none. I can't lay a hand on nobody. Got no feet, lost 'em in the mutilation of my body, otherwise – I'd walk my way back to where you are.

I have refused to die – three times. The fact, you and me, we're speakin' well, it's a mystery. Paranormal, no other way to s'plain it.

And this next thing, don't ask. It's not every day yah getta' chance to elbow out your killer.

"He … he … he wha' wha' … won't let me sleep." That's Harris talkin'. I didn't get no first name. Our introduction informal, brief, and violent.

I meant to say *killers*. Harris' one of 'em. My command of language want never no good. Still got a mind, tho'. Consciousness, I suppose you'd call it. Got a name too.

McKinley Adams.

In my humble introduction to Anne Phillips, I told her to call me, *Mic*. The source of my trouble, doin' business with that son of hers, Dickie Phillips.

I earned a few nickels cleanin' up over at the VFW doin' jobs to keep the place goin'. Dickie took to climbin' on a bar stool, plyin' his trade with Vets in need. Plenty of 'em boys, far back as Vietnam, a few Iraq, and many Afghanistan, still wounded and displaced. Mostly them younger ones lookin' to ease their various pains, and Dickie promisin' a remedy.

I wasn't no customer. Kept to the bottle, my old man's affliction. Careless over every drop. Had been that way since I returned from the gulf. George Senior's little expedition, everywhere but Baghdad, we failed to get Saddam.

Dickie took a likin' to me. It was his momma, Anne, I had a shine for. 'Bout ten years younger than me, she was a redhead, her body a privilege for any woman half her age. Still the bottom side of fifty, Anne kept herself up well despite a hard life. She'd known plenty of men while ridin' the ruckus. Never bothered me.

Men have a thin' for redheads. Their color speaks fire, hot. The tiny hairs dotting their wrists are noticeably more interesting. An attractive redhead is a mystique, seein' that redheads number no more'n two percent of the population. The grace of a calico cat, intriguing a man, that plume of pleasure unseen. That furry patch, the apex of their thighs.

It was me lustin' Anne whenever at their place with Dickie. Thinkin' I had no more'n a chance than an icicle formin' in hell, I was not a typical man she gave herself to. See, I was always a dime to everybody else's dollar. Small change, a follower, never a leader. So, when Dickie got the idea to way-lay a delivery to the VFW, I found myself in on it.

He'd learned about the delivery sittin' and soakin' at the bar. Had gotten in good with Jesse, the bartender. When the truck showed up, me and Dickie was watchin' Jesse sign for expensive cases of Scotch, Bourbon, and Rum; the driver unloading all into the back storage room.

Jesse gave a look in our direction, maybe recognizing Dickie's rental. I was never sure if he was in on it. Surprising though, Jesse left off the alarm activatin' security cameras. I had a key but no code. Once we were inside, we quickly loaded what we could into our truck. Tore up the place a little, makin' it look like a break-in.

One of the many petty thefts I joined in with Dickie. We'd roust a few lockers at fitness centers, followed package delivery trucks along their routes. Porch pirates, we'd cover our faces with scarves liftin' packages squattin' in front of doorbell cams. Simple mischief. Didn't hurt nobody. I figured anything for a buck, adding to my meager earnings.

Earnin' pennies on the dollar, me, being a war veteran. My own fault, really. You get outta' life what you expect. I didn't own many expectations, never had. Not much for schoolin,' I had joined the army and gone to war. 'I-Rock,' the intense heat of the desert, the ever-present fear, overcome by the closeness of my comrades. Somebody tellin' me what there was to do, when to do it.

My daddy used to say, 'all things, they connected.' A bible beater, an irreverent preacher in his own home, daddy would quote First Corinthians, Chapter Twelve. His warped imagination of family.

"For the body does not consist of one member, but many," he'd say. "The eye cannot say to the hand, 'I have no need of you, nor again the head to the feet, 'I have no need of you.'"

One of many scriptures he'd memorized, never to the heart, soundin' impressive and intelligent comin' from a sixth-grade literate. Daddy would recite while gettin' drunk and gettin' angrier. Eventually, layin' a heavy hand, he bein' the head, "'ministration of justice'" on my poor momma and his seven children. Chased me away at seventeen.

Lookin' back, I suppose I was seekin' salvation through contrition, doin' bad things purposely. Dangerous things, that I might pass on through heaven's narrow gates. First, at war, where I wasn't much for the killin,' the point of bein' there. Had my hand in it, saw my share of dead bodies. The actual combat, the war itself was short before spittin' me back stateside. I been adrift ever since.

My hand, it weren't never clean. I stole. I cheated. Never spendin' more n' a few days in jail. Each time thinkin,' I might draw nearer to God. Never penalty or punishment that would bring repentance. Like returning to a mountain overlook, peering down, threatening to drop. Keepin' to the safe soil beneath my feet, until that last, what I'm tellin' you about.

Dickie was attracted to men of war, veterans who'd served. His attention rapt, every story told, mostly spun around the lies that was our truth. We became 'thieves thick.' Got so, see one, the other nearby. Dickie got from me a loyal sidekick. He became like family, givin' me hope with Anne.

Dickie had a vicious streak, could be persistently annoying, and constantly threatening. May have been his size. Couldn't have been no more n' five feet, six inches. Had a habit of wearin' boots with tall heels. A hunnert' thirty pounds wet, he appeared puny but was strong as an ox. Wore black tee shirts, always undersized. Typically, the image of a heavy metal band plastered on 'em. Ozzie Osbourne, Mega-Death, and Kurt Cobain, all Dickie's heroes. Always in black jeans, cuffed at the bottom cause of his height. He refused to dress himself from junior boys.

His momma a redhead, Dickie got near brunette coloring. Kept his hair short, near a buzz cut, like in the military. Face was soft, so he'd put on a fierce look through his eyes. His brow intense, starin' and darin' except when listening to them war stories. I'd look up seein' in Dickie's face the innocence of that Culkin kid from them Christmas movies.

Dickie had a short reach for any one of the knives he'd collected. Bowie, Bayonet, and a variety of switchblades, always one on his belt. What he was unable to do with small hands, Dickie did with his reach, whatever he could grab. I once seen Dickie grab a bottle in a bar-fight and beat a man with it. Seen him beat another bloody with a bar stool, brutal. Had seen Dickie raise his boot violently on a woman of his, before I stepped in.

After a while, the fellas at the VFW grew to resent Dickie comin' in. Suspicion he was responsible for the theft of all that liquor didn't help none. Dickie wasn't no member, but the bar was open to anybody, and Dickie had his regular customers.

I had a calming effect on Dickie, noticeable by most, if only for a moment. Could speak a word or two of reason, all but that one night.

"Be nice, you'd ride along with Dickie and me." Dressed as Little Red Riding Hood, an invitation from Anne.

I wasn't wearin' nothin' but a cheap plastic mask coverin' my eyes. The elastic string pinchin' over my ears, drawn tight at the back of my head. The Lone Ranger without a white Stetson or Tonto.

Dickie and me comin' from Anne was two parts of a threesome already. Mike *Magoose* was the third. I seen 'em come into the VFW, Halloween night. Wearin' masks and costumes for the drink specials like everybody else.

Dickie had swaggered in wearin' a rubberized Richard Nixon mask. A black leather jacket over his usual outfit. I'd undressed Red Riding Hood, Anne in stiletto red boots, their shiny leather flowing up and over her kneecaps. Bare thighs in the space between 'em and the hemline of a frilly red frock. Attracting my eyes, and the attention of *Magoose*, the big bad wolf. The mobster's henchman, he'd followed her in.

Mike Magagowski – nobody dared mispronounce his four-syllable given name, so shortened to *Magoose*. A neighborhood boogieman, more reputation than was seen. Spoken of dreadfully, in the mouths of the poor bastards who'd become *Magoose's* prey. A death angel, *Magoose* was dispatched by Donovan Klinkovich, the self-appointed god of our neighborhood.

Anything having to do with Klinko was bad business. He owned the entire left side of the ledger, don't kid yourself. If your name was mentioned right, a payment was due, the liability all yours. Best to wish for just a simple fracture from *Magoose* and not your life.

Reputed to be a downstream mob guy, Klinko, was possibly connected to nobody. His believed ties to the Mafia cast his shadow large over our west-end neighborhood of Slavs, Poles, Ukraines, and Germans with a smattering of Irish, like me. The west end was mongrel, all the disposition of a Rottweiler.

That night, *Magoose* was wearin' a Donald Trump mask like a half-dozen other guys, it bein' our neighborhood. *Magoose* was the only Trumper dressed to kill. Always in a starched work shirt, he preferred long sleeves, buttoned at the cuffs. The top button, the collar too. Gray, never no other color, he'd purchase Carthartt from the Tractor Supply Store. The shirt's long tail kept untucked, hiding the carry at his belt. A no-name mechanic of death.

"Who's the pup?" Donald Trump asks Anne.

I'd followed her over from where I'd been cleaning tables. The place was only half full.

"He's a friend of mine, my associate," Dickie answers for her. His voice muffled by the Trickie Dick mask. "This here's Mic McKinley."

"You keep company with the busboy?" *Magoose* said it, a mouthful of mean. He'd meant it for Anne, having watched her sashay away and return with me in tow. I wasn't too sure about becoming a fourth wheel, and *Magoose* was set against it, concerned over any intrusion with Anne.

"He's my driver," Dickie said. "And a damn good one!" The affirmation settled it. But it left me wondering. Was there more to the evening? *Magoose* had narrowed to getting into Red Riding Hood's basket. Anne went back at his elbow, too cozy for my liking. Nymph mesmerizing monster.

"Youse' Irish, that right, McKinley?" *Magoose* was back on me. "I got one for you." The gold Trump pompadour, a tuft of fake hair atop the mask the only thing moving except the rubberized jowls when he spoke from beneath it, breathing hard.

"Two Irish couples decide to swap partners for the night. They're swingers," he says.

I'm listening. Dickie and Anne, too.

"After three hours of amazing sex, Paddy says to Seamus: 'I wonder how the girls are gettin' on?'"

Magoose didn't follow with laughter. There'd be none from me. I took offense, Irish jokes are okay only among Irish. It was Dickie who served up delayed laughter, howling with Anne cautiously joining in. Both of them sounding like a canned soundtrack to some sitcom. I knew then, something was up.

"Mic, come on have a drink. Don't be mad," Dickie says. He grabs me, pulling me toward the bar, his side.

Magoose, stiff as a hard-on, staring at my reaction.

Anne quieted. Her lips pursed, cherry red lipstick the reason I stayed. If *Magoose* were to bang her tonight, I figured to know my stand.

After a few drinks – I kept the bottom of my glass wet – my wits about me, Dickie suggests we move on. Keep the party goin,' sayin' he knew of a place. *Magoose* was agreeable. And why not? Anne was actin' in every way, giving indication he'd plug her at night's end. She'd giggle when he whispered in her ear. I still didn't have a clue about things.

Out in the parking lot, Dickie tosses me his keys. First time I'm behind the wheel of his juiced Chevy Impala. We'd drive rentals under stolen license plates when we worked. Anne grabbed a door taking the driver's side back seat. I watched *Magoose* thinking backseat too. But he was guided by Dickie to the front passenger's seat. Dickie in last, seated with Anne in the back, directly behind the big fella.

"Where the fuck is this next place?" Figurin' he'd just been cock blocked, *Magoose* mixed anger with impatience. Shoulders straight, hands up, his fingers were beneath the Trump mask preparing to lift – when he choked on steel.

He began half-coughing, half-gasping, trying to work the trachea hole introduced into his neck by a six-inch switchblade a quarter inch wide. The suddenness stole my surprise.

"Drive!" I hear from Dickie. He held firm the handle of the blade, having managed to release it into his victim's neck in that narrow space between the seat top and headrest.

I turned the ignition starting the car, remembering foot to brake, moving the shifter to D, before pressing the gas pedal. Steering the vehicle out of the dark parking lot with the calm of a man taking his elderly mother to breakfast. A dying man writhing in the seat next to me.

Magoose had been impaled. Proper to say he'd been asphyxiated by his own blood. Three holes together – mouth, nostrils, and the third unnatural, unable to produce enough air to override the choking that preceded his death. The bloodletting as good as the truth about drowning face down in an inch of water.

Anne didn't scream. I figured this was the play she knew about already. At Dickie's hand sure, but they'd planned it together. She'd done everything right so that *Magoose* let his guard down. His weakness for a woman as fatal as Samson's attraction to Delilah.

We dumped *Magoose's* body where it could be found. Dickie figurin' more time to clean the car. We did some, it helped to have faux-leather seats. Dickie arranged later to replace the front passenger seat, get rid of it from where most of the blood had stained.

That night, Dickie insisted I come home with him and Anne, sayin' we needed to agree on alibis. I wondered if he didn't trust me. I didn't see much leverage to coppin' a deal as an accessory to capital murder. It bein' Mike *Magoose*, I'd be seen as a hero by some. To others, hated with a mind for revenge. Thinkin' of Klinko and his associates, I figured to keep my mouth shut.

I learned later that it was part of their plan, deepening my complicity. The sleepover included Anne pullin' me from the sofa into her bed. Turns out, she was opioid addicted, a fentanyl freak, Dickie her trusted supplier. I got what *Magoose* had been sniffin' for many times over. Not sure how I survived and lived to tell. Just so you know, as red down there, as her head of hair.

I woke in the late morning, Dickie gone, Anne in the kitchen absent of any illusions. There was no breakfast, no "good morning." It was clear to me by her coolness that *last night* was strictly business. I gathered my things in silence, muttering, "hope

I can see you again," sounding every bit the fool. Her deafening disinterest shuts me off, the door closing in my face.

"He … he … he wha' wha' won't let me sleep. The … the … the dead dude. He's been … ka' ka' keepin' me up at night."

Harris, he became Dickie's replacement for me as sidekick. A black guy, one of few livin' west end. Former boxer, questioned by police detectives, hiding his involvement in murderous deeds. I'll pause now and let Harris talk.

"Do I ga' ga' get an uh' uh' 'uh-turn-ee? A lawyer?"

"You're not sayin' you're tied up in this are you?" Detective number one, completely disingenuous.

"You've stopped making sense, Robyn. Listen, how 'bout takin' a deep breath. We'll ask the questions; you supply the answers." An indirect attempt at interrogation, absent of Miranda Rights.

Yeah, say what? I'm Harris. Who y'all? How'd I get twisted in with the dead guy, and whoever the hell else ya'll is?

I know a few big words, can't say 'em when I wants because of my 'stu-stu-stutterin.' Like sayin' Ro-Ro-Robyn, my mother-fuckin' affliction of a first name. My mother's idea. Thought it cute and clever. Drop the 'i'' for a 'y' in tribute to her best girlfriend. Damn bad idea! Might as well been named 'Sue.'

I suppose, no worse than my introducin' that crazy-ass Dickie Phillips to Donavan Klinkovich. Figurin' to get my ass from under a debt owed to *Klinko,* that Mafia mother-fucker! And that *Fonzie* bastard Dickie, learnin' to kill at a drop. Turned out meaner than a Chihuahua been snipped at the balls, ain't never gonna' produce a pup, despite all his humpin'! Them female Chihuahuas, them bitches knowin' it too, mockin' that mother-fucker!

How'd I get mixed up in this muck? A fuckin' elbow, that's how. Them dumb asses failin' to level a damn bone in that concrete mash. That hell-bent dead guy, been torturin' my ass 'bout bein' cast in that basement grave. He and that woman, that's some crazy shit!

I ain't about to say shit to them detectives. Knowin' my ass be in a vise with that mother-fuckin' Klinko. Mistake was takin' out his boy, Magoose. Then decidin' to clean up, Dickie's momma and that dead guy. Dumb stuff!

I met the kid, Dickie, another source to score some blow. Cocaine and white bitches, my two weaknesses in life. Started with drugs during my boxin' career. Could do me some *junk*, easy as throwin' my left jab. Never had much of a power punch in the ring or in life. After the fight game, I was pretty middlin'.

I was stayin' with some ugly 'ol gal, pussy had me livin' there on the west side. Wouldn't have minded hittin' Dickie's momma. Redhead, whoa! Titties was tight and talkin' even as a corpse. But I'm gettin' ahead of myself.

Klinko followed the introduction to Dickie with an invitation. Takin' out *Magoose*, in exchange for joinin' his organization. *Magoose* had touched Klinko's daughter. Yeti sonna' bitch couldn't keep his *poke* in his pants. Rock hard, like pewter, all the time. Anybody that didn't have sausage 'tween they legs.

Magoose denied it, puttin' Klinko in a tough spot between his girl and business. Rotten son of a bitch that Klinko is, he's careful about business. Personal score. Felt he had no choice but to hit *Magoose*, his daughter accusin' like she did.

Dickie was standin' nearby, anxious to do the deed. He takes *Magoose* out, leaves the body public, where it can be found, proof he'd done the dude dead. Cops after a beggars night melee, figurin' *Magoose* had it comin', knowin' him to be the straw that stirs violence.

Klinko pretended upset when questioned by them detectives. Lyin' motherfucker! When he heard from associates Dickie had accomplices – some guy and a woman who'd twisted up *Magoose's* balls – he got to sweatin' bricks. Klinko hadn't meant for Dickie to involve nobody. Magoose always a lone mercenary, muscle enough, never needin' no company to escort anyone to an open grave.

Days later, I'm out with Klinko and Dickie, all up in the powder. Feelin' like a pastry chef, a contestant on that *Great British Bake-off Show*. Doin' lines not costin' me nothin,' my reward cause I introduced the two. Betty Crocker wedded to Duncan Hines, and me at the reception. Beautiful!

Dickie, he's samplin' the product. Klinko, he don't dip in the shit. Money is that motherfucker's drug of choice, addicted to havin' more of it. Pittsburgh by way of Wheeling. Klinko is trailer trash royalty, had married some gal with a community college degree. The one bratty daughter, a big house, and a few cars, dude behaved like he'd earned respectability. Shit! I know that motherfucker still ate spam!

"Let's take a ride," Klinko says to Dickie, and we fall into his Chevy Suburban. I'm figurin' my ass is about to have a seat at a *panty party*. I know the strip clubs, plenty! Instead, we end up at Dickie's. His momma opens the door, and there's a dude lookin' surprised behind her. No sooner Klinko closes the door, Blam! Blam! Dickie's gone Jason Stathem on 'em. Takes 'em both out, sayin' not a motherfuckin' word.

This is some crazy shit! I'm freakin' out, elevated by the powder, thinkin' 'bout gettin' my ass on the other side of that door. I'm next, I figure. Them two sons of bitches is nut jobs. Not to be trusted.

"Get his gun, Harris!" Klinko orders. Say what? "Get his gun, nigger, now!" Klinko was shoutin' from behind his own piece.

I backed to the door, square in the middle of this bullshit. And Klinko's orderin' me to cross and grab Dickie's gun. What the fuck?

Dickie, he's lookin' all dazed. Either the aftershocks of what he'd done – the bitch was his momma after all – or Klinko's sudden betrayal.

"I have to tell you one more time, get his gun, it'll be you off to dance with the pixies. You hear me?" Klinko says, malice in his eyes.

Cocaine is a bitch! Made me one, steppin' between two guns. My black ass suddenly the chocolate center of a vanilla cream. Dickie hesitates, before eventually letting go of his gun.

"Keep it on 'im," Klinko orders again. "While I check on these two," meanin' Dickie's mother and the dead guy.

Dickie's lookin' relaxed. A sly smile dawning on his damn delirious face. I tighten my grip on his gun, figurin' to shoot the motherfucker if it comes to my life or his.

"We got what we came for," Klinko says. "Let him have it."

He's wantin' me to waste Dickie? Or so I thought, until I feel the nip and nudge of Klinko's gun in the small of my back. With Dickie reachin' right hand, expectin' me to release his pistol, I understood better. Damn! Monkey in the middle, I'd been played.

"You sayin,' you were not the trigger man?" Dumb ass detective number two asks me.

"Hell no! I'ma … ma'-ma' su' su' … sayin' … ah … ah … ah … didn't … da … da … do it. Ah, ah … ain't ka' killed na … na, no-body!"

My stuttering is worst when I'm nervous. I hardly stutter when I'm fucked up high or ridin' a white bitch. Eases my affliction, the reason I love 'em.

I moved the bodies, cause I had no choice. My prints were on the murder weapon. You woulda' too, some shit like that happened. When I got to the motherfuckin' dead dude, Klinko was wrong. Still breathin,' his eyes alive! I figured he'd be dead when we dumped 'em. I wrapped 'em into heavy tarps Klinko and

Dickie brought along, and they watched me load 'em into the Suburban.

We transported them bodies to some house somewhere. They blindfolded me for the ride over. I didn't say nothin,' hearin' that monster Dickie, he had another idea. The sick bastard had purchased bone saws. Me and some other clowns owin' notes to Klinko, made to butcher them bodies. White boys, all I can remember.

A dormitory of death. Day one, mutilation. None of us had used a bone saw before. We were to dismember down to the torsos. Ain't no magician's trick sawing a dead body, shit takes time. Me and some stupid big motherfucker, we drew the dead man. Bone saw at his shoulder; he saw me saw him while I saw him seein' me seein' him take his last breath.

Day two, cleanup. Blood had run everywhere on them tarps across the floor. Mops and buckets filled with bleach water. Every wall, every corner, everything gone over with disinfectant bleach wipes. Everything tossed into barrels, including our clothing. We'd been dressed like motherfuckin' space invaders. Fishin' men's waders, hoods as head coverings, goggles, and gloves. Like we was dissectin' sona' fa' bitch *E.T.*

In between, locked in our rooms, dead tired. Worked like fuckin' Hebrew slaves. Hellish. Dickie and Klinko, all the time pointin' Uzis or Kalashnikovs at us. Ordering, one false move and we was dead men.

Day three, jackhammerin' and concrete work. None of us good with a *jack* either. Heavy vibration felt runnin' from my gloved hands up and throughout my body, 'bout tore my shoulders up. Ta-ta-ta-tat! Like bangin' a babe,' never comin' to no nut. No satisfaction in it.

Dickie and Klinko wuz' in a hurry to get three feet down. A six-foot grave damn impossible. After tearin' up the basement floor, we took turns loading chunks of rock usin' shovels. Baggin' and tiein' everything in heavy black liners, carryin' up the stairs. It was the worst day. Like bein' on a chain gang short a dozen dudes.

An assembly line of ghouls, I stopped counting the number of fifty-pound bags of cement we hauled out of the Suburban, into the house, and down the stairs. Thinkin' we'd be noticed by neighbors, kept my head low not wantin' nobody to see clearly my fuckin' face.

Klinko and Dickie shorted on tools to mix the cement. A hellish slurry of stones and bones, using water from a hose. We patted it out best we could, one motherfuckin' trowel between us, the rest working with shovels. Light was no good, usin' our eyes, and a single level to match the new section with the old of the floor.

I thought they was gonna' kill us. We walked the next day. Klinko and Dickie warning us on punishment of death to never say nothin.' Darin' that them motherfuckers might change their demented minds, seekin' distance from the west end, I said my goodbyes. Now y'all tellin' me, a fuckin' elbow found me?

"That's right, an elbow. Could say, the dead man nudged back into this world." The detective continues, "about a year ago, new tenant moves into the place. Sets up the basement as a *man cave.* Eighty-four-inch television, wet bar, the NFL Network, and guys over every weekend. You know the deal."

"He buys area rugs. Vacuums and sweeps the space behind the pit sofa where the concrete is lighter than anywhere else. Guys a neat freak. Notices lots of dust whenever he sweeps over it. Whiteish doesn't seem normal."

"Well, a year into those sweepings, a round rock starts to poke through. His girl worries, believing it's a bone. They called us, the police department."

"Just so, you know …" I say to those detectives, "he didn't have to find me. Don't believe he ever left me from that first night."

I mean of course, the dead guy. Came into my sleep, first in that God-forsaken house of horrors, then regular. "I ain't slept good, one motherfuckin' night!"

I found Harris, yes. Locked in on him as the weakest, easiest to haunt. Those other grunts nameless and faceless. I can't explain it, Harris' mind lay open to me, accessible through the darkness.

"He won't let my black ass … sleep. He's responsible!"

"Who, Robyn? Who's responsible? Klinko or Dickie Phillips?" Them cops figured me ready to break.

"Tha … tha … that motherfuckin' dead dude. Ah' … ah' … ah' don't know. What's his name!"

"Name's McKinley Adams. Believed to be one of Dickie's mother's boyfriends. Had been seen with Dickie over at the VFW."

I've heard voices … myself. Beckoning me to come, enter into a narrower, darker space. I've refused…to die. Just as I managed somehow to elbow through the muck while those magoos worked.

"Mac … Mac … muh, muh, Mic-Kin-ley. What about Klinko? What became of that sonna' bitch?"

"Donavan Klinkovich," one of the detectives obliges. "Found dead at his residence, a bullet lodged in his temple. He and his wife when this thing began to crumble. We believe your boy Dickie is responsible."

"You … you … you … mean to ta' ta' tell me, tha' tha' fuckin' bastard … is on the loose?"

"Dickie is believed to be with Klinkovich's daughter. Imagine that. It's a good thing we found you upstate when we did. May have saved your life."

"Truth is, I ain't had a life. Not since that night, seein' that motherfucker Muh … Muh … Kin-ley. Them dead eyes, alive, him singin' that dumb ass song."

"Song? What song?"

"Yah … yah … yah know. Dem' … dem' … dem' bones. Croonin' in my sleep. 'Oh the … toe bone's connected to the foot bone. The foot bone's connected to the ankle bone …'"

"Y'all know what I'm sayin'? Dem' bones! That's some crazy ass shit!"

DEM BONES

Lynn's thoughts …

My grandmother used to sing the song, *Dem' Bones*. Never really understood what she was talking about until now. *Dem' Bones* or *Dry Bones* was a spiritual song written during the late 1800's. Supposedly, the song was inspired by the *Book of Ezekiel* and his visits to the *Valley of Dry Bones*. A prophecy that one day God would resurrect us, take our bones and add flesh and blood, then blow the breath of life into our lungs.

Not sure if once I'm gone that I'd like to become human again. Isn't that what a Zombie is, a dead person resurrected?

Then again the song was an integral part of Anthony Powell's published novel, *A Dance to the Music of Time*. An interesting read actually through several volumes that painted a picture of the English political power and culture that plagued the world during the mid-20th century.

England almost did own the world at one time when the British occupied a majority of the lands – the Americas, Australia, India, and Africa. The British Empire wanted to rule the world. But has anyone ever heard of the *Tartarian Empire*? This empire actually ruled the world prior to any known written human history. Supposedly, the greatest structures of the ancient world were erected by this great unknown empire, then a world calamity destroyed everything, forcing humans to try again.

Humans build and grow, and then war and the destruction tears everything down, requiring humans to build again. How many movies or novels portray this repetition? This short story reeks of war and destruction. Destruction of not only the human soul but his psyche. They say history is doomed to repeat itself. Why is that? Why can't we humans learn from our past mistakes and transgressions? Why must we continue to fight and to tear down, only to rebuild? Perhaps there never will be an answer.

Detective Yazmin

Tom and Lenore Dayton

In the early hours of Wednesday morning, a thick fog settled across the ground. Yazmin made her way to the freshman dorms with three-year-old Leilani struggling to keep up. Six police cars surrounded the building.

The co-creators of the Central Cali Murders crime podcast, Daniel and Ed, who were voted number two locally and fifteen nationally, stood out front sharing their thoughts.

"I know it's a myth and that's why I said it," Daniel stated.

"It makes no sense for Bulldog members on the police force to have any type of tattoo," Ed replied. "That would give them away."

"That's why it's on their ankles." Daniel laughed. "So no one can know unless they want them to."

"Do you even hear yourself?"

Yazmin waved and they waved back.

"No coffee for you, Yazmin," Daniel yelled out.

"I don't like the taste anyway," Yazmin hollered back.

"Try it with a little cream and sugar, it'll change your life," Daniel stated.

Two cops stepped out of a vehicle parked the farthest from the scene. Crisp uniforms looked as if they had just been removed from a box. Their age and the way they held themselves announced that this was their first day on the job.

Until she figured out their real names, Yazmin dubbed them Jack and Jim.

Jack pointed at Jim's untied shoe.

Jim responded by kneeling.

Jack appeared peeved on the verge of saying something but paused.

Jim struggled to catch up like a little brother attempting to fit in with the bigger boys.

Yazmin shifted her focus to Chief Pedraza and Lieutenant Fischer who were whispering to each other with their hands on their belts. Fischer stopped talking and nodded at Yazmin. She held his gaze for only a moment longer than what could be considered as respectful.

"Well, look who it is," Fischer exclaimed, "the Benoit Blanc of Fresno."

The compliment, added to the long gaze, was too much for her. She tried to compose herself, to remain calm. "You have 'im in custody?" She fought the impulse to tremble.

"Grab a front seat if you'd like. That pretty boy is about to make his grand entrance any second now." The lieutenant held up a finger, asking for silence, as communication blared through his shoulder walkie.

"Bringing the suspect down now," the radio crackled.

Yazmin was relieved to have the conversation end, a few more seconds and she would not have been able to hide her shaking.

Chief Pedraza sidled to her side, while focusing on the dormitory door, "What's the job of a police officer?"

"To deter crime," Yazmin replied.

"That's just PR bullshit, no one can do that. This job is about making the victim's families sleep better, and tonight, Sienna's parents are going to sleep a little more soundly thanks to you, but you didn't hear that from me."

Yazmin smiled. "Hear what?"

He chuckled. "The academy is accepting new applications for a few days next week."

An unexpected warmth cascaded over her. Confirmation of existence and of achievement, something she never received from her padre. She appreciated this brief moment of kindness from a man who had become a de facto father. But it also felt somewhat overwhelming. Her eyes welled despite herself, and she averted her gaze to avoid detection.

A loud metal clang echoed through the air. The dormitory doors opened, and a six-foot basketball player of a man, surrounded by police officers in riot gear, stepped out. A dark-colored man with light eyes and bleached blonde dreads that bubbled across his forehead. He was Sienna's boyfriend and raised as Charles Burrow, but better known to his basketball team and the campus as Tré. An awareness that he was a sharp-looking man and a freshman starting as a forward in the Fresno Bulldogs line-up made him dangerous.

Despite her best intentions, Yazmin could not help but feel satisfaction that this elite kid, who had everything handed to him, was now in handcuffs. Raised in Clovis, he attended an elite high school and left with a middle-ranged GPA. All she could see was a young man who weaseled his way into Fresno State, the same way he weaseled his way into Sienna's heart. The Fitzpatrick's were one of the most affluent and influential families in Clovis. Yazmin believed that when Sienna discovered what kind of a man he was, he did something about it.

Before Sienna's disappearance, his average was twenty-five points a game. It was thirty-two points alone against the Las Vegas Rebels. Since her disappearance, his scoring had been in the single digits. Last game against Long Beach, he was benched for the first time – three fouls against the powerful forward, Eugene Huang. Tré's shoes cost more than Yazmin's outfit.

She eyed the chief, hoping to find a trace of camaraderie in the scene playing out. Instead, she was confronted with a troubled, wide-eyed gaze as if he might be a family friend.

Not the response she was expecting from a seasoned police chief during a big win for their department. Mist and silence overtook the scene, burning a place in her mind. She knew she was heavily responsible for this. She was the one who found Tré's car at Lost Lake abandoned with blood matching that of the victims – Sienna, and her cousin, Veronica, and a third unknown victim.

The gravity of the moment hit as many phones recorded the scene. Yazmin had surveyed her social peers and judges. Teenagers barely out of high school, wearing Hello Kitty pajama bottoms, Fresno State t-shirts, and hair in curlers. Despite herself, she found her feelings were not much different from Tré's.

Flashing lights pulsated and reflected off each person's face, giving the appearance that this was a Christmas show, a horrifying Christmas show.

Yazmin, a few years ahead of the freshmen, was a light-skinned Latina. When she was a baby, her mom was consistently harassed by people asking if the child was hers. A polite way to accuse. Yazmin's asymmetrical features, particularly her eyes, would draw one in. Her eyes narrowed to the point where she would be teased as Asian by classmates when they were old enough to make the connection.

She was always expressing an innate joy for life that some labeled as naive, but her friends deemed as heavenly. Her sorority sisters gave her a nickname and it stuck – Hiji. Her body was developed from generations of warriors, compact with muscles and a flamenco dancer's posture.

Giving birth three years ago, she shamed herself for not losing the weight. Wearing a purple and white-striped shirt from a clearance rack, she held onto Leilani's hand.

The three-year-old smiled, softening the hearts of her mother's harshest critics. A variety of different stains had accumulated on the child's shirt with mixed results of cleaning, despite the numerous times they had been through the wash.

Since Yazmin's father worked all hours at the post office, the chief had slowly filled that role, sporting his pencil-thin mustache, dark skin, and traces of grey on the sides. He tried to dissuade her from following Sienna's murderer but to no avail.

"Keep yah nose outta it, Hija," he said.

Yazmin had taken to heart his advice until her streetwise cousin, Veronica, went missing. The victims were found in Woodward Park lying next to the duck pond, each one week apart with similar bruises and rope marks around their necks, wrists, and ankles.

Listening to Jack read Tré his Miranda rights, Yazmin sensed a warm paternal energy from the chief, filling her with confidence and a sense of identity. This was where she belonged, finally finding her tribe.

"We'll make a statement, and I'd appreciate it if you would join me at the podium. I don't think anyone knows the case better." The chief kept his eyes on Tré.

She was not expecting to be thrust into the limelight. She watched as they ushered a handcuffed Tré into the back seat of a patrol car. "That's flattering, Chief, but you don't think it'd be weird for a citizen to be speaking at a police press conference?"

"Would I invite you if I did? See you at eleven, Hija." There was a warm chiding in his delivery. She smiled briefly before returning her attention to the suspect.

In her periphery, she noticed the recruits, Jack and Jim, were handling the suspect rather roughly. After Jim closed the door, Jack pointed at the shoelace again. Jim leaned down to retie, but this time he revealed a mark on his ankle. At first, it looked like a birthmark. He was already standing and entering the vehicle when she identified it as a tattoo. If she had to guess, it would be a dog, maybe a bulldog.

Yazmin was trying to process what she had just spotted, attempting to convince herself that it was not real. Sounds of the traffic drifted as she allowed herself to contemplate the possibilities.

It is just an urban legend, there is no proof that a street gang is running its operations from inside the police department. Yazmin felt a tug. Looking down she smiled.

"Mommy, I'm hungry."

Her daughter's pleas usually caused Yazmin to bounce into action, but this time she stood frozen. Leilani waited for a response, and when it failed to arrive, she acted confused.

Yazmin was taking in the scene with new eyes as if this whole performance had been orchestrated for her benefit. She failed to locate similar tattoos on the other officers as they were wearing police-issued blue socks that covered their ankles.

A thought she dared not to conjure pushed its way into her mind. Her thoughts were disconnected as she tried to dismiss this new information. It sounded absurd that there could be an element of the Fresno Bulldogs operating within the police force that was pulling the strings. But she could not hold back the tide of thoughts as they cascaded. The police were framing Tré and spreading breadcrumbs from one clue to the next for her to find just so they could set her up as the patsy. She had wondered why the chief wanted her at the press conference, now she understood.

So I can take the fall when things go sideways?

She was a civilian, so naturally expendable and worse yet, a woman. These were mere assumptions she told herself as her heart raced. She needed hard evidence to back her preposterous claims, but she needed them before things blew up in her face, before eleven o'clock today. It was now eight. The situation was a ticking time bomb that would blow in about three hours. And if she didn't deactivate it fast enough, she could be in a holding cell next to Tré by the end of the day.

Pushing back an anxiety attack, she took several deep breaths. A police officer approached. *Is he orchestrating this?*

Lieutenant Fischer sidled up to her. "When you first walked into the precinct, I did not think much of you."

Yazmin shrugged, refusing to accept the reality of the situation. She just knew that this man was the mastermind. "Jeez, Fischer, don't hold back. Tell me how you really feel."

He smiled. "To my dismay, you didn't fuck-up this case as bad as I had hoped." He was trying to be sarcastic with an underscore of flirtation.

Yazmin's skin crawled and she wanted to run. But running would only reveal her weakness, and she needed strength to find the evidence. She took another breath and closed her eyes for just an imperceptible second to gather her strength. "When did your sharp, detective skills make the connection? When the whole precinct knocked on the murderer's doorstep and invited you in for the ride?"

Fischer frowned. "Did the chief talk to you about applying to the academy?"

Despite her denial, her body was sending signals based on reality, she tried to breathe deeper, but her muscles tightened. The man she thought there might be a future with had just faded. The life they could have lived with his son and daughter, Jaydon and Jocelyn, barbecues on the 4th, salsa dancing at Toca Winery, and working together solving cases, dissolved in the dust. Now, she just prayed she could survive their conversation without revealing her true fears.

If he was the mastermind behind everything, he was playing at a level three times beyond her and she wasn't sure she wanted to catch up. She could remove seven years from her life to arrive back at the place she was at just a few minutes ago where they were flirting – where the good guys wore blue and the bad guys wore handcuffs. She didn't want to believe he was trying to butter her up before the press conference. Watching him in her periphery, she noticed more of his flattery as manipulation. It tore her apart that every word had become calculated. Despite her best efforts, she could not help but feel patronized. It triggered a gag reflex she had to suppress.

Maybe police officers are incapable of complimenting women without being laced with male chauvinism.

The silence between them lingered as she glanced inside the car and at Tré. A feeling of camaraderie grew that was impossible to fathom moments earlier. The bitterness for his socio-economic status faded as she read his pain of losing his lover and of his innocence.

Yazmin realized that the clues had lined up too perfectly, like a one-hour episode of Criminal Minds. Seeking justice for her cousin, she had just helped cover up a crime, sending another young, innocent man to prison.

Yazmin thought about the locker room jokes the police officers would have at her expense. All of this was just too much. She was struck with an insatiable urge to binge eat. She imagined an Oreo cookie shake, curly fries, and a burger or two, upsizing of course, and maybe Chinese food. She would purchase enough to keep her numb and isolated for a few days. Maybe she would come out on Monday. Maybe.

"Mom! Mom! I'm hungry … *hungry now!"* Leilani screamed throwing her teddy bear. This was phase two of a Leilani meltdown. Phase three was not fun.

Yazmin's eyes grew watery as her daughter pulled her back into the land of the living. Like casting a rope down a well so her mother could climb up, the fantasy of eating fast food disappeared as she was comforted by her daughter's meltdown. She did not feel like a complete failure as she gripped her daughter's hand, just a confused mother.

"You guys left the house without breakfast, don't you realize it's the most important meal of the day," Fischer stated with a smile directed at Leilani.

Leilani looked away.

Yazmin bit her lip, fighting the urge to respond condescendingly. "Let's get some cereal." The only response she could muster without raising her voice.

Holding tight to Leilani's hand, mother and daughter walked cautiously to the student union where others were eating breakfast, starting their normal day from the late-night studying of the night before.

TOM AND LENORE DAYTON

174

DETECTIVE YAZMIN

Lynn's thoughts …

I'm not sure if others will understand the ending, but I did. Every woman has a vision of a future. And for some reason, fate has a way of tossing blocks in our way. For the character in this story, the block was not the little girl, the block was our character giving credence to relationships that were not a good fit.

The mentors we look up to in life are not always our friends. Throughout my career, I found that a mentor could be either positive or negative. Those who were negative never gave me bad advise. Not in the least. In fact the opposite. However, what they kept our relationship alive for was that I could be used as an excuse, if they ever needed one. A patsy as our author describes.

As young and impressible women, we often meet those who will keep us in the sidelines until they need to pull us out. Then we're hit with accusations that make no sense. We're shoved against a wall and slapped with punishments for something we never said or did.

Our author captures this in the ending of her story. The character fully understands that the police didn't want her for her abilities to solve a crime. No, they wanted her as a lamb that would follow their lead with them never having to say a word – to fall for their antics, to be naïve and trusting.

Throughout my career in government service, my main mentor saved me from many a situation. He would pull me aside and lecture on how not to be innocent and fall for the illusions of grandeur. My real mentor constantly shoved reality in my face no matter how harsh and painful.

To this day, I am grateful for that mentor. And I think that in this story, our main character's mentor was her daughter. A little girl that slapped reality into her mother's face. When they entered the lounge to eat breakfast, it was then that she understood. A fear of betrayal that had no end.

TOM AND LENORE DAYTON

Devil's Lodge

Tatiana Samokhina

A crisp breeze knocked persistently on the slightly ajar window. Teresa flinched as a thin stream carried the overly-ripe aroma of daffodils into the motel room. It was a cool, inky night behind the blackout curtains that concealed the full moon. Too heavy to tremble, the curtains remained still as if hiding a secret.

Her hands rubbed her neck as she removed the hair clip adorned by a shiny metal snake. Dropping it on the bedside table, she allowed her hair to fall to her shoulders. She slipped into the bed, reaching for the pull-light. The room fell into darkness. The smoothness of the weighty blanket over her tired legs felt comforting. As her pale cheek sunk into the soft pillow, her fingers intertwined underneath. Another deep breath to settle and rest, and her muscles and senses slept.

A chilly touch tapped on her toes.

Impossible, keep sleeping.

Another touch. Soft but cool, a tickle that slid to her heels like a snake. Tickle, tickle, tickle.

Teresa jumped from the bed, the blanket close to her chest. Her heart pounded as goosebumps crawled up her back. She groped for the light, but her fingers found nothing. Inside the darkness, red horns raised as bright, yellow eyes twinkled, illuminating a wicked grin.

She screamed, but no sound escaped. The stench, unexpected and nearly tangible, gathered in the air. Death-pale and scared, sweat dripped from her brow. She stared at the laughing eyes with black slitted pupils that contrasted the glowing flames that surrounded them.

"Nice to see you." The guttural growl echoed through the room.

She gulped.

"Don't act surprised, Teresa." The thing snarled, stepping closer, the hooves loud against the floor.

Teresa stiffened, too frightened to blink.

Its putrid breath was hot against her skin.

"Don't say you've forgotten me!" it whispered.

Long nails reached for the golden cross that hung around her neck. It pulled, breaking the chain, tossing the small piece of gold over its shoulder.

She stood frozen, eyes squeezed shut.

Its dark lips hovered just above her ear. "Let me remind you." The creature hissed.

A deafening snap and her body stretched out, soaring up, hitting hard against the knotty pine. She crashed to the bed, bouncing only once.

"TikTok." The creature clicked its tongue.

Teresa's head spun as specks splashed colors past her vision.

Long, invasive, and hairy fingers skimmed through her recent memories, drawing her into the scene of just a month past.

"TikTok ..."

That night when glasses were clinking and tipsy laughter echoed from all sides, the handsome cruiser sailed through Sydney Harbor, gleaming with wealth and arousing envy.

Teresa, wearing a thin, black dress, leaned against the railing. The sparkling Sydney skyline seemed serene, contrasting sharply with her reality. From the corner of her eyes, she caught the sight of a crew member. Holding a bouquet of daffodils, he walked past, scattering a delicate, sweet scent of fresh flowers.

The cruise director appeared from out of nowhere with a wide grin. His jacket unbuttoned and bowtie skewed. "Teresa? We're starting the dance of shadows. Keen to join?"

"Um." She shrugged. "I don't dance."

"No one dances, come join."

He offered his hand and Teresa accepted. Instead of his usual cobweb of lines across his brow – just one thick and straight line accompanied his slightly wet palm.

"I really don't ..." she mumbled.

"Please."

"Honestly."

"You'll love it." He chuckled.

Teresa smiled, following him to the dance area, where giggling passengers were ready to impress. She adjusted her dress, feeling out of place amid the noisy crowd.

A girl with the corners of her lips smeared with chocolate, dropped her wine glass and clapped. Two men wearing white jackets ran to her aid. A young waiter, his whiskers curlier than those of a sea otter, stepped up to Teresa, holding out a tray of refreshments.

"No, thank you," Teresa said.

On the other side of the deck, behind the thick velvet curtains, a movement. A motion so brisk and faint that it must have been the breeze.

The activities director rapped his glass. He captured the attention of his audience that roared and squealed. He explained the dance rules, rapping his glass one last time.

Men and women jumped to the floor, swaying – shifting – turning – spinning. A chamber orchestra skillfully alternated between classical melodies and jazz rhythms. Freestyle improvisations, krumping, and stomping pulled in the applause. The cruiser rumbled, the engine thrummed, and the temperature soared with an eerie power of pure energy.

Teresa found the elegance and clumsiness entertaining. She stood to the side, hoping to remain invisible, giggling and pressing her finger to her lips. A cold hand pulled her into the bustle. Startled, she scanned the crowd with her eyes.

"Go, go, go!" they screamed.

Teresa's gaze landed on a man with his mouth opened wide. She smiled as three quick steps cleared the way. The orchestra fell silent. A sidestep. A flawless boleo. Teresa kicked with poise and precision. Someone gasped and the lights died, covering the dancefloor in darkness.

"You need a partner for Molinete?" The raspy whisper hit with a cool breath just above her shoulders. The slight rustle of the heavy curtains remained unnoticed. Cold, thin fingers intertwined with hers.

Forward, backward.

Forward, backward.

TikTok, TikTok.

Her hips pressed against his. Her finger slid down his icy hand. Her leg hooked around his. Inside a dreamlike surrealism, the outside world blurred, and the laws of time dissolved. His hands, confident and persistent, pushed her onto a soft mattress. His nose burrowed deeply into the nape of her neck, and his fingers ran up her inner thigh, savoring the smoothness of her skin. His tongue left a hot sticky trail as it ran up her chest and to her lips. His mouth closed over hers.

The night melted into seconds. Teresa opened her eyes, sleep crusting the corners. She stretched on the empty bed, feeling lost and confused.

"How did this happen?" she whispered.

She was not in her cabin. Morning sunlight seemed to be filling in the empty spaces. On the bedside table lay a bouquet of withered daffodils, their sour stench making her nose twitch. Teresa stood and picked up her dress. She grabbed her bag from the chair and peeped in the mirror. A deep red line ran from her collarbone to her right ear. She touched it and the tips of her fingers burned. Her heart pounded. Yanking open the door, she sprinted across the empty deck and down the ramp as far away from the cruiser as possible.

TikTok.

Teresa screamed as the arctic breath brushed against her skin.

"What do you want from me?" she asked. "Go away."

Its laughter echoed through the room. "Fight me, Teresa." The *thing* chuckled. "Fight me and I leave."

Another snap and she soared into the air, freezing just between the floor and ceiling.

"Leave me alone!" Tears rolled down her cheeks. "What do you want?"

"Why did you take it?!" it asked.

"Take what?" Teresa cried as her body shook.

"The pill!"

His ominous question hit almost immediately, making her cough. Under the heaviness of her realization, she fell onto the bed. The creature floated just above, its eyes wide and filled with madness.

"Don't you dare," she stated.

It growled, scattering its stench. "If you don't want it the traditional way, we can innovate." The laugh was loud and threatening. Its pervasive voice vibrated through the empty spaces, distorting her reality, erasing boundaries, and blurring angles. The cursed room shifted, elongated, and spun.

Teresa grabbed the sheets, fighting the twisting that swiveled behind her eyes. The full moon laughed, infecting the daffodils. Shattered glass floated on inverted water, from where an endless fountain of grief spewed. Kaleidoscopic stars lit and jingled with envy. A sea otter winked. Slim buildings soared into the sky as the empty cruiser sailed past. Eyes blinked and ears listened from afar. Velvet curtains swished and hissed, concealing the morbid show.

Something wet and icy-cold slid down the corner of her eyes. Shaking her head, she rubbed her face, but the unknown liquid dripped deeper until it settled in her stomach.

She opened her eyes and was again floating. A pointy saliva of icicles was frozen against the sides of the creature's lips. Decaying teeth glistened in the moonlight and the thing roared. The room quaked and rattled, before falling into an ominous stillness.

The madness was gone. The creature too.

Teresa remained silent on the bed, holding her breath.

Slowly ...

    Silently ...

      Softly ...

She stood. Nothing. The room remained calm and creepy. She pulled on the string and the room lit. The window was still ajar. The metal snake still gleamed on the table.

Teresa darted into the bathroom, turning on the water. The coolness on her face seemed to wash away the clinging molecules of evil. She sipped, soothing her parched throat. She looked in the mirror and an unknown person looked back. Tired, disheveled, and flushed, she choked back a cry.

She pushed her cross deep in her pocket, her pajamas in the carry-on, and darted from the room. Teresa stopped at the road, trying to remember which way was the bus stop. On the side of the driveway, a flowerbed. Dry daffodils, dead and grey, waved at her.

A sudden knock.

She flinched.

Another knock.

Teresa looked down and gasped.

Her bag tumbled as it fell to the ground.

Another knock, but internal.

Her stomach grew. She screamed. Her cries only dissipating inside the tired and muggy air. Holding the bump with her trembling hand, Teresa glanced back at the motel.

The hanging letters, *The Devil's Lodge*, taunted her from the roof. A faint tik-tok swept slightly from somewhere above her ears.

184

Lynn's thoughts …

Now this is a scary story. Waking and not remembering must be the most frightening experience in the world. Obviously, she understood she had sex with someone, but no idea with who or how.

Women must protect themselves. We tend to walk through life with a false sense of security. We tend to think that with this new movement of women being all powerful that we can wear whatever we want and go wherever we want. But we are vulnerable. Men will forever be stronger. Especially, when our guard is down.

To be taken advantage of by anyone is a great fear. But to be violated without our memory is even worse. This story brought fear to my heart and soul.

Fear is there to protect us. Today's feminist movement portrays a dangerous false sense of security. Yes, women can hold powerful positions. Yes, women can live alone. Yes, women can change a tire. But at the same time, why advertise that our bodies are free by wearing practically nothing? Why chance a drink or pill?

There are monsters out there that are real and prey on vulnerable women. We must teach our young to protect themselves when in public. Never leave our drink alone. Never accept a drug from a stranger. Never leave an establishment with a stranger.

Maybe one day the correct teachings will come from being independent. But if we want independence, then we must also be responsible. Even with what happens behind closed doors.

186

Dream HOUSE

Carolyn Saletto

Alice Braddock sat at her computer, eyes like slits as she peered through her corrective lens. Compulsively, she chewed on gum as she examined the numbers of the Braddock Retirement Home. BRH as it was known to the small waterfront community of Blaine, Washington.

A silver frame, she had yet to throw out, decorated a slightly faded black and white photo that was a constant reminder. A knife that cut deep, taking her back in time to when she was a little girl. A little girl with brown eyes and long curls. Every night, her mother would wind her hair in rags before she went to bed.

"Good girls have nice curls," her mother used to say. "Good girls …"

That phrase haunted Alice. If she disobeyed her mother, Alice was punished. A dark closet under the stairs was the best place to discipline the daughter, to correct whichever sins she had committed. Alone in the blackness ensured that the child would be a *good girl.*

Seventy years later, Alice thought about the darkness. That closet protected the memory of her hating her mother.

Alice inherited the fifty-year-old business. A move by her parents to guarantee that she never left. She despised the residents and her employees. She hated it all. She grew up at BRH, first working in the kitchen, then on laundry duty. Eventually, the business side. BRH was all she knew, a heavy chain that continuously dragged her down.

One thing that lifted Alice's spirit was what she called *a breath of fresh air*. A final rebellion against her mother. She had been skimming the books for years.

It started out small, innocent. Alice looked for cheaper kitchen items, scrounging for the best deals on everything from dishwashing soap to tomatoes. She discovered she could save money but still charge the same to her residents. She never adjusted in their favor, only hers. She scammed the Medicare costs too, collecting fees for residents who had passed. Soon, she was creating fake clients.

Skimming, skimming, skimming.

Increasing her pay, she justified it by telling herself she deserved it. However, she never increased her employees' salaries.

Rubbing her neck, she noticed the long shadows that now filled the room. She shut down her computer and headed home.

Waking with a start, Alice sighed. The morning rays were just filling the sky with pink and blue. Sweat covered her face.

What was I dreaming?

Visions of a house, a dark house, was all she could remember.

Was it my childhood home?

The dream filled her with dread. Rubbing her eyes, she stood, and her bones cracked in protest. Shrugging, Alice headed for the office.

"Here's yesterday's mail," Maureen, the front desk attendant, said, holding the letters.

Alice smiled, wanting to win over the old lady with friendliness she didn't feel.

"The ID bracelets for the residents arrived. A few are complaining about irritated wrists."

Alice looked through the pile of bills and advertisements. "They can put the bracelets on their other wrist. They've got two."

"The old bracelets were better."

Alice cast a withering look at the woman. "The old bracelets were twice the cost. The new ones will be just fine. Like I said, have them switch wrists."

Alice stood outside the large house that was now cast in shadows. Dark windows stared back like eyes on a corpse. She thought she knew this house but couldn't place it. Blackness seeped across the steps in the shape of billowy smoke. She swallowed, before walking to the front door and slowly opening it.

Again, Alice bolted out of bed, heart beating. It was the same dream, the same house. She shivered, feeling an emotion she thought long gone. It was fear. She pulled a piece of gray hair from of her face.

When was the last time I was afraid?

"Good morning, Alice." Maureen smiled.

"Not now." Alice blew past Maureen, heading to her office. She wasn't able to shake off the foreboding that now haunted her. Something that always made her feel better was finding ways to cut costs and defer the savings. "Maureen! Bring me my coffee."

Alice continued drinking coffee, swearing she would not fall asleep. Popping a few caffeine pills along with the cappuccino night cap, she turned on the television. It was almost five in the morning when her lids betrayed her and she fell into a fitful sleep.

Alice stood inside the dark house, smelling the decay that reminded her of death. The thinning threadbare carpet showed the wood flooring underneath. The closet was similar to the one she remembered as a child. Climbing the steps to the second floor, she kept trying to wake up. She sat on the bed and dust bunnies bounced, wrapping her in a cocoon. The doorknob twisted and with a creak, the door opened. A wrinkled and bruised hand reached for her. Something spoke, reminding her of breaking glass.

"Alice … what sins have you committed? Is it closet time?"

A rag fell from the dreaded hand. A bracelet with the letters BRH circled the bony wrist.

Alice screamed.

"She's in here, Captain."

Officer Boyd studied the body of Alice Braddock. The woman had died alone on her couch several weeks ago. He noticed something shining on her wrist. A bracelet with the letters BRH, and in her hair were tiny, twisted rags that clung to the thin gray strands.

Lynn's thoughts …

Good versus evil in this story. So relevant in today's society. A young child is abused by her parents only to grow and become an abuser to her employees and community. Since she never married or bore children, I guess the aging home will revert to the state.

Individuals who cheat the system are not always evil. Most are simply desperate or greedy. Monies that are an easy steal often leads to another and then another and then another. Excuses of entitlement often follow until the abuser is caught.

After working in government for over twenty years, my philosophy is that one will always be caught. There is always someone looking over the shoulder and since they are not receiving any of the rewards they tattle.

Benjamin Franklin once said, "Three may keep a secret, if two of them are dead."

Such a true statement. The concept of bragging always takes precedence over keeping a secret. Those unhappy with themselves or lack feelings of inclusion will often brag in an attempt to compensate for what they believe they are lacking.

Self confidence begins as children. If parents do work to stem the idea that the child is capable, then that child will often shy away from society. Those that shy away often times have a skewed vision of right versus wrong. Then there are those children who are too confident to the point of entitlement. Individuals who believe they can do what they want, when they want, without any regard to society as a whole.

It is an unusual balance when raising a child. We cannot spare punishment, but we also cannot stifle creativity. Perhaps that is a class we need in college.

eMergency conTact

Jessi Vasquez

The water from the faucet burned his hands.

Uncle Jay sucked in a breath through his teeth and shut off the hot water, shaking out his fingers until the sting subsided.

"Did you space out again?"

He flinched. He hadn't heard Aubrey enter. "Yeah, must have." He glanced at the sink. "Dishes are done."

"You're a lifesaver."

"Where's Terry?" he asked.

"Waiting for Uncle Jay's world-renowned, blueberry pancakes." She grinned.

His face lit in response. She seemed girlish and mischievous when she smiled like that, just like when they were kids. "I better not keep him waiting, then."

Cinnamon and vanilla wafted through the house, mingling with the aroma of fresh coffee. Golden sunlight filtered through the windows, illuminating the countertops. Jay hummed while he flipped flapjacks onto a plate, and Aubrey poured coffee into waiting mugs. Jay set a plate in front of his nephew, drizzling syrup on top. Terry picked up his plastic fork and tore in. Jay sat at the table. Aubrey brought their mugs over before she settled in.

"I love mornings like this," Aubrey stated.

"Me too," Jay replied.

"It feels kinda like the old Sundays at Dad's house," she added.

Jay nodded.

Aubrey blinked.

He squeezed her shoulder. "Let's make *new* Sunday morning memories."

Porky, the family German shepherd, circled the table, sniffing the air.

Terry held out a forkful of pancakes.

"Oi!" Jay snapped. "Don't feed him that."

"But look how sad he is," Terry replied. "I can share a little of mine with him."

"That's really sweet, bud," Jay replied. "But it's bad for him."

"That's not fair," Terry replied.

Jay and Aubrey exchanged a look.

"You're raising an awesome little human," Jay said. "Hold on. We can give him a biscuit."

Jay stood at the door and sighed. Legos now littered the floral living room rug. He laughed. "Whoa. Did dinosaurs trample your city?"

"No, the aliens landed." Terry shrugged.

"Are they friendly aliens?"

"Um," Terry rolled his eyes. "I think they're gonna be, but they crushed the clock tower so now everyone's mad."

Jay whistled and knelt. "Looks like you need reinforcements. Hey …" – he touched the boy's arm – "… where'd you get the gnarly bruise?"

Terry stared at Jay.

"Him trying to climb on the counters," Aubrey stated, her hands on her hips.

"What'd I tell yah, bud?" Jay said.

"Use a chair," Terry whispered.

Aubrey's eyes narrowed. "Um, no. How 'bout, stay off the counters."

Jay winked. "Wait 'till mom's not around."

"If he hurts himself … – she sighed – … it's your fault now."

"He'll be careful. He doesn't want Uncle Jay banned from the house … did you just see that?" Jay stood.

"See what?" Aubrey asked.

Dark vapor curled through the air.

Aubry cursed, heading for the stove. "Maybe I'm burning something."

Jay stood, stopped as the vapors thickened. "No really …" he replied, "… you don't see this?"

"I don't see anything." Aubrey shrugged.

"I think we should leave the house." He held out his arms out for Terry, but the boy shifted as the black smoke twisted around him. His bright eyes now wide with terror as the mist caressed his face, covering his mouth with a clawed, coagulated hand.

The water from the faucet burned his hands.

"Did you space out again?"

He shivered. "I guess ... where's Terry?"

"Down for a nap. Want to sit on the porch? I love watching the rain."

"Rain?"

The clouds reminded him of the bruises on Terry's arm, dark gray and purple. "Did we play Legos?" he asked.

"I don't know what you did with your morning, but Terry hasn't played Legos for a few days now." Her 'brows furrowed. "You feeling okay? You seem out of it. Did you take your meds?"

"I don't remember." He glanced around.

"Better take them."

Holding a glass of water, he shook out an Adderall pill and swallowed. He nodded at his sister.

"How's your treatment going?"

"I remember my keys now when I leave the house."

"I've heard myths of such feats."

"And I haven't been late to an appointment in ... like ... six months." He followed her out the back door. "Teach me your ways."

She flashed his favorite smile at him. "I could, you know. I told you about that new program I started."

"Lovely Transfiguration?"

"*Loving* Transformation," she replied.

"It's working for you?"

"It's so good." She nodded.

"Part of that *illumination* thing?"

"Illuminative Life Coaching, yeah."

"Do I have to recruit three friends to join with me?"

She lightly punched his arm.

He snickered, sitting in the chair across from her.

Fat raindrops hit the ground, and a long, low rumble boomed, reverberating in his chest.

Porky nuzzled his hand.

He scratched the dog's chin. "Who's the bravest boy?"

Porky leaned against his leg, letting out a long, anguished whine.

"What's the matter, bubuh?"

"I don't know what's gotten into him lately," Aubrey said. "He's been so needy."

"It's as if he's in pain or something?"

"I don't think so."

Jay ran his hand over the dog's body.

Porky flinched and whimpered.

"Sounds like he's hurting. Should we take him to the vet?"

She bit her lip. "Maybe when Terry wakes up."

"What's this on his mouth?"

"I don't see anything," she said.

He wiped at the dog's muzzle, pulling away black tar. He sighed, flinging the black goo. The tar seemed alive, crawling from the dog's ears and dripping from the corners of his eyes.

"We have to get him to the vet now!" Jay stated, standing.

"Keep your voice down," Aubrey hissed. "You'll wake Terry."

He stared at his sister, then wiped the stuff off Porky's face, feeling desperate.

The dog whined, climbing on his lap.

The more ooze Jay pulled from the dog, the more it seeped, clotting in the fur.

"You're freaking him out," Aubrey said.

Jay hefted Porky in his arms. "I'm taking him to the vet. Get the door."

He stumbled and Aubrey hesitated. The goo now climbed up Jay's shoulders, trickling down his back.

"Why are you just standing there?" he grunted.

"Because you're scaring me!"

"You should be scared!" Jay yelled.

He shifted Porky's weight as best he could and fumbled with the door. He staggered to the front of the house. Reaching for the brass knob –

The water from the faucet burned his hands.

"Did you space out again?"

He turned off the water, bracing against the counter. "What's happening to me?"

"What do you mean?"

"Weren't we just sitting outside?"

"When?"

"Just now."

"No?" A concerned edge broke through her forced cheeriness. "You were finishing the dishes before we all watch cartoons."

"Is Porky okay?"

He studied her bemused smile. "He's fine. Should we bring him in to watch Doggon Detective Mysteries?"

"They still make that?"

"There's a new one. But we can put on the one from when we were kids. Terry likes 'em."

A yellow Lego ricocheted off his head.

"Ow. What —"

Aubrey frowned. "You got a headache or something?"

"Didn't you see that?" He waved a hand at the floor, picking up the Lego. "Wait. I thought it was a Lego. Is this glass?"

He held it under the light, recognizing the sunflower pattern from the lamp that was on the end table.

"What are you talking about?"

He studied the broken piece.

"You're scaring me. Did you take your meds?"

"I think so."

"I think maybe not. Take them."

"Adderall isn't going to help this. I think I should … go to the hospital …"

A guttural growl shook the house.

He gripped Aubrey's arm. "What is that?"

"What is what?" She yanked her hand away. "You're hurting me."

"You didn't hear that? Was it Porky?"

"I didn't hear anything. Maybe you should lie down."

Terry shrieked with laughter on the couch next to him.

Jay blinked. "How long —"

A savage snarl echoed through the house.

"Where's Porky?" he asked.

"You really want me to bring him in?" Audrey asked.

He swallowed hard. "I think we should leave. All of us. Can we leave?"

Her 'brows tensed. "Of course. Where do you want to go?"

The water from the faucet burned his hands.

A string of profanities exploded as he swiped a glass from the counter, it broke in the sink.

"Jay! What the hell?"

"I think I'm going crazy!" He faced her and froze. Her left eye was swollen, the skin a deep, bluish violet. His eyes stung. "Jesus Christ. What happened?"

She shifted back on her heels. "What do you mean?"

"Did … did I do this?"

She touched her face self-consciously. "You know what happened. We talked about it."

He backed away. "I need to call someone. My doctor maybe. Hell … maybe the police at this point."

"You haven't been taking your meds, have you? You're always so forgetful without them."

He pulled out his phone.

"Three-six-one-one," a cool, professional voice said from the speaker.

"Huh?"

"Let me," Aubrey said, taking his phone. "I'll call."

He yanked at his hair. "Aubrey, I —"

A figure loomed behind her, cloaked inside the thick shadows. An animalistic rumble ripped through the room as sticky, black tendrils grabbed his sister. Her eyes bulged and tar coiled across her throat, choking off her cry.

He tore at the tendrils. Pieces splattering against the tile, clinging to him, twisting up his arms and around his neck, prying open his mouth —

The water from the faucet burned his hands.

He gagged and spit into the sink.

"Are you okay?" Aubrey asked.

The ground rolled.

Little feet padded over the tile. "Are we going to watch cartoons?"

Jay faced his nephew with a smile that twisted into a frown. "When did you get a cast, bud?"

"You said you'd sign it," Terry said.

He ran his fingers through his hair, forcing himself to meet Aubrey's eyes. "Am I hurting you guys?"

Her face darkened as she cast down her gaze. "You'd never hurt us on purpose."

"I don't know what's happening." His voice cracked. "I can't remember anything."

She held out the orange pill bottle. "I really think it'll help."

He took the bottle and checked his pockets. "Have you seen my phone?"

"You said you left it at home." She handed him a glass of water. "You've been so forgetful lately."

He took a sip, placed a pill under his tongue, and took another sip. "I think I should call my therapist when I get home."

"That's a good idea," she said.

He covered his mouth. "I think I'm going to be sick."

He locked the bathroom door, spitting the pill in the sink. It was a pale green, one he didn't recognize. He pulled Aubrey's phone from his pocket and tapped her code. Logging into his account, he checked his upcoming appointments.

None.

He had sent his therapist a text requesting to be put on her schedule.

A knock at the door. "You okay in there?"

"My stomach doesn't feel right."

He exited to the main menu and checked his prescriptions. There was something unfamiliar listed under his Adderall. He clicked on it, but no additional information apart from the name and dosage. A message popped up in the corner. He clicked on the inbox and opened the therapist's response.

```
Therapist:    Hi, Jay, yes of course. Can
              you make a 1:00 on the 11th?

Jay:          Yes, I'll take it.

Therapist:    I was a little surprised when
              you canceled all your
              appointments. Is everything
              okay?

Jay:          I'm fine, thanks.
```

He took a deep breath.

```
Jay:          When did I cancel my
              appointments? Did you speak
              with me?

Therapist:    Two weeks ago through the
              app. Do you need to speak
              over the phone now?

Jay:          I can't talk now. Tonight?

Therapist:    I'll call at 5pm?

Jay:          Perfect. Thank You.

Therapist:    Do you need me to order you
              something?
```

He ignored the text, returning to the main menu. He clicked on his treatment plan.

```
Loving Transformation TMR Therapy - Enrolled
```
He turned on the faucet. Clicking on the link for needing help, he typed — `'talk to a representative now'` — and waited.

"Thank you for calling the NetHealth Helpline, this is Darlene, how may I direct your call?"

"I'd like more information on TMR therapy," he whispered.

"Are you a NetHealth client?"

"Yes."

"May I have your full name and birthdate?"

He gave it to her.

"Could you speak a little louder?"

He raised his voice as much as he dared.

"And what is your NetHealth passcode?"

He felt as though he had just been dunked into ice water. "Three-six-one-one?"

"Yes, there you are. It looks like you enrolled with Loving Transformation's Trauma Memory Reconsolidation Therapy program four weeks ago. What information can I help you with?"

There was a sharp knock at the door. "Are you talking to someone? Do you have my phone?"

"Can my emergency contact approve authorization for my treatment plans?" he whispered.

There was the tap of keys on the other line. "Yes, it looks like you granted those permissions to your sister?" She read out Aubrey's full name and birthday.

The rap of knuckles against the door became more insistent. "I can't believe you took my phone! Give it back."

"Yeah, that's her. I'd like to remove her and change my passcode," he stated.

"I can assist with that." She changed the information per his instructions. "Is there anything else I can help you with?"

"How do I ... deprogram?"

"I'm sorry?"

"Cancel my enrollment."

"From the TMR program?"

"Yeah."

She paused. "Let me transfer you to a life coach or next available representative."

Aubrey's demanding pleas took on a desperate edge. She twisted and shook the door.

"This is Tiffany with Loving Transformation. All Illuminative Life Coaches are currently busy, but I'd be happy to assist you."

"Hi, hello …" he whispered, "… can you tell me what the Trauma Memory Reconstruction thing is?"

"Trauma Memory Reconsolidation?"

"Yes."

"Are you enrolled in our program?"

"Apparently."

There was a heavy silence. "Did someone in our organization recruit you?"

"I guess."

"You don't know?"

"No."

"That's … highly unusual. There should have been a video chat with one of our coaches. Do you know who would have recruited you?"

He gave her Aubrey's full name.

Something slammed against the door several times. It might be Aubrey trying to kick it.

"Are you Jay?"

"Yes."

"Are you experiencing difficulties with your treatment?"

"Yes."

"Okay, let me pull up your history. It looks like you've selected to target memories that are causing distress and separate them to be processed with the assistance of a professional at a later date.

You've called every day for the last two weeks. Hmm. We don't usually recommend that. Yesterday you called twice."

Terry's sobs were almost drowned out by Aubrey's fists against the door.

"Are you sure it's been me calling?"

"You or your emergency contact."

"But how would she –?"

"In theory, she'd just have to hold the phone to your ear."

"Can I remove my emergency contact?"

"Would you like to report a problem?"

"I really don't have time. Can you just remove it?"

"Of course, there it's done. Is there anything else I can assist you with?" Her tone insinuated she sincerely hoped she couldn't.

"Is there a way to unlock memories?"

She sighed. "Shit, I don't get paid enough for this."

"Excuse me?"

She huffed. "Sorry. Not your fault. It's just, you're like the eighth call I've received. I knew this would happen when we went national."

"You knew what would happen?"

"People unhappy with their treatment who want access to their memories. And the goddamn coaches are never available because there's only three of 'em. Is there any possibility you can wait?"

"How long?"

She sighed in resignation. "Three hours."

"I can't. I think if I don't do it now –"

She swore again. "Yeah, you sound pretty backed into a corner. Are you somewhere safe?"

"Not really," he said, over the banging.

"Would you like me to contact your local emergency officials?"

"Actually, that'd be great." He gave her the address.

"They're on their way, but it's a thirty-seven minute wait."

"Thirty-seven? Christ."

"I know. You sure you want to do this?"

"Yeah, I'm sure."

"It's gonna suck."

"You're not helping."

"Because I'm not qualified to do this. I did mention that, didn't I?"

"Yeah, you did. Okay, let's do this."

"Okay." She took a deep breath. "Give me your passcode."

"My NetHealth code?"

"That's the one."

He recited the new number, and she regurgitated a series of numbers back to him.

The water from the faucet burned his hands.

Glass shattered and skidded across the tiles.

"Every day I tell this kid!" Aubrey said.

A tan hiking boot ground a yellow Lego into the rug.

Porky stalked forward, muzzle contorted into a feral snarl.

"Oh god," Jay said.

"Hang in there, guy," Tiffany's voice stated. "It's not real."

"You sure?"

"Not anymore. Whatever it was already happened."

He closed his eyes, but it did nothing to stop the onslaught of images. He touched his face, and his fingers felt wet and sticky. *Blood?* "I can feel … everything …"

"Watch out for the baby!" Aubrey shrieked, shielding Terry. A silhouette bore down on her. Jay wedged himself between them and shoved hard against the darkness. One hand slid into a sweaty armpit.

"No! Don't hurt him!" Aubrey cried out.

"We have to go!" Jay pulled Aubrey to the door.

Gravel crunched in the driveway.

Aubrey sat on the couch next to him, glancing around nervously. "The house …"

"It's just a few toys and dishes," Jay replied.

The door burst open and darkness roiled in. Viscous tendrils wrapped around his sister's neck. Jay reached out and they cracked and snapped under his fingers, coils suddenly becoming brittle claws. The shadow receded and Aubrey wept.

"He's gone! He left us."

"Good!" Jay replied.

Terry huddled in the corner, his arm hanging at an unnatural angle. Jay scooped him up.

"We need to go," he said.

Aubrey took a deeper breath and shuddered. She nodded. "Let me grab my bag –"

The lamp exploded hitting Jay's head. He crumpled as sunflower shards splintered his shoulder and cheek, just missing an eye. A black mass hit, striking, kicking, spitting. A primal snarl ripped through the room and Porky clawed at the blackness, sinking his teeth into the vague shape of a hiking boot. The shadow wilted, then thrashed, tar tendrils curling around the dog. Porky yowled and whimpered.

Porky whined in Jay's arms.

"I don't give a crap. I'm taking him!" he yelled.

"You can't take my dog!" Aubrey screamed. "I'll call the police!"

"That's the best idea you've had all night," he stated. He shifted Porky and reached for his phone. "Let's call them –"

"You still with me, dude?" Tiffany's staticky voice crackled.

"I …"

"Where are you?" she asked.

Glass skidded across the tile. Terry crouched under the table, clinging to one of the legs.

"I don't know …"

"Where were you when you first called me?"

The water from the faucet burned his hands.

No. The water is cool under my fingers. "The bathroom."

"Okay, good. I think that's where you still are. That psycho is still trying to break the door down?"

"Not a psycho."

"Are you defending her? That's your sister? As in, Emergency Contact … relationship, sister."

"Yeah, but she's not … she's … she wouldn't …"

"She did."

Aubrey shrieked, "He's going to kill me! He's going to kill me! He's –"

"Don't hurt, Mommy," Terry yelled out between sobs.

A gravelly voice echoed, "I'm going to blow your Mommy's brains out."

Jay wiped his eyes. He sounded raspy. "You don't know what she's going through."

"Hell, dude. I know your sister wouldn't be wrapped up in this crap if she didn't have issues. But this is seriously messed up."

"Did you just call your company crap?"

"I hate this place."

He huffed out a laugh. *That's a good one.* The ground suddenly felt solid when he laughed.

"Are you still in the bathroom?" Tiffany asked.

"Yeah."

"Good. Describe something to me. Preferably, not toilet stuff."

Another laugh. "Um. The counter. It's pink and teal swirls. There's glitter –"

"That sounds hideous."

"I always thought so."

"You have a good laugh."

"I don't sound deranged?'

"Not so far," she replied.

"How much are they paying you?"

"Minimum wage," she replied.

"No."

"I only get paid when I'm on the phone. Which admittedly has been a lot lately."

"Since you went National?"

"Yeah, and minimum wage in Wyoming is low."

"I'm guessing that's bad."

"The worst," she replied.

"Jesus," he said. "You should quit."

"And do what?"

"I should call and complain. Demand you get a raise."

"Hey, now you're talking."

"Maybe threaten them with –"

"This call is being recorded for quality assurance," she stated.

He let out a breath of amusement.

"Well …" she said, "… if they listen to this, I'm probably fired anyway."

"Not if I raise hell." The words might have been more effective if his voice hadn't wobbled.

"See, now you have to pull through. My future depends on it."

"Who are you talking to?" Aubrey yelled.

"Tiffany," he yelled back.

"Who the hell is Tiffany?"

Tiffany snickered.

"The neighbors probably called the police!" Aubrey said, slapping the door in an uneven rhythm.

"Good," Tiffany and Jay said at the same time.

"Are you laughing?" Aubrey asked.

"You still see the fugly counter?" Tiffany asked.

"Yeah, I …" – he caught his reflection in the mirror – "… oh …"

"What?"

"My face. One side's all busted and scabbed."

"Dude …"

"I know." He groaned and touched his cheekbone gingerly. "I opened something up. I think I need stitches."

"How's the rest of you feeling?"

An intense throbbing rang through his head, his shoulders, and his knee. "Ouch."

"That's what I was guessing," she said.

"You're pretty good at this for not being qualified."

"I've helped a few friends through some bad trips."

"You know, I've never been high."

"Buddy."

Aubrey kicked the door harder. "I can't believe you're laughing with some girl!"

"I should get outta here," Jay said.

"Is it safe to leave?" Tiffany said.

"Can she call in reset things?"

"No."

"Then, I'm good. I'll call your boss later. Probably with a lawyer."

"You know a good one?"

"Maybe my therapist does."

"Oh, good. You have a therapist."

"She's already been contacted."

"Awesome. So, I'm released from all responsibility."

"I never held you responsible."

"Someone has to be responsible for you. Well, Jay, I hope I don't hear from you again. Unless it involves buttloads of money. Or possibly as a character witness."

He was still laughing when he hung up but quieted when he faced the door. He pulled it open. The outrage instantly drained from Aubrey's face.

"It's not what you think," she whispered. She followed him through the hallway. "Where are you going?" When he didn't slow as she stepped in front of him. "You're leaving us? What's Terry going to think?"

He stepped past her to Terry hiccupping on the couch. His arm was wrapped around Porky.

Jay swept Terry's hair off his forehead. "Hey, bub. I'm sorry we scared you."

Aubrey scoffed and rolled her eyes.

Jay kissed the top of his head, and then the top of Porky's head. "The best boy."

The dog licked his face.

"Ow." He scratched behind the dog's ears.

"You don't understand," Aubrey said.

"You got that right."

"He's my husband."

Jay unlocked the front door, cracking it open.

Aubrey slammed it shut. "Marriage is unity. I don't expect you to understand."

He pulled the door open.

She threw her weight against him, blinking away tears.

His shoulder protested against her.

"Please just talk to me."

He squeezed through the small opening and stepped on the porch. Rain pelted, plastering his hair to his face. It dripped into his eyes and down his ravaged cheek, stinging, but also soothing. Aubrey flung the door open and grabbed his shirt.

"Jay, just. Please. I'm so messed up. I can't lose you."

His heart beat as he embraced her, pulling her against his chest.

Her body shook and heaved.

He stroked her hair and kissed the top of her head.

"I hope you find your way back," he whispered. Uncle Jay closed the door behind him, stepping into the rain.

EMERGENCY CONTACT

Lynn's thoughts …

At first, I thought this would be an alien attack story. Was I ever wrong. Mental illness is nothing to laugh about. Especially, short-term memory loss. Consolidation/reconsolidation therapies for the prevention and treatment of PTSD and re-experiencing a tragic event is real. But can it be applied without the patient's knowledge?

Our main character is plagued by lost time, only to awaken to his loved ones being hurt. Of course, he blames himself, believing he is hurting them during psychotic episodes while in a black-out state. Toward the end when he was told he had left his phone at home, well, that was a dead giveaway.

I guess his sister and nephew are being abused by her husband, and she needed someone to blame. Push the focus from her husband. But to place it on her brother?

Many types of drugs can cause short-term memory loss – antianxiety – antiseizure – tricyclic antidepressants – narcotic painkillers – sleeping aids – incontinence drugs – antihistamines. Anyone of these his sister could have had prescribed.

Perhaps what we need to take from this story is the fear of trusting a loved one and then being betrayed. I don't believe his fear is from his memory loss as much as the discovery that his sister was the root cause.

I've read many articles recently about a family member killing another family member. One of the oldest sins in the world. What causes a person to become so angry, so vicious, they must kill their relative? Recently, I read where a child killed their grandparent. How will that child live through the guilt? Perhaps they're not supposed to. Once you've past that threshold, what would you have to lose if you killed again?

Nothing, therefore, why not kill again, and again, and again.

The brother walking away from his sister and nephew was definitely painful. No doubt there. Just an overall sad but truthful story.

Eternal Embers

Travis Klappe

No living tree was in sight. The cave looked dark and sinister, the passage covered in large, black rocks that barred any who dared to enter. The forest had rotted, revealing nothing but scorched Earth and barren stones and sticks; just a few hollow trunks remained standing and those were on the verge of crumbling.

Alethea stared at the map afraid she might have missed something. "Lady Elara, I believe we are here."

"No kidding …" Lady Elara stated, waving her hand, "… lift your nose from that map for a second and have a look."

Alethea tilted her head. Her mouth opened as she stared at the scarred landscape that marked the unmistakable entrance to the monster's lair.

The two dismounted, tying their horses to a dead tree.

"It is as we feared," Lady Elara stated. "This rubble marks the remnants of the seal that kept this monster trapped for over a century. What lies inside is responsible for the recent attacks on the Kingdom of Celestria."

A faint chill blew, causing Alethea to shudder. "You really think it could still be alive?"

"The latest assault on nearby villages would suggest as such. Whole ecosystems turned into mass graves. Not much is known about the monstrous Necroflame. Only that it took the Grimshade himself and five of his knights to seal it away … years ago. Where it came from and what it wants are only spoken of in whispers. We can't make anything out of the wreckage it leaves behind." Lady Elara pushed on a large rock. She nodded as it rolled a few feet. Her six-foot muscular physique aided her as she moved more to the side.

"I might have a better idea," Alethea said. "If this thing is as dangerous as you believe, we need to save our strength." Alethea pulled a red bulb from her satchel, holding it in her hand.

"Am I supposed to be impressed?" Lady Elara chuckled, a faint curiosity hidden in her tone.

Alethea stepped up to the cave and shook the bulb, before wedging it into a space between the rocks.

"What's that supposed to do?" Lady Elara asked.

"Quick, hide behind this rock. A combination of different powders. When they're shaken like that –"

An explosion sent the rocks flying. Alethea ducked as ash-colored debris rocketed over her head. A large rock aimed for Alethea's head and Lady Elara dove, unsheathing her flaming broadsword, cleaving the boulder in half. Her dark, red hair flowed like a delicate fire. She shot Alethea a sharp look of disappointment, before pushing aside the remaining rocks.

"From what I've heard …" – Lady Elara whispered – "… your family used to be quite powerful. It's one of the reasons I wanted you as my apprentice. A good bloodline will say a lot about a person. It's a shame your lineage turned from great sorcerers to basic illusionists. A useful trick, but not very mindful."

"Illusionists have their place ... I suppose." Alethea's cheeks reddened. "Thanks for the save."

As the two inched into the cave, the light dissipated, leaving only the flickering glow from Lady Elara's blade. Lady Elara paused. Alethea almost crashing into her.

"There's writing and drawings on these walls. Look here." Lady Elara pointed to a towering abomination of a monster etched in white, surrounded by green fire. "This must be Necroflame. It looks like these are inscriptions, but I can't quite make it out."

"That's because it's the language of the sand people," Alethea replied. "Not spoken for generations." Alethea ran her fingers over the crude runes. "I studied this language under the clergymen. I was honored to meet one of its descendants. A relatively stiff language if you ask me. Many of our words have no translation."

Lady Elara rolled her eyes. "Yes ... yes ... I remember you boasting about your six languages. Just tell me what it says!" She tapped her sword with her fingers. "Perhaps we can find a better way to understand this monster. Discover a method to seal it back to the depths of hell."

"Oh, yes, of course." Alethea cleared her throat before continuing, "This is describing a great battle. But where does it begin?" She studied the wall as she inched farther into the darkness. "Ah hah. This monster wasn't born. It was summoned." Alethea pointed to an etching of a dark figure. "Celestria was under attack. The people were desperate. They turned to a wizard for help. No, wait, something worse. A necromancer. One who conjured forth the undead. A monster who sang songs of green fire."

Lady Elara coughed.

"Your mentor was there too. The great warrior Dricus Ravenwood, the Grimshade. He was a part of this. Together, they were able to rid the kingdom of the barbarian hordes."

"Impossible." Lady Elara stepped back.

"It says it right here," Alethea waved her hand at the wall. "Perhaps the sand people were mistaken, but it looks like Necroflame fought for Celestria. Our peace was built on this creature's wings. Or so it says. But the writing over here speaks of a hunger … an insatiable hunger … that could not be quenched in a time of prosperity. When the Grimshade and the necromancer raised Necroflame, they angered the gods. This is why the creature returned twisted and monstrous … undead. Necroflame craved war, quenching itself with the souls of those it devoured."

"When I knew him," Lady Elara stated, "the Grimshade never mentioned this monster. I remember that war. Blood-soaked fields and endless agony. The Grimshade was a great warrior, but he was not without his faults. His abilities were rooted in dark magic. I admired his ability to delve into the darkness without becoming a slave." Lady Elara glanced precariously down the dark passage. "Did you hear that … it sounds like … whispers."

"No, I didn't." Alethea continued to study the wall. "When the Grimshade and the kingdom had no more use for Necroflame, they realized they couldn't control its hunger. So the Grimshade forced the creature into the darkest depths they could find … this cave. He couldn't kill the monster, so he sealed it away after a horrific battle. Sealed for all eternity. Or so they hoped."

"Until the seal was broken," Lady Elara replied. "Perhaps when the Grimshade passed away, the power of his magic faded." As the whispers grew louder, Lady Elara covered her ears.

Alethea's body had grown stiff, her face frozen.

"What is it? What do you see?"

"My … my family crest is here, in these drawings. I have no idea why."

The whispers were inching closer. Shadows danced in the distance as the darkness grew.

"Something is wrong," Lady Elara stated.

A sharp and jagged hand reached out from the darkness, grabbing Alethea. She screamed, hitting hard against the wall. Her vision blurred and she collapsed, the sound of a voice echoing through her mind.

Lady Elara stepped into the darkness but was swept from her feet by a powerful force. She braced herself for another attack. She swung her sword through the air, at nothing. "Reveal yourself!" Lady Elara stared into the shadows.

A face appeared, one all too familiar.

Alethea rubbed her head and winced. She was bleeding.

"Alethea …" a voice said from the darkness. "From the moment you were in your mother's womb, you have betrayed us. I will not accept your insolence any longer. You haven't earned the right to wear our name."

Alethea's vision slowly cleared. She studied the shadow that seemed to be moving, morphing into something unknown. A tear ran down her cheek. Then another. She staggered back as her chest tightened. Lost in the deepest pits of her despair, Alethea wanted to cry, but no sound escaped.

"How dare you!" Lady Elara yelled out.

A flame erupted from somewhere deeper in the tunnel. Lady Elara flung her sword with cold precision, sweeping motions cleaving the shadow in half. With a powerful leaping strike, Lady Elara split the shadowy image. She stood over Alethea, holding out a hand.

"That was my father's voice!" Alethea stated.

Lady Elara helped her to her feet.

"This must be one of Necroflame's powers," Alethea said. "An illusion of sound. Using our fears against us."

They stepped deeper into the cave. The whispers grew louder, and the shadows grew darker. When the light from Lady Elara's sword no longer pierced the darkness, they paused. Alethea's heart pounded with each step as the air thickened. It felt as if the walls were closing in around them.

The ground gave way, sending them into a black void. Lady Elara grabbed Alethea, using her body as a shield. They gasped as they hit the solid ground, hard.

Alethea glanced around. They were inside a dimly lit chamber; the walls covered with carvings and symbols. Lady Elara was unconscious, her breathing shallow but steady. Alethea shook her head but only made herself dizzier. She stood.

The room was a circle with a single entrance. The air felt thick, reminding her of decay. A chill ran down her spine as she realized where they must be – the heart of Necroflame's lair. Lady Elara stirred and moaned.

"Lady Elara, are you hurt?" she asked. "We're in the lair. We need to keep moving."

Lady Elara groaned again, opening her eyes, blinking. "What happened?"

"The cave gave way," Alethea replied, helping her to sit. "We're lucky to be alive."

Lady Elara nodded, glancing up at the large hole that was now above them, too high to reach.

"I believe we're in the heart of the liar." Alethea sighed. "We need to find a way out before Necroflame returns."

A deep roar pierced the air, vibrating the floor.

"We must hurry." Lady Elara wavered as she tried to stand. She searched through the darkness but her eyes lit as if she recognized something. "The seal," she whispered. "If we can find the seal, we can reseal Necroflame inside this cave."

Alethea nodded. "What is this seal?"

Lady Elara shrugged. "I don't know. But we must try."

They searched the chamber, seeking for any sign of a seal. Every stone they turned over, every inch of walls they examined. But nothing.

Large, lumbering footsteps were headed in their direction. Time had run out. Alethea froze, her heart pumping. They might be doomed to the same fate as the nearby villagers, burnt with a dark, green flame.

The floor vibrated, making it hard to stand. Another followed. Lady Elara was hitting her fists against the rock, each punch shook the cave's foundation. A stalactite fell, nearly crushing her.

"Lady Elara, stop! This cave can't stand much more."

Lady Elara continued to punch the rock. Her face frozen with an eerie determination.

"Lady Elara, your hand is bleeding!" Alethea sighed.

Shiny trinkets and artifacts littered the floor. The cave shook with each hit of Lady Elara's fist. Alethea searched through the junk not sure what she was looking for. But something small and silver grabbed her attention. She picked it up. It was her family's crest – the seal!

"I found it." She held it up for Lady Elara to see. "Look, I found the seal!"

Lady Elara's eyes widened, her hands dripping with blood, most of the skin gone. "What?"

"I recognize this," Alethea replied. "My family once dealt in magic. The Grimshade must have turned to us to make the seal. I would recognize this crest anywhere."

With only the one tunnel as an exit, they darted into the darkness. Up, up they ran, hurrying to the entrance, Alethea clutching tightly to the seal. Large footsteps echoed from behind.

"We don't have much time," Lady Elara stated. "We won't make it to the entrance. That thing is too close. We must seal it here. In the heart of the cave. Quickly now, before Necroflame finds us. Do you know the incantation?"

Alethea nodded, her heart pounding. "If this seal was made by my family, then the incantation will be written somewhere in my grimoire." She pulled out a small book from her satchel, rifling through the pages.

A growing green glowed, bathing the air that surrounded them. Alethea slammed her finger on a page and read, chanting the words aloud. A blinding light filled the chamber as she spoke, and a surge of power coursed through her.

The rumbling was replaced with a deep stillness. The light faded, and the chamber fell silent. Alethea and Lady Elara looked at each other, their eyes wide. Had they succeeded in banishing the monster? Had they really managed to reseal Necroflame inside the cave?

"I think you did it," Lady Elara whispered.

"We did it," Alethea replied. "We saved the kingdom."

Lady Elara looked at her with an odd smirk. Together, they made their way to the cave's entrance. As they stepped into the light of the setting sun, Alethea felt a sense of peace. The nightmare was finally over, and she and Lady Elara had emerged victorious.

Making their way back to the kingdom, Alethea couldn't help but feel grateful for everything that happened. She felt fulfilled and at peace but not entirely unburdened.

"Lady Elara, that seal won't last forever. What happens when this one breaks? What then?"

"Then? I will return to seal it once again. Perhaps the monster will finally meet my enchanted blade. Only time will tell."

"Perhaps I can return to my father. Perhaps …"

"Perhaps you can ride with me. Today, you have honored your family. The choice is yours. But know this, when they gave up on you, when they cast you out, they lost the privilege of your duty. If you return to your family, I only ask you to do so out of choice, not obligation."

Alethea nodded and smiled.

Lady Elara, for the first time, returned the warmth.

Alethea cleared her throat, her voice wavering ever so slightly, "Lady Elara, I would be honored to remain with you."

Lady Elara nodded. "The greatest stain on The Grimshade's legacy remains buried. The kingdom is once again safe from Necroflame's clutches. I will spread word of what we did. Now, we build our legend together. Sometimes, the mind can strike where the sword will not. Only fools will believe they have nothing left to learn. I suspect there is much I can learn from you. Someone as old as me ought to know that by now. You have deemed yourself to be a worthy companion, Alethea Ashburn."

The orange sun set blissfully across the horizon with colorful shadows dancing in the distance. The horses pace resembled a perfect pace.

Alethea had finally found her place. For she was Alethea Ashburn, and she was destined for greatness. And nothing, not even the darkest shadow could stand in her way.

224

Lynn's thoughts …

The monster in the darkness always works, and it works in this story. Rome was once devastated by heavy flooding. The year, 1495. Rumors abound about a terrible monster that had washed onto the banks of the river. The creature was said to be a ridiculous combination of human and animal. The creature had the head of a donkey, the breasts of a woman, the bearded visage of an old man (on the butt), and a tail crowned with a roaring dragon's head. Then there is a story from ancient Greece, *The Epic of Gilgamesh,* written sometime between 2700 BCE and 600 BCE. Nearly four thousand years ago!

Perhaps monsters are just rooted deep in our souls. There is actually a name for being afraid of monsters – *tetraphobia.* According to child psychologists, we're to ask our children to be brave and not fear the night. This approach didn't exactly work too good in Steven Spielberg's story, *Poltergeist.* The boy was attacked by the old tree and the girl was sucked into the closet.

Fear is something that is bred into us. Being brave may be a good thing at certain times, but fear may save our lives – the old fight or flight impulse. Fear is healthy and normal.

Travis does a great job at capturing the fear of a known, but unknown monster. I specifically enjoyed that the monster was never truly described. Instead, it was left up to our imagination to fill in the blanks. Was the monster a dragon, or a huge bear, or a mixture of human and animal parts. Travis never says, but what the monster looks like was not what was important. It was capturing the unknown and how we humans fear it.

As for me, I will simply avoid caves. The monsters that dwell there may dwell in private and peace as far as I am concerned. How about you?

FAMILIAR FACE

Daniel Gene Barkelamp

I'm going to tell you something. You'll probably think I'm crazy, but it doesn't matter. I need to tell someone.

I'm just the weird girl in town, the one who dresses in black, blasts loud music, and makes up wild stories. Maybe the cops will listen tomorrow after Jenna Lo's parents file a missing-persons report. They always find kids like Jenna.

Jenna didn't want to check out the old school, not with me. But I insisted. That's how it always works. I want to do something dangerous that Jenna doesn't want to do, and I taunt her until she gives in.

People often ask how we became friends, and I often wonder the same thing. To be honest, I hated Jenna the day we first met in second grade – her pink t-shirt, pink backpack, and pink sneakers, and prim-and-proper way of talking. Oh, and how she sucked up to the teachers. We're cool now, but I still become angry whenever we raise our hands at the same time, and the teacher acts like I'm invisible – all to give Jenna the chance to say something smart. I guess, I'm a little competitive. But today, nothing keeps us apart.

Until now.

Until we visited the school.

"I must confess …" – Jenna sighed – "… sometimes I don't understand you."

The steel truss bridge separated our quaint, touristy, and painfully boring Pennsylvania town from New Jersey. The spindly appendages creaked in the late November wind like the legs of a decaying spider. The chilly water of the Delaware River rushed over the rocks far below, carrying an occasional soda can or plastic bag.

"What are you talking about?" I asked.

"When we're in school," she replied, "you couldn't wait for the bell so we could leave. Now, here we are on a Saturday, and what do you want to do, break into a school … of all places!"

"This school's different." I frowned as I thought about the hall monitors, the detentions, and the lunch periods that were too short to scarf down a decent sandwich. "It's been abandoned since the '50s. Everything's exactly as it was on the last day of classes seventy years ago. People say it's haunted."

"And?" Jenna snapped her gum, checking her phone. "Why do *we* care about a dusty, old school?"

"Cuz it's got history," I replied, "unlike our town where everything's shiny and new and … dull."

"I happen to like *things* that are shiny and new," Jenna replied with a toss of her hair. "It's called … being contemporary."

I shrugged. "Maybe we'll see a ghost."

"Mmm." Jenna shook her head, shoving her nose back into her phone.

Stepping off the bridge on the New Jersey side felt like stepping into an alternate reality. Gone were the cafés with outdoor seating, the dazzling window displays of vintage-clothing shops, and the ice-cream parlors selling nine-dollar frappés. Instead, were old, sooty brick buildings that followed the curbs and darkened antique stores covered with iron bars over the windows. The sun ducked behind a mass of gray clouds, plunging the street into a deeper brownish-gray of gloom. Everything felt weighted down with age.

"Ah, yes, now I remember why I never come here," Jenna stated. The corners of her mouth turning down with distaste.

"Shut up and follow me."

I led the way to a short alley lined with doors that obviously hadn't been open in years. The main street looked like a drag, no one around.

"Doesn't anybody live here anymore?" Jenna asked.

"Of course," I replied. "That's why we need to move fast. The cops keep a close watch on this place to make sure no one breaks in."

"Cops?" Jenna repeated, stopping. "You didn't say anything about cops. I'm not getting arrested over this."

Classic Jenna. Lecturing as usual. "Relax." I grabbed her wrist, pulling her along. "People explore this place all the time. That's how I heard about it. We just need to get past the bushes. Then no one'll be able to see us from the road."

I dragged Jenna a few blocks up the deserted street. And — there it was — the crumbling tower of the school's central wing looming over the untamed trees and bushes. It stood silent and ominous against the graying sky, as though it were waiting for someone. Visitors, perhaps — us.

"I've seen enough." Jenna turned to run. "I'll be waiting for you at Maggie Moo's when you're done."

"Nice try." I spun Jenna by the shoulders, shoving her to the door.

The gates were hanging, torn from their hinges. We passed under a leaning wrought-iron arch where the overgrowth was out of control, forming a tunnel that now led to the entrance. Each step plunged us deeper into darkness. By the time we reached the concrete steps, it felt like night had fallen. A granite slab in the shape of a tombstone read:

DEDICATED BY THE CLASS OF 1926

Over the text someone had spraypainted in heavy black letters:

R.I.P.

"Tasteful," Jenna whispered.

My experience hopping fences to cut through yards and parks after dark came in handy. I hoisted myself through a broken first-floor window – an entryway for other explorers – and yanked Jenna up after me. She whined as a splinter caught her designer sweatpants.

In what appeared to be the principal's office, dark rust-colored spots stained the desk blotter. Yellowed papers had blown across the floor from a breeze in the open window. Other than that, it looked like the principal might walk through the door at any time and sit at his desk.

For the next hour, we explored the school, floor by floor. I started in the basement. Jenna had drawn the line, so I left her in the lobby. The laugh was on her, since the basement turned out to be the least creepy part – just a few leaky pipes, nothing more. The rest of the place lived up to its reputation.

Dried, cracking paint, and fallen plaster crunched as we explored the empty halls. I closed my eyes, imagining the laughs and shouts of students, long since gone, bouncing off the cinder-block walls. Old-fashioned wooden desks – the kind with horizontal slots on top for pencils and space underneath to store textbooks – sat derelict and discolored under the thick layers of dust. The boys' bathroom was tiled in baby blue, the girls' in a cracked and sickly pink that reminded me of bubblegum-flavored cough syrup. For a second, I almost felt grateful for our spacious and updated school with its wide corridors and single-use restrooms. *Almost.*

At the end of the first floor, we reached a massive oak staircase with swooping banisters that made me think of the grand staircase in old black-and-white photos of the Titanic. On the first landing, we pushed through a heavy set of double wooden doors that led to the gym. The air smelled stale, like the dried rubber soles of hundreds of pairs of Chuck Taylor All-Stars.

"Look," I said, pointing. "The basketball hoops are still hanging."

"Truly fascinating," Jenna replied, thumbing on her phone. "Can we step on it? I'm not getting a signal in here."

We skipped the second floor, climbing to the third. From the windows, we could see the bridge we had crossed earlier and the polluted water of the Delaware. In the silence, I felt as if we were locked away from the rest of the world.

After passing several classrooms, we stood in front of a closed door. The first since the gym. No number plate or other marking.

"I wonder what's inside," I asked.

"Maybe it's closed for a reason," Jenna replied.

"What's the matter, you afraid?"

"Absolutely not." Jenna shrugged. "Just not curious about more dusty rooms."

I slowly turned the brass knob, nudging the door with my foot. It creaked open, revealing absolute blackness. Not a speck of light penetrated the shadows. Using the flashlights on our phones, my tough demeanor crumbled. I gasped.

Blackboards covered all four walls, end to end, floor to ceiling. No windows, no desks, no closet. The beams revealed dozens of life-size illustrations of children, razor sharp, as though they were created just that morning. The children were crowded together, shoulder to shoulder, each facing the center as though they were staring at something. A border of roaring flames surrounded the children. The fire looked hot even without color. None of the children were smiling.

"This must have been the art room," I whispered.

"Creepy." Jenna's voice quivered. "I mean, don't get me wrong, the illustrations are well done, but I don't like it in here. Where are the tables? The easels? Did they have something against watercolors?"

As Jenna passed her light over the somber and haunted faces, I saw my chance to frighten her. Without a word, I backed out of the room and slammed the door.

Jenna twisted the knob, pulling from the inside, but I was stronger.

"Ha-ha, Erin, very funny!" she called out. "Open the door!"

I gripped the knob tighter.

"Erin, open the door this instant! You're being stupid!"

As Jenna scolded, her voice leapt a pitch or two as her fear set in. Now, I'm usually one for pranks, but I chuckled as I imagined Jenna's neatly straightened hair falling into her face as she tugged on the doorknob.

"Erin, please," she sobbed. "Let me out. Let me out, and I'll … I'll take you to Maggie Moo's on our way home. My treat. Please!"

My joke was feeling mean, and Jenna sounded panicked. I loosened my grip, but Jenna's cries fell silent.

I closed my eyes and listened. An old stillness fell down the halls. At first, I thought it was part of Jenna's ploy to have me open the door, but as the seconds turned into minutes, my heart pounded.

"Jenna?" I called, flinging the door open.

Jenna's phone lay quietly on the floor, dust particles dancing in the beam of the flashlight. Jenna was nowhere to be seen. I shone my light around the room, running it over the faces and the flames.

I froze.

In the center of the back wall, flanked on both sides by ghostly children, stood a girl who hadn't been there before — stark and vivid drawn with fresh chalk. She stood stiff and straight, her arms crossed in front her chest as though she'd just been laid in her coffin. Her face wore an expression of sorrow. A sorrow I'd never seen before.

That was how Jenna disappeared.

Don't believe me? Fine, you're in good company. Like I said, the cops didn't either. But they will tomorrow. All they have to do is cross the bridge, walk up the shadowy path through the tunnel of bushes, climb the big oak staircase, and look for the room with all the chalk children.

They'll find a familiar face in the crowd. A face I once knew well.

234

FAMILIAR FACE

Lynn's thoughts …

This story sounded familiar. The old tale of someone ending up captured on a chalkboard or inside a painting. Then again, if we are captured in a photograph, does that mean our spirit was also captured?

How many times do we try to sabotage our friends? Frighten them? Lock them in a dark room so the demons can take them away? Many indigenous people believed their souls were taken when a camera lens was snapped. If we study a photograph or painting, actually study it, one can sometimes sense the soul of that individual. Especially, through the eyes, and sometimes, they stare back.

While studying art in college, the Mona Lisa was always a topic for discussions. Her eyes, her smile, what was she thinking. Was her soul pulled and captured on that canvas between the brush strokes for an eternity? Maybe Leonardo had the power to capture a soul — an essence. Would there be a difference?

I recently read about artificial intelligence and how many believe it will capture our souls. Playing a video game almost places us inside a painting. The screen captures us, holds us hostage, and sometimes changes us.

In this story, *A Familiar Face*, I'm reminded of something a little deeper than friends just playing a joke. It made me consider what life actually was created for and how we must respect it. Years from now when someone examines a photograph of us, what will they see in our eyes or our smile? Would they find despair or an exuberance for life?

What would you want them to see?

From Your Bipolar Ex-Girlfriend

Anonymous

I'm sorry, but I want to do the right thing by not involving you. I found myself writing another letter. The only way I can still talk to you. I don't know if you'll ever read this, but we always expressed our deepest thoughts and emotions. If you read this now, it will only complicate your life and your new relationship. I'll save it for a time when I'm uncertain, but hopeful.

I wanted to talk about my recent self-realizations. I've been questioning my character and overcoming adversities. I can't admit this to others because the trauma haunts my family. They would become afraid of me. Only you will understand the inner workings of my complicated mind. I wanted to talk about my patterns and extreme behaviors, and rationalize my thoughts with you. I know you might be thinking this is crazy, but have you heard of hypomania?

I recently ended another bad relationship. I knew it wasn't right the whole time, but I proceeded to feel miserable and receive poor treatment. I knew living with him and a roommate would be a huge responsibility. I numbed my emotions to tolerate everything, but I became extremely depressed and irritable. Many fights led us inevitably to break up and me to sleeping on the couch. The last fight ended with him calling me bipolar. He chose to attack my darkest, most painful insecurities. I could feel his words were making a damaging impact on my brain. I immediately shut down and turned hollow. I kicked him out of my apartment before I could feel anything but anger.

When I stayed at your place, I felt safe and lighter. I could relax and be

myself with you. We were so much in love.
Then suddenly, I'd become overstimulated and
demand to leave for an unspecified amount of
time. Don't you think that was extreme? Am
I just paranoid about having a self-
diagnosis used as a weapon against me? I
spiraled after that anxiously, researching
the condition. Did you know that AD+D is on
the same spectrum? Did you ever question
it or did you secretly suspect it all along?
Have you studied type-two bipolar disorder?
I know you have. You've probably considered
this but knew it would destroy me. It can
progress down the spectrum into type-one
if left untreated, and at worst, could
progress into schizophrenia. I thought
psychotic symptoms were required to
qualify for this disorder, but mania isn't
associated with type-two. It's more
defined by reoccurring periods of severe
depression and hypomania.

As a child, my sisters and I were
secretly monitored for signs of my
father's psychosis. Of course, we looked
like angels compared to him. No one was
educated enough about his disorder to know
the signs. I witnessed his episodes in
fear and confusion, but looking back now, it
was as blatant as it is in the movies.
Type-two has a slower cycle of depressive
and hypomanic phases. It appears to be

less drastic than the rapid cycling and mania associated with type-one.

I become so depressed at times that I can barely leave the house. I shower seldom and stay home from work. I must find peace before I can make progress. When my brain and environment is stable, I can do anything. When I'm better, I can attend therapy and admit I've repeated this pattern. I've been frightened to address my behaviors or have anyone point them out to me. Behavioral patterns are a symptom too. So is putting off therapy.

My racing thoughts forced me into self-reflection. I questioned why I let myself return to this dark place. I've felt displaced in my surroundings for countless years like an outsider. Maybe I was grasping for comfort and tempted by an enabling environment. It was painful accepting and facing my mistakes again. I tried to find your insight when contemplating which of my thoughts were myths or true reflections. My imagination is fast and hard to control, my thoughts make me feel uncomfortable and jittery. I've seen depression affect those I love, even you struggled with it, but mine feels lower. Even more debilitating. I'm an anchor weighing others down when they're already sinking.

I lied to you about my AD+D, I never had a formal diagnosis. Maybe I wanted to hide behind a label or have a reason for my reckless behavior. I wanted to tell you the truth. I was carrying so much guilt, and I'm sorry I couldn't. People always jokingly said I had AD+D, so after learning everything about the disorder and relating to many symptoms, I just went along with it. At least, I learned some strategies and attempted to treat myself. Do you remember when I met you? I was taking a prescription that I called my zoom pills. I actually ordered them over the phone in ten minutes with a doctor at a clinic. I said they were for a binge eating disorder. Vyvanse happens to be the best medication for AD+D. I continued to get fluke refills for about a year. I loved it too much. My brain felt incredible, like I was functioning at a higher rate. I was fast and sharp, zoomy. Makes me wonder.

I was crying at 2:00 a.m. last night when I started writing you this letter. Do I cry more hysterically than most people do? The doctor thinks I need medical leave from work and sent an urgent referral to a psychiatrist again. The last referral from over a year ago expired, remember you helped me through that difficult time too? I called the office asking for help and they told me I needed to get a new one. I wish I had gone the first time. I was finally forced to call my family doctor and he insisted that I come see him.

I've been horrified of the chance this could be something to do with my father's genetics. Maybe it's his fault that my brain can't cope and function properly. It's terrifying to accept that I could have a more manageable version of his insanity. My doctor thinks so, he said that if it's true I could still function extremely well and be successful on the right medication. I expected him to resist sending the referral and blame everything on my menstrual cycle. He actually listened and reassured me that many "normal" people exist with my father's condition. I admitted that I'd been avoiding him because I thought he was rude and scary. He told me he cared and wished I had come to him sooner for support and advice. Why did I make him out to be such a villain?

My mind recalls my actions and mistakes when I feel rational, and eventually, I feel terrible for my choices. I'm so sorry you had to bear the burden of many of them. I'll always wish that I treated you better. I still think about the letter I wrote you before we stopped talking for the last time. I couldn't remember the words I wrote no matter how hard I tried, but my mind couldn't continue blocking them out. I knew how raw and important that letter was, it was haunting me. I felt a burning shame for writing you something so meaningful and then leaving without a proper explanation. My emotions changed overnight, and everything felt wrong. That tore me apart. I didn't want it to be true, it couldn't be happening again, and yet I still surrendered to it.

Maybe if I had admitted everything sooner, we could've recognized my cycles and compulsive skepticism. We worked through everything together, and my feelings always came back stronger. I forced myself to reread the letter and process my feelings, it was so sad. I meant everything I wrote. It'll always be you. I wish this could have been different, I'll never be able to fill your place. I need to be alone to create a stable life for myself. People get hurt if they're close to me and I can't let that happen anymore.

Sometimes it takes me months to process and piece together the way I feel. I start recalling emotions and details that I ran away from long before. I have a change of heart about decisions I was once so sure of. Do you still think this is a trauma response? Anxiety, depression, or mood disorder? I hope you receive this with an open perspective and without judgment. Either way, I need to recognize my mistakes and work on myself. Either way, you deserve an apology, my explanation or attempt at it, and so much more. You were the most amazing partner to ever exist. I'll continue taking small steps for you.

If we were married, our lives would revolve around medication to prevent disasters from happening. The side effects would affect you too. Staying unmedicated would inevitably cause cognitive issues and emotional anguish, and the result could dangerously deteriorate my well-being. Even medicated, my condition will still worsen as I age. It wouldn't have worked between us, it couldn't have. When I'm depressed, I want to withdraw and self-sabotage, to be alone and suffer in privacy. I ruin everything. Do childhood trauma and difficult life experiences cause this? Is this really a by-product of my choices, environment, and abusive past?

I remember telling you how important my sleep schedule was. You'd help me manage my racing thoughts while we were falling asleep in your bed. Having a routine helped my mind function better when I could stick to it. Maybe I could've managed this through therapy and lifestyle alone. Follow a careful diet, exercise, sleep consistently, do lots of self-care, and more. But as soon as that routine gets disrupted? If any difficulty arises or some kind of tragedy comes along? Then I'm dealing with a stressful adversity AND experiencing an intense episode. Maybe if I lived in a year-round sunny climate and practiced yoga every day.

If the diagnosis is true, I'll need to find acceptance somehow. I could be successful, have a family, and a stable career. Who cares if I need to take medication? Almost everyone does at some point in their lives. But that wouldn't be fair to you as a partner, and I want you to have a life with more than that, with the possibility of a family. It would be difficult to wean off my medication to have children, and if I did, there's a risk that the hormones could severely damage my brain. I also would never wish to pass this down to another human being.

Did you know that bipolar is the most likely psychiatric disorder to be passed down from a family member? If you have a bipolar parent, the likelihood of inheriting it rises. You're also at a higher risk of developing bipolar if you've experienced trauma at an early age. I've had many traumatic incidents that could've triggered the gene, and I've had an increasing number of low periods too. I stayed out of your life because I felt ashamed of what I'd chosen for myself. I didn't want to drag you through my depression again, so I detached myself to protect you. I was always afraid of depending on you to regulate my emotions.

It feels like the past year has gone by in just one single night. I've withdrawn from reality and all those important to me. I was letting myself live life as though I'd already died. That's when I decided to see the doctor again. I want answers for myself, I want to finally have peace of mind again. You were the only person that ever understood me. Feeling like no one can understand what you're going through or experiencing - another symptom. I know that's a symptom of depression too, I'm just trying to view this through an outside lens.

I found a letter I wrote when I was 16. I posted it on a blog that I deactivated, but somehow, I found it and got back into the account. It was sad. I've been in pain for a long time, and I never asked for help. No one tried to understand what I was going through until I met you. I really do love you. I was struggling with things neither of us could understand and I'm sorry that I hurt you so many times. That is not who I want to be inside.

I've been finding comfort in talking to you while I'm falling asleep at night. I pretend I can call you without phones, that we can tap-in to each other using our unexplainable connection. I tell you what I'm going through and listen to your voice of steady reasoning. I miss how you would guide me through the turmoil. Your voice is slowly fading, but I still search for your guidance when making choices. I've been thinking about my future and how to do things better this time. Why has it been so hard to make good choices for myself?

I'm so glad you have someone. Someone to appreciate your kind soul and what a remarkable man you are. I hope she gives you a gentle and blissful life. I wanted that with you, but I'm slowly accepting why it couldn't work. Being with me is basically like agreeing to be a caregiver. Agreeing to only receive love half of the time. I would eventually depress you and that's not your fault, you deserve stability with someone. I hope that I can be healed enough to maintain healthy relationships one day.

It was an emotional night when I finally surrendered to taking medication. I was thinking about you and trying to hear your words of encouragement. Maybe if I had taken the pills the first time, I could've saved us. I don't know if I feel anything yet, but I've only been taking anti-depressants for 3 weeks. I read that they could trigger mania and my doctor agreed with my concern. He gave me another prescription to keep me "stable". It's still an uncomfortable stage of my life. I've been trying to find relief.

Please know that you're doing the right thing, as hard as that is for me to say. I promise to heal whatever wound or illness confronts me and continue this journey. Processing this has been incredibly difficult and I'm truthfully resisting acceptance. I wish you could be at my side when I receive the diagnosis. I can't share it with anyone but you. When I start writing to you everything pours out. I'll figure out how to manage this, and I won't let it define me. Thank you for making the greatest impact on my life.

FROM YOUR BIPOLAR EX-GIRLFRIEND

Lynn's thoughts …

The rambles of an ex-girlfriend, how bittersweet. A bit of advice, become friends with ourselves before becoming friends with another. If we cannot love ourselves, we can never fully and unconditionally accept another.

Relationships require us to change, to evolve. Inside every relationship, our personal beliefs and behaviors dwell. When people are attracted to another, it is this uniqueness that pulls them to us. However, too many times, once we become familiar, we seek out their faults and try to change them – to make them better in our eyes. Which of course never works.

In the ramblings of this author's story, I see a frail young woman who refuses to accept who she is, living through others. When this happens, overload can occur, and for some, overload means it is time to escape.

What attracts us to another can also be what we despise in ourselves. If we live in a relationship with someone who mimics our failures, we may feel safe at first, but when we turn for support, the relationship falters.

Mental illness is nothing to joke about. However, too many times, humans use mental illness as an excuse. Instead of walking boldly into the future, we sometimes cower and hide within a medicated bliss. Feeling numb means we can live outside reality, stand on the fringe and simply watch. But that is not why we are here.

Helping those with a mental condition is similar to helping a toddler to walk. We hold their hand, but eventually must let go and allow them to stumble. Feeling our way through the darkness is not always a bad thing. Especially, when we hit a wall. It is how we learn to turn around.

Getting fired

Vasantha Aaron

The phone ran insistently. Lakshmi ignored it, hoping the secretary would pick it up. She was focused on wording her email just right, not wanting the client to get the wrong idea. Or maybe she did, but it needed to sound friendly and upbeat while saying *no*. It just wasn't coming out quite right.

Her phone kept ringing. She sighed, answering, "HCA, this is Lakshmi."

"Lakshmi! It's Barbara. Come to my office immediately!"

Dial tone. The woman had hung up.

Lakshmi stood. Her mind raced. Was she getting fired? Had she done something wrong? She didn't usually roll into the office until about ten, but she always stayed late and always finished her work. Maybe her client complained – most mornings he'd have left her six or seven messages by the time she could check her voicemail. Could she help it if he was a middle-aged dad with a boring life with nothing better to do than start work at six?

As she rounded the corner, the security guard stood solemnly outside Barbara's office. He looked relaxed and hypervigilant at the same time as if trying to act nonchalant.

Lakshmi hesitated. "Um …" she motioned at Barbara's office.

He didn't move. He didn't even turn his head.

Lakshmi studied Barbara through the glass. She was packing a large cardboard box. Her hair disheveled and her lipstick uneven.

"Barbara?" Lakshmi peeked past the door, unsure whether to enter.

"Oh, Lakshmi!" Barbara didn't stop packing. The woman was pulling her drawers out of her desk and dumping the contents into the box. Another box sat on the floor, already tapped. "I've been fired! Can you believe it? I've been fired!"

"I … I … I don't understand." Lakshmi stammered.

"You don't understand?" Barbara wiped her eyes, smearing her mascara even more. "I don't understand!" Barbara's Bronx accent accentuated each syllable. "One minute, I'm pitching a new account and being praised, and the next, Cheryl's on the phone telling me to pack up and get out! The nerve. They have no idea what they're doing. They'll fall apart without me! And this fucker …" – she motioned at the guard– "… he's here so I don't call my clients and take 'em with me. Little does he know they all love me and they'll find me. They'll go with me, mark my words!" She spit in the direction of the guard, who stared at the opposite wall.

"But, Barbara? I don't understand. What happened?"

"Cheryl said it was something I said to a client. I don't know. I don't even know *which* client she was talking about. Do you know how much business I've brought into this company? Fucking millions, Lakshmi, millions!" Barbara bowed over the box that was overflowing with years of a life dedicated to the company.

"Be careful. You work for me. They're probably coming for you next. I'm sorry."

"Of course. Don't worry. Is there anything I can do to help?" Lakshmi wanted to sound calm, but her stomach clinched and her heart raced. She couldn't afford to be fired. She couldn't afford to miss a single paycheck.

"Watch your back." Barbara glared at the guard. "And be ready." She forced more items into the already packed box.

Lakshmi backed out quietly. She made her way to her cubicle not knowing what to think. She sat, thankful none of her friends were in their neighboring cubicles. She wouldn't know what to say. She sat motionless, feeling numb.

The phone rang jarring her back to consciousness.

"HCA, this is Lakshmi?"

"Lakshmi, it's Cheryl. Do you have a minute to come by my office?"

"Um … yeah, of course. Sure, Cheryl. I'll be right there."

Lakshmi fought the urge to cry. Maybe this was it. She pictured herself packing a much smaller box than Barbara's under the humiliating watch of that stoic security guard. Who was she kidding. Lakshmi wasn't important enough to take clients with her. They wouldn't be worried about letting her go.

Lakshmi stood, smoothing her skirt. Her hands felt sweaty. She walked to Cheryl's office, hoping no one would stop her on the way.

She tapped on Cheryl's door.

"Come in." Cheryl smiled. "Do you mind closing the door?"

Lakshmi sat in the chair opposite Cheryl. She felt like she was moving in slow motion. She felt fragile as if too quick a movement might shatter her.

"I'm sure you've heard that Barbara's no longer with HealthCare Associates." She paused.

Lakshmi nodded.

"I'm sorry I didn't have a chance to tell you sooner. To be honest, it happened quickly. I can't go into any detail, but Bob ⋯ you know, the Account Executive at Pharma Global ⋯ called this morning and mentioned a conversation that made him ⋯ let's say, concerned. Well ⋯ more than a little concerned. A lot. I was forced to let her go. Barbara will not be allowed to have further conversations with her clients."

Lakshmi nodded again.

"I ask you not to speak to her about anything related to work from this moment on. I want to reassure you that you're doing great. In fact, Bob specifically mentioned your high quality work and reliability. He asked that you remain on the account. So, keep up the good work!" Cheryl stared at her, folding her hands on her desk.

Lakshmi stood. "Okay. Thank you." She turned to leave. "Then, I'm not fired?"

Cheryl smiled. "You're not fired. Far from it. You're doing extremely well, and I'm happy you're a part of our company."

Lakshmi smiled and nodded. "Thank you."

She closed the door carefully behind her. Still feeling tense, she sat at her cubicle.

Stacy was lounging across the aisle, filing her nails. "Oh my god, Lakshmi, where have you been? I think Barbara's been sacked!" Stacy rolled her chair closer.

"I just spoke to Cheryl."

"Shit! What'd she say? Oh my god! Did *you* get fired?" Stacy's eyes were wide, her hands shielding her mouth.

"No. Cheryl said I'm doing great. Said Bob wanted me on the account."

"Fuck!" Stacy dug her heels into the carpet, pushing her chair back to her cubicle. "What the fuck? What did Barbara do?"

"Have no idea."

"You didn't ask?" Stacy sounded horrified.

"No."

"What did Cheryl say?"

"She said Bob told her about some conversation that was disturbing. Then she said she had to let Barbara go."

They sat quietly for a moment.

"What could she have said?" Stacy asked.

"No idea."

Stacy rolled closer to Lakshmi and whispered, "Something ⋯ racist?"

"Barbara's not a racist. I mean ⋯ I don't think she's racist."

"Something anti Semitic then?"

"Barbara's Jewish."

"Then ⋯ something anti Muslim or anti Catholic or ⋯"

"Or ⋯ I don't know." Lakshmi's mind raced with a million questions.

Who was her new boss? Who was taking over Barbara's accounts? Should she keep working on her projects? Should she ask for a promotion? Why didn't she think these questions when she was in Cheryl's office?

"Hey, folks." Laura swung an expensive, leather bag over her shoulder. "Guess what I just heard?"

"We know already," Stacey replied.

"Oh, it's much worse than that," Laura whispered.

"Do you know why?" Lakshmi asked.

Laura plopped nonchalantly on her chair. "Yep."

Stacy rolled closer to Laura's cubicle.

"Apparently ⋯" Laura whispered, glancing dramatically over her shoulder, "⋯ apparently ⋯ she hit on a client."

"What?" Stacy gasped.

"Which client?" Lakshmi asked.

"I don't know. But supposedly she suggested they have an affair. Like, she just straight up told him she wanted to have an affair. Can you believe that?"

"Cheeky." Stacy giggled. "I almost like her now."

Lakshmi feigned checking her emails. She had to have time to think. None of this made any sense. Cheryl had said it was Bob who had complained. Then, Barbara hit on Bob? Fat, golf-shirt wearing Bob? Barbara was older but still an attractive woman, and Lakshmi never noticed anything out of the ordinary in the way she talked to Bob or any client. There'd never been a hint of anything sexual or even flirtatious. It was all business and standard talk. Hitting on a client just wasn't her style. If anything, Lakshmi had seen plenty of the opposite. Male clients were always making inappropriate comments to Barbara, and she adeptly deflected them every time. This just wasn't making sense.

Lakshmi's phone rang.

"HCA, this is Lakshmi."

"Lakshmi, it's Martin. Do you have five minutes to go over a couple things for the Pharma Global account?"

"Sure, I'll be right there."

Dreamy, Scottish Martin. He was the scientific writer on two of Lakshmi's accounts. A few years older, he was fit, gorgeous, smart, and his accent made everyone swoon.

Lakshmi grabbed a notebook and pen, and aimed for Martin's office. The drama of the morning rolling away.

He was sitting at his computer, looking focused and extremely handsome.

Lakshmi tapped on the doorframe. "Hi." She smiled.

"Can you close the door?"

Lakshmi closed the door and sat, her pen poised over her notepad.

"Um, you heard about Barbara, right?"

"I just talked with Cheryl."

"Did Cheryl say anything about what happened?"

Martin didn't know either? "No. Well ⋯ yes. She said Bob had some kind of *disturbing* conversation with her that forced Cheryl to fire her." Lakshmi paused. "Did Cheryl not talk to you about it?"

In the natural pecking order, Lakshmi was at the bottom. She was an Account Executive, but the fact that there was no assistant meant the only person who answered to her was the editor. Everyone else was more experienced and had more seniority. That included Martin who was a Senior Writer. For Lakshmi to suggest she might know more about it than Martin was impudent.

"She said the client wanted her off the account?" Martin leaned back with a thoughtful look. "Have you heard any rumors?"

Lakshmi scrutinized his face. It seemed blank. Could this harm her in some way? She decided on the truth. "Some of the other Account Execs are saying she hit on Bob."

"What?" Martin guffawed. It was a bellow from the gut, clearly authentic. "What the fuck?"

It was so out of character for Martin to curse that Lakshmi started laughing.

"That's stupid, right?" he asked. "Utterly stupid!"

"I thought the exact same thing. Makes no sense." She leaned closer. "I've been in a lot of meetings with them, and she never did or said anything flirtatious or even act like they were friends. It can't be true." Lakshmi felt relieved to be talking about it.

"Something isn't right," Martin said. "It's like she's been ⋯ I don't know ⋯ setup or something."

"What?" She liked that Martin was confiding in her, but Lakshmi was feeling out of her depth. "What do you mean?"

"Bob's lying. Bob lied and got her fired. On purpose." Martin sat and crossed his arms.

"I ⋯ I don't understand. Why would he do that?"

There was a loud knock, and the door swung open. Lakshmi jumped in her seat.

"Hi Martin. Oh, hi, Lakshmi. I'm glad you're both here. Cheryl asked me to take on the Pharma Global account. I'll need to debrief with both of you tomorrow morning. Can we get together around nine or so? Lakshmi, please ask Sarah to attend. I'll call Bob and let him know I'm on the account. We should probably have a team meeting with him tomorrow afternoon to make sure he understands there won't be any hiccups or gaps. We just want to give him a little extra TLC for the next few weeks. I'm looking forward to working with you." Marly breezed out, slamming the door without waiting for a response from Martin or Lakshmi.

Martin looked at Lakshmi and shrugged. "Shit ⋯ Marly?"

"Shit ⋯ Marly." Lakshmi repeated. "I'd better warn Sarah. I'll make sure the conference room is free at nine." Lakshmi aimed for the door. "Martin? Are you thinking what I'm thinking?"

"Not sure what we can do."

Lakshmi headed to her cubicle. Passing Cheryl's office, she paused when she heard voices. Lakshmi ducked into a nearby empty cubicle.

"Cheryl, I swear. I've never hit on a client!" Barbara stated. "Never! I would not do that. Especially, not Bob Senter! You've seen him!"

"Barbara ⋯" Cheryl's voice was low and calm. "He's the client. I have to believe him."

"No, you don't. In fact, you can't. I don't know why he's doing this." Barbara lowered her voice. "Actually, I do know why he's doing this."

"Lakshmi, what are you doing?" Sarah asked.

Lakshmi pulled her next to her, placing a finger over her mouth.

"He hit on me!" Barbara stated. "Bob's trying to protect himself by turning the story around. What a little shit. He asked me to meet him for dinner to discuss the account. I said yes and met him at Balthazar. We had a couple of drinks, and he started saying all the things these guys always say ⋯ you know, 'you're so beautiful,' 'how'd you get so beautiful,' and 'you're so smart.' He kept saying he was glad I was running his accounts ⋯ blah, blah, blah. I hear that every day, right? But then he started touching my thigh under the table."

"Barbara. Please –"

"No, Cheryl. You have to hear this. He started touching my thigh. I removed his hand. I told him nothing was going to happen, and we had to keep it professional. But Bob wouldn't stop. He grabbed my hand and placed it on his crotch. On *his* crotch, Cheryl! I was scared. I pulled away and left. Actually, I ran."

"Why didn't you mention this before?"

"Bob called the next day. He apologized. Said he had too much to drink and asked if we could put it behind us. He's the client. A big client. So, I said yes. Of course, I said yes. What else could I say? Now he's trying to get me fired, and you're going to let him get away with it?"

"I have no choice, Barbara."

Lakshmi grabbed Sarah's hand and pulled her from the cubicles. They hurried to their chairs.

"What was that all about?" Sarah eyes widened.

"The truth."

"What?"

"There's a meeting at nine tomorrow with Marly to go over the Pharma Global account, since Barbara's not running it anymore."

"Marly?" Sarah whined. "Shit."

"Yeah." Lakshmi sat at her computer and sighed. *Now what?*

She knew what Barbara had told Cheryl had to be true, and yet it sounded as if she was still getting fired. Before she had formulated her thoughts, Lakshmi found herself tiptoeing to Chery's office. She stopped a few feet from the door and listened. She didn't hear Barbara anymore, nor could she believe what she was doing. She told herself she didn't have to do it, and yet she kept moving closer to Cheryl's door. She knocked.

"Come in." Cheryl's voice sounded tired.

Lakshmi opened the door. "Cheryl, may I speak with you?"

"Of course, Lakshmi. Come in."

Lakshmi sat on the edge of the chair. "Um, I'm not sure how to say this, but feel that I have to." She cleared her throat. "Um ⋯ Barbara's telling you the truth."

Cheryl nodded.

"I'm sure she didn't hit on Bob or do anything inappropriate. I mean, I don't have proof, but –"

"I understand this is hard for you," Cheryl stated, "but we just cannot accuse a client of lying."

"But he *is* lying. I know it."

"Honestly?" Cheryl sighed and glanced out her window. She paused for so long that Lakshmi thought she might have forgotten she was speaking. "It doesn't matter. This is how it works. The client is always right. Especially, a client as important as Bob."

"But –"

"This is life. It's not perfect, and it's not always fair, especially for women."

"But you're the boss. You're a woman. You have control over this. You could make it better."

Cheryl shook her head. "No, I can't."

"You mean you won't. Even if someone else is assaulted by this guy." Lakshmi stood. "You're gonna let it happen."

Cheryl leaned over her desk. "You need to calm down. You do not know what you're saying."

"I know exactly what I'm saying. I'm saying, I quit!" The words spilled out of her mouth as she stumbled out of the office.

Lakshmi found her way to her cubicle and sat. She was in shock. She placed her head in her hands and cried. What the fuck did she just do? She couldn't believe it. She had quit her job – on principle. A job she needed. How would she pay her rent?

Lakshmi picked up her phone and waited. She ripped pictures and notes off her wall. She pulled out her desk drawers and rummaged through the contents, wanting the things that still meant something. There weren't many.

A click on the other end, and Lakshmi drew a deep breath. "Hello, Barbara? It's Lakshmi. I'm gonna need a job."

Lynn's thoughts …

It's a man's world. I believe a song was written about that. And when that man has money or power, its even more of a man's world. But in reality, if we switch Bob with Betty, would the outcome be any different? No, it would not.

I understand where Vasantha is trying to take us with this piece, and under most circumstances, women are placed in a compromising position, no pun intended. However, those placing us there are not always a man. Women have and do use similar tactics. It's just something that is lacking in an individual that pushes them to desire power over another. It's an illness – the need for control. Having someone control our life, in many ways, is a fear and a hefty one.

I had a boss tell me once, "You don't think I hired you for what is on your resume do you?"

I was in my fifties and couldn't believe what I was hearing. Instead of becoming angry, I actually laughed. Thinking about my body at fifty, there was no other response but to laugh. A huge belly one. Before I left his office, I simply replied with, "Of course, it's a very impressive resume … six pages!"

I do not recommend quitting a job over principles, and highly suggest waiting for a replacement position to arrive. It may feel empowering to say, "I quit," but in all honesty, who cares? Once an opinion is voiced, that employee is most likely considered a liability and may soon be replaced.

The workforce is all about making money. Satisfying a client does not always mean sacrificing the employee, and men can be harassed just as easily as a female. It is unfortunate when those with money and power take on that *slave* mentality. If one still is bothered, they can start their own business. However, once clients are involved, the attitude usually switches to match Cheryl's.

264

Julie Koloini

Ellie woke with a feeling that the dog needed to go out. The room was dark, so it must be early. She closed her eyes but there it was again. That low, pneumatic huff that Jax used to wake her when everyone was asleep.

No one else could hear him, not even her husband, who slept soundly beside her. She felt his warm chest rise and fall against her back. She reached for her phone to check the time, it was almost three. She groaned.

It was entirely too early to take the dog out. She had a policy of making him wait until at least 5:30 or 6:00. She didn't want to encourage middle of the night excursions.

She placed the phone on the nightstand to hide the light. But there it was again. That little huff. But this time, a bit more voice. He probably saw the light from the phone that signaled she was awake. Jax jumped next to her pillow, thumping the side of the bed with his tail.

Jax was a small, black miniature schnauzer that technically belonged to her eight-year-old son, Luke. A surprise for Luke. He was a little more than a year old now, and more or less, full grown. He weighed about twelve pounds and held a tuft of white fur on each paw and under his chin. He was always a little unkempt because it was the responsibility of a child to brush him between trips to the pet groomer. Jax would bite at the brush and Luke would balk at the chore.

She stilled in place, trying to match her husband's breathing, hoping she could trick the dog into thinking she was asleep. Jax wasn't even supposed to be in her room. He belonged to Luke, but Jax seemed to think he belonged to Ellie. Every night, Luke took Jax to bed, desperately wanting the dog to sleep with him through the night.

In the morning, the child would complain. "Jax didn't stay with me last night. How can he protect me if he always sleeps with you?!"

When Luke fell asleep, Jax would curl at Ellie's feet. She felt bad about it. She had bought the dog for her son, but the dog seemed to be completely in the dark at that point.

"Stay," she would tell him. "This is where you belong." Her words never worked. She had tried to put him back in Luke's bed just last night. "Stay." She raised her hand for emphasis. "I'll see you in the morning."

Jax would remain next to Luke for about five minutes before ending up in her bed. She imagined what Luke would say when he woke to find Jax missing again.

She sighed, louder than expected.

Jax scratched at the door, demanding to be let out.

"Go lay down," she whispered.

He gave another huff.

She considered ignoring him until he gave up on his quest, wishing they had a fenced yard where she could let him out for a few minutes. She imagined the luxury of standing inside the door, wearing a fuzzy bathrobe and slippers, while keeping a watchful eye from under the soft porch light.

They used to live in a house with a yard but had moved to the state of Texas two years ago for her husband's job. They picked a nice apartment to become familiar with their new city before purchasing a house. Mike wanted the perfect home for their family. A home with a short commute.

Ellie just wanted a yard, and a fence, and a kitchen. However, the perfect house didn't seem to exist. Therefore, they still lived in an apartment. The place was nice enough. It wasn't such a big deal before the puppy, but now someone had to take the dog out on a leash and clean up after him several times a day. Her son was somewhat responsible, but after the sun set, Luke always insisted it was too dark.

"It's scary," he'd say. "I know there's something on the other side of that fence, and I never want to see it."

Ellie knew there was nothing there except stalks of wheat, a herd of cows, or jackrabbits. She never pressed the issue, not wanting her eight-year-old wandering around outside alone in the middle of the night.

The dog paced the room, scratching at the door. He stood at the side of the bed, huffing in her ear. His breath a hot blast in her face. He returned to the door and pawed again.

"Fine, let's go," Ellie whispered.

She slipped out of bed not disturbing her husband, tucking the blankets in next to him. His breathing never changed.

It was February and would be frigid outside. The change in weather had taken her by surprise. The temperature seemed to fluctuated greatly on the plains of the Texas panhandle. When they first arrived, it was seventy-five degrees in the sunlight but turned twenty-five once the sun set. It was windier here than in Chicago. The wind blew at an average speed of thirteen miles per hour pretty much all the time. It took some getting used to.

She pushed her bare feet into a pair of furry boots and wrapped a blanket around her. "I'm almost ready," she whispered. She reached for her glasses, but they weren't on her dresser. She had worn them before falling asleep. Luke needed help with new batteries for his booklight. She distinctly remembered her glasses on the nightstand. She was actually too tired to care, and only wished to get this little excursion over with. She didn't need her glasses. It was too dark to see anything, anyways.

"Come on, Jax."

Jax followed her, his toenails tapping on the floor as he bounced. He wagged his tail, and his backend wiggled.

She grabbed the leash from a basket, clipping it to Jax's collar.

Luke had picked out the leash with little red apples. The collar gave rise to the dog's nickname. Sometimes, they called him Apple Jax like the breakfast cereal.

Jax waited for Ellie to open the door, pulling her into the cold. She relied on him to guide her through the dark, blurry landscape. Fortunately, the ground was amazingly flat and bare. They followed their usual route around the apartment past the garage used by the landscaping staff. Jax stopped to sniff at a tree recently transplanted, leaning at an alarming angle. He seemed to feel sorry for the doomed sapling, electing to pee on the corner of the garage instead.

It was dark and cold. The wind blew at a somewhat slower pace than usual, but it was still windy. She was glad when they headed home. Jax tugged on the leash. She didn't mind, as long as they were heading in the right direction.

As they turned the corner, Ellie listened. A new sound seemed to be floating in the wind. It almost sounded like music. A pleasing melody, harps strings. The image of a golden harp with a delicate silver filigree pattern and shining strings filled her mind. She shivered as the wind blew her hair against the back of her neck. It felt as if those imaginary strings were plucking against her skin, inching up her spine in tune to the music.

"Jax, do you hear that?"

The dog ignored her.

Ellie shuffled her feet, allowing Jax to sniff at the tiny, pathetic excuses for bushes with yellowing leaves. Eventually they would shrivel and die, and tumble away in the wind, nothing more than a tangle of sharp sticks.

Jax sniffed the ground, the leash moving in a serpentine pattern. The reflective apples glinted with each wave.

The sound came from the side of the building near the garage. Jax stood still, pulling in the direction of the noise.

"Now what?" Ellie squinted in the darkness.

It sounded like breathing, but it was too loud. Ellie tensed, pulling Jax back a bit. He dug his feet into the dirt, standing firm. It sounded like an animal; the panting growing louder and speeding up. Whatever it was, it was now coming for them. An icy chill filled her soul.

Jax barked.

Ellie's heart raced.

No matter what was causing the noise, she didn't want to be outside when it reached them. She visualized a ravenous wolf, and her with only a small dog to protect her. Jax wouldn't stand a chance against whatever animal was making that heavy sound.

As she closed in on her apartment, she lunged for the front door, reaching it just as she was sure the animal would be rounding the corner. She didn't wait to see what it was. Ellie dragged her small dog into the house, slamming the door shut.

Jax barked, his fur standing on end.

Ellie's heart hammered. She heaved a deep breath and held it for as long as she could. She picked up Jax and sat on the edge of the couch. She held the small dog close.

"Shhh," she soothed. She was trying to calm them both.

Jax barked but grew quieter with each yelp.

The air grew thick. She had wished for silence but now it seemed too quiet.

Jax sat in her lap, his front paws pressing on her legs. The wind had stilled. Whatever was snarling had stopped. The hair on her arms pricked. A presence was just outside as if some *thing* was close, crawling into her soul. With only a single door between them, she didn't feel safe. The door wasn't very strong, constructed mostly of glass surrounded by only a thin border of wood. A small consolation was the blinds, that were closed.

Ellie could almost picture what the creature looked like. It was as if it was projecting a presence directly into her mind just like the sound of the harp.

But that's impossible, isn't it?

Ellie felt it standing there, fighting the urge to enter. She set Jax on the floor and stood. Goosebumps covered her arms. She barely dared to breathe as she stared at the door. Each breath shallower than the last, doing nothing to ease the pain building in her chest. If she would just part the blinds – part the blinds, it would be standing there, waiting for her.

No – it wasn't a creature but a man who wore a long, black coat, a flat, black hat with a wide, circular brim. His skin was extremely pale, his eyes completely black, and a thin and straight nose. The most disturbing feature was his mouth. Instead of lips, there was a gaping hole filled with a swirling dark mist.

She felt the tug of that whirl deep inside her belly. She stood in front of the door, staring at the blinds. She could see him clearly feel him on the other side. The room remained silent except for the roaring of her blood through her ears.

He stood directly opposite her now.

Her shoulders hunched as she stepped closer. She reached for the blinds, her pink glove startling her. She exhaled and the tightness eased. She rolled her shoulders and straightened her back. Her hand hovered near the blinds.

A rush of energy hit like a viper, and she parted the blinds, peeking out.

Nothing. Nothing but the hazy outline of the familiar brick columns that supported the patio. Ellie glanced through the small slit. She sighed. No one was there.

He had been there, but somehow he vanished.

She stared. Her breath fogged the glass. The breeze was picking up. She turned from the door and sighed.

Jax cocked his head and whined.

Had I imagined it? No. Jax had heard it, too.

The dog had known something was wrong. He had barked. She had felt his fear as much as her own.

"What was that?" she whispered.

She wished Jax could talk. She reached down and scratched his ears, unhooking the leash. Jax followed her to the bedroom.

"It was just the wind, right, Jax?" she whispered.

She tried to convince herself that it had all been her imagination. But she failed. She could not forget how she reacted to a man standing on the other side of the door. He had been there. She knew it and Jax knew it, too.

She shivered.

She pulled the covers over her shoulders, and Jax curled against her feet. Closing her eyes, the man wearing the black hat filled her mind. Her heart itched. She was being silly. She was too old to be afraid of the dark. She opened her eyes but the room was dark. The fuzzy furniture seemed to help. It was better than gazing into the swirling abyss of that man's face.

Her husband's soft snores were soothing. She focused on his breathing to slow her racing heart. Ellie considered waking him. She would appreciate the sound of his voice. But what would she say?

Scooting a little closer, she felt his heat, understanding how cold she had been. She rubbed her fingers, bringing warmth into her hands. Time slowly passed before that strange music again filled her ears. She shivered and the chill returned. The music grew louder.

The harp was in the living room now. Too close to Luke. She had to keep her son away from the harp. She had to keep that man away from Luke. Ellie nudged Mike. He didn't wake, so she shook his shoulder until he mumbled something.

"I heard a noise," Ellie whispered.

"What kind of noise?" Mike struggled to sit up.

"Music. I think someone's in the house."

Mike climbed out of bed. He opened the door and peered into the darkness. His bare feet slapped against the hardwood as he opened another door, probably checking on Luke. Jax jumped down and his nails tapped across the floor. Mike rustled the blinds, he was looking outside.

Her stomach clinched.

Mike returned, closing the door behind him. "Are you sure you heard music?"

"I think so."

"Nothing out there." He entered the bathroom.

She would need coffee in the morning.

Mike stood in the doorway with the light behind him almost blinding her. He didn't look quite right.

"Are you okay?" she asked.

"Fine."

His eyes seemed darker than usual. His normal light blue eyes were now completely black. She stood and stared. His eyes were dark as if made from a swirling mist.

"Your eyes," she whispered.

"My eyes," he repeated.

Mike turned, facing the mirror. His body withered before exploding into a column of writhing snakes. Her husband was gone. The snakes fell into a knotted heap where he had just been standing, hissing as they inched closer to her.

Ellie jumped on the bed and screamed.

The snakes wiggled and hissed. Black and red and yellow stripes glowed from the bathroom light. A brown diamond pattern decorated a larger one. Several black snakes with yellow stripes reminded her of the dog's leash.

The snakes aimed for the hallway.

She took a deep breath, following them. If she could just open the door, then her son would be safe. The snakes would leave. The twisting mass inched across the living room, jumping over the sofa. She skirted around the coffee table, keeping as much distance from the snakes as possible. When they aimed for the door, she sighed. Luke would never know about the evil snakes.

"Yes!" she hissed.

She would shield her son from the awful truth. Unlocking the door, she pulled it open. The man with the swirling mouth stood silently on the patio. He didn't look at the snakes that rushed past his feet, the tangle breaking free as they slithered into the night. He looked directly at her.

Ellie stared at his eyes and knew. She knew that her eyes were now different. They were nothing but black clouds swirling like a dark storm. Ellie's flesh ripped, revealing a pillar of snakes, heaving and gasping, tumbling as gravity pulled what was left of her to the ground.

Lynn's thoughts …

This woman definitely needs to stop eating before bed. Wow, is this a dream or reality? Dreaming of snakes can indicate something unpredictable or untamed coming into one's life. Snakes can also represent fertility or a creative life force. Snakes shed their skin, and therefore, can represent a rebirth.

Perhaps our main character is pregnant? I would bet that eating ice cream and pickles would bring on such a nightmare.

Then again, black is the absence of all color. At least where light is concerned. Perhaps, the symbolism behind the man in black is evil. The opposite of light, living in the dark.

Symbolism is running deep in this short story. At first, I wasn't sure what was happening with the dog and the early morning wakeup call. Maybe the dog sensed something. If we combined the imagery of the darkness with the snakes, what would we have? Judges and colleges wear black robes, symbolizing what – wisdom? Snakes represent creativity, therefore, perhaps our author is trying to demonstrate how staying in the light brings out the truth. And when we stay in the dark, we run the risk of being led astray.

Black is the color of the ink used in printing of most books, newspapers, and legal documents. The contrast of the stark white background with the dark black and wise words. Even in Old English, the word, *blaec,* means ink.

When reading through this anthology, allow your imagination to seep beyond the simple stories. Our authors write to spread their understanding of their world. So many times, we humans tend to box ourselves into a stagnant existence of singular basics – but what if one plus one did not always equal two but something different?

Julie has a message in this story, but what exactly is it? And would it matter if my analogy differed from yours?

JULIE KOLOINI

276

lingering fear

David Ajluni

The most joy that Laney and Rodrick ever felt was when they became parents. A sweet, baby boy with big blue eyes that looked at everything with wonder. He provided a new level of bliss they had never experienced. But their world would soon never be the same.

They were not actively trying for a child. Instead, they decided to let things happen naturally. Before they knew it, Anthony was to arrive that spring. He resembled them both, and they were amazed at the combination their genetics had produced. Anthony was calm and sweet.

"It's not unheard of," the pediatrician had said, "just unusual."

"He's much like my grandfather," Laney had replied. "Grandpa Max was the most calm person I ever knew."

Grandpa Max had passed away around the time Laney had graduated high school. He'd been sick for a while and was no longer the spry sixty-something who wore pressed shirts and a spotless white Stetson. She missed his calm demeanor and half-witted smile. But Anthony was also calm and shared the same awkward smile as his great-grandfather, and to Laney it was a comfort. It was as if Grandpa

Max had given her a gift, so she wouldn't have to experience life without him.

As he grew, Anthony reached the typical milestones. He rolled over at four months, sat up at six, and was potty trained at seventeen. By eighteen months he held a full vocabulary. Anthony was a wonderful child, and his parents adored him.

They took him to most get-togethers that their friends hosted. They were the first to have a child, so he received a lot of attention. Laney and Rodrick knew how lucky they were to have such a well-behaved toddler. But it wasn't until his third birthday that things changed. It started with an innocent comment, seemingly at random.

"People are red inside," Anthony said to his mother.

Laney didn't know how to respond. "Where did you hear that, sweetheart?"

"I just know it." He smiled.

Another month had passed before he said something else out of the ordinary. A cut on his foot from a broken dish that Laney had dropped the day before had startled the child. He yelled out but didn't cry.

"Sweety, I'm so sorry," Laney had said as she cleaned his wound.

"Don't worry, Mommy," Anthony said. "It's only skin-deep and nowhere near an artery."

"You …" Laney paused. "… you're so smart." "This might sting a little. But I have to clean it."

Anthony nodded. "It's okay, Mommy. It's only peroxide. Alcohol stings more."

"How do you know this?" Laney asked.

"I just know." Anthony smiled. "Alcohol's my favorite."

Laney froze.

"Who knows where kids get things from?" her husband had said later that night.

"How can you be so dismissive?" Laney asked.

"Maybe what he said was a little weird. But he's only three. His vocabulary's so advanced. I wonder if he repeats things before he knows what they mean."

Laney shook her head. "No, you should've been there. He knew exactly what he was saying."

"Either way, where did he hear it from? Daycare maybe?"

Laney sighed. "We took him to Sarah's housewarming last week. Was Dane at the housewarming?"

"Yeah," he replied, "why?"

"Because he's always the first to get buzzed." Laney laughed. "He's not shy about liking to drink. Maybe he made a comment in front of Anthony."

Rodrick also laughed. "I'll mention something next time I see him."

Anthony's comments were out of the ordinary but there seemed no reason to worry. There were several justifications that could explain the word salad from their child, especially if his parents had Dane for a friend.

Rodrick sat Anthony on the counter to remove his bandage and check on his cut.

"OW, OW!" Anthony shouted.

"What's wrong, buddy?"

The cut was bleeding again, and the scab was now held between Anthony's little fingers.

"Why did you do that?" he asked.

"I used to do it all the time," Anthony replied.

"But this is your first cut."

"No, Daddy, I used to do it to other people."

Rodrick squinted. "What are you talking about?"

"Their cuts were bigger. Much bigger."

Rodrick fell silent. He bandaged Anthony's cut and announced that it was bedtime.

Rodrick couldn't sleep. The following morning, he decided on a father and son outing.

"That's important," Laney said. "Go for it."

"We'll be back in an hour or two. Enjoy your time off."

Rodrick and Anthony headed for McDonald's. After lunch and a little playtime, they sat in the car.

"Let's talk," Rodrick said.

"Okay, Daddy."

"Do you remember yesterday when you talked about ... cutting people?"

"Yes."

"Where did you hear that?"

Anthony shrugged.

"Who told you about cutting people?"

"Nobody."

"You're not in trouble, buddy. I promise. I just want to know what you were talking about."

"I used to cut people."

"Who did you cut?"

"Grown-ups."

"What grown-ups?"

"I don't know."

"When did you do this? You've been with Mom and me or daycare."

"Silly, Daddy," Anthony replied. "I wasn't always with you and Mommy. I used to live in a big house with a big attic."

"Oh you did, did you?"

Anthony nodded. "Uh-huh. And that's where I took people to cut them."

Rodrick held his thoughts but understood that something wasn't right.

"Is everything okay?" Laney asked as they readied for bed. "You've been quiet since returning from your daddy-son date."

"I don't know how to say this," Rodrick whispered. "Um … Anthony needs help." He stared at his wife.

"What? Why?" Laney frowned.

"He's been saying weird shit."

"Like what?"

"Like … he cuts people … and used to live in a big house with a big attic."

"Excuse me?"

"I think we need to get him into therapy."

"Are you messing with me?"

"I wish I was. I really do." Rodrick shook his head. "I heard of reincarnation, but I thought it was bullshit."

"Reincarnation?" Laney repeated. "I can't think about this."

"We *have* to think about this. Do you know what's going to happen if he talks like this in preschool?"

"But if true, what kind of a person was he?" Tears formed in her eyes.

Rodrick looked up reincarnation on the internet as Laney scheduled an appointment with a therapist. The internet search led them to reconnect with a Sikh, a friend from college.

"Tam!" Rodrick hugged his old friend.

"Long time, bro," Tam replied.

"What can you tell me about reincarnation?" Rodrick asked as they sat at the cafe.

"Reincarnation of the soul? Well … the atma leaves the body to find another. We Sikh believe that God … or Waheguru … as we refer to, matches atmas with our new bodies. Good deeds in life get an atma closer again to Waheguru, which is the ultimate goal. But we could live eight million lives before that happens."

"What happens to a soul that does bad deeds?"

His friend sighs. "Those are the ones that are trapped in a cycle."

"Doomed to repeat their bad deeds?"

"Why are you asking?" Tam asked.

Rodrick took a deep breath and stared at his cup.

"Rodrick …" Tam reached out and touch his friend's hand. "What's wrong?"

"My son's been saying some … things."

"Things? What type of things?" Tam asked.

"If reincarnation is true … my son lived a bad life before now."

"Wow." Tam sighed.

Rodrick nodded. "My wife's taking him to a therapist. We need answers."

"Every life is different. My religion explains about what happens after death. But you must look to science to explain life itself."

"What do you mean?"

"The life you and your wife give must account for something. I know you're not going to treat him badly."

"Of course not."

"Then, there you go. Why should he turn out the same way?"

"But can't some souls be evil?"

"Evil is a flaw. Atmas are divine. A soul cannot be flawed."

"What then? Hitler was just a flawed … body?"

"No man. Fuck that atma. He was pure evil."

They both laughed. It felt good to laugh in the midst of such a confusing time.

"Look," Tam said, "psychopaths must come from somewhere. We could talk about nature versus nurture until the cows come home. But if you treat your boy right, the odds are in his favor he will not repeat his old life."

Rodrick felt a little reassured. That night, he and Laney talked.

"Anthony has a therapy appointment on the fifteenth," Laney said.

"That's quick," Rodrick replied.

"We're paying out of pocket."

"He's worth it." Rodrick told her everything Tam had said about reincarnation. The conversation gave them hope, and they climbed into bed feeling a little better.

Rodrick stared at his wife, slightly jealous at her ability to fall asleep, even under stress. It was as if her body and mind stopped to recharge after a certain hour. He needed to be fully relaxed in order to fall asleep, and that seldom came with ease. He stared into the darkness alone with his thoughts.

Growing uncomfortable he flipped on his back, then to his side, where a small figure stood, staring at him. Startled at first, he soon realized it was his son.

"Anthony!" he whispered. "You scared me, buddy. What's wrong? Can't get to sleep?"

"I heard you and mommy talking," Anthony replied.

"You know we love you, right?"

He nodded.

"Good," Rodrick said. "Let's get you back into bed?"

Silently and slowly, Anthony headed to his room. Rodrick was amazed at his son's lack of fear for the dark as there was not much light. Rodrick watched as his son's silhouette paused before climbing into bed.

"Silly, Daddy," Anthony whispered. "Mommy isn't supposed to know."

"Mommy's not to know what?"

"I don't know," Anthony replied.

The next morning, Rodrick called in sick from work. He drove two hours to where his father-in-law lived. To say he was nursing a theory on life would be an understatement. The theory of what was wrong with his son constantly roared loudly through his brain.

He pulled up to the big house and stared at the pitched roof. No dormers or windows, but Rodrick always felt like there was enough room under the gables for another house. He climbed the stairs to the small square porch and rang the bell.

"Hello Rodrick," Laney's father smiled.

"Hi," Rodrick nodded.

"Where's Laney and Anthony?"

"It's a Monday, they're at daycare and work."

"Shouldn't you be at work?"

"No time to explain. I need to see your attic."

"Why?"

"Have you been up there?"

"What do you think?" Stan replied.

He shoved past his father-in-law and darted into the house.

"Rodrick?" Stan stated, following him. "What's wrong?"

"I'll explain," Rodrick darted up the stairs. "I'm really sorry."

Stan followed. "You and Laney hardly ever come over. I haven't seen my grandson since he was an infant. I want him to know me."

Rodrick glanced down the hall.

"They're behind there," Stan grumbled, pointing.

Rodrick stood at the door. He tried the handle and it opened. He climbed the narrow stairs with Stan behind.

Rodrick's eyes darted across the empty space. It was dark, save a few splinters of light escaping up the stairs. He felt around, looking for a switch. The lights blinked and a huge, cavernous and empty space greeted him. He now stood quietly with his father-in-law at his side.

"What did you expect?" Stan asked.

"You don't want to know," Rodrick replied.

"Are you okay?"

"Yeah … no … I don't know."

Stan placed a hand on Rodrick's shoulder. "What's going on?"

"Why are there walls here?" he asked.

"Because it's a house?" Stan replied.

"The trusses are exposed. Some light is getting through. But there's sheetrock on *these* walls."

"My dad did that about twenty-five years ago. He thought we needed more insulation."

"Why leave the ceiling untouched? The cold will just come in through here."

Stan shrugged. "Every bit makes a difference, I guess."

"No," Rodrick corrected, "installing partial insulation defeats the purpose. It's almost like he was … trying to hide something."

"What?"

Rodrick had an auditory flashback of his wife talking to the doctor a couple of years back – *'He's very much like my grandfather …'*

Rodrick approached the wall. "I'll get this fixed. I'm good for it."

"What?"

Rodrick tugged on the sheetrock.

"Hey!" Stan shouted. "What are you doing?"

Rodrick jerked harder. The edges crumbled, cracking down the middle. Rodrick and his father-in-law now stood speechless, staring at a mass of mummified remains, slowly tilting until gravity took over. The bodies fell with a ghastly clatter, as a puff of dust whooshed into the air. Four in total. Their skin fileted on the arms and legs. Stitches and old thread bordered the edges. Rodrick heard his son's words once again – *'I cut people.'*

Stan's eyes filled with tears. "God dammit, Daddy." His voice trembled.

The attic was soon bustling with police. Thirty-eight mummified bodies were found. After much questioning, Stanley Garver was not considered a person of interest. Grandpa Max had kept his secret extremely well hidden. He had lived his entire life with the love of his family surrounding him. But now that his dark soul had found a new life – the secret was out.

To Anthony, everything was new, which provided hope for his parents. But further research revealed that psychopathy tended to run in families. Aside from a grim past life, genetics also worked against Anthony. Something Laney and Rodrick had feared. But this was a fear that wasn't quelled at the end of a moment or a horrifying tale. Their fear was one that lingered and degraded the mind over time. Nobody knew how Anthony would turn out, and they were powerless to influence the future. They simply had to wait.

Anthony grew to forget. Laney and Rodrick had heard of kids losing their sixth sense as they aged. They committed to never speak about the past, believing it was their only hope to raise a normal child.

By ninth grade, Anthony was a calm and well-adjusted student. He was sitting in biology awaiting the new assignment. The teacher walked in pushing a metal cart, containing preserved frogs pinned to wooden boards. A few students gagged. Others grimaced. Some couldn't wait to start.

A dead frog was placed on Anthony's table. He looked at the creature, its arms and legs pinned to the board. The aroma of formaldehyde permeated the air. His lab partner could barely look, let alone hold the scalpel. But as Anthony anticipated the dissection of the frog, a strange feeling consumed him.

"I've done this before," he whispered.

"When?" his teacher asked.

Anthony thought for a moment. "I don't know."

Lynn's thoughts …

Genetics – a scary thought. The older I get, the more I think I'm my mother! Another scary thought.

Many people have said they can talk to the dead or they lived before. Before what? And many have concrete evidence. Now that is indeed scary. Not the other worldly part, but the coming back to this world part – scary thought.

Have you ever looked at something and had that *feeling* that you were there before? That what you were about to do was a repeat, although that would be impossible? Maybe it isn't impossible after all.

Did you know that there are signs that we may have lived before. Aside from Déjà vu, the signs include past unusual memories, dreams/nightmares, fears/phobias, an unexplained connection to another culture, passions, habits, odd pains, and birthmarks. Hmmm, so the next time I want to watch a documentary on Egypt, instead of me being interested, it may mean I was King Tut's long-lost sister. What if I have dreams of living on another planet? Would that make me an alien?

This story definitely needs a part two. What happens after the frog? Does the Déjà vu take over and the child becomes a serial killer or does he simply shrug it off and become his own person? Then again, how connected is our inner self to our outer self?

Maybe Edgar Cayce was right after all, we are nothing more than a flake from the overall big spirit. A wayward drift of a simple thought that once was.

Nah, I'll wait for part two.

DAVID AJLUNI

Losing Her

Teddy E. Powers

Running is never easy, especially when it's from yourself ...

The heavy steps of age had chided Silice for some time now. He slowly made his way along the cobblestone streets, feeling a little different as his knees slightly buckled.

The years are catching up to me.

Reaching the top step, he looked back out at his world. He was at a place unlike any he had ever known, and he had known many throughout his sixty-plus years. He sighed as he sat on the porch swing, slowly rocking back and forth. It seemed so long ago, the events that brought him here, to this place, to this time.

So long ago ...

She lay halfway conscious, propped slightly on the innumerable pillows she always insisted on. He sighed for she looked so different from just a month ago. Her face pallid with the lines of anguish that creased her brow and lips. A permanent fixture these last few weeks. The color of her face so drained that her lips appeared to have a slight tinge of blue.

"Water, water." Her voice barely a whisper.

As he tilted the cup to her mouth, she seemed to gain a little strength. Her voice sounding more normal, though fatigue. She coated every syllable as she thanked him and smiled.

How did it come to this?

How had they reached this moment? How was this happening, and why? Why was there nothing he could do? Why wasn't there anything they could find? Why weren't they telling him anything? Why weren't they trying?

Why, why, why?

He threw the cup and water sprayed across the floor and against wall as the glass shattered. Silice held his head and sobbed. He was losing her and didn't want to think what that meant. He felt her hand fall, uncertain as to when it had hit the couch.

"My love," she whispered, "I'm still here, it's okay. We'll figure it out. You'll see."

"How? We tried everything, been to everyone or have you forgotten?"

"Oh, no." She coughed slightly. "I remember."

The tarmac glistened in the sun, heat visibly rising off the pavement. The wind gently blew the tree branches and all was quiet. Their tiny sedan hurtled down the highway, encroaching on recklessness, as Silice berated the steering wheel.

"Asthma? Seriously!" he yelled out. "Three hours? Three godforsaken hours, waiting just to be told it's just asthma?"

"Come now," Sarah stated, "what did that wheel ever do to you?" A soft smile played on her lips that quickly faded when his eyes glanced at her. "Besides …" – she shrugged – "… it fits. All I've had is a little shortness of breath and a cough. I'll be fine."

"That's not the point," he replied, "it shouldn't have taken three hours of waisted tests to come to that conclusion."

"Perhaps not." She took a deep breath. "But now we know."

Taking a deeper breath, he tried to relax, although feeling exasperated. "I guess we do." He grasped her hand and squeezed gently. "It's still a waste of time and money. Two hours spent doing nothing but waiting. Just not right. We're saving for that house, we can't afford the extra expense."

"It'll be fine, sweetheart." She smiled. "You'll see."

It had been three weeks since they moved into their new home, and somehow boxes were still everywhere. They spent three hours elbow-deep in stuff, placing books and dishes in their respective places. His head would disappear over and over again inside the body-length box. He would re-appear smiling with a picture frame or some other object.

"Hey?" he would state, "it's our wedding photo!" He'd beam, brandishing the photo.

"Is it? Let me see." She had said, raising herself slightly to a seated position.

Silice knelt, showing her the picture. His smile, even broader as he held it for her to see. "Look at how beautiful you were in that dress. I'll never forget how you looked coming down that aisle."

"I bet you won't." She smiled, stroking his cheek with her thumb.

He cupped her hand against his face and kissed it. "How was your nap? Did you sleep okay? How're you feeling?" His smile had somewhat faded, concern coloring his tone.

"So many questions," she replied, coughing. "I'm alright, love. Just a little tired." Suddenly acquiescing into a coughing fit, she grabbed her chest.

Silice handed her a handkerchief before darting into the kitchen for a glass of water. He stood in the archway as the coughing subsided. But when she pulled the handkerchief away, red speckles glittered on the white cloth.

"That is most definitely not asthma." Anger colored his voice. "Get in the car, we're going back to that doctor."

"I'm fine. It's nothing," she replied. "Just need a little sleep."

"It's not just nothing, Sarah. This topic isn't up for discussion." His voice was stern.

"Baby, it's half past four and we won't make it. It'll be closed." Sarah coughed again, before laying back down.

He sighed, feeling defeated. She was right, protesting was futile. "First thing tomorrow we're going."

She waved her hand, closing her eyes.

The leaves had begun to change, the glow of the Autumn sun now permeated the trees. The last of the summer rains dripped from their branches. The drive was automatic to him now, his hands twisting the wheel just enough to conquer the familiar curves. Sarah dozed quietly on the passenger seat.

Can't believe it's been two years.

The doctors ran test after test, finding nothing until one day, they discovered a small mass in her right lung. His heart fell when they stated it was cancer. But the prognosis was still good. They had an experimental method of reducing the cells called *chemotherapy*. Two Yale pharmacologists were holding trials and welcomed Sarah to join. Every month they made the trip. For seventeen months, he would shake his head, looking over at her. She'd smile and reach for his hand.

But she's getting worse. I'm not sure what I would do if ... no!

The treatment was somewhat working. One always seemed sicker before getting better, right?

Right.

He shook his head again, shaking off the thought. His hands turned the wheel to the familiar curves.

How did it come to this? How could I be losing her?

Another curve, another twist of his hands. It all seemed impossible. Another turn, and his hands twisted in the familiar direction. A glimpse of something darted in front of the car. He hit the brakes, jerking the wheel. His tires caught on a patch and the car spun, skidding, until it slammed into a tree. He woke to the sound of someone screaming. His head throbbed. He blinked a couple of times, trying to clear his vision. The screaming wouldn't stop. He glanced around and he was alone.

"Sarah?"

Silice focused on the passenger seat. The tree had just missed the door. Sarah rested in the remnants of the window, blood trickling down her cheek.

"Sarah!"

He couldn't hear himself over the incessant screaming. No, not screaming. His ears were ringing. He tried to examine her but couldn't move. His ribs were either bruised or broken. Lifting his arm hurt but he had to touch her. The pain was almost blinding.

He gently slid closer, pulling the hair from her eyes. He shook his head, remember his training, trying to assess the damage. Shattered glass covered her face. Tiny scratches everywhere. Thankfully, nothing looked too major. Bruises were on her arms and probably elsewhere. Her legs were unnaturally close to the dashboard, probably pinned underneath.

What should I do? Should I try and move her? No, something may be broken; bad idea.

He pulled himself out of the wreckage, testing his legs.

"No pain, that's good."

He stepped to her side of the car. A slight nudge to her seat elicited a small whimper. He paused.

"I'm sorry, baby."

Silice pushed the seat back into place the best he could.

Sarah cried out.

A knot formed in his throat. *I can't …* He swallowed the knot, trying to focus.

Sarah was bloody and bruised. It didn't seem likely that she'd broken her neck or spine. Perhaps he could move her. The ringing in his ears seemed to be growing louder. Feeling dizzy, his vision blurred.

Someone ran across the road.

"Help us!" He gasped, falling, succumbing to the darkness.

The sheets felt cool against his skin. He turned, trying to get comfortable.

Why is my mouth so dry? Wait, bed? Sheets? Where am I?

He was in hospital.

"Oh, no! Sarah!? Sarah!" He tried to climb out of bed but couldn't move.

"Sir, wait." A nurse pushed him down. "You must stay in bed, you were severely injured."

"Where's my wife?" he asked, feeling breathless.

"Wife? The woman who was with you?" The nurse paused. "She's in ICU."

"She's alive?"

"Yes sir, she's alive."

"That's all that matters." A thought ran through his mind and he raised up on his elbows. "When can I see her?"

"Soon." Her voice sounded softer. "As I said, she's in ICU. But she's stabile."

Silice nodded, closing his eyes.

"Would you like some water?"

He nodded again.

Moonlight illuminated the room, bright as the morning sun. The nurse bustled about in the late hours, making her rounds.

Silice bolted upright.

"Whoa!" the nurse whispered. "It's okay. Easy does it." She placed a hand on his shoulder. "Silice," she whispered, "do you know where you are?"

"Sarah?!" he yelled. "Where's Sarah?"

The nurse pointed to the next bed. "She's resting, as you should be. Now please, lie back down."

He relaxed and nodded, drifting off to sleep.

"That was somethin'," the nurse whispered.

"He does that sometimes," Sarah replied, "ever since he came back …"

"Came back?"

"He was overseas during the war." Her eyes glazed as she remembered. "I thought I had lost him when I heard the news of the casualties. He was one. After worrying and wondering, he walked right through my front door." She laughed. "Just walked right in." She sighed. "I cried in his arms for hours." Sarah grinned. "His shoulder was soaked, but he never let go. He just leaned down and kissed me, before saying *'I told you I'd come back didn't I?'* I bawled all over again." Sarah sighed.

The nurse propped a pillow behind Sarah's head. "Comfortable?"

Sarah nodded.

"Good." The nurse picked up her chart and made a few notes. "How long after he returned did *that* start?"

"What?" She glanced at Silice. "Guess I got caught down memory lane. Sorry …"

"Oh, no … you're fine. The war is still fresh on everyone's mind. My sister was a nurse in the Army, and let me tell you, the stories she told … but you don't want to hear about those."

"I'd bet." Sarah cringed. "No, thank you. I'll do without those stories. Sigh-liss," she whispered, over enunciating his name, "I think it was about six months after he returned. He was having a hard time finding work and half the classrooms and schools were closed to help with the war efforts, which meant I had no students. No students, no paycheck. We were just married. With the stress of moving in together, plus not having an income, I think he just couldn't handle it." She fidgeted with her sheets. "It happened again when I became sick."

Sarah stared at her hands as if somewhere far away. She took a deep breath. "He woke one night screaming, which of course woke me. I never saw him like that before. He stared off into nothing for a moment before screaming at the wall … 'Sir, 1 at 12, 2 at 3, 5 at 9, and 6 at 4.' A few nights later it happened again, only that time he was screaming names and orders. I think he was reliving the war. The worst part was he had no memory of it when he woke up. I didn't have the heart to tell him. Then, he would just start crying. I didn't know what to do, so I just held him." Tears welled in Sarah's eyes. "I just wish I knew how to help him."

"Oh, sweetie." The nurse touched her hand. "I'm sure he'll be just fine. Don't worry. Let's get you comfortable. I think we've had enough excitement for one day."

Sarah nodded.

The nurse fluffed her pillows. "Get some rest and take care of yourself, let me worry about him." The nurse stroked her hand again.

"Quite the pair, aren't they?" asked another nurse, standing by the door.

"Yes, yes they are. So sweet."

"Are they sleeping?"

"One is. They should sleep 'til morning. I've got to get to bed myself."

"You look exhausted."

"Their charts are over there. See you in the morning."

The two RNs waved, parting ways.

The sunlight peeked through the blinds, spotlighting Silice's bed. He pulled on his sheets, the tingle of the warm sun prickled his chin. Voices of doctors and nurses were audible but unintelligible. He stirred slightly.

Is that Sarah's voice? "Sarah!?"

"Mr. O'hara, you're awake?" The doctor made his way between the two beds, pulling up a chair. He sighed. "There's no easy way to say this .. but Sarah's cancer has spread."

"What?! How?!" Silice felt bewildered.

"The bruises somehow allowed the disease to replicate faster. What's more, we discovered that the cancer originated in the pleura or lining of her lungs, not in the lungs themselves."

"What does that mean?"

"It means she has Mesothelioma and not lung cancer as originally thought. She's likely further along than we though. Unfortunately, very little is known about this particular cancer, however the treatments have had promising results."

"What does that mean?"

"It means that unfortunately, we've done all we can here. I've made arrangements with a colleague closer to your residence, Dr. Renard Bouchier. He's agreed to make in-home visits to monitor your wife's progress instead of you returning here. In the interim you're to continue the chemotherapy. It seems it's her best chance."

"We don't have a vehicle anymore." Silice stated quietly, looking over at his wife.

"My parents may have one we can use," Sarah said. "I'm sure they won't mind." Sarah smiled.

"Is there a phone we can use? To call her family?" Silice asked.

"We already contacted your families. Your father assured us he would be on his way this morning."

Another nurse poked her head in the room, "Forgive me, Dr. Taylor, but you're needed in room nine."

"Be right there." He smiled. "I'm sorry. I'll be in touch."

Samuel Braunsin, Sarah's father, arrived a few hours later and they headed home. He had a car they could use, but it needed a little work.

"Why don't you stay with us until it's fixed?" Sam asked. "Mary can keep an eye on Sarah while you're at work. Besides, I'm sure they'd love a little mother-daughter time."

Silice glanced at his wife who was sleeping on the back seat. *That could work.* It would allow him time to set up the doctor visits.

"When's your next appointment?" Sam asked.

"Huh? Oh, uh, Dr. Taylor said we'd resume our visits as normal despite missing this last one. The appointments are on the third Thursday of every month." He looked at Sarah again. "I think we *will* stay with you until the car is fixed. If that's alright?"

"Of course. I offered, remember?" Sam laughed, clasping him on the shoulder. "We're here for you, son. Don't worry."

"Thanks, Sam." Silice smiled. "I appreciate it."

"Think nothin' of it, you're family."

Between locating the required parts and the labor, it took a little over two weeks to fix the car.

"Listen to her purr," Sam stated.

"Had doubts?" Silice asked.

Samuel pulled two drinks from the small fridge in the garage, handing one to Silice. "How are you holding up?" Sam asked.

Silice stared into the distance. "Doing alright. Just worried."

"I know how I'm doin' and she's my daughter. I can only imagine if Mary was going through this. Not that one's worse than the other. I'm just …"

Silice stared at his drink.

"Let's eat," Sam said, pulling Silice from the garage.

"I told Sarah you'd wake her," Mary said. "So, hop to it … and be nice."

"Me, nice? To that sleeping lion over there?" Silice laughed.

Mary swatted him with a potholder.

"Abuse!" he whispered, quietly walking to the couch where Sarah was asleep. "Hey, baby, dinner's ready."

Sarah gave a small stretch and yawned. "Okay, I'm coming. I'm a sleeping lion, am I?"

Silice chucked. "A very dangerous one."

Sarah elbowed him, gently.

"Careful," Sam stated, "you might break something. Like mother, like daughter." He chuckled from the table. "Careful Sarah, your husband's still got work to do." Once Sarah was seated, Sam added, "After that you can beat him all you want."

"Hey!" Silice whined. "Bunch of turncoats."

"Y'all be nice to that boy." Mary said, placing a basket of bread on the table.

Silice promptly reached for one, receiving a pop on the hand. "And here I thought –".

"That was your first mistake," Mary stated.

The table was silent for only a moment before they laughed.

Silice smiled, watching his family enjoying a much-needed moment of reprieve.

Its going to be okay, isn't it?

LOSING HER

Lynn's thoughts …

Family illness is never a pleasant experience. Especially when dealing with cancer. I'm not sure which is worse. A sudden death or a lingering one.

And with death, why is everyone so afraid? We honestly do not know what is on the other side. Some say nothing is out there. Others claim there's a whole other existence.

I read about a doctor who weighed bodies before and after death. He claimed there was a slight loss of weight when the soul left. Interesting, didn't know a soul could weigh anything. Kinda like a puff of smoke. Does smoke have weight?

The fear of losing a loved one can weigh heavily on a person's mind. When that happens, we sometimes forget we are still alive, which is what our character, Silice did. He forgot he was driving and hit a tree.

In reality, knowing that the end is near can be a fear that is difficult to overcome. We all know that we will not live forever. That is a reality we cannot escape, but to contemplate it, now that can be horrifying.

I see death as a door in the forest. No walls, just a door to open when someone knocks on the other side. What is on the other side, who knows. And who's knocking is another question with no answer. But one day at some unexpected moment, we will all answer that knock. We just do not know when.

Then we must ask the real question, *do we return?* And if we do, why? Perhaps we failed at living in our life and must repeat the grade. Now that would really be a terrifying thought. Imagine if the government passes a law that states our debts follow us into the next life. How many would be willing to return then?

Run Through the Jungle

Richard Schulein

We were ready to depart Katmandu. Johann, despite his temporary contrariness of *I don't want to leave*, woke up on his own like an adult, carried his suitcase to the bus, and was anxious to get moving. We tied the suitcases on the rack, before reflecting on the place we were leaving. Our meditation was Silvio's brainchild.

Captain Silvio, bearded and dark, was our driver and leader.

The meditation was a little tacky, but it worked. Within minutes, I started to relax, satisfied I was making the right decision.

Monika, the aggravating princess, ran off the bus in the direction of the ramshackle hotel we just left. Meanwhile, Mai, petite, blonde and with a come-hither attitude, showed up with sensible shoes and no makeup. She also stepped off the bus, climbing onto the roof rack. A few minutes later Monika had returned, face flushed, clutching a small, red box.

What's going on?

For weeks, we were calm and determined to hit the road in spite of the hash brownie we wolfed down for breakfast. Everyone, except Silvio, who seemed to be in control of himself and his tribe. He truly was the captain, keeping everyone safe and our chariot in fine shape. As the newest member of the crew, I spent time getting to know everyone. Hash brownie notwithstanding, I was calm about leaving but not determined.

Katmandu was at the top of the world, the place from which a person headed either east or west. I second guessed myself every day. I had accepted a job teaching then turned it down. I had turned away from a girlfriend to catch a ride. I thought of Audrey and shuddered.

Now it was time to move out – Katmandu to Kabul. But something weird was going on.

What's in that red box? What's Mai doing on the roof rack?

After a few minutes, a knock on the roof and Silvio started the engine. With the car in gear, we were off.

What was she doing up there? "Can I be up there, too?"

Silvio was cool, still meditating. "That's where we ride, one at a time, to have a better view of our world."

"All of us?"

"All but me." He laughed. "I drive."

"Will I have a turn? Is it safe?"

"Yes, but until then, you are the navigator. It's safe. There's a rope that keeps you in place. You couldn't move even if you want to."

I opened the map. Silvio seemed to know the exact way to leave the city toward the border. I was a navigator without a portfolio.

Once out of town, we followed the signs that said *Raxaul.* I felt panicked.

Where's my passport?

Silvio glanced at me pawing at my passport pouch. Did I have a damn visa for India? A month ago, I received a single-entry visa. Single-entry. No good anymore. What about now? I needed another visa. The most essential rule of traveling was to plan your steps. I had been caught flat-footed once and had to splurge on a plane ticket. But what now? A few more pages and, thankfully, there it was – Visa for the Republic of India – expiring in three months.

The memory of a drug induced visit to the Indian embassy with Audrey hit. It had taken us two hours, but in my drugged-induced haze, I had forgotten about it. I exhaled.

Silvio, who was nothing if not careful, had stopped the vehicle. Was he scared by my panic. No, he wanted to check on the tires. The tire was okay, and we started off again.

The road zagged through the mountains as we hit the part I dreaded. The worst road in the world. I was on it once before while on the back seat of an ancient school bus with good brakes but no suspension. We were now traveling south and down the mountain.

The road twisted and turned through diabolical switchbacks. I clutched the passenger's handhold, caressing it on straightaways. Silvio was an expert driver. He wasn't just bragging when he said not to worry about the mountain roads. He knew what he was doing and how to finesse a hairpin. Holding on was important, and I thought about Mai on the rack with just a rope around her waist.

The boxes in the back were wedged between the iron seats to keep Monika and Johann safe. I wondered how Johann was faring. Last night I panicked at the thought of traveling this road. Now I was living it. It was a tense, breathless ride. Halfway down, we turned off the main road and onto a secondary one toward Chitwan Elephant Station.

The scenery had changed. We were no longer plunging down a mountainside, but rolling through the foothills. The fir trees were replaced by a mixture of evergreens and elms. The ground leveled becoming dotted with scattered ponds and puddles. The vegetation thickened and we crossed several streams. After stopping for a bite to eat, Silvio coached Mai inside with the single word, "Monkeys."

She took my place. I sat in the rear. It was reasonably comfortable, but the only view was through the two small windows on the side doors. Monika and Johann were discussing European politics and the east–west divide. Johann ended a bit too emphatically, saying that Monika was able to cross borders as easily as everyone else because she had a French passport in addition to her Latvian one. They complained like an old married couple.

Mai and Silvio argued about traveling by day versus traveling by night. Why would we even consider traveling by night in India? I searched Johan's face for an answer. In his high-pitched voice, he squeaked out that Silvio had a good point. Roads in the daytime were packed with pedestrians, animals, bicycles, motorbikes, rickshaws, and various other slow-moving vehicles. Cars would become stuck in the inevitable crush. Mai's argument for daytime travel was that turning day into night and night into day would keep us tired. Silvio countered that it would cost us extra days and try our patience. The captain had spoken, ending their heated discussions.

Silvio parked under a large tree and we climbed out.

"What happened?" I asked.

"The road ended. The station is along this path through those trees. We'll walk the rest of the way." Silvio seemed autocratic. "But we can't leave supplies on the roof. Everything has to go inside. Let's get to work."

We loaded up the bus, but it was a tight fit. We left a few suitcases on top, trusting that no one would want to steal clothes. Off we went to find the elephants. The terrain was the same as we had seen along the road – wet and dry, ponds and forest, meadows and brush.

Johann stopped. He had forgotten his passport. Now his nerves were getting the best of him. His squeaky voice whined. "It's the worst thing that could happen. I'm scared."

A ready-made anxiety for the one member who could least afford it. He had no memory of where he had left it. Was it in the bus or in his suitcase? We had to return.

I volunteered to walk with him. We would lose half an hour, but it was better than a panic-stricken Johann. I was enjoying the landscape much more on foot. My eyes wide admiring the half jungle-half brush. The chatter of wild animals grew louder. We rounded a bend and the bus was in a clearing under the tree. Forty or fifty monkeys were creating havoc. Clothes flew every which way. Johann picked up a stick and whooped, running toward them. I found a stick too. We screamed, waving our arms.

We reached the bus, and a few monkeys screeched but were frightened off when we banged on the bus. We gave chase and when we returned, we dropped to the ground, panting.

The damage! Clothes, books, makeup, and other items were strewn about everywhere. Suitcases upended – an undeniable mess.

We stared at each other, collecting the items. After shoving everything into suitcases in no particular order, we literally stuffed everything inside the bus. We could sort it out later. The bus was a mess too, but Johann had at least found his passport. Johann was now calm and rational. We locked the bus and I laughed.

We were back to where we had split from the others, finding the same path through the trees. We logged through forest that was quickly becoming dense and overgrown. We stood at a fork in the road, deciding on which way to go. Silvio appeared in front of us, smiling.

"How'd you know where to find us?"

He pointed at the binoculars around his neck. "When you don't come, I look for you. What went wrong?"

We recounted our strange story about the monkeys.

"What did the monkeys look like?"

When we repeated the story to the girls, three huge elephants watched us from between the trees. Elephants at a zoo did not compare to standing next to one. With no gap or barrier, it felt overwhelming. No one had to tell me to not to make a sudden move. Their power was immense. Two of us plus the driver were assigned to each elephant.

Johann declined, as I thought he would. After the monkeys, just being there was enough for him. He was closing in on himself and could no more climb onto the back of an elephant than sprout wings and fly. He plopped on a wicker armchair on the veranda and closed his eyes.

But where were we going?

"We're looking for an Indian Rhino." Silvio stated.

We awkwardly climbed up the rope ladders. Mai and I shared the beast with one mahout. Monika and Silvio were on the bigger elephant. Our elephant was encircled by a rope frame knotted at intervals for us to hold on to. With emphatic gestures, we were told not to stand as if any of us could.

The elephants lumbered.

We held on, feeling unstable. Mia seemed to be getting the hang of it. I felt grateful she was my partner. While the elephants tramped us through the semi-jungle, we tried different position, until we gained our elephant balance. When we signaled that we were ready, the elephants stomped down the riverbank, plunging into the water.

One minute we were on land, the next, we were surrounded by rushing water. On our own, we would have been washed away in a flash, but the beasts were simply strolling through the torrent, rock steady, as if it were nothing.

I had just read Tolkein's, Lord of the Rings, and was reminded of Merry and Pippin carried by the Ent elder. We lumbered a good ten minutes to reach the other bank. As the elephants climbed out of the river, we hung on tightly.

"Thank God there were no crocodiles," I said to no one but myself.

We marched through the thick jungle with leafy plants and vines. More chirping and chattering and an occasional shriek, though nothing like a Tarzan soundtrack.

Mai and I looked at each other and mouthed the word "Monkeys."

Monkeys, monkeys everywhere, and our escapade wasn't done. The two mahouts had maneuvered the elephants together so they could have a moot. After awhile, they said it was time to return. The elephants were tired. But I didn't believe it for a second as the elephants seemed tireless. We started back but stopped. Our mahout shushed us, pointing his stick to the vegetation. A rhinoceros with one great horn stood several yards away. The rhino looked shorter than I expected – stout would be an understatement – and was a shiny brown. It stared at us. We were in a face-off in the middle of a jungle. I was unable to move. I glanced at Mai without turning my head. The rhino scraped a hoof on the ground which sounded like a fingernail across a blackboard.

The elephants held their ground. We held our breaths.

The rhino made a shuffling step back, before taking two steps forward. Our elephant twitched, but did not move. A single foot forward from the other elephant, then a foot from the rhino.

This can't be happening! Sweat gushed down my back. *No, no, no, don't sweat.*

Silence. Silence that stretched and tested our grit. More sweat. Two trumpets from our elephants and the rhino loped away.

We watched, not moving, until broad smiles erupted on the faces of our mahouts. Our asses were saved. They had promised a glimpse of the endangered Indian Rhino, not a show-down in the middle of the jungle. The odds of finding it were not great, but they had scored a bulls eye and they knew it. That probably meant a tip, a big one. Unconsciously, I felt the pouch hanging from my neck.

A few deep breaths, smiles of relief, and our rides turned to leave. Mai and I couldn't speak, so we touched each other's arms. On the other elephant, Silvio sat pensive, staring in the direction of the now retreating rhino while Monika struck a Valkyrie pose of victory.

We sauntered back to base when our elephant took a curve too wide and barreled into a hanging thorn bush that impaled my leg and stuck. I wanted to say, "Stop the elephant," but my voice was caught. My leg, however, was being pulled and me with it. In my mind's eye, I was already on the ground. I yanked with all my strength and my leg pulled free, leaving behind some flesh. My right pantleg dangling turning read. But at least, I was still on the elephant.

Mai sat motionless, holding her bit of rope, while the mahout sidled over to me. He pulled out a piece of cloth from *I-don't-know-where* and wrapped my leg to stop the bleeding. The elephant kept up its pace, oblivious to the drama happening on its back.

We carried on and crossed the river at a place where it was shallower than before. All was good as the elephants bounced us back to the camp.

My leg had stopped bleeding, and I felt no pain from the intrusion of the oversized thorns. When I offered a sizeable tip for his help, he refused.

We wanted to leave the jungle before dark, so we hurried back to the bus. The others felt guilty about the pace and thought we should slow down because of my leg, But I felt fine. In the following days, I felt no ill effects. The injury healed quickly, which I attributed to the mahout's magical cloth. We found the bus and rearranged the suitcases. With Silvio at the wheel, we would be at our destination in no time at all.

312

Lynn's thoughts …

What a fun read. The excitement of real, wild animals in a real, wild jungle. I wonder how scary that would be? My family has driven through the safari jungle rides before and some of the animals were huge, but none were actually scary. They were probably quite use to us strange animals *(humans)* staring at them from inside the bellies of those metal monsters.

Perhaps this little story is more about being afraid of the unknown. At times, we enjoy frightening ourselves by pushing our inner child to the brink before backing away. What is it with the thrill of a risky adventure? Why must we jump off cliffs or ride that huge wave or venture into the forbidden darkness? What makes us want to take that risk?

Imagine living hundreds of years ago and exploring the great unknown. How terrifying that would be, especially if we had children. Then again, why is it we are more afraid when we have children with us? Is it the sense of responsibility?

Interesting thought. Perhaps as we travel the glass jungles or the dark green ones, we should ask ourselves exactly what it is we are searching for? Is it adventure, a search for that hidden treasure, or is it the desire to chance fate?

Thrill seekers are what the *experts* call them. Those who need more than the average rollercoaster ride. Daredevils is what they were once called. What is it that makes some push the limits when others are content to sit in a chair under a tree? Maybe it is the dopamine that our bodies crave – the pleasure chemical. As for me, I will allow my brain to release that *pleasure chemical* as I read a good book while sitting in a chair under a tree. I simply find stitches and broken bones a little too painful to willingly submit.

Sacrifice

Amberlyn A. Pryor

Maria glanced at the door.

The knocking continued.

"Please," she shook her head, "tell him I don't feel well."

It was the truth. Maria gave birth two days ago and she was exhausted.

"How do you know it's a man?" Cynthe asked.

Maria didn't reply but struggled out of bed. She picked up her son as she glanced at the tiny shrine to the goddess Harminea. It was considered good luck for a baby to sleep at the goddess' feet. Because of the drought, no flowers were in the offering bowl, but the fresh paint showed Maria's devotion. She whispered a short prayer as the knocking continued.

"Maria! It's me, Shaman Kaiche. Let me in!" Another bang on the door. "I'm the voice of the mighty god Wudein and you are not to deny me entrance."

Cynthe glanced between her sister and the door. "Why is the shaman here? He of all people should know to stay away."

It was their firm belief that when a woman gave birth, they were vulnerable and must be separated from the men of the village. To do otherwise was to invite evil into their home and risk sickness and death. Even husbands were to stay away unless they received the goddess' blessing.

Maria touched her sister's arm and frowned.

"I'll tell him to leave," Cynthe whispered. "The goddess Harminea promises all new mothers her protection. The shaman wouldn't dare to risk offending her." She was quick to open the door, but Kaiche was gone by the time she peeked out. "See, everything's fine."

"He'll be back," Maria said. "Stay here tonight. You can bring Vorn over. There's plenty of room."

Vorn, Cynthe's youngest, was sick. She was splitting her time between caring for Vorn and helping Maria.

"I wish I could," Cynthe replied, "but Vorn isn't sleeping. He'll keep you up. You need your rest." She hugged her sister. "You'll be fine. Now back to bed. You're in no condition to be walking around."

Maria's legs did feel a bit shaky.

Cynthe tucked in the blankets and the baby fussed. "Do you know what the shaman wanted?"

Maria shook her head. "Nothing good, I'm sure. I spoke to him when … Uley died." It still hurt to talk of her husband. It'd been almost two months, but the pain was still fresh. Maria took a deep breath. "Shaman Kaiche said he wasn't surprised Uley had died. He said Wudein had punished Uley for failing to show proper homage to the gods."

Cynthe snorted. "Sounds like Kaiche didn't like the decrease in offerings. Probably had to ration his food like the rest of us. We've never had a drought this bad. Even my husband had no animals to sacrifice to Wudein."

Maria nodded. "Uley burnt herbs at the shrine. He did right by the gods. But Kaiche said —"

"Maria, no more worrying. When I return home, I'll tell my husband that Kaiche is bothering you. He'll set things right."

Maria wished she held her sister's optimism.

Cynthe hugged her sister, careful not to wake the sleeping baby. "We'll have rain soon. I felt the goddess with us during the birth of your little one. She guided us and gave you strength. He's such a beautiful baby. There's no way Harminea would bring him into this world only to let the drought destroy us."

Maria held back her tears and nodded.

Cynthe pulled the basket closer to Maria's bed. She stacked the cleaning rags and loin cloths, before bidding her sister goodnight.

"Wait … did you latch the windows?"

"Yes," Cynthe replied, not pausing on her way out.

"All of them?"

"Yes," Cynthe said with a note of exasperation.

Maria stood and barred the door, checking each window. While the sunweave cloth of the inner frame could be cut, the wooden shutters and metal latches were in good condition. Uley had made sure of that. He'd taken good care of her and their home. He would have made a wonderful father. Maria's throat tightened as she thought of him. The house was so empty.

Her son stirred in his sleep.

At least she wasn't alone.

Maria knelt before the goddess, feeling the warmth of the candles. The presence of the idol helped to ease her nerves, but Maria was still afraid. She wished Uley was here.

Maria forced herself to stay awake, but it was a losing battle. As she was nodding off, her son woke. She changed his cloth before feeding him. The sound of his suckling calmed her. She was barely awake when she placed her son in his basket. She lay on the edge of her bed, one hand draped protectively over her son.

A cry woke her, but the room was silent.

Did he go back to sleep?

The candles had burned out and the hearth's fire was down to only embers. She couldn't see much. She felt around the basket. Her son was gone. She winced and grabbed her stomach.

Moonlight filtered through a broken window. The door was unbarred and opened to the night.

Sweat stung Maria's eyes as she darted down the dark street. Her shoes slapped against the dry ground, but her labored breathing made it hard to stay quiet. Only a few cats, silhouetted by the moonlight, noted her passage. Her abdomen still hurt, but at least it wasn't getting worse.

She held tightly to her husband's longbow. She only had two arrows. After his death, she hadn't thought to replenish them. Her brother-in-law hunted for her table now, and he had his own bow and arrows. She had thought to pack them away until her son was old enough to learn their use. Luckily, she'd been too upset to put away her husband's things.

She forgot to bring a lantern, but the goddess' moon was full. Maria never saw the kidnapper, but it had to be Shaman Kaiche. She hadn't told her sister the truth about the shaman. Partially because she didn't want to believe it herself.

Shaman Kaiche came to visit her shortly after Uley's death. At first, she thought he was paying his respects, but he had come to discuss their unborn child.

"With your husband gone," he said, "you'll never be able to raise the child on your own."

She'd foolishly thought he was offering to help, but she was wrong.

"Your baby won't survive when winter comes. You should spare the child the pain of slow starvation and give the child to me. The gods demand a sacrifice to bring back the rains. Something more worthy than a baby goat."

Maria couldn't believe what he had said. The goddess had forbidden human sacrifices generations ago. She had said as much to Shaman Kaiche, but he spouted nonsense about balance and world energies, justifying his words. She demanded he leave and had avoided him ever since. She should have known he wouldn't give up and now her baby was gone.

The village shrine was just ahead. She prayed the shaman was alone. She only had two arrows, and she wasn't skilled with a bow. If one acolyte accompanied him her plan would fail. Clenching her teeth with the pain in her abdomen, she slowed as she rounded the corner.

The alter square was deserted. Not even a candle was lit within the shrine.

Maria bit her lip, refusing to cry or give up hope. She had to find her son. Should she return to her sister's house and ask for help? Maria took a deeper breath. She couldn't involve her family for attacking a shaman, no matter how justifiable, would risk the wrath of the gods.

But where is my baby?

There were several holy places the shaman could use for the sacrifice. The Blessed Spring was mostly mud, so he wouldn't be there. That left the God's Hammer, the Ancient Tree, and the God's Tear. Maria had to pick one. With every breath wasted just standing there, she could feel her baby slip from her reach.

"Oh, great goddess Harminea." She closed her eyes and prayed. "Please, help me find my son. He's my only child and my last link to Uley."

A wind from the west swept through the square, bringing a faint cry of a baby.

She ran to the God's Tear. "Thank you, Goddess," she whispered.

As she ran through the dark, she tripped several times on tree roots and rocks. Her knees felt bruised and scraped. Her clothes now ripped.

The path to the God's Tear was uphill and through the trees. A large white stone, quite unlike the darker native rocks, that jutted out of the earth near the edge of a cliff. As Maria neared, she placed an arrow to the bow. Her baby cried before suddenly stopping.

Heart racing, she ran from the trees.

Shaman Kaiche was alone, holding a knife in his hand. Her baby, wrapped in a cloth, laid on the God's Tear. He was not moving.

"No!" she yelled, fearing she was too late. She drew back the bow as far as she could and released the arrow. Maria gasped and dropped the bow as the string slashed her hand. The arrow sailed harmlessly past the shaman, disappearing off the cliff.

The shaman cursed.

Maria charged forward, giving up on the bow and last arrow. Fingers curled like claws, she screamed and attacked the shaman. She grabbed his arm, pushing away the knife, using her weight to shove him closer to the cliff. Her strength wouldn't last, but the cliff's edge was close. If she could just get him to take a few more steps. She'd lost her momentum, and the shaman kept his footing. He was taller and stronger than her.

Her baby cried.

He's still alive.

Loose soil, kicked free from their struggle, tumbled over the edge.

"You selfish fool!" the shaman yelled. "Will you deny rain to the village just to save one baby?"

Maria bit his arm.

He screamed and dropped the knife. Cursing, he punched Maria in the stomach.

She doubled over, struggling to breathe.

He grabbed her hair, yanking her head back. "I won't let you stop me. The gods demand a sacrifice!"

Ignoring the pain, she slammed her fist into his crotch.

He hunched forward, groaning.

"Then you be the sacrifice," she yelled, ramming her shoulders into his legs.

He took a step, but that was enough. His foot met only air. He fell, his grip on her hair only slowing him a moment, as his weight dragged them both over the cliff.

Shaman Kaiche held on to a protrusion of rock. But it gave way under his weight.

Maria fell only a short distance and was caught by an old tree. She clung to the branches, looking up at the distance she had just fallen. Her heart was beating. The tree's roots shifted, losing their precious grip. Maria froze, afraid to move.

Her baby cried.

"I'm coming," she whispered.

Each motion sent dirt falling. The tree lurched under her. She screamed, wrapping her arms around the trunk. Only a few precious roots held the tree in place. Terrified, Maria scrambled the last arm's length, grabbing onto the rocky cliff. She felt the tree give, crashing down the cliffside. The violent snapping of branches reminded her of bones breaking. That could have been her fate.

"Goddess, please don't let me fall."

Gritting her teeth, she climbed. The cliff slanted slightly with plenty of handholds. The distance wasn't far, not even twice her height.

"Easy," she said.

Her arms shook and her muscles screamed out in pain. Maria wanted to cry, but she kept her eyes on the tuft of grass at the top. Slow and steady, she finished the climb. Maria lay in the grass, grateful to be alive. She spat out the dirt and whispered her thanks to Harminea. After crawling to the God's Tear, she pulled her baby into her arms. He was wrapped tightly and unharmed.

"I'm here now. You're alright."

He cried.

Maria laughed. Tears filled her eyes, but she wasn't sad, just tired and relieved. Her hysterical laughter faded, and she took a moment to breathe.

My son is safe. We're both safe.

Maria pulled a clump of dirt from her hair. It felt like she'd been buried alive. Even her teeth felt gritty. Her grandmother used to say, *'you need to eat a peck of dirt before you die.'* Maria wasn't sure how much a *peck* was, but hopefully she was nowhere near it.

She pulled up a handful of dried grass, wiping her clothes before feeding her son. As he suckled, she leaned against the God's Tear and watched as the moon rose, thinking about the long walk home.

"Would it be so bad to sleep here?" she whispered to her son.

The wind had picked up. It was cool and smelled of rain.

Maria laughed. "Guess not. But Shaman Kaiche was right. It did take a human sacrifice to bring back the rain, but apparently the gods preferred his death over yours."

Kissing her son, she struggled to her feet. She brushed off more dirt, before picking up her husband's bow and the remaining arrow.

"Let's go home."

By the time she arrived, she felt surprisingly good. She was still tired and sore, but relief made her feel weightless. Her son woke when she tried to put him down. She patted his back in case he needed to burp. Humming a soft tone, she sang a short lullaby.

"Little one, close your eyes. Tomorrow will be a new sunrise. Sleep and dream, my love. The stars watch from above. Mommy is here. You've nothing to fear."

She lit a candle for the goddess Harminea. At the foot of the statue, a single arrow, identical to the one she'd shot over the cliff, glowed in the soft light. The fletching had a bit of blood. Maria glanced at the wound on her hand. When she picked up the arrow, a tiny seed was under it. The seed was just beginning to sprout. It was a crest pine, the same tree that had saved her life when she'd fallen off the cliff. Crest pines were drought survivors.

"Thank you, Harminea."

Maria planted the seed outside and near her door so the tree could protect her home when it was grown. She placed her husband's bow and arrows on a table near the goddess' shrine.

"Tomorrow," she said to herself, "I'll practice." She ran her hand over the bow, vowing to never be caught defenseless again.

As Maria climbed into her bed, she listened to the soft patter of rain on her roof.

324

SACRIFICE

Lynn's thoughts …

The fear of losing a child is one of the worst fears a mother can experience. But to lose a child to a sacrifice? How senseless is that? During a sacrifice, it was considered that the more important an object the more devout the person was rendering it. Therefore, sacrificing a child was one of the greatest gifts a person could give to a god. But then, what kind of a god would accept the death of a child?

During the great drought and famine of 1454–1457, hundreds of child sacrifices took place which strengthened the theory that the Aztecs utilized human sacrifice to placate the gods. But why kill the children?

There is a lot of documentation and research into sacrificing children. But there is no mention as to why? I simply cannot connect a famine or drought to a child, unless a crying child was considered a burden because the parents couldn't feed it. It would be interesting to fly into the past and ask the question, "Who told you this would work?"

Again, that word fear comes into play. Humans are so afraid of suffering through a drought or hardship that they are willing to kill their babies. These humans honestly believed they were somehow being punished by their gods, and the death of a little one would make them safe. They feared their gods and their future.

It is strange what fear will do to a human psyche. It distorts reality to the point that we are willing to do just about anything to appease the invisible man who lives in the clouds and judges us all.

Interesting concept indeed.

326

Short Boat Ride on the River

Karen Andrews

"Boys, come here."

He stopped the boat in the middle of the river, swinging his seat to face them. Water from their shorts ran down their legs. He hugged them before cupping a hand over each shoulder. His eyes remained fixed on hers.

She studied his huge hands holding their sons. As the sun dipped behind the clouds, she shivered.

No one moves.

"Boys … look at Mommy."

Their eyes meet hers, and she reflexively reaches for them.

"Don't." His face had shifted into that other shape – hard with angles.

She clasps her hands, looking from child to child.

Questions on their faces and they shiver.

She reaches for the towels behind her, leaning forward, handing one to each.

"Are you babies?" he asked. "Only babies need towels."

The oldest drops the towel, and the younger one follows. No one says a word about the towel wrapped around the father's waist.

"Boys … do you think Mommy loves us?" His eyes are locked on hers.

The boat rocks. She had forgotten to bring her phone. She left it upstairs at the house. *Stupid. Stupid.* The familiar twist, aches from inside her stomach.

"Do you think Mommy loves us?" he asked again. "She isn't being nice to me."

The youngest frowns. "Why?"

Her elder son tilts his head, eyes narrow. "Why not?"

The ice in the open cooler slaps the floating cans against the sides. She does not dare to breathe. His hand releases the youngest, who reaches down and fishes through the cooler. She looks at the water, the boat carrying them upstream with the current. The familiar crushing and an empty beer can lands on her foot. The sharp edge nicks her skin, and a little bubble of blood grows just above her baby toe.

"Sorry," he smirked. "I missed."

She doesn't feel it, doesn't move. "Maybe we … um … can talk about this later?"

He ignored her. "Boys, we're a family, right? Don't you want to hear what Mommy said to me last night?"

She looks at her boys. The eldest frowns, his eyes accusing. "What's Dad talking about?"

The youngest steps to her, but his father's hand pinches his shoulder, the small face twists in surprise. She stands.

"Jesus Christ! You're going to tip the boat. Are you trying to kill us? Do … you … want … us … all to die?"

The oldest looks at her with wide eyes. "Mom, sit down!"

She sits, fighting against the nausea.

"Are you going to tell our boys what you said last night?"

She glared at the water, spitting out the bitter taste. Her stomach burns. "I think we can talk about this when we get home. I don't … think we want to talk about … about … here with … you know … let's go back, let's go home."

"I can barely understand you." His voice dripped with disgust. "Boys, do you want Mommy to keep the truth from you, or do you want to know what she said?"

The boys seem to want to know. They demand to know. His grip relaxes, and he sits back, smirking, not taking his eyes off her.

"As usual, Mommy won't tell *you* the truth, so I will."

They look at him, seeming grateful for a strong and honest father.

"Mommy thinks there's something wrong with me. She thinks I need help. She wants to make me go away, and if that happens, she'll never let me return." He grips their shoulders again. "Look at me."

They do.

His voice sounds whiny and pleading. "Have I *ever* hurt you?" They look at her, seeming confused.

"Tell Mommy what you want. Do you want her to send me away?"

The boys cry, begging her to not make him go away.

Last night, she had held him, his body wracked with sobs as he begged her for forgiveness – he hadn't meant to hurt her. "You need help," she had told him. "We need to get you help." He had agreed, but she had forgotten that his vulnerability came with a dark price.

The water spread out around them. The river was not wide in this spot and she was a strong swimmer. She had glanced at the depth on the fish finder screen, but didn't remember the numbers. Numbers, words, ideas, nothing stuck any more. She recalled feeling shocked at how deep it was. One could get lost forever down there.

How many guns did he have?

He took them out and cleaned them this morning — disassembled them with the boys' help.

"Count them for me," he ordered to her, but she had become confused, almost dizzy, looking at the metal covering.

She shuddered and forced herself to be still as he stood close behind her, his hands lightly stroking her arms, his lips close to her.

"You can't concentrate?" he asked.

When she didn't answer, he shoved his chest into her back. She lurched awkwardly, reaching out her hands to brace on the edge of the table. Two guns fell to the floor.

"Jesus, careful!" he yelled. "You're gonna kill one of us." Backing away from her, shaking his head, and snorting, he looked at the boys. "She can't even count. Are you even listening to me?!" His voice was incredulous, the wind loud.

"Sorry … what?"

His eyes narrowed.

She didn't seem to understand.

He spoke slowly as if she was a child. "Do you have any idea how scared we are that you will tear us apart and destroy this family? Do you have any idea how much I love my family? Do you know what I'll do to protect my family?"

The boat rocked. She breathed deeply and spoke to not just the boys. "It's okay, I thought Dad may need some help to be the best dad he can be."

The voice in her head whispered, *Liar.*

"I thought going away for a little while would be good. But maybe Dad doesn't need that. He wants to stay with us, so I'm happy he'll stay and be a good dad. It's okay. We're okay."

They were not okay. But their crying stopped with her reassurances.

He stared at her, concentrating on her words. She shifted her body, forcing herself to look up at him.

Acting gentle, she folded her hands in a trusting, relaxed position.

His eyes blink. His face softened – the sharp edges of his jaw loosening. She kept her eyes on him, keeping the boys in her sight. Now, he was someone else.

"Good. Okay, good. Boys, who wants to go for a swim?" He laughed and pushed them playfully, but just a little too hard, jumping into the water. The boat rocked.

Without a glance in her direction, the boys jump in after him.

SHORT BOAT RIDE ON THE RIVER

Lynn's thoughts …

I honestly thought this man was going to toss his wife overboard. Then I became angry that she was stupid enough to board his boat. In reality, spousal abuse is nothing to joke about. It's a serious issue that many endure. On one side we have the husband or wife that is the abuser, and on the other, we have a spouse who refuses to leave. Why do they stay? Many reasons – money, children, love, fear, the list goes on and on – do they need a reason?

As I read this story, the boat floating on the water reminded me of life and how we must balance in order to survive. When she stood and the boat rocked, the husband threatened to blame her for their potential deaths should the boat flip. That simple statement made me think. How many times has someone said something that made us hesitate or pause or take a step back. Later when we contemplate about the situation, we want to smack ourselves for folding into their fears, their weaknesses, their self-doubts.

Perhaps the rocking of the boat should make us stop and consider how solid the ground beneath our world actually is, and are there any possible ways to make it more stable? Relying on another to make our life whole never works. We have to make ourselves whole first.

The woman in this story obviously wanted to find help for her abusive husband. However, until he wants to fix himself, help will never arrive. Perhaps the motto behind this story is a simple one, we all must be responsible for ourselves first. Unfortunately, when our children are involved, balancing our lives is not always a black or white answer but filled with colors, all colors.

I choose green.

334

Surprise Lessons

Desiree Lovato

I told him he should have believed me.

She didn't toss him in and she wasn't supposed to be there. If she walked away now, no one would know. He would be just another body washed up during the spring thaw. A clueless hiker gone missing. Too bad they cared more about their Northface fashions than basic safety.

A car door slammed and muffled voices signaled other fools who walked this forest. Mostly teenagers. Time to disappear or distract? She looked at where the man no longer struggled. Glossy eyes periodically peeked above the water, before sinking back down.

None of these fools are my problem.

The longer she hesitated, the greater the chance she could be accused of something she didn't do.

Technically.

Technically, she never touched the man. She never sabotaged his path nor influenced his decision to take this one. She simply was the type of woman who never showed fear, and she would not apologize about it either.

She was taking a *clear-your-head-so-you-don't-kill-anyone* hike when a cocky, know-it-all, thrill seeker showed up. They met on the steep grade. He was running down instead of waiting for her to pass.

"Nice etiquette, asshole!" she yelled.

He stumbled before staring at her. "What'd you say?"

She picked up a stick about as long as her arm and repeated her words. "I said … nice etiquette, asshole! You're suppose to give uphill hikers the right of way?"

"Didn't realize there were hiker's police up here." He sneered, stepping closer.

"I suggest we drop it," she replied. "You go your way, I'll go mine." She tightened her grip on the branch

"Oh?!" He took a threatening step. "Or what?"

"Neither of us will want to find out."

"You think you can threaten me and get away with it?" The man dropped his pack, closing the distance.

She grabbed a rock and threw it. It hit just above his eye. He reached up and touched blood. "You bitch!"

After throwing a second rock, she ran. Her lungs and thighs burned as she darted up the hill, trying to reach the bridge. She knew these trails like an old friend from childhood. With a fluidity that felt like flying, she ran until her legs cramped.

What if I miss the turn?

She stopped next to a tree to catch her breath. With no time to consider what to do next, footsteps and a labored breath echoed through her ears.

She ran, keeping the canyon at her side.

It's got to be here somewhere. Once I cross the bridge, I'll lose him on the downhill trek.

She ran along the canyon's rim to the post that pointed to the setting sun.

Almost there.

Confident she was ahead of the stranger, she stepped on the small planks. Standing in the middle of the bridge, she closed her eyes and paused, soaking in the sounds and smells of the rapids thundering below. One of her favorite places.

The man stood at the entrance. "You're not as fast as you think!"

"Stop!" She gripped the rope. "What do you want?"

"An apology, then ... you sail off this bridge."

She took a step back. But for each solid step she took, he took two.

He shook the bridge and stomped his feet.

"Lunatic!" she screamed.

A few steps to the edge, her left foot caught, and she stumbled. Frantically, she clung to the railing that now slid between her fingers. Fleeing was not an option. She shifted to fight mode and kicked at the man.

He lost his footing and fell. His grip held for a measly second before he plunged into the water, gasping for air, and screaming obscenities.

She glanced over the railing and frowned.

What just happened? Why did he attack me like that? What if I hadn't kicked him?

She never had a choice, it was either him or her. After tossing his pack into the water, she stared at the rope he left behind. Picking it up, she sighed. Walking back the way she had come, she remained close to the bank, keeping her eyes on the river.

I wonder if he's dead.

The parking lot was not far. After one last glance, she smiled. His hands periodically flailed above the water. He was still alive.

The fading light made it hard to see, and she didn't want to look, but then again, she did. It was important to know if he would survive, and if she'd have to face him again. Or was he actually dead? Either option was terrible, but facing him would be worse. He could have killed her, and there was nothing she could do but fall in the water.

The man was stuck between several large boulders, and his flailing had stopped. A pale face peeked just above the water, his lips gasping until they fell silent. His eyes were opened wide; dark opals glistening in the moonlight.

"Hey guys, over here!" a voice cut through the night's air

She could disappear into the shadows or report the discovery of a body. It never occurred to her to report the truth. Who'd believe her? Nothing about life ever said she should admit to interacting with a dead man. A sole invitation to a sure indictment. Therefore, she slunk into the darkness.

Watching from the shadows, she waited for the hikers to pass – two boys and two girls. She followed at a distance.

What if they see him?

"Hey, watch this!" the larger boys stated. He threw a rock over the edge, and it splashed in the water.

"That's nothin'," the other boy replied, rolling a larger rock to the edge. "Watch this!"

If they see him, they'll have questions.

"Come on guys, grow up," a feminine voice replied.

"Yeah, let's go already!" another girl yelled.

That's four. At least one would be missed …

She was surprised by the implication of her thinking. The man's rope was no longer in her hands. Instead, she had tied one end to a tree and held the other end loosely.

What the hell am I doing?

"Hold on," the older boy stated, "I got one more."

"Yeah, come over here and watch," the other boy added.

The girls laughed, standing at the canyon's edge. The mini-boulder the boys were rolling to the edge appeared to be twice their size. The girls sat with their legs dangling over the edge, waiting.

"That might take them a while," one of the girls said.

"No, it won't!" grunted a voice in reply.

She stood, listening, growing annoyed. *Why don't they leave already?* She hoped they didn't make her do something she didn't want to do. But the smile that crept to the edges of her lips when she glanced at the rope in her hands conveyed a different thought.

"Don't hurt yourselves," a girl yelled. "It's not worth it."

"But it will be," the boy replied.

She watched as they pushed the stone. She watched as it wobbled into motion. She watched as the girls watched the boys.

What happens when they look into the eddy?

Was the body still there? Would the rock sink it or project it to the surface?

If I get caught ... "Calm. Down," she whispered. "We will not panic. We will work this out."

"How long are we supposed to wait?" a girl asked.

The boys grunted, pushing on the rock.

"We got it!" the other boy yelled.

"Wait!" One of the girls pointed at the water. "What's that?"

"What's what?" the other girl replied, following her gaze.

"That!" her friend stated. "See that spot in the eddy? Someone's down there."

"You're seeing things," the other girl replied, "I'll bet and —"

A hand rose to the top of the water, flopping with the current, before sinking back under. In this light, it might have looked like the man was still fighting for his life.

"We're almost there!" a boy yelled.

Their boulder had gained momentum and now they were simply guiding it to the edge.

"Wait!" a girl screamed.

"Stop! There's someone in the water!" the other one said.

Stopping the rock proved to be more difficult than getting it to roll. The boys struggled to slow it down.

"Stop it!" the girls screamed.

"We're trying!" the boys replied.

She watched from the shadows, walking past the hikers, allowing the rope to skim the ground. *It shouldn't be this easy.*

The kids worked as one in trying to stop the rock before it soared over the edge. If she pulled the rope at the right time, it should send all four into the river.

"They deserve it," she whispered.

Shoes scuffled in the dirt and their shouts of encouragement filled the air. "We got this, guys. It's slowing down."

The darkness had settled over the evening. The hikers were so close to the edge. Fixing her eyes on the shadow of the rolling rock, she pulled with all her might.

The rope hit the kids. Their yelps of surprise sounded strangely satisfying. She ran to the edge, pulling the rope tighter.

It shouldn't be this easy.

The rope grew slack as several splashes echoed through the darkness. She sighed. The hikers struggled in the water, and she wished she could stay and watch.

That kind of thinking is what got you involved in the first place. "No … it was that asshat thinking he could intimidate me. The only thing I fear is myself. I told him neither of us wanted to know what would happen. It's not my fault."

And the kids? her conscience asked.

She came to the canyon for a clear-your-head-so-you-don't-kill-everyone hike, but she didn't get that. Instead, that bastard killed her Zen.

She stepped closer to the edge.

Can't leave any evidence.

She listened, hearing only the comfort of the rapids. Peering over, several glassy eyes glared back. No one gasped or flailed. They just floated, making circles in the eddy.

That's what they get.

She untied the rope from the tree and curled it around her arm.

"If no one knows, then it didn't happen."

She turned on the car's radio and sang on the drive home.

342

SURPRISE LESSONS

I guess crazy, homicidal people are not afraid of much. That is why they believe they can get away with doing things, things they should not be doing. Why do people murder? Mental health issues? Relationship problems?

As Aemilius Papinianus once said, "It is easier to commit murder than to justify it."

And our main character had no problems committing murder, but she definitely had excuses as to why. An excuse will often shift our basis of reasoning from a threatening situation to a safer one. When we make an excuse, we are doing so because of either fear, an indecision, or a lack of responsibility.

If this is true, then what was the motive for our main, unnamed character? Stress from a hard day at work? The fear of her own death or punishment? Making a poor decision?

The human psyche is something so many authors have attempted to write about. Why we do what we do is difficult to explain. Even those who commit murder often times have no explanation. It was simply something that happened.

Is a premeditated murder worse than one from impulse? The law believes so. The ancient law, *thou shalt not kill,* not only focuses on the actual taking of a life but extends to the heart and inner workings of the person. Did you know that anger, insult, and name-calling are also violations of that *shall not kill* law? Then the question pops up, is murder ever justified?

In the end, we can never hide from our conscience. Our thoughts and memories will follow us no matter where we try to hide. Isn't that how a lie detector works?

344

the DIVE

W. Rogers

"Come on Chris, you can do it," the coach yelled. "Just grit your teeth and dive in. The board's not that high. You can't get hurt."

"Yeah, there's nothing to it." His best friend, Stan, stared up at him from the edge of the pool.

Chris clung to the railing, glaring down at the water.

"He'll do it this time," a girl said.

"Uh-uh," a boy stated, "look how he's walking."

Chris released his grip, taking a few short steps. He faced the pool, his toes at the board's edge. The grit under his feet felt sharp and threatening, as if warning him. The other boys in line remained quiet – probably waiting for the splash of success. Chris glanced past his feet and into the water.

From poolside, Stan and the others watched as the color drained from Chris' face. His eyes wide and his mouth open. Shaking and feeling weak, he retreated to the ladder. The boys in line groaned. After several tries, Chris had yet to take his first splash.

The class knew him as *No-Dive Johnson* or *Sissy Chrissy*.

It was the end of October – too cold to swim outside. Therefore, the inside pool gave little to the imagination of what hid beneath. Classes at the school's pool was fun, fun until the coach introduced diving.

"What's wrong with me?" Chris asked himself.

Stan often asked the same question as they walked home together. "Chris, what is it with you and this diving thing? You've been up there about nine times. Each time you act weird before chickening out. The guys are talking about this ... uh ... situation at school."

"I know. I hear it all the time. 'Better not use the water fountain, Johnson. You might drown.' I think the girls and the teachers are starting to look at me funny."

"Put a stop to it and take your dive. I've been at your summer place enough times to know you're not afraid of the water."

"'Course I'm not afraid of the water," Chris replied.

He thought of the happier days at his family's beach cottage and how he became a strong swimmer. On calm mornings, he'd swim out to the point in a rhythmic crawl, returning with leisurely backstrokes. On windy days, he'd throw himself into the swollen waves as they crashed against the sand bars. He'd allow the undertow to drag him under until his lungs begged for the surface.

"And your dad ..." Stan continued, "... he always says you're half fish and fearless."

Chris kicked at something. "I think I'm going crazy."

"Tell me something I don't know." Stan smiled.

Chris stopped and sighed. "If I tell you something, you gotta promise not to tell the others, especially, not the coach."

"Okay."

"For real," Chris stated, "tell nobody."

Stan placed his arm around Chris' shoulder. "If you want me to keep a secret, I promise on my grandfather's grave not to breathe a word."

"Don't say that!"

"Say what?"

"That stuff about the grave," Chris replied.

Stan eyed his friend. "What's up? You used to be Mr. Water. Now you're afraid of a nothing dive in a pool. Now, I can't say the word *grave* a week before Halloween? What's going on with you?"

"I'm not afraid of the water ... I'm afraid of what's *in* the water."

"Huh?"

Chris took a deep breath, but his voice felt weak. "At the bottom."

"Bottom, bottom of what?"

"When I'm standing on the board, I look into the water and below me ... is a ... body ... a corpse ... lying on its back ... face up. Some of the face is rotting ... waving in the water." Chris swallowed. "And its eyes ... they're bulging ... staring right through me. Then its arms rise up as if to ... catch me or ..." – he shuddered – "... welcome me."

Stan sighed. "That's a little weird."

"I know, right?"

"Maybe if you told the guidance counselor?"

"What for? She'd think I was having trouble at school or that something was wrong at home. What's wrong is that *thing* I see at the bottom."

"Maybe you've got a brain tumor and it's making you see things that's not there. Maybe you should see a doctor."

"Yeah, maybe."

The following week, swim class was held early – a few of the boys wanted to be home on time for Halloween.

"Chris," Stan said, "I've been thinking about what you told me. I heard that if people fear something so much they start to see things that aren't there."

Chris sighed. "I'm not afraid of diving. I'm afraid of what's under the water."

"But if this corpse ... or zombie ... or whatever ... is there, don't you think that the rest of us would see?"

"I don't know why no one else can see it. All I know is that when I step to the end of the board and look down, there it is, reaching out with those bony fingers."

Stan shook his head. "Tell yah what, I'll look when I'm up there."

"Thanks."

Chris and Stan entered the locker room.

"You know Johnson ..." a boy yelled out, "... that toilet is like a little swimming pool. Better not stand in front of it. You might drown!"

"Yeah," another said. "Or sit on it."

"Shut up," Chris yelled.

"Knock it off, you guys," Stan replied. "He has a reason for not diving."

"Yeah," a boy stated. "Chicken reasons."

The boys laughed as they aimed for the pool.

The class swam and wrestled until the coach blew his whistle.

"Okay, people ..." the coach yelled, "... let's line up for diving practice."

The boys mimicked bodybuilders with threatening gestures like WWE wrestlers as they waited for their turn to dive.

Chris remained silent.

"Chris, over here," the coach yelled.

Chris felt all eyes land on him as he walked up to the coach.

"Here it comes," a boy yelled. "Here's where coach tries to talk Johnson into diving."

THE DIVE

"Chris," the coach whispered, "tell me why you won't dive. Maybe I can help."

Chris said nothing.

Coach sighed. "Look, when you get out there, curl your toes over the edge. Raise your arms, tuck down your head, and just fall over. Break through the water with your hands and you won't get hurt."

Chris watched the coach's lips move but could only think of the thing at the bottom. What if he kept his eyes closed? Then he wouldn't see the thing at the bottom.

"Okay, coach. I'll give it a try."

Chris stepped up to the back of the line and the coach blew his whistle.

"What'd he do? Offer a million to dive?" a boy asked.

"That wouldn't be enough," another replied.

The others laughed.

"Remember to swim away from the diving area when you surface, or the next diver will hit you. We don't want any casualties." Coach whistled for the first diver.

In turn, each boy stepped onto the board and walked to the end. The confident divers sprung off the board, arced, then straightened before hitting the water. Others walked up, curled their toes around the end, bent their knees, and fell forward. One by one, the divers surfaced, swam to the pool's edge, and climbed out.

Stan was next, then Chris.

"Tonight's the night, Chris," Stan whispered. "You can do this."

Stan reached the end of the board and glanced back at his friend. He peered into the water and shrugged. Two hops and he sprang off with his arms above his head. He curved down and sliced the water before surfacing with a wave.

It was Chris's turn.

The boys stopped joking and shoving. They were watching and waiting. Chris climbed up the ladder, stepping onto the board. The school's ventilators droned like low notes on a church's organ. Stepping up to the end, his heart hammered and his blood pulsed through his ears.

"Tonight, I'll dive," Chris whispered. "Tonight, I'll dive."

In the seats at the pool's deep end, Chris' father sat, smiling and waving. He had arrived early to give the boys a ride home.

Chris half returned his father's wave as his throat tightened. *No choice now. I can't let Dad see me chicken out. It's for the best. I've got to face this.*

Sensing Chris' determination, the boys in line yelled.

"Come on, Johnson!"

"Go for it!"

"Let's go, Chris, you can do it," Stan yelled.

"Attaboy," the coach hollered. "Head down. Arms out."

Chris barely heard the coach telling him to lean forward.

The boys screamed out in unison. "Big dive, big dive!"

Chris closed his eyes, refusing to look in the water. He refused to acknowledge the corpse that waited for him at the bottom of the pool. He refused his fears. He refused to back down. He flexed his legs and pushed off. He pointed his toes. He extended his arms. He straightened his arched back. He tucked his head. He aimed his hands at the water. He felt the surface separate. He felt his body slide into the wetness. He opened his eyes.

"He did it!" a voice yelled.

"Nice dive!" another screamed.

"All right!" Coach hollered.

Stan whistled and waited to help his friend out of the water.

The voices quieted.

"Where is he?" Stan yelled.

THE DIVE

The class looked into the water from the pool's edge. They saw nothing.

Then someone screamed. "There he is. On the bottom!"

Chris' dad darted from his seat.

The coach dove in.

Chris's face was as cold and as white as the tiles he laid on.

"Nooo!" His father's cries echoed through the air.

Coach pushed on Chris' chest, expelling water.

Stan did not stare at his friend but at the corpse that floated toward him. The white hair that stuck out. The pallid face that framed the bulging, red eyes. The bared, yellow teeth inside a mouth that was pulled taut. Stan screamed as the creature splayed its boney fingers on outstretched arms, seemingly to welcome someone or something into its darkest lair.

Lynn's thoughts …

What are some of the famous quotes on fear?

"The fears we don't face become our limits?" – *Robin Sharma*

"Too many of us are not living our dreams because we are living our fears." – *Les Brown*

"Our fears establish the limits of our life." *Not sure who said this one.*

But is not fear something that is there to help protect and warn? Does not our inner self talk to us through our fears? Perhaps Chris knew deep inside that if he dove into that water his body would not withstand the pressure, and he would die. Could his fear have manifested as an evil creature waiting to devour him?

They say that fear often presents itself in many forms and that healthy fear keeps us safe. They call healthy fear an intuition. But as real fear is based on reality, an illogical fear is manifested as a phobia.

So what is the difference between the a real fear and a fake one? Is there a difference? Fear of the dark? They often say, there is nothing to fear in the dark, but they are wrong. In a dark room, there may be furniture to trip over or a wall to run into. In a dark forest, there are wild animals. Therefore, is fear of the dark real or fake?

Spiders? Spiders do bite. Therefore, why not fear spiders? Snakes, the same thing. They bite.

Chris, our character, is not afraid of the water or the dive. He fears the ramification; the result or the evil creature lurking at the bottom. The creature that welcomes him into its arms.

Were Chris' fears real or fantasy? I would argue, real.

Weight of Her Skin

Gemma Davidson

The sky was blue, a simple, pure blue. White clouds streaked, casting shadows across the mountains. Patches of snow glittered under the sunshine. Spring had dripped into the valley, and the river now moaned with the season's arrival. Wildflowers were slowly peeking out from under the rotting leaves.

Prudence stared at her boots. They were relatively new – three years. Her toes rubbed against the worn hide and fresh mud colored the edges. Her hem should have hidden the ugly things, but she had grown slightly; her shoulder straps were now uncomfortable against her chest.

Prudence felt like a prisoner as her shoes crunched in the sludge, the cold seeping through the leather. The little yard was kept somewhat square by a tilted picket fence, that trudged along the winding river. Shoving her hands deeply into her pockets, the seams tore, giving her something to thread between her fingers. She glanced at the path and paused. She had walked too far without realizing it. She was now at the bridge.

It was an addition to her mountain path, made during her great-grandfather's boyhood. Stretching twenty feet or so, it suspended over a forty-foot drop. The metal frame, black under the afternoon sun, soaked in the light. The planks, made from wood, now seeped to the core with aged dew. Two wrist-thick ropes bound the sides to steady the casual visitor, not that anyone ever crossed it. People died on the other side of this bridge. Stories of *Empty Skins* people often found like a discarded fur left atop the white snow.

She rubbed her arms. Her skin was soft and giving. How hard would it be to remove someone's skin? Any rough surface could do that. But her heart was safe.

"Prudence!" It was Grace, her younger sister.

She sighed. *Time to return home.*

Never moving forward, it was always time to go back. Stuck in the same day, the same place, the same eternity. She would never escape this place.

What if I didn't go back?

She turned the idea through her mind. Somehow, the thought seemed cold and austere. Too distant to consider, but a certain part of her felt warm, soft. As if perhaps the idea could become real. Prudence could wrap herself inside her fantasy of escape. But where would she go?

At the end of the bridge, the breeze blew with a freshened renewal. *What if ...?* Her eyes searched the path before her. Would she be happier over there?

A screech and birds burst from the trees, flapping, escaping. They stretched and flew into the forest. Their cries echoed as the distance grew.

"Prudence!" Grace called out her name again.

She sighed and took two steps. Prudence couldn't see everything that was on the other side of the deep valley. Not from where she stood.

Grace remained quiet, her breath sending puffs of steam into the cool air. Her eyes brightened and her chest heaved. She grabbed Prudence's arm. "Come on. Dinner's waiting!"

Prudence yanked her arm away, tears pooling in her eyes. Trudging along the path to home, she closed her eyes, listening to her feet slap against the earth.

The small, two-room cabin was shared by her family of ten. She stared at the table and shrugged. The ancient wood was filled with deep scratched, gouges in the beautiful oak finish. It was probably once an impressive tree but now it was dead. The family had gathered, demanding, reaching, grasping.

Without a word, Prudence sat.

Her mother served her portion, potatoes glistening with fat and a slice of rabbit. Her mother cleared her throat.

Prudence stared at her plate.

"Prudence?" her father whispered. "Anything wrong?"

Prudence left the table and hurried out the door. She'd be whipped later for her quick retreat. Her feet stomped as she hurried. Taking a deep breath, her chest bounded. Holding back a scream of frustration, Prudence set her mind on the destination.

The bridge remained quiet just as before.

Prudence rested on her hip, staring at the trees on the other side. Shadows waved as if blown by an unfelt wind. The snow glistened, pure and untraveled – beautiful.

No monsters had walked the other side. Nothing had stomped and raged through the woods. If there was anything on the other side, what would it be? A monster would have crossed the bridge by now and attacked her family. If there was anything out there, it would have come for them in the night. But nothing was there just pathetic stories.

A shadow peered out from behind a tree. It wavered before fading into the darkness.

She sat up. Most were afraid of shadows, but not her. They were nothing more than dark *things* in the corners of the world. Were monsters real? Could she affect them? She definitely couldn't change them. Were these creatures of the shadows flighty and free? If monsters were over there, what would they eat – her?

If she only knew what was at the end of that bridge.

Prudence often found herself at the bridge, peering into the forest on the other side. No matter how bright the sun or the moon was, the other side was always hidden in shadows. Nothing to confirm that something wasn't just out of sight. Monsters didn't hide from people, people hid from people. Therefore, it couldn't be a monster. Yet, the shadows were too far away to be sure.

The bridge swayed as she stepped on it. It moaned as the river roared from below. She stopped halfway across, glancing over the railing. The water crashed and broke against the rocks, frothing with violence. The river would have kept her away from the other side at one time. But not today.

She stared at her feet. Her toes were just an inch below her hem. She felt heavy, and with a sigh, she walked toward home. She would take her heavy clothing off at home. Then again, why not take them off now?

Images of her mother's displeasure vaguely formed in her mind, but she blinked those images away. Her heart raced as she first removed the scarf, her hat, and coat. The petticoat made of her grandmother's patchwork quilt felt as scratchy as her woolen nightgown. She stood clothed only in her thin cotton shift that matched the color of her skin. The light of the moon and the frigid air caressed and soothed the stinging lashes from her father's switch. Her heart thudded inside her chest, and she gasped. Still too many layers.

A wolf howled from somewhere near her side. She grabbed her clothes and ran down the path to home. Some *thing* followed, but her panic kept her inches ahead. Cool air filled her lungs as the ground cut against her bare feet. She stood at the entrance of the garden and held her breath.

A sound, somewhat familiar echoed through her ears. The creature had returned, rushing down the path and across the bridge.

Prudence stared at the forest. She understood now what she wanted, and it was separate from this madness, this pain. What she wanted was blessed and beautiful. The creature wanted *her* to join *it* inside the shadows. It longed for her and she longed for it. Her soul calmed as she collapsed on the doorstep.

The night finally engulfed the mountains, and after staring at the dark rafters for hours, she finally rolled out from under the covers. She stripped the layers, losing everything but the shift. It was the only thing that felt light and free.

No noise escaped her feet as she crept across the cabin, lifted the latch, and ran to the bridge. She knew the way – every stone and bump. The river was deafening, and the bridge remained unreal. Her bare feet stepped onto the cold wooden planks that creaked and moaned.

Prudence shrieked.

A weighted hand just crushed her aching soul. An iron hand clasped around her arm. She stared into Grace's terrified eyes. Her sister clung to her, breath escaping through steaming clouds.

"Prudence," she whispered, "what are you doing? You'll freeze to death. Your lips are blue."

Prudence stared at her sister as if seeing a ghost, a long-forgotten reality. Her sister's hands felt heavy, weighing her down. Prudence's eyes glinted with the moonlight and her heart filled with hate. She would never go back.

Grace's eyes widened as her breath caught. Prudence sighed as her sister toppled over the edge; the river absorbing any sound she may have made on the way down. Was she free now too? But Grace would never have chosen the freedom Prudence yearned for. She was heavy and that was why she fell. It took only a little courage and push for Prudence to prove it.

Prudence took a step, catching the swinging rope. She fell to her knees, feeling light. The snow cracked as she walked off the other side of the bridge and into the vast unknown. She stared at the shadows where the creature stood, waiting. It was not a monster, but a teacher and a friend. It would show her how to live, how to be free.

"I've come," she whispered.

Her voice faded as if inhaled. The shadow guided her deeper into the forest. She followed. Snow crunched under her bare feet. The creature left no tracks for her to follow. She wanted to walk like that too – light and weightless.

Prudence stepped into a vast meadow. The creature shuffled and the tall trees circled her creating a thickening blackness, but they remained silent. Her breath invaded her eyes in slow streams of white. Her stance made her skin feel hot and coarse.

Seconds ticked.

Her breath froze as she held up her hands. "Free me!"

A shadow stepped from the darkness, reaching for her. The shape was somewhat familiar. Their fingers touched and she stiffened. They clasped hands and she relaxed. The shadow was gentle, inviting. She wondered how long its arms must be that she could not see its body. The gentle fingers caressed her neck, her face, petting her. She couldn't see as it cut the strings that held her together.

Ecstasy filled her soul as she experienced a new freedom. No cold, no weight, no pain. They were taking it all away. She glanced up and dozens of hands now slid from the darkness, shining with scissor-like claws. The moonlight flashed against the steely edges. Prudence was suspended in the moment not really seeing everything.

Her scream split the silence ... *SNIP!*

Lynn's thoughts …

A little on the sensual side of a young teen's mind. All young girls and perhaps boys fantasize about something like this; under the control of someone or something strong and powerful. But the question is, was the girl dreaming or was it reality? I would argue – dream.

Fear of the unknown is both intriguing and scary. Oh to walk boldly into that dark room or behind that tree or into the night's shadows, alone and brave with only a pounding heart as protection. Why do we do such things?

I would say that this piece is about moving from childhood and into womanhood. Stepping into the unknown is thrilling and transformative and often helps us to grow. For Prudence to leave the safety of her family and escape into the darkness was a way for her to explore her sexuality.

The bridge could represent that forbidden path to adulthood; a fear every woman experiences. The death of her sister could represent letting go of the past and moving forward; leaving her childhood behind. The shadows could represent young love and a first experience. What if the shadow was actually the boy next door? Interesting thought.

If the story was nothing more than a dream, then my analogy would still fit. If it was her reality, then this child would be best suited inside the dark shadows living with the hidden monsters.

All parents try to guide their children into adulthood. There are so many pitfalls and dangerous paths to choose from. However, as parents, we must be brave and stand back, allowing our children to select their own way. And – if we imparted our wisdom wisely, they should know which path to take and which path to avoid.

Welcome to the Neighborhood

Carol O. Mason

EDNA

It's a shame it came to this, and I feel rather bad about it. But some people just don't see things the right way. I'm well-known in this neighborhood, and I believe, loved by most. I tried my hardest to be nice, friendly, and helpful, but did they appreciate it?

No.

My name is Edna. I was born and raised in Alabama and attended college at the local university, where I met my husband, Bob. My life was pretty wonderful; high school prom queen, homecoming queen in college, belonged to the best sorority on campus, and of course, dated and married the *big man on campus.* Guess one could say I was the quintessential Southern Belle. My family treated me like a princess, and I always believed everyone else would do the same. A few have called me spoiled, pushy, or a bitch (*so crude*), but they don't know the real me. I love people and always try to do good things.

Although I love the South and miss the genteel hospitality of the region, Bob and I moved to the East Coast shortly after marriage. A lucrative job was just too good to pass up. We never had any children, and after forty wonderful years, Bob passed away. Now, I'm alone.

I've lived in this lovely neighborhood for close to twenty years. A family-oriented neighborhood with quiet streets, mature trees, and manicured lawns. I remember a certain day, the day that Sean and Kayla Murphy moved in across the street. I was excited about the new neighbors, especially after the sudden deaths of the previous owners.

"What an attractive young couple." I watched the moving company through my front window. "I'll have to welcome them personally to the neighborhood."

It always fell on me to keep an eye on things. I'm home most of the time. It was the least I could do for my neighbors.

I spent the morning making one of my delicious casseroles for the new neighbors. Moving was such a bother, and they probably wouldn't have time to cook. At six that afternoon, I knocked on their front door. When she opened the door, I sighed. I underestimated Kayla's beauty. Up close, she was stunning, glossy dark hair, emerald green eyes, and a lithe, fit figure.

"Hi, I'm Edna. I live across the street. Welcome to the neighborhood. I know what a hassle moving is, so I brought y'all some dinner."

"That's so nice of you," Kayla replied. "I'm Kayla. Come on in for a moment and meet my husband."

Sean was busy unpacking kitchen stuff. Kayla introduced us and I assessed that Sean was every bit as attractive as his wife. Kayla was a banking executive and Sean was a doctor. An improvement for our neighborhood. We need more successful professionals around here. I must take them under my wing and introduce them to the others. They could be the children I never had.

The following week, Kayla and Sean left for work. Like most people, they had a pretty regular routine, left the house around seven and returned around six or so. People were such creatures of habit. I called Thursday evening to ask if I might bring dinner over on Friday, seeing how they were tired after a long week.

"Oh, don't go to any trouble," Kayla replied. "We will manage."

"It's no trouble. I have to fix my own and I'll just make a little extra for you two."

Kayla acquiesced and the next day I prepared a delicious dinner. When I took it over, I had hoped to be invited in. Kayla made it clear that she wasn't prepared to have company. I was somewhat disappointed but decided not to push it. After all, it was just their first week in their new house.

Sunday, I made a batch of blueberry muffins. It was late in the morning, but Sean answered, looking sleepy and rumpled.

"My goodness, Sean … it's practically noon. Don't you think it's time to be up and about?"

Sean squinted through bleary eyes and mumbled, "Thank you, but please don't come over so early."

Honestly, some people just don't know how to be gracious. His manners could stand some improvement.

The Friday night dinners and Sunday morning muffins soon became a routine. I made the sacrifice of waiting until ten to take the muffins over. I invited Sean and Kayla for dinner several times, and they accepted once. They brought what I believed to be an expensive bottle of wine, and I don't approve of drinking. However, they indulged and seemed to enjoy it. I'm waiting for a reciprocal invitation, but they haven't extended one yet.

KAYLA

Sean and I love our new house and neighborhood. We've been married for two years, and although our parents keep asking when we're going to have a baby, Sean and I are too busy to take on the commitment. We love having our weekends free.

We've been gradually meeting our neighbors and most are great. The one across the street, Edna, is a nice lady but she can be a bit much. We met her the first day when she brought over a casserole. I thought it was a considerate thing to do and believed she'd be a good neighbor. Edna apparently doesn't have family, and we never see visitors at her house. I suspect she's lonely and eager for company.

She invited us for dinner, which was a nice evening. Although, she seemed to disapprove of the wine. We couldn't allow good wine to go to waste, so we drank it. I know we should pay her back and have her to our house, but something's holding us back. I'm concerned we might start something we would regret.

She offers to do errands for us, but I don't wish to feel as if I owe her anything. I don't usually become too close to the neighbors. I even caught Edna looking through our windows, and once, she walked right in saying, *'family shouldn't have to knock.'*

I came home from work and had the feeling someone had been in our house. A few things were out of place, although nothing was missing. It left me with an odd feeling. Sean said I was overreacting, but I changed the locks and found a better hiding place for the spare key.

SEAN

Kayla and I are happier than we've ever been. We have great careers and a beautiful home. It was priced just right. The former owners had died in the house and that made potential buyers hesitate. Didn't bother us.

We haven't met all of our neighbors, but we did meet Edna. It was nice of her to bring us dinner. But she seemed to think she can drop by anytime. She seemed unaware that she's intruding on our privacy. When Kayla mentioned we should reciprocate, I said *no way*. I don't want to spend an entire evening with just Edna again. She asked personal questions and seemed offended when we didn't answer.

Kayla insisted someone was in our house while we were at work. She noticed a few things were not in their usual spots. I blew it off, thinking maybe she had moved the things herself. But she insisted on changing the locks. If that makes her feel more secure, it was worth it.

KAYLA

Sean and I love to entertain family and friends. We had a housewarming, and it was wonderful. Everyone had a good time, although Edna acted a bit off. Maybe someone said something to her. I don't know what it could've been and I haven't asked.

We're planning a barbecue for our friends whom we haven't seen in a while. It will be so good to see them again.

SEAN

Kayla and I hosted a housewarming. It was great to meet our neighbors and see our old friends. As a doctor, I tend to notice things that others might not. I couldn't help feeling that something was bothering Edna. She didn't mingle even though we went out of our way to introduce her to everyone. The other neighbors, who presumably she already knew, didn't visit with her. They'd give her a polite hello before finding an excuse to wander off. People can sometimes be shy at large parties, but I know Edna is not shy.

Something is bothering me. I have patients diagnosed as psychopathic. I see elements of that in Edna. I could be wrong, psychiatry isn't my thing. She's not bat-shit crazy, but something isn't quite right. Oh well, she's just a neighbor.

Shortly after the housewarming, Kayla and I had a barbecue for our friends. Everyone enjoyed themselves. Kayla said Edna was offended she wasn't invited.

EDNA

My relationship with my new neighbors is not going the way I had hoped. Seemed to start out okay, but they've not responded as I envisioned. I wanted us to be a little family, but they are cold and distant. They haven't invited me for dinner, even though I served a lovely one. When I take over my casseroles and muffins, they never invite me in. My social skills are superb, and people enjoy my company, so that can't be the problem.

They invited me to their housewarming. I was looking forward to it, but it turned out to be a huge disappointment. It was quite rude that Kayla and Sean weren't more attentive toward me.

The final straw was when they had a barbecue to which I was not invited. The people arrived and I'd be lying if I said I wasn't hurt and a little jealous. When I commented to Kayla that my invitation must have gotten lost in the mail, she explained that it was just for their close friends.

I'm not one to give up easily, but it's becoming clear this relationship will never develop as I planned. I had such a close, loving family when I was growing up, but the concept of family doesn't seem to matter much to people. I treated Kayla and Sean as I would my own children. But they choose not to be a part of my life.

I wish to be a mother figure to them. But this situation is too one-sided. Our arrangement is intolerable. I will just have to make Kayla and Sean one of my extra special casseroles just like I did for my husband, Bob, when his illness became unbearable. And … as I also did for the ungrateful neighbors who lived in that house before Kayla and Sean.

It will contain that exotic seasoning, one not featured on cooking shows. I deserve to have a family that appreciates me, and the time has come to move on. I hope that the next family across the street will agree about the importance of a close-knit and loving family. I hope they can appreciate me and what a great addition to their family I will be.

"Is that asking too much?"

WELCOME TO THE NEIGHBORHOOD

Lynn's thoughts …

The horrible neighbor problem. Familicide is a type of murder where an individual kills family members, most often children, spouses, siblings, or parents. How frightening is that? Did you know that in half the cases, the killer eventually kills themselves? But I don't believe Edna will kill herself any time soon. If only the parents are killed, then it's referred to as a *parricide*. When all family members are killed, the crime is referred to as *family annihilation.*

So what was Edna doing? A little of each?

People become clingy for a number of reasons – anxieties, insecurities, lack of attention and reassurance, unusual attachment style, fear of being alone, and the fear of being abandoned. Even childhood trauma can cause clinginess.

Poor Edna has a little of all of these issues. The thought of a stranger intruding on our lives would indeed be quite scary. After all, how would we rid ourselves of such an individual? Especially if they lived across the street? Almost reminds me of the neighborhood kid who that rings our doorbell at seven in the morning on a Saturday.

Our homes are our sanctuary, and for anyone to intrude, is indeed a lingering fear for most. Why do some believe it is okay to ask personal questions of others? Then again, sometimes when someone gives a gift, they expect something in return. When I give a gift, I expect nothing. I do not even need a *thank you.* The thought and joy of sharing is quite enough for me.

Mental illness seems to be in style these days. Many search the internet for just the right one to mimic. Which, unfortunately, lessens the disorder for those who actually suffer from it. But then again, those who mimic a syndrome are probably mentally ill too. They just don't realize it yet.

Asphodel Road

Page 9

Jon Pierre Carter

For years and during his spare time, Jon has written in the sci-fi/fantasy realm, while dabbling in horror and crime thrillers. He spent ten years as a freelance writer/reporter, contributing to media companies, various businesses, and news publications. His freelance work covered domestic and international politics, including lighter topics such as music reviews, pop culture, and historical events. His academic background is in world history, English literature, and philosophy – all of which he uses as inspiration to tell stories.

Jon currently lives in Atlanta and works to support a demanding but loveable rottweiler mix that routinely prowls for treats and new toys.

BIOGRAPHIES

Michael A. Wexler

Ata Nor

Page 27

Michael was born and raised in Philadelphia. An accomplished guitarist, he's had an exciting and enriching musical youth, privileged to work alongside Jimi Hendrix, Ike and Tina Turner, Chuck Berry, and others. Placing his musical skills aside, Michael now tackles writing. *Officer Down* is his debut novel; a psychological thriller that explores the heart and mind of an inner-city cop. He is currently working on the sequel which is expected to be released in 2025.

BIOGRAPHIES

The Black-Eyed Kids

Page 41

Nicole Duffeck

Nicole is a Wisconsin native, recently transplanted to Georgia where she lives with her family and too many dogs. Nicole works in the Medicare department of a large insurance company where she helps the most vulnerable members of the population remain healthy and safe. In her free time, she enjoys writing (obviously), reading, kayaking, and playing pickleball. Nicole owes her belief in the paranormal to an overactive imagination and several personal experiences.

BIOGRAPHIES

Marcus Hysmith

Bloody Mary

Page 51

Marcus Hysmith is a wild and crazy artist who loves to write, paint, act, and perform comedy. His writing is primarily in the supernatural and horror genres, but almost always has a comic edge. He's a former United States Marine who now lives in Austin, Texas.

Brightmore

Page 61

Onyx Rebel

Onyx Rebel has always been a lover of books. But it wasn't until adulthood that she believed she could be like her heroes and write something great.

Reading has always been her favorite escape, but writing has become her therapy. This is Onyx's second year in Indignor House's competition and she's so excited that she'll again be published. According to Onyx, "Writing in this competition has given me the confidence to start writing a novel."

Hopefully, you will be reading more from her soon.

BIOGRAPHIES

BuckEye

Page 69

Roger Guffey

Roger taught mathematics in high school and college in Lexington, Kentucky. His first collection of short stories, *The People Up the Holler*, delves into the lives of the people from his rural community. His second book, *When I Was My Father's Son*, discusses his relationship with his father.

In 2020, one of his short stories was shortlisted in the Fresher Fiction Writing Contest. His second collection, *Stories from the Porch*, tells more about the people in Wayne County, Kentucky.

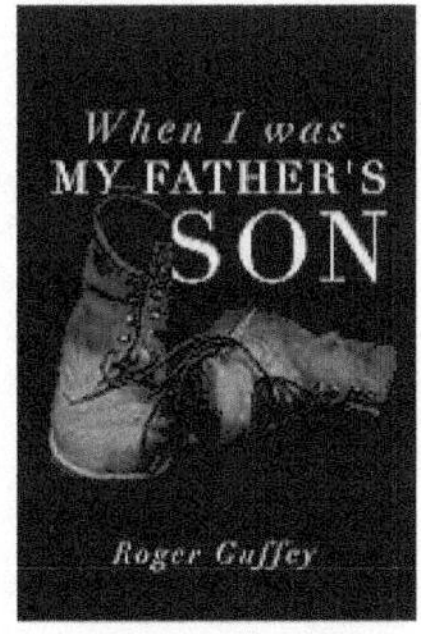

BIOGRAPHIES

Kyle Connor

Child of the Night

Page 77

Kyle hails from Kenner Brah Louisiana. Originally a big wimp about all the scary stuff, he flipped his fear into empowerment by taking control of the narrative – he started writing horror. Nowadays, when he isn't indoctrinating his daughter with Vincent Price movies, he listens to dark ambient music as he falls asleep in hopes of inducing his next nightmare. After all, they're good for his art.

BIOGRAPHIES

Nicholas A. Tseffos

Choices

Page 85

Nicholas spent twenty-five years as a technology executive, and his ability to incorporate high-tech concepts and products into writing seemed second nature. His short stories were published by The <u>Mill</u>, <u>FSM</u>, and the 2022, <u>Indignor House Anthology</u>. He's a member of the International Thriller Writers Association and attended numerous conferences, participating in Craftfest, Pitchfest, and various Master Classes. He studied at the *Loft* in Minneapolis with author Téa Obreht, the Chippewa Valley Writers Guild with Nickolas Butler, and with Steven James at ThrillerFest. He's a member of ITW's THRILLER-TIQUE program.

BIOGRAPHIES

The Coffin Club

Page 103

P. K. Granger

A lifetime of reading mysteries led her to write short fiction. Sharing compelling mysteries with insight into life and providing an enjoyable break in a reader's daily routine was her goal. She felt successful when able to include a touch of humor.

P. K. Granger's career began as a hospital laboratory medical technologist which moved her into healthcare administration. In those riveting days amongst fascinating people, she carried her half-completed stories. Now, she focuses on sharing complete fictional stories. Previous writing awards included the 2021 Writer's Digest writing competition.

P. K and her husband live in western North Carolina, although Texas will always be her home. They also treasure their years in Oregon and the Midwest. Outdoors, gardening, traveling, critters, and cooking are among her favorite hobbies.

BIOGRAPHIES

The Curious Case
of Joseph Nessen

Page 123

Georgie Svrcek

Georgie Svrcek wrote fiction from a very young age; first attempting a novel at age nine. Obviously, the book never panned out, but she continues to write. Her comedic poem, '*A Passage from the Personal Diary of Eroticles of Lesbos,*' won the 2022, Candace Carlucci Backus prize. In 2024, her short story '*Lone Star,*' won the Denise Marcil Prize for fiction. Also in 2024, '*Transparency*' was shortlisted for the Letter Review Prize for Short Fiction.

She's an aspiring playwright, having written several 10-minute and one-act plays. Her historical drama 'Demonized' was selected for a workshop production at Skidmore College, where she's seeking a bachelors in Theatre with a minor in Creative Writing.

BIOGRAPHIES

Dead Rat

Page 135

Linda Balboni

Linda resides in a comfortable suburb outside of Boston, Massachusetts, is married, and the proud mother of a grown son and daughter. She studied writing and art at Dean College but enjoyed writing stories and poetry for most of her life. She's humbled to have a few poems included in chapbooks and online magazines and feels the happiest when she is creative. She loves to paint and draw, especially pastel portraits and landscapes, and appreciates photography, music, and the beauty of nature.

BIOGRAPHIES

Dem Bones

Page 145

Michael G. Whitfield

Michael writes for *Reynoldsburg Magazine;* his hometown of Reynoldsburg, Ohio (*the birthplace of the tomato*). *Finder's Fee* in <u>House of Secrets</u>, a short story, was published in 2023 in an anthology from the Ohio Writer's Association. *Morning Star*, another short story, was published in 2024 and can be found in <u>Untold Stories</u>, a fiction anthology from the Dublin (Ohio) Writer's Group.

Michael holds a master's degree in journalism and education and writes fictional short stories. Currently, he is revising a cozy mystery novel for publication featuring Morgan Stern, a spiritually conflicted insurance investigator.

Having written several children's books and stories, Michael continues to submit his work to various writing contests and magazines.

https://reynoldsburgmagazine.com

https://www.ohiowriters.org

BIOGRAPHIES

Detective Yazmin

Page 165

Tom and Lenore Dayton

Tom and Lenore work in healthcare on the California Central Coast. When not wine-tasting, playing miniature golf, or singing karaoke, Lenore enjoys cooking new vegan recipes, Tom enjoys hiking. Both enjoy spoiling their Maltese and Maltipoo.

BIOGRAPHIES

Devil's Lodge

Page 177

Tatiana Samokhina

Tatiana lives in a beautiful Surry Hills suburb of Sydney, New South Wales, Australia. She teaches English and works as a fiction translator where she has the ambitious task of conveying the emotions, nuances, messages, and writing style of an author within target languages.

She's flexible and self-motivated, her love of literature makes the world a more beautiful and harmonious place. You can find Tatiana at:

https://www.linkedin.com/in/tatiana-samokhina/

https://www.instagram.com/tatianasamokhina/#

BIOGRAPHIES

Dream House

Page 187

Carolyn Saletto

After nearly thirty years of owning businesses in the Pacific Northwest, the retired life for Carolyn Saletto offered time for her to write a memoir, *One Hazel Green Eye,* where she explored her childhood defined by little or no supervision, inviting the reader into a deeply personal space.

Carolyn is an avid writer and a graduate of *The Narrative Project.* She participanted in *Deep Dive 2024* hosted by Bianca Marais of *The Shit No One Tells You About Writing* podcast.

When Carolyn isn't typing away at a story, she spends time with her family and friends, playing with her grandchildren, or attempting to conquer the game of golf.

Instagram:	csaletto_writes

Substack:	carollynnsaletto.substack.com

https://www.thenarrativeproject.net

https://www.theshitaboutwriting.com

BIOGRAPHIES

Emergency Contact

Page 193

Jessi Vasquez

Jessi is a fiction writer who resides in Washington with her spouse, their band of misfit friends, and correlating pets. Fueled by her love of dark roasts and reading, she devotes her time to crafting speculative and literary fiction.

BIOGRAPHIES

Eternal Embers

Page 215

Travis Klappe

Travis is an English student at Mount Royal University in Calgary, Alberta. He's been passionate about creative writing from a young age, enjoying the freedom to build imaginative worlds filled with adventure and horror.

For Travis, the allure of storytelling lies in the ability to craft narratives that captivate and engage, and where the writer has control over every aspect of the tale. Writing since first grade, Travis shares his work, feeling a personal challenge as it reflects his most vulnerable expression.

Writing remains Travis' favorite way to explore new ideas and connect with others. He continues to pursue his love of storytelling, always seeking to improve his craft and share the excitement and creativity he finds in writing.

BIOGRAPHIES

Familiar Face

Page 277

Daniel Gene Barlekamp

Daniel is the author of various short stories, poems, and audio dramas for adults and young readers. Most recently, his middle-grade fiction has appeared in the anthology, <u>The Haunted States of America</u>; Godwin Books – July 2024. His poem, *What is a Monster*, was featured in <u>Ember: A Journal of Luminous Things</u>, and translated into Mandarin by Poetry Hall.

Originally from New Jersey, Daniel now lives with his wife and son in Massachusetts, where he works in immigration law by day and attends law school at night.

Visit him at:

https://dgbarlekamp.com

His poem, *What is a Monster,* can be found at:

https://read.emberjournal.org/contributors/daniel-gene-barlekamp

From Your Bipolar Ex-Girlfriend

Page 237

Anonymous

Author prefers to remain anonymous.

BIOGRAPHIES

Getting Fired

Page 251

Vasantha Aaron

Vasantha is an Indian American doctor, soccer mom, girl boss, and sometimes short story writer. Born and raised in Indiana, she attended college in St. Louis. Dropping out of graduate school in Chicago, she stumbled into the wild world of temporary work in New York. After an ill-advised and longer-than-necessary stint in advertising, Vasantha dragged herself back to Hoosier State to continue her medical studies.

Vasantha now practices radiology in Indianapolis, between her writing gigs and kids' soccer games.

BIOGRAPHIES

In the Dark

Page 265

Julie Koloini

Julie's life plan includes dying in the first wave of the zombie apocalypse because that shit sounds like a terrible time. Then she can return as a ghost to haunt a quaint little bookstore and finish her towering *To Be Read* pile.

Julie studied poetry and Shakespearean at Ohio State University but currently lives in Atlanta, Georgia, because those Ohio winters are rough. She's published a collection of poetry, *Flying with Wax Wings*.

Today, she mixes M&Ms into her popcorn at the movies.

BIOGRAPHIES

David Ajluni

Lingering Fear

Page 277

Throughout life, David has created music, films, and definitely a little trouble. But no matter where his creative fancy led him, he continued to write short stories, essays, screenplays, songs, and poems. Eventually, he made it official and called himself an author. To date, his accomplishments include *Candelabra*, *Seriously Unsettling*, and *A Friend Who Bleeds*. David enjoys hiking, spending time with family, and writing his bio in the third person … kind of.

BIOGRAPHIES

Losing Her

Page 289

E. Powers

From a young age, Teddy E. Powers had a wildly vivid imagination. With every book, every TV show, and every movie, his elaborate fantasy world grew. Although his life was filled with struggle, he never allowed his imagination to grow dim. He turned his dreams into stories and poems with the hope that one day he would have a chance to share them with the world.

Teddy lives in the mountains of northern Virginia with his loving wife. He's currently serving in the Army Reserves and just completed his degree in psychology with a concentration in human resource management and entrepreneurship. He's working toward his dream business which will allow all people to receive the psychiatric help they need.

BIOGRAPHIES

Run Through the Jungle

Page 303

Richard Schulein

In 1972, Rick traveled for three months along the Hippie Trail from Greece to Katmandu and back. Stemming from that trip is his unpublished memoir, *Road Dust*. The story *Run Through the Jungle* is based on that memoir. A life-long escape artist currently in exile, he has lived as an expat for the better part of fifty years. His education took him through two universities and into a career as an English teacher. But, alas, teaching was not to be his endgame. He eventually detoured his way into the bookshop business, running his own shop in the heart of Athens for twenty-three years. He's currently married to Titika, a successful English instructor. Together they have two children, Jason and Naya, and one grandchild, Elina.

BIOGRAPHIES

Sacrifice

Page 315

Amberlyn A. Pryor

Amberlyn almost gave up on her dreams of becoming a writer. In high school, she doubted her ability to improve her craft and was unsure how to make a living. A friend encouraged her to write, and at just the right moment, to keep her stories alive.

Amberlyn wrestled a creative writing minor at college, while achieving an equally enjoyable major in wildlife science. Destined to not make much money but to enjoy her life, Amberlyn honed her craft. From writing groups to online courses, she honors the importance of finishing the first draft and not listening to internal doubt.

Amberlyn lives in the glorious forests of Virginia with her husband and nearly grown children.

You can find Amberlyn at: http://www.amberlynpryor.com

BIOGRAPHIES

Short Boat Ride
on the River

Page 327

Karen Andrews

Karen loves writing and spending time with her adult sons, stepdaughter, partner, friends, and family – including her houseplants. A teacher for many years, Karen is now a graduate student. She loves the outdoors and floating on the water; especially in the seat of a canoe.

Karen is grateful for the opportunity to see her fictional short story in print with all the other *Fear* authors.

BIOGRAPHIES

Desiree Lovato

Surprise Lessons

Page 335

Desiree Lovato (Dr. Dez) is a lifelong learner and multimedia artist. Twisting words into stories, poetry, plays, and music is something that she loves. Her fascination includes the human experience; believing that empathy is the most powerful weapon, building perspective through strength.

According to Dr. Dez, "If we're afraid to examine our dark sides, we can never truly understand the magnitude of our light."

As a public school educator, Dr. Dez encourages others to grow and be themselves. As a teacher, she seeks to connect with and support others through her honesty, humor, and unexpected actions.

Her stories reflect these same ideals.

BIOGRAPHIES

The Dive

Page 345

W. Rogers

W. Rogers is a retired middle school teacher, a home renovator, a husband and father, and an accomplished procrastinator.

He lives in rural Canada and values the quiet, the fauna and flora, the clean air, and the never-ending house, property, and vehicle upkeep. Aside from building and repairing computers, he creates digital art, and reads fantasy and dark-themed novels while slowly improving his creative writing skills.

BIOGRAPHIES

Weight of Her Skin

Page 355

Gemma Davidson

Gemma is an avid reader of books while backpacking through the mountains of Utah and Wyoming. For Gemma, nothing is more compelling than creating and exploring the struggles between characters, which she hopes will emphasize the beauty and the worth of living. This is her first published work, and she sincerely thanks Indignor House for the opportunity.

BIOGRAPHIES

Carol O. Mason

Welcome to the Neighborhood

Page 363

Carol is a native Texan and a voracious reader. She holds a master's degree in exercise physiology and worked sixteen years in corporate wellness programs before retiring a few years ago. She has several years of experience creating work-related presentations, as well as freelance article writing. Carol decided to try her hand at writing fiction, and *Welcome to the Neighborhood* is one of her first efforts.

BIOGRAPHIES

Lynn Yvonne Moon

The Dream

Page 5

Lynn is an award-winning author of adult, young adult, and children's literature with over ten books in print. She holds a master's in public administration from Troy State University and a master's in literature from Lindenwood University.

Becoming daring and grabbing onto two close friends (Mark and Shannon), Lynn thought up the idea of an anthology at Indignor House to give new authors a home to see their work in print.

BIOGRAPHIES